THE SMILING MAN

www.penguin.co.uk

Also by Joseph Knox

Sirens

THE
SMILING MAN

Joseph Knox

Doubleday

LONDON · TORONTO · SYDNEY · AUCKLAND · JOHANNESBURG

TRANSWORLD PUBLISHERS
61–63 Uxbridge Road, London W5 5SA
www.penguin.co.uk

Transworld is part of the Penguin Random House group of companies
whose addresses can be found at global.penguinrandomhouse.com

First published in Great Britain in 2018 by Doubleday
an imprint of Transworld Publishers

A CIP catalogue record for this book
is available from the British Library.

ISBNs 9780857524409 (hb)
9780857524416 (tpb)

Typeset in 12/15 pt Adobe Garamond Pro by Jouve (UK), Milton Keynes
Printed and bound in Great Britain by Clays Ltd, Bungay, Suffolk

Penguin Random House is committed to a sustainable
future for our business, our readers and our planet. This book
is made from Forest Stewardship Council® certified paper.

1 3 5 7 9 10 8 6 4 2

For Stephen K.

'It's as if I know something and don't know it at the same time.'

Thomas Ligotti, 'The Frolic'

————

It started with a knock at the door.

When he thinks of that now he grimaces. Closes his eyes and runs a hand across his face. It's a bad memory in a head full of them, and the smallest thing can spark it. The electricity in the air before a storm, or the lancing smell of ozone after heavy rain. Sitting across the table from a new girl or a new colleague, and caught off guard like this, he might allow himself to drift off into it, knowing that neither one of them will last anyway. His vision blurs and a haze of sunspots passes in front of his eyes, like he's staring into a bright light.

'I think there's someone outside,' he'd heard the old woman say.

It was after ten on a Sunday night and they'd probably been on their way to bed.

Their house was a stubborn mid-sized Tudor-build, designed to withstand everything, apparently, but the rain. Through the pane of smoked glass set into the door, the boy could make out two or three buckets in the hallway, collecting dripping water, and perhaps that's why they hadn't heard him at first. He knocked again, stepped back and looked at the house. It seemed too big for one old couple, but it had something he didn't associate with the narrow, thin-walled rooms he'd lived in, some personality.

It had to, out here in the middle of nowhere.

The old woman got to the door first. When she opened it she called out for her husband. He looked even older than she did, and it seemed like a struggle for him to get around. When his head appeared over his wife's shoulder, when he saw the small, shivering boy on their doorstep, he adjusted his glasses in surprise. The boy was rake-thin, glass-eyed, pale. Wearing just a T-shirt and trousers, both soaked through by the rain. The old couple looked about him, but it seemed like the boy was on his own.

The woman frowned, crouched. 'Are you OK, sweetheart?'

The boy stood there shivering.

She squinted into the night again then took him by the wrist, led him gently inside and closed the door. 'He's frozen,' she said to her husband, drawing the boy past him and into the front room. The old man re-locked the door, pushed the deadbolts back into place and followed them through, looking at the wet footprints on the tiles.

The boy wasn't wearing any shoes.

'I'm Dot,' said the old woman. 'This is Si.'

When the boy still didn't answer, Dot shrugged. Found a blanket and went to boil some water. Si sat on the sofa, worrying his hands. He guessed the boy was about seven or eight years old but aged prematurely by the dark rings around his eyes. He didn't look about the room, or even focus on the things in front of him. He just stared blankly ahead. When Dot returned with a hot-water bottle, Si reached up and put an affectionate hand on his wife's arm. The boy's eyes flicked suddenly on to them, as if unfamiliar with the gesture.

'Can you tell us your name?' said Dot, lifting the blanket and pressing the hot-water bottle against the boy. His shivering intensified, until his teeth sounded like a baby shaking a rattle. He forced his eyes shut and clenched his jaw to control it. 'Should we call the police?' said Dot to her husband. He was nodding, already getting up, glad of something practical to do. She rubbed the boy's head while she waited. It felt like his blood was boiling.

'Dot . . .' Si called from the hall.

'Hold that thought,' she said.

When she left the room the boy smoothly removed the blanket from around him and went to the light switch beside the door. He flicked it off and on, off and on. He put his head out into the hallway and watched. Si and Dot were both frowning at the phone, which they'd discovered wasn't working. The boy went to the porch, walking on the balls of his bare feet, unlatched the front door, drew back the deadbolts, and opened it.

A shape dislodged itself from the shadows and moved slowly towards him. The rain had stopped and there were stars visible now that the boy had never seen in the city before. As the shape grew closer it stood out against them, looking somehow darker than the night.

'Good lad,' said the shape, the man, nodding at the boy. The man's face was flat and angular as a blade, and he wore a trained inexpression that gave nothing away. It was his body that said everything, erupting with messy, overlapping networks of muscles and veins, like the storage device for all the hate in the world. He had a claw-hammer in his gloved right hand and used his left to tousle the boy's hair.

He stopped, retracted the hand in awe.

He'd produced a coin from behind the boy's ear and held it out for him to take.

'What do you say, Wally?'

'Thanks, Bateman,' said the boy, accepting the coin solemnly.

He sat on the porch as Bateman went past him, inside the house.

'Hey . . .' he heard the old man say. 'What are you—'

There was a wet thud and something heavy hit the floor.

The old lady started to scream. 'No,' she shouted. '*No—*'

Another wet thud, the sound of something else hitting the floor. Straining, the boy heard a low moan coming from inside. A determined gurgle and perhaps another word. Perhaps her husband's name. Then there two more footsteps, a final blow and total silence.

The boy closed his fist around the coin Bateman had given him and stared out into the darkness. His mouth watered and sunspots started to pass in front of his eyes. They were just a shimmer at first, then they came thicker and faster, until they were roaring down in front of him like the rain. Like he was staring into a bright light instead of pitch-black darkness.

———

I
Midnight City

1

The heat that year was annihilating. The endless, fever dream days passed slowly, and afterwards you wondered if they'd even been real. Beneath the hum of air conditioners, the chink of ice in glasses, you could almost hear it. The slow-drip of people losing their minds. The city was brilliantly lit, like an unending explosion you were expected to live inside, and the nights, when they finally came, felt hallucinatory, charged with electricity. You could see the sparks – the girls in their summer clothes, the boys with their flashing white teeth – everywhere you went.

There's a particular look on their faces between the hours of midnight and 6 a.m. Falling in and out of bars, kissing on street corners, swinging their arms along the pavements. Whatever's happened to them before is long gone and, for a few hours at least, they feel like tomorrow might never come. Most of them are students, sheltering from the economic downturn in degree courses they'll never pay off. The others work minimum-wage jobs and live for the weekend. When I see them they're living in the moment, for better or worse, and the doubt, their default setting during the daytime, is replaced by some kind of certainty. I was on my 120th night shift in a row. Six months into what felt like a life sentence.

My own kind of certainty.

So I watched their faces, the young people, between the hours of midnight and 6 a.m. I watched life literally passing me by. I nodded when they did, smiled when they smiled, and tried to stay in the moment. I kept my head down and took the positives, the sparks, wherever I could get them.

We were already on Wilmslow Road when the call came through. An enormous interconnecting through-line, it runs almost six miles, linking the moneyed properties south of town with the struggling city centre. It's the busiest bus route in Europe and always alive with taxis, double-deckers, commuters and light. And lately, with fires that someone had been setting in the steel dustbins lining the road. Because these fires were low priority, likely meaningless, and always set after dark, they fell to us, the night shift.

There were only two permanent members of the team.

Young detectives rotated through, just to say they'd done it, and some of the no-hope floaters did a few shifts a month to cover our days off, but permanent night duty meant one of two things. No life or no career. In my few years on the force, I'd managed to satisfy both requirements.

The dustbin fire was already out when we got there. My partner and I arrived to smouldering cinders, asked some questions and had begun to pack it up when we saw a crowd gathering on the other side of the road. I checked the time and drifted through the traffic towards them.

They were preparing a midnight vigil for a kid called Subhi Seif. Supersize to his friends. Until a few hours before, Supersize had been an eighteen-year-old fresher, living in a city for the first time in his life. Then he'd seen a girl being mugged and gone after the man who did it. He'd run into the road without looking for traffic and been obliterated beneath the wheels of a bus.

The mugger got away.

Alongside the torches, UV lights and flowers already laid in tribute, ten or so of Supersize's friends were standing marking the spot. They played sad songs from their phones and passed sweating cans of beer to keep cool. I reminded them not to stray out into the road themselves, then crossed back to the car where my partner was waiting. We drove an unmarked matt-black BMW that criminals could still spot at a glance. Mainly because of the man usually crammed into the passenger side. My superior officer, Detective Inspector Peter Sutcliffe. At a glance he could only look like a cop or a criminal, and I still wasn't sure which was closer to the truth.

'How are the Chicken McNuggets?' he said, not looking up from the sport section. Sutcliffe was one of life's great nature–nurture debates. Was he a born shit, or had he just grown into one because of his unfortunate name? His suit jacket, filled to breaking point by his body, looked water-damaged with sweat, and he was giving off so much heat that we sat with the doors wide open.

'What's on the radio?' I said, nodding at the scanner, the reason he'd waved me back over the road.

He turned a page, sniffed. 'The Hamburglar's struck again.' I waited and he sighed, folded the paper. 'It was sexual harassment, or assault, or something . . .'

'Sexual harassment or something?'

Sutcliffe's face, neck and body were swollen in odd, ever-shifting places, and his skin was deathly pale. He looked like he'd survived an embalming. We never used his full name, just called him Sutty to avoid distressing the public any further.

'Jesus Christ, this heat.' He ran a hand through his glistening, thinning hair. 'Feels like I've had a blood transfusion from Freddie fucking Mercury.' He looked up, remembered I was there and gave me a yellow smile. 'You know me, Aid, I zone out as soon as I hear anything "sexual". We're going to Owens Park, though, if you wanna crack on . . .'

Sexual harassment or something.

The only thing Sutty hated more than young women was me. I watched him as he began applying the alcoholic skin sanitizer that he used compulsively, whenever I got in or out of the car. It made him look like he was rubbing his hands together with glee. I gave him a smile to keep things interesting. Then I indicated and pulled out into the road.

2

It was almost midnight when we arrived at Owens Park. The largest halls of residence in the city and home to more than two thousand students, most of them first years. Set in spacious, leafy grounds, the campus comprises five main blocks, including one tower which can be seen from the street, glowering out over the trees. Grey buildings clash hard with green surroundings. The baby-boomer wet dream. It had been built to last in the sixties but was looking its age now. There was talk of tearing the lot down and starting from scratch but it would be a shame when they finally got around to it. So much of the city already looked like a building site.

I parked up and looked at Sutty.

'You coming?'

'That's a personal question. Just give us a call if her knicker-drawer needs searching.' He returned to his paper. 'You're always so good with the little girls . . .'

I got out of the car, ignoring his tone, frankly grateful not to be taking him with me. Sutty and I were two different kinds of bad cop. Our being partnered together was a sort of punishment for us both, and we each tried to make things as difficult as possible for the other. It was the only thing we had in common.

I walked through the gate. Followed the stark white lights, blazing in the darkness. I smelt the freshly cut grass and felt a flicker of excitement. I'd never lived here but had visited a few times when I was younger, crashing parties, seeing friends. It was strange to think that I wasn't in touch with any of them now, that dozens of people must have occupied their rooms, their beds, their lives, in the intervening years. For a moment I felt like I was walking into my past, going through a gateway into Neverland. I heard a scream of laughter and saw a teenage girl run by, being chased by a boy with a super soaker. Looking over my shoulder, I watched them melt into the darkness, still laughing. It reinforced a cruel, universal truth. I would age. Owens Park would always be eighteen.

I consulted the campus map, found the block I was looking for, buzzed a first-floor flat and waited. The grounds were eerily quiet now and I turned to look around. Felt the latent power of a day's heat, humming up from the grass. Across the path stood another firm, grey block of buildings – lit windows glaring at me. I heard the bolt of the door click and turned to open it.

3

I went through the hallway. Past some street bikes, under a bare light bulb and up the stairs. The block was badly ventilated, built decades before in a city where heatwaves were unimaginable. I felt the sweat spiking out of my skin. There were listless, conversational voices behind closed doors. Adolescent smells of deodorant, drink and drugs.

It felt like a pressure cooker.

On the first-floor landing there was a teenage boy, pacing back and forth. He was black. Handsome and wearing a smart, dark tracksuit. He took a swig from a large, frosted glass and frowned when he saw me.

'Thought you'd be a woman.'

I stopped. 'What kind of service were you expecting?'

He snorted, took a step closer and lowered his voice. I could smell the mint in his glass. 'I called about my friend. And she doesn't know that I did. Thought they sent women for girl stuff . . .'

'Girl stuff?'

He nodded. 'Said when I called. You all not on speaking terms?'

'Dispatch aren't as articulate as you are, Mr . . . ?'

'Earl.'

'That a first name or a surname?'

'Only name you're getting. What do they call you? To your face, I mean?'

I smiled. 'Waits.'

He looked at me for a second. Thought about it. 'Heavy,' he said, finally. He led me into a kitchen-cum-communal space. 'Park here, I'll find Soph.'

I could hear ambient sounds from the hallway, a steady hip-hop beat, but there was no one else in the room. Because it was dark outside and the lights were on, I could see myself reflected in the black mirror of the window. On the table there were trays of crushed ice, mint, sugar and lime. There was a row of jelly glasses and a wet bottle of rum.

Through a door I heard a girl say: '*What?*'

I sat there, beneath the blazing fluorescent lights, and waited. A minute or so later, Earl came back into the kitchen, went to the trays and began fixing a strong drink without looking at me. He had the practised movements of a professional cocktail maker, even going so far as to spin the rum bottle in his hand.

He saw me notice. 'I mix in The Alchemist,' he said. A celebrated Spinningfields bar where you could do permanent damage to your body and bank account. 'Here.' He slid me the glass he'd been working on. A mojito.

'I'm on the clock,' I said, catching it.

'Not *for* you, Sherlock. Maybe she needs one?' He walked out into the hallway, nodded at the door he'd come from and then went to his own room. I picked up the glass, so cold that it hurt my hand, went to the door he'd indicated and knocked.

I didn't know what to expect.

'Hello,' said a shaky, southern voice. The room smelt faintly of suntan cream and the girl inside it was young. Sitting on the bed in denim cut-offs and a vest. Her shoulders were starting to turn red from the weather but the rest of her skin glowed from weeks of vitamin D. She had freckles about her eyes and a heart-shaped face, and as her desk fan strafed the room it tousled her hair, brown with the tips dyed blond. There were some bruises on her legs but I was glad to see she didn't look upset or in distress. Just a little embarrassed. A little put out. She closed a laptop and pushed it to one side.

'I expected someone older . . .' she said.

'I've got the liver of a man twice my age.' She almost smiled and I handed her the glass that Earl had given me. 'My name's Aidan Waits, Detective Constable.'

'Sophie,' she said.

'We could talk in the kitchen if you like, Sophie?'

She considered me for a moment. 'Here's fine. Would you close the door, though?'

I did, then motioned to an absurd pink chair at her desk. 'May I?' She nodded and I sat down. 'Sounds like your friend out there's worried about you.'

'Earl's a good guy . . .'

'Tight-lipped, though.'

'I was surprised he called you at all. He hates the police. I mean—'

'Don't worry, I basically agree with him. We do have our uses, though. I'm guessing if he picked up the phone it's something serious. Why don't you tell me about it from the start?'

'Well, I'm a first year . . .'

She said it like it explained everything else.

'No crime there. What are you studying?'

'English lit?'

'I've heard of it.'

'Probably not much use in the real world.'

'Sometimes the real world's not much use itself . . .'

'Yeah.' She put the glass to her forehead for a second, rolled it from right to left and then took a drink. 'So, last week I went to a club. Actually.' She reached over to the desk and handed me a crumpled flyer.

Incognito.

The picture was of a young woman, dressed in school uniform. The copy pitched hard to entice freshers to a club night. *Free entry (pardon the pun)*. Free birth control, too, as the rumour went. Most girls went once, 100 per cent in on the joke. They took the free drinks, absorbed the heated stares of the regulars and then left. You still heard the odd horror story, though. Entry for men was twenty quid a go and most of them wanted their money's worth. I'd seen the queues, sliming their way down the street.

I handed back the flyer. 'I've heard of that, too.'

'I met a man, Ollie. Older but, y'know, nice. Well dressed and stuff. He seemed like a big deal in there, anyway.' I had a good idea of what a big deal in Incognito might look like. Sophie rubbed her palms, unconsciously, on the bed. 'We went back to his flat . . .'

'We can have a female officer here if you'd prefer?'

She shook her head. 'We slept together, it was fine.'

'Those bruises?' I said, referring to the marks on her legs.

'Oh, no, I'm a cyclist. It's one of the things I love about it here.' She paused. 'Look, the night was fine, it's just that he filmed us—' She stopped abruptly, looked down at the bed.

'And now he's holding it over you.'

She blushed, nodded. 'I didn't know people actually did that.' She took another mouthful of her drink. 'He said,' she stopped. 'He *implied* that if I don't see him again he'll leak it on to the internet.'

'I take it you don't want to see him again?'

She shook her head.

'Do you have a surname for Ollie?'

'What will you do?'

'I'll talk to him.'

'Now?'

'There's no time like the present.'

'Isn't it a bit late, though?'

'The later the better, it might give him some idea of how serious this is.'

'. . . And is it serious?' I could see that she was trying to talk herself down.

'Your friend out there seems to think so. I think I agree. Ollie's

15

trying to blackmail you into doing something. For some men it's the only way they know.'

'I didn't get his surname.' She looked away. 'God, you must think—'

'I don't think anything. Can you describe him?'

'Older than you, maybe mid-thirties? And, I guess, he was a little chubby. He had sort of light red hair, like it was losing its colour.'

'And he got in touch with you about the video. Did you swap numbers?'

She shook her head. 'In the morning I got up and bolted. Stupidly, I left my jacket with my student ID in. He messaged me today.'

'Where did Ollie live?'

'The Quays. I'm not sure which building, though. I think the big one.'

'Can I see the message?'

She made eye contact for a second. 'I'd rather you didn't.' It was the first time she'd sounded anguished, and I was glad Earl had made the call.

'It'll be a big help if I know the nature of the threat. If I know everything you do.'

'So, is this official already? It's just, I didn't call you, Earl did.' She paused. 'My parents would kill me.'

I thought about it for a second. 'If you show me the message, I'll know as much as you do. If I can find him, I can have a word informally if you like.'

'There's a picture.'

'It'll stay between us.'

'You don't look much like a priest. No offence . . .'

I sat back, gave her some space. 'Nicest thing anyone's said to me in months.'

She made up her mind. Opened the laptop, turned the screen towards me and then stared at the wall. *Loved your debut, think you could be a star. Should the world see this, though? Maybe you can come back around and convince me otherwise ;) xxx*

Beneath the text there was a gif. It repeated one second of video on a loop. In it, Sophie was naked, sitting on a bed laughing. I thought she looked high. I turned the screen back towards her, got up and left my card on the desk.

'Leave it with me.'

4

I went back to the car and climbed in. I could smell the disinfectant that Sutty had wiped the surfaces down with, and when I picked up the radio it was slippery in my hand.

'Complainant doesn't want to make a formal statement at this time, over.'

That closed the case as far as Dispatch was concerned.

'How'd it go?' said Sutty, stirring. 'Think you can finger a suspect?' I opened a window so I could breathe, started up and pulled out into the road. 'Let me guess. She had a face like a boiled arse but says some bloke risked his liberty to kiss it.'

I just drove.

Sutty had no family and no friends that I knew of. The rumour was that he'd once been a promising detective, before he became addicted to human tragedy and was slowly seduced by the night shift. That had been a decade ago. Now it was all that he lived for. Ours was essentially a patrol duty, prowling around looking for trouble. This gave the shift the illusory promise of real detective work. The chance to see something through to the end. This promise was generally broken by our handing cases over to the day shift. Often we inherited them back the following night impossibly transformed, or with basic follow-ups not done. We were plain-clothes detectives, officially reporting to CID, but they rarely acknowledged it. Uniform treated us with the minimum amount of respect that they could get away with. I was here because I had to be.

But Sutty was in love with it.

He was at once attracted to, and repulsed by, the people. The boys were all snowflakes and fuckwits, the girls were easy or, worse, feminists, but he'd happily sit in cells, listening to them all night, he'd even drive them home when they were lost or drunk or both. To the untrained eye, these instances could look like sympathy, but in truth he enjoyed seeing people cast low.

In truth, he encouraged it.

He'd routinely let the names of informants slip to violent criminals, he'd drop young girls working as escorts in the worst parts of town. He told me he'd once attended an AA meeting, poured a bottle of vodka into the free coffee and waited, watching, as people got drunk. 'Took this blue-haired slag home afterwards,' he'd said. 'Screwed her until the hair dye was running down her face.'

Our partnership was a war of attrition.

He openly despised me, but any obvious reciprocation seemed to feed something inside him. So I tried to keep the condemnation out of my voice. He'd say and do outrageous things and I'd smile back, swallow them, refuse to give him the satisfaction.

Although he was a large man, and although we often disagreed, I'd never been physically afraid of Sutty. He enjoyed our status quo too much to change it. Mentally, though, it was a different matter. Once, we'd been parked in the lay-by of a car accident hot spot, our lights out as we watched the road for speeders. It was three or four in the morning and he'd been talking, idly, about old cases. Finally, he got around to his first go at the night shift. He'd responded to a disturbance at a dog shelter.

'So there's this witch at the entrance, yeah? Long black coat, fingerless gloves, the whole bit. Except she's twitching like someone put a thousand volts through her, listening to the ghosts in her hair or whatever. And the voices are especially vicious tonight. Three-part harmony from Hitler, Ho Chi Minh and Fred fucking West.

'So I go up the path, Mr Nice, and get up alongside her. She starts giving me all this Jesus stuff, asking if I'm saved. Says he's coming back, he's on his way, etcetera, etcetera. I said I think he's outta town tonight, sweetheart.

'Anyway, turns out she's broken in, given the dogs their first holy communion or something. Wait here, I say. I get halfway down the hall and the smell's killing me, just unbelievable. Every cage I look in, the dogs are sodden, I mean soaking wet.' He laughed. 'She'd only gone and baptized 'em in petrol. Then I see her at the door and she's got her back to me, shuddering. I realize she's striking matches. Mad bitch has put us on God's guest list.'

Sutty lost his eyebrows and most of the hair on his head before he got outside. He collapsed on to the lawn, coughing his lungs up, listening to the dogs howling, barking, burning alive in their cages. At first light he'd traced the woman's footprints. They went one hundred feet into the trees and stopped suddenly. As far as he knew, that was the last anyone saw or heard of her. The story wasn't remarkable in the context of the night shift, which is filled with haunted people and impossible dead ends.

It was Sutty's reaction to it that disturbed me.

'That's when I saw it,' he'd said. 'All the famine and war and children in need. We've been born right into the end of it, Aid, straight into the death throes. The whole race is suicidal, it's hard-wired into us and something's flicked the switch. We're the last generation there'll ever be.' As he talked, I realized that he was being sincere. Worse, that he was in love with the idea.

The night shift meant different things to different people. To our superiors it was a demotion out of sight, almost out of reality. To me it was an act of cowardice. Somewhere I could hide out from my own life and let it pass me by. But to my partner it was life itself. It was his front-row seat to the end of the world and he was on his feet, applauding, in standing ovation.

5

'What did I tell you?' said Sutty, dowsing himself, face, neck and chest, in sanitizer. 'The window-lickers are out in force tonight.'

Incognito ran out of a loft bar off Piccadilly, and we watched the line of men, oozing outside the door and round the corner. They were standing in packs, smoking and swearing, driven half-mad by the neon and the heat. By the girls in their summer clothes who didn't even notice they were alive. Most of the men wore sharp buzzcuts and shapeless going-out shirts, and they seemed to share one low, booming voice that happened to possess them at different times. 'Yeurgh,' said Sutty, opening the glove compartment. He found his wet wipes and leaned over me to clean the steering wheel I'd just taken my hands off. 'Someone really let one go in this gene pool.'

Although he was including me in his dim assessment of the men, looking out at the line it was hard not to agree. It was like watching one personality, stretched paper-thin across twenty people.

'Fancy a walk?' I said.

He balled up his wet wipe and threw it out the window.

'I could stretch my legs, yeah. Ever met the guy who runs this place?' We climbed out of the car and I shook my head. 'Bloke should've been a handjob. A real beauty. Looks like the singer off a cruise ship that hasn't docked in a decade.'

Two girls walked, arm in arm, to the front of the queue. The men nearby stopped braying for a second and drank them in. The doorman winced like he'd just done a shot, then stood to one side so they could pass, watching as they went up the stairs. His hair was shaved so closely that I could see the veins, gripping his skull. Any shorter and I could have seen what he was thinking.

He looked at Sutty. 'Back of the line, darling.'

'Try Detective Inspector. And get it right first time.'

All emotion drained out of the doorman's face. 'Apologies, Detective Inspector. How can I help?'

'We want to talk to the owner . . .'

He didn't move. 'There's a few heads with a stake in Incognito. Let me know which you're after an' I'll make an appointment.'

Sutty was laughing again. 'An appointment with Guy Russell? That's not a little black book I want my name appearing in.' The doorman still didn't move. 'Come on, you know the bloke. Personality like a contraceptive. Hairpiece that could place runner-up at Crufts. I know he's here and I know you haven't been ID-ing those girls tonight, so best we talk to him off the record, eh?'

'Pat,' said the doorman to a colleague. 'Work the line a minute, yeah?' He gave us a dull, gold-toothed smile that sent the veins pulsing across his skull again. 'Right this way, gents.' We went inside, across the sticky, fly-trap floor and up the stairs. The doorman walked ahead, easing people out of our way with one arm. The blending smells of perfume and alcohol felt intoxicating, and the air throbbed with bass and thick, numbing heat. We emerged next to the bar, in a half-lit loft space with around a hundred people in it.

'Wait here,' said the doorman. I looked at Sutty, his eyes caressing the men and women in the room. It was almost an even split between them. Most stood separately, some cautiously mingled, and one or two had paired up on the dance floor, grinding into each other with the music. The real action took place in the booths lining the room. You'd see four or five girls crammed into one side and two men on the other. Nothing between them but gleaming steel buckets, filled with cheap bottles of prosecco and ice.

The doorman emerged from the dance floor. 'Mr Russell can see you now.'

'I'll wait here,' said Sutty, eyes bobbing from table to table. 'Secure the bar.' When the lights caught his face he looked like a spoiled, sweating chicken.

The doorman led me across the dance floor, to a booth in the corner. A man in his mid-forties was sitting beside a young girl. He was staring at me while she scrolled idly through her phone with one finger. The man perfectly matched Sutty's description. Carefully dressed, but strangely out of time. His black shirt was tight and had the top four buttons open, creating a long V shape beneath the neck. He gave me a practised, peroxide-white smile and motioned to the seat opposite him. I slid into the booth. The girl, who hadn't looked up from her phone, wore clothes that seemed designed for the room. Wild colours that caught ultraviolet lights at suggestive angles. She wore frosted eye-liner and atomic pink lipstick, and she must have been twenty-five years younger than the man beside her.

'Someone looks thirsty,' he said, over the music.

I didn't say anything.

'Alicia,' he said to the girl. 'I'm thinking . . . two Jack and Cokes.'

There was an ice bucket with a bottle of Dom Pérignon on the table but apparently I wasn't worth it. Alicia stood without looking at either of us. I saw that she was wearing UV contact lenses. They made her seem vacant, dead behind the eyes. The man watched her go, glowing through the crowd, before he spoke again.

'Name's Guy Russell,' he said. 'And you've got until she gets back.' Russell was sitting facing the dance floor, and a dull red light washed across his face. I guessed it was his regular seat, a look he cultivated.

'There's a customer of yours I want to talk to.'

'Yeah?' He leaned forward, smiled into the light. I could see the seams of several, overlapping plastic surgeries. 'What's her name?'

'*His* name,' I said. 'Ollie or Oliver.'

'Don't tell me it's work-related?' I nodded. His smile was like a strobe light, flicking on and off continually, and I assumed he'd snorted his dinner. 'Ollie or Oliver, you say?'

'Mid-thirties, going to fat, light red hair losing its colour.'

'Not a lot to go on . . .'

But I thought he was stalling. Backing away from a name he recognized.

'He's a regular,' I said. 'He was high-rolling it here last week.'

He beamed at me through his lidless, unblinking eyes. 'As you can see, I have a lot of regulars, Mr . . .'

'Detective,' I said. 'Aidan Waits.'

'I have a lot of regulars, Detective Waits. Most of them "high-rolling it". Can I ask what this is about?'

'No.'

He shifted in his seat. 'But you're not flinging shit at Incognito?'

'Who'd notice?' I said. His smile flicked off again. He took a breath to speak but before he could, Alicia returned with our drinks. She set them before us and sat back down again. She looked like she'd stepped in from another dimension.

'Sorry, mate. Time's up, can't help ya.'

I didn't move and he clicked his fingers at me.

I leaned in. 'Don't act like the real thing, Guy, I've seen it close up.' We glared at each other while the girl pretended to concentrate on her phone. 'Ollie or Oliver,' I repeated.

'What do you think the most important part of this business is?'

I looked at him. 'The condom machine.'

'I mean to me personally.'

'Same answer.'

'Appearances,' he said, starting to lose patience. 'And not just mine. Not just Alicia's. But an appearance of understanding, discretion. Anonymity. A lot of these lads are in relationships. Married even. Would they be coming back if they thought I was passing out their card numbers?'

'The man I'm looking for's sexually harassing a teenage girl.'

Alicia stopped scrolling through her phone. 'She was one of your customers as well.'

'Look at that bar,' said Russell. Through the dance floor I could see dozens of men, holding up cash and cards, trying to get served. 'Teenage girls don't pay my bills, Detective.'

'You think those men are here for the music?'

His smile flickered and finally died out. He looked at me for a moment, then picked up my untouched drink and poured it into the ice bucket.

'Alicia, it looks like our friend's dry again.' The girl stood, taking the hint immediately. As Russell craned his neck to watch her go, I saw the fold of skin behind his ears from a facelift. It made him look as though he wore a mask that was slipping. I turned to see Alicia at the bar, talking to the doorman. 'Eyes back in your skull, Detective.' Russell was leaning across the table now. 'I took a girl back last night. She's on her knees sucking, and I do mean sucking, my fingers. Thought she was gonna dislocate 'em. And I tell her, you don't get the rest until you've agreed . . .'

'Agreed to what?'

'Incognito, baby. No names. The best deal in town, and I've cornered the market. Y'know what? In a place where every club's a front for one fucking thing or another, I think you just can't take a bit of honesty.'

'What is it you're being honest about?'

'That men want to screw young girls. That, guess what, young girls want to pop men. But that doesn't suit someone who's looking for victims, does it? Well you won't find any here, pal. It's a room full of people doing what they want, with who they want, when they want. The name of a guy in last week?' He laughed. 'Get real, and get the fuck out of my club.'

It was my turn to smile now, and I stood up, happy at least to have seen his real face. 'You've been very helpful, Mr Russell. Thanks.' Alicia returned with a fresh Jack and Coke in hand.

'Take it,' said Russell. 'It's on me.'

I accepted the drink and dumped it on his head. 'Look at that, you're right about everything.' I handed the empty glass back to the stunned girl just as the doorman closed his forearm across my neck, dragging me across the dance floor by the head.

Sutty was laughing like a drain. 'Tried to tell ya,' he said. 'A dog doesn't know what shit is unless you rub his nose in it.' We were crossing the road back to the car.

'*Hey*,' someone shouted. I turned around, saw the girl, Alicia, coming towards us. 'Who the fuck do you think you are?'

'Do you collect these girls or what?' said Sutty yawning. 'I'll be in my office.'

I turned, walked into the middle of the road, met her halfway. 'Excuse me?'

'You heard. What, you go round fucking people up?'

'The only thing I fucked up were his hair plugs. Have you got something to say to me?'

She looked at me through those unreadable UV lenses. 'A few things, actually, yeah.'

'Come on,' I said, leading her back to the pavement. 'How old are you?'

She thought I was asking if she was legal to drink. 'Eighteen,' she said, defiantly.

'Well I just spoke to a girl the same age who met a scumbag here last week. All I need is the guy's name to go and set him straight. Your friend in there thinks that's too much to ask. Do you?'

'Depends on the scumbag.'

'Ollie or Oliver something.' She didn't move. 'Look, if you know who I'm talking about, do me a favour. His surname, anything.' I stepped closer to allow a group of people past us, into the club.

She folded her arms. 'Cartwright,' she said quietly.

'Oliver Cartwright?' She nodded almost imperceptibly. 'You wouldn't happen to know where he lives?'

'Do you know Imperial Point?'

'The Quays?'

She nodded. 'Flat 1003.'

'Tell me about him.' But she'd already turned and started for the club, her arms wrapped around herself. 'You knew,' I said to her back. She stopped walking. 'As soon as I said sexual harassment to Russell, you knew who I was talking about.'

She half turned. 'Me and Ollie were a bad match, y'know? We both liked being in control.'

'Let us drop you somewhere,' I said.

'Like where?'

'Like home.'

She smiled. It was just a flicker at first, then the real thing. She ran the back of her hand over her mouth, like she was trying to wipe it off her face. I saw the hot-pink lipstick, smeared across her wrist.

'This is as close as I get to it.' When I didn't say anything she laughed again. 'Guy Russell's my dad.'

6

The Quays were only a twenty-minute drive from Piccadilly, skirting around the city centre, and the roads were clear at this time of night.

'What's all this about?' said Sutty.

'It wouldn't interest you.'

'Suit yourself,' he said, turning to look out the passenger-side window. 'Just don't drag me into it.'

'Drag you into what? Doing your job?'

'Whatever it is,' he said. 'You and those fucking girls again. Last year not enough for ya?'

'If anyone can turn a blind eye, it's you, Sutts. You've got two of them.' He shot me a look but didn't say anything else, and we drove the rest of the way in silence.

It was around 12.30 a.m. when we arrived at the Quays. Formerly the site of the city docks, a port on a busy stretch of the Manchester shipping canal, they'd fallen into ruin when the industry went abroad. In the eighties the boomers had swept in and redeveloped everything into half a billion pounds' worth of shiny, ultra-modern high- and low-rises, glittering out on to the water. The buildings were uniformly steel and reflective, jutting out from the ground at crazy angles like enormous shards of anti-climbing glass. The architecture, and the economic reality of the people living in it, made for an uncomfortable fit with a lot of the city's down-at-heel housing.

I got out of the car and went for the building's entrance. When I looked back at Sutty he was already running a wet wipe along the steering wheel.

Imperial Point had been the first high-rise here, and still stood tallest. The tower had a slanting, asymmetric shape. It looked like the visual expression of a slumping stock market. Unlike Owens Park the streets and the buildings were quiet, and I felt no pull from my personal history. I'd only ever visited the area to break up domestic disturbances. There were either some especially thin walls here, or some especially unhappy people.

I found the entrance, rang the bell and explained myself to the bleary-eyed doorman. He'd been wedged in behind a desk and I got the feeling that I'd woken him.

'I can take you up . . .' He was tucking his shirt in.

'I'll manage,' I said, already going for the lift.

I stepped out on to the tenth floor, felt the quality of the valeted carpet underfoot. Air conditioners hummed overhead and the walls, when I touched them, were like blocks of ice. Automatic lights came on as I passed beneath, dimming again once I was out of their range. The corridors were quiet, still and identical. I got turned around once or twice but eventually found 1003. There was a peephole set into the door and I had the sensation of being watched. Before I could knock, it opened a couple of inches on the chain, and I saw a man squinting out at me.

'Ollie Cartwright?'

He considered me for a moment. 'And you are?'

'Detective Constable Aidan Waits.'

'It's the middle of the night, Detective Constable. What's this about?'

'Perhaps we'd be quieter inside?'

He looked at me.

I looked back at him.

He closed the door and I heard him taking the chain off. When he opened it again he spoke to me through literally gritted teeth.

'Right this way.'

I went in, past some hung-up jackets, noting a well-worn denim one that stood out against his shoulder-padded blazers. I went into the beige-grey living room. The furniture was brand new and there was a TV on the far wall that was bigger than the front door. There was an upright hard-shell flight case beside it. I sat down, felt the chill of the air conditioning. In the corners of the mirrored coffee table, I thought I could see powder residue.

Oh, happy day.

Cartwright stood in the doorway watching me. Trying to look like he meant business in his monogrammed dressing gown. He was a big man, older than I was, somewhere in his mid-to-late thirties, as Sophie had said. His hair was thinning and his cheeks were two fleshy pouches hanging off a red, booze-tanned face. I felt a twist of jealousy that the girl I'd spoken to earlier had actually spent a night with this man, and I decided to take it out on him.

'Take a seat,' I said. As he crossed the room I saw he was wearing flip-flops, that he dragged them across the floor when he walked. I closed my eyes for a moment then opened them again.

Cartwright collapsed into the chair opposite. 'What's this about?'

'I want you to tell me that.'

He glared at me, radiating annoyance.

'I'll wait, then.' As I said it, I felt my phone vibrate in my pocket. I ignored it. 'Tell me about yourself.'

'Like what?'

'Full name, job description . . .'

'Not a big TV watcher?'

'Are you more annoyed that I woke you up or that I don't know who you are?'

'Badge first,' he said with a sniff. I passed it over. Watched him memorize my name before handing it back. He gave me a meaningless, bland smile. It did look familiar.

'Name's Oliver Cartwright. I'm a commentator for Lolitics.' His inflection went up at the end of the sentence like it was a question. It was a name I associated with vengeful, right-wing web journalism. The odd talking-head appearance on TV that always meant it was time to change the channel.

'I'll look out for it. What's the luggage about?'

'Dubai on Tuesday.'

'Business?'

'Stag week . . .'

'You're single?'

'Yeah, look this is harassment—'

'Harassment. I'm glad you brought that up.' He started to respond but thought better of it. 'What's your social life like, Ollie? Where do you drink?'

'Wherever they serve it. Something wrong with that?'

'Ever get along to Incognito?' He sat back, uncomfortable. 'You might lie for a living, but remember you're breaking the law when you do it to a police officer.'

He smiled at me. He looked like a man checking for food in his teeth. 'I haven't lied, Detective.'

'You know why I'm here. There's a girl's jacket hanging up in the hallway. Somehow I don't think you've got the shoulders for it . . .'

'Oh, classic,' he said, watching me through half-open eyes. 'She has a one-night stand and it turns into rape a week later.'

'What makes you think that?'

'These girls fall off the fucking assembly line unable to live with themselves. Any instinct they follow's just something new to regret the next day. And she was well up for it, if that's what you're asking.'

'Difficult thing to prove,' I said. 'And we have to take these things seriously . . .'

He smiled again, almost as though it were him interviewing me. 'I can prove it, actually.'

Somehow I was surprised when he shrugged, took his phone from his dressing-gown pocket and started scrolling. I hadn't thought he was stupid enough to volunteer the video himself. He smiled when he found the file he was after and handed it to me. The still image was of Sophie. I pressed play and breathy sounds filled the room. The video showed the girl, flat on the bed as Ollie laboured on top of her. The expression on his face was priceless. He couldn't believe his luck, either.

'Looks like a pretty satisfied customer, wouldn't you say?' There was a leer creeping out from the corners of his lips. I felt like slapping it off his face. I stopped the video, erased it, then went to his deleted items and cleared that, too. He snatched for the phone but I moved it in time.

'Is that the only copy?'

'Yeah, you—'

'Sit down, Ollie.'

'What?'

'Sit down.' Hesitantly, he did. 'OK, tonight's main story.' He rolled his eyes. 'I don't believe that this is the only copy.'

'I don't give a shit what you believe,' he said, re-folding his arms. I looked at him for a moment then ran my middle finger along the corners of the coffee table, holding the powder residue up to him.

'Think you can make me believe this is dandruff?' He blushed. 'I don't believe it's the only copy,' I repeated. I felt my phone vibrating in my pocket again. 'So we'll have a look at your computer. Once we've deleted it from there, I'm going to go and you won't hear from me again.' I looked at him. 'Sophie won't hear from you again, either. Will she?'

'No,' he said, holding eye contact. He took me through to his study and showed me the files saved on his computer. We trawled through various video images but none saved in the last week. My phone was vibrating again and I looked at the screen. *Sutty.*

'Excuse me,' I said, stepping into the next room to answer it.

'*You moving into one of these fucking flats or what?*'

'I'll be five—'

32

'*We've got a job. You'll be at the main entrance in sixty seconds or you'll be walking.*'

He hung up and I went back into the study.

Cartwright looked at me. 'I'm telling you that was the only copy.'

I didn't believe him but the fear seemed real enough.

'Fine,' I said, walking back through the living room towards the front door. 'But if you're lying to me you'll be making your next sex-tape in prison.' In the hall I stopped for Sophie's jacket and unhooked it. 'And I'm taking this with me,' I said, holding it up.

'Good riddance.'

'You're getting off light, Ollie. Have a nice life.'

I could feel my heart beating when I got back to the car. Sutty was standing beside it, leaning on the roof. He was squinting into his phone, trying to type a text message with the knuckle of his index finger.

He looked up when he saw me coming. 'Oh, finally . . .'

'Everything OK?'

'Reported break-in, Palace Hotel.'

I climbed into the car and started up. Felt Sutty's slick disinfectant on the steering wheel again. 'Why can't uniform catch it?'

'It's money,' he said. He looked at the girl's jacket I'd thrown on to the back seat. 'Don't even tell me what that's about.'

7

The Palace is an enormous Victorian redbrick on the corner of Oxford Road and Whitworth. It sits opposite the Grand Central and the Thirsty Scholar, with the Black Dog Ball Room around the corner. I could see the clock tower, two hundred feet above us, commanding the skyline. There had been nights when I'd gotten so drunk and so lost that I'd used that tower like a lighthouse. In the bad old days I'd even stayed at the hotel once or twice, sometimes with girls I'd just met, sometimes when it was too late to even try and get home. I'd thought it was a shame when it was shut down. Renovation implied change, and the Palace was heritage, one of those rare things in life that should stay the same. It had been a while since the doors closed, and I'd read nothing in the press about them reopening. As we got closer I saw that even the clock tower, something I'd always relied on, was telling the wrong time.

It was 1 a.m.

The entrance was a grand, architectural statement. A fifteen-foot marble archway set into the red brick of the building. A young woman was waiting outside. I was surprised to see her breath in the air until I noticed the glowing blue tip of an e-cigarette between her fingers. She was smartly dressed, projecting the kind of confidence that made her look cool against the listless, hot and bothered nightlife. As we approached she was staring into the middle distance, exhaling synthetic smoke, and we had to wait a second for acknowledgement.

'Police?' she said, placing the e-cig in her purse.

'I'm Detective Constable Waits and this is Detective Inspector Sutcliffe.'

Sutty cut in. 'We hear you've got yourself a visitor, Mrs—'

'Ms,' she said.

'Well,' he smiled. 'I stand politically corrected. Ms . . . ?'

'Aneesa Khan.'

'And what's your connection to the Palace, Ms Khan?'

'I work for Anthony Blick Solicitors. We're currently negotiating the sale of the hotel.'

'Hadn't realized it was on the market,' said Sutty. 'I might've made you an offer . . .'

She gave him a smile that was there and then gone again, like a shrug of the face. 'Misdirection, Inspector. Renovation sounds better than the truth.'

'Which is?'

'Shut down due to the costly acrimonious split of its owners.'

'So the place is empty?'

'It should be.' She frowned. 'I suppose we'd better go inside and find out.'

The lobby was enormous, and the only light came from the hotel's front desk on the far side of the room. It was an impressive, overwhelming space, somehow insulated against the heat from outside. Many of the furnishings were originals from when the Palace was built in the 1800s. It had been the headquarters of a prominent life insurance company and had a sense of style and grace rarely seen in modern architecture. The ceiling, which must have been thirty feet above us, was a stained-glass dome. The floors were gleaming, glazed stone, and enormous pillars lined the room, keeping the roof above our heads. As the world became more cramped, it felt remarkable to walk off a congested street at one in the morning, into a wide open space.

'The alarm was triggered about an hour ago.' Aneesa spoke quietly but her voice reverberated about us. 'When no one switched it off, they called me.'

35

'Not unusual for something to fall over in a building this big . . .'

'We have a night watchman, though. Ali. I haven't been able to get hold of him.' All three of us looked at the unmanned front desk. The lamp that had been positioned to shine out at the doorway, right into our eyes. Its glare shrouded the far side of the room in darkness.

'Is that his workstation?' I asked. Aneesa nodded, not taking her eyes off the desk. 'I'll check it out. You can wait here if you like.' I turned and walked towards the light. After a moment I heard her following me, heels echoing on the stone floor. There was a sigh, then the cheap squeak of Sutty's plastic shoes.

I reached Ali's workstation and moved the light out of our eyes. It was hot to the touch and must have been on all night. There was no one behind the desk, and the only objects on its surface were a phone, a key card and a coffee. Sutty squeaked towards me, leaned over and touched the mug.

'Cold as ice,' he said.

I moved round the desk, held up the mobile phone. 'Could this be his?' Aneesa nodded. I pressed a button and the screen lit up. Five missed calls.

'They're all me . . .' she said.

'Could he be doing his rounds?'

'Without his phone?'

Sutty yawned into his armpit. 'He's probably sleeping it off in one of the rooms.'

'Sleeping what off?' said Aneesa.

'*It*,' Sutty replied.

'I don't think he's the type.'

'Must just be my faith in humanity,' he said. 'On the blink again . . .'

Aneesa looked between us. 'I was called out because the alarm was triggered and no one switched it off. Ali's not at his post, so where is he?'

'OK . . .' Sutty went to the lifts and pressed the call button. 'Let's have a look around.'

'They haven't been signed off yet,' said Aneesa. He shot her a look. 'They don't work, Inspector.'

'Something in common with your security guard, then.' He looked at the steps which led up to the palatial, famously grand staircase and shook his head. 'I get nosebleeds above sea level anyway. Up you go, Aids. We'll search the ground floor.'

I gave Aneesa a glance and went towards the staircase.

'I'll come with you,' she said. Sutty snorted but didn't comment.

Once we were out of earshot she turned to me. 'Is he really your boss?'

'Yeah, he can be quite nice when you get to know him.'

'Really?'

I shook my head. 'I was actually hoping he'd try the stairs. He might've been dead by the third floor.'

She smiled, but nervously. 'I have a sudden urge to see your ID.' We stopped. The staircase was dimly lit. 'You don't strike me as much of a policeman . . .'

'Very perceptive.' She raised an eyebrow and I searched my pockets. 'I'm not much of one.' I showed her my card and we began climbing the stairs again. They went endlessly up, with two large flights between each floor. 'Tell me about your security guard.'

'We have two, on alternating shifts. Ali's our night man, a really good guy.'

'How long's he been with you?'

'About as long as I've been involved with the Palace, which is as long as it's been closed. Six months or so . . .'

'One guard at a time isn't much for all of this. There must be, what, two hundred rooms . . . ?'

'Closer to three hundred.'

'And all of them locked?' I asked, as we reached the first-floor landing.

'That's the idea . . .'

The corridors on each floor were linked, forming a circuit that would bring us back to the main stairwell. We went left, into a low, ambient buzz. The anti-noise of a cavernous, empty building. Lights, pipes and appliances in chorus. The air was thick and stale up here, having gone too long without human interruption, and I could hear the static carpet, lisping beneath our heels. I tried the handles on two or three rooms as we passed them. They were all locked, and I took it as read that the rest would be too.

'Have you ever been here before?' said Aneesa. 'When it was open, I mean . . .' There was a forced note of cheer in her voice and I thought she was probably nervous. It felt unusual to be walking through an empty hotel with a stranger in the early hours of the morning.

'Once or twice,' I said. 'My main memory was getting lost in these corridors.'

'It's a bit of a maze.'

'Maybe that's what happened to Ali.' I'd meant it to sound reassuring but it just brought her attention back to him.

'You don't think so, do you? You or your partner?'

'In our experience, security guards aren't usually that proactive. They tend to clock in and put their feet up for a few hours. The first and last patrol of the shift's usually when they hand over to the next guy.'

'Ali's not like that. We even pay him extra to go room by room.' We'd completed our circuit of the corridor and began climbing the stairs towards the second floor.

'Why extra?'

'To run the taps, flush the toilets – things can go stale in an empty hotel without some movement.' She saw a look pass across my face. 'What is it?'

'Well, the doors are all locked.' She frowned and I went on. 'If he was doing his rounds, he'd have taken his key card with him.' As she turned this thought over, the lights flickered and went out.

There were no windows in the stairwell and we were suddenly in total darkness.

'What's happening?' she said, reaching out for me. I found the torch in my pocket, clicked it on and held it in the space between us.

'Probably the trip switch. Do you know where the fuse box is?'

'Main one's on the ground floor, I think.'

'OK. Why don't you head back downstairs and call my part-ner?' I dug out my phone and gave her his number. 'Tell him where I am. If you can get the lights back on, even better.'

'Sure,' she said, her voice faltering. I couldn't tell if she was scared or disappointed. She started down the stairs anyway, hold-ing her own phone up like a lantern. I reached the second floor by torchlight, cautiously moving its beam about the landing before I moved on. The corridor was so long that the thin spot of light didn't even reach the other end. I started forwards, the closed doors either side of me igniting a peculiar kind of claustrophobia. I tried the handles of the first few. All of them were locked.

About halfway along the corridor I stopped. Absorbed a wave of paranoia. I clicked the torch off and stood still in the darkness, trying not to breathe. Feeling the blood beat through my ears. Then I turned the torch in the direction I'd come from and switched it back on.

Nothing.

I carried on, made a full circuit of the corridor and found myself back where I'd started. I climbed the stairs to the third floor and stopped on the landing. I could smell something now. Just the mem-ory of a scent. I couldn't tell if it was perfume or cologne but the edge of alcohol was unmistakable, standing out against the bland, heavy air. When I reached the mouth of the corridor and strafed the torch beam from side to side, I saw something and took a step back.

There was a man, a few feet away, lying face down on the carpet. I could see the blood on the back of his head, a fire extinguisher on the floor beside him.

'Hello,' I called out. He didn't move. I shone the light above him, straight down the centre of the corridor and began walking.

Reaching the man, I realized I'd been holding my breath. I exhaled, crouched beside him and placed a hand on his shoulder. He groaned.

'Can you hear me?' I said. My eyes fixed on the far wall. The thin spot of light from the torch. We were almost exactly halfway along the corridor and I felt exposed in the darkness.

'What happened . . . ?' he said, reaching for my arm.

I helped him sit up.

'Ali?'

'Yeah.'

'I think someone hit you. It's OK, I'm a police officer. Did you see anything?'

'I . . . I don't know.' As he spoke, a shape passed through the torchlight at the far end of the corridor, and he gripped my arm.

'It's all right,' I said. 'My partner should be here any minute. I have to follow them, OK?' He nodded, forgetting his head, wincing in pain. I stood and walked in the direction of the movement, covering as much of the corridor as I could with the light. I dialled Sutty and spoke quietly when he answered. 'I've found the security guard. Third floor. He's got a head injury and needs medical assistance. I'm pursuing an intruder to the end of the corridor. Request back-up.' I hung up as I reached the corner. Took a breath and then stepped around it.

Nothing.

As I came back to the staircase I heard a sound, like moths tapping at a window, and I realized the lights were dink-dink-ing back to life. I looked all around me, letting my eyes adjust, and saw that I was holding my torch with both hands. I clicked it off, pocketed it and started up the stairs to the fourth floor. Something felt different. It was even hotter up here and there was a subtle change in air pressure.

I thought I could hear a low, hissing sound.

I felt a draught against my skin and followed it down the left-hand corridor, to a fire exit, slightly ajar. I opened it all the way with my foot and looked down the staircase. Street sounds and a blast of cool air. If someone had just gone through it, they were outside by now. I let out a breath, more relieved than anything, and began retracing my steps. As I did, I saw there was a light coming from one of the rooms I'd passed.

The door was wide open.

Room 413.

It was raised on a slightly higher level than the rooms either side of it, with its own short staircase leading up. I climbed the stairs feeling suddenly dizzy, suddenly lost in the labyrinthine corridors.

'Hello . . .' I called out.

No answer.

I walked through the doorway then stepped back against the wall. Room 413 was a large suite, at least double the size of any I'd ever stayed in. The light came from a desk lamp and gave the room a moody, intimate tone. The window was closed but I could hear faint sounds of traffic down on Oxford Road, still going at gone one in the morning. The glare of the city outside cast moving, kaleidoscopic shadows across the walls.

At the far side of the room was the solid, immovable silhouette of a man.

He was sitting in a chair, facing the window. He didn't respond as I drew closer and I felt a cold sweat, itching out from my scalp. I wiped my face with my forearm, eyes not leaving the shape. As I came alongside him I saw that he was dead. His own sweat was glazed across his face, and I thought I could feel the heat pouring out of him. He looked well groomed for a midnight intruder, cleanly shaven with a sharp haircut. I stopped when I saw that his eyes were wide open. They were cobalt-blue and staring into the next life like he was done with this one. It was his teeth that sent me out of the room, though. The muscles in his mouth had contracted viciously, and locked into a wide, wincing grin.

8

Aneesa waited with Ali for the paramedics to arrive. I'd told Sutty there was something he needed to see on the fourth floor and taken him up to 413. The corridors were unventilated and warmer at the top of the building. By the time we reached the room his pale skin was bubbling with sweat. He looked like he was being boiled alive.

'Better be good,' he said, wheezing up the narrow staircase. He playfully rapped his knuckles on the open door and shouted: '*Housekeeping.*' He stopped when he saw the body, then looked back at me. Jabbed a wet finger in my chest. 'You fucking touch anything?'

'No.'

'The light?'

'On already.'

He stared at me for a second then turned to the man. With the window closed the room was oppressively warm. When Sutty shrugged off his jacket I followed suit. His shirt was saturated with sweat.

He paused, taking in his surroundings before going any further. There was the usual king-sized bed, alongside some teak walls and furnishings. It felt more like a smart, city-centre apartment than a hotel room. Sutty nodded at a plastic key card lying on the floor.

The man was sitting in a leather chair which had been moved to face the window. There was still some light, bleeding through the curtains, casting shapes on the walls.

'You need to see his face,' I said.

'Pretty boy, eh?' Sweat poured out from Sutty's skin and I mopped my own brow in response. 'Well, lead the way.'

The desk lamp was too dim for the full effect, so I clicked on my torch, went towards the man and lit him up. The light caught his teeth, that rictus grin, and Sutty winced, waved at me to lower it.

He licked his lips thoughtfully. 'Makes you wonder what's so funny . . .'

I didn't say anything.

When I lowered the torch beam on to the man's lap I saw an odd pattern on one trouser leg. A circular shape in orange stitching. I was about to take another step when Sutty clicked his fingers at me. Shook his head.

The man was middle-aged. Wearing a dark suit. My first impression, from his rich brown skin, was that he was of Middle Eastern origin. The effect was somewhat undone by his piercing blue eyes. They, in conjunction with the vicious smile on his face, made him look like he knew something that we didn't. Some awful knowledge right at the edge of sanity.

'Homeless?' said Sutty.

I shook my head. 'Clean clothes, no smell. He looks more like a don or a teacher than a user . . .'

Sutty grinned. 'Well, it's all academic until forensics arrive. I wanna talk to that security guard, though, before the paramedics get rid of him. Take the mountain to Mohammed.'

'I think his name was Ali.'

'Yeah-yeah,' he said, crossing the room.

I followed him to the door, stopped, and looked back at the man. Outside, I could hear the traffic on Oxford Road. Piercing through it all were the sounds of sirens, two or three sets, moving in different directions through the city.

9

Ali had been lifted on to a gurney and moved to the lobby. Two paramedics stood beside him, discussing his vitals. Aneesa watched, anxiously, at a distance. Several uniformed officers had arrived and one of them was talking to her, taking a statement.

Sutty approached the lead paramedic. 'We need a word before you cart him off.'

'I'm afraid you'd have a one-way conversation. We've given him something for the pain.'

'Well, give him something else.'

'It doesn't work that way, Inspector. We're taking him to St Mary's, so you can catch him there tomorrow morning.' Sutty started to speak but swallowed the insult and nodded. Then he shouted across the room at the uniformed officer talking to Aneesa.

'Oi, hot fuzz.' The officer turned. 'You go with 'em. He's a witness or a criminal, a flight risk either way.'

'Sir. It's just that my orders were—'

'Your orders have changed, sweetheart.' The officer didn't move. 'You'd better be pissing your pants now so you don't need to go on the ward, son.' The officer went bright red, turned and followed the paramedics outside.

I looked at Sutty. 'You're a class act . . .'

'And you're lucky there's someone more trustworthy than you around. Right,' he said, clapping his hands. 'Can everyone dressed like a male stripper gather round.' Aneesa crumpled into a chair

44

and Sutty rolled his eyes. 'Make yourself useful and get rid of her.' He briefed the officers to secure the building and begin a search of the premises. 'No one goes up to the third or fourth floors without my say-so. Repeat that back to me.' They did and Sutty grunted. 'Good, now get on with it.' They filed out of the lobby in different directions, leaving Aneesa and me alone.

'Are you OK?' I said. She nodded but didn't look up. 'It's been a night. Let me call you a cab.'

She paced up and down the road while we waited, like she was trying to walk off the memory of Ali's attack. The lapsed detective in me wondered if there was something between them but I immediately dismissed the idea. She was young and successful, a city girl at least twenty years his junior, going places. When the car arrived she climbed inside and started to close the door before pausing.

'The fourth floor . . .' she said.

'What about it?'

'You found Ali on the third, you said. Why did your boss say they couldn't go up to the fourth? What else was up there?' I didn't answer and she came to her own conclusion. 'Before the paramedics put him under he was scared. Really scared . . .'

'Scared of what?'

'Voices, he said.'

I passed her my card. 'We'll need to speak to you again, but call me if there's anything you want to talk about in the meantime.' She closed the door and stared at the back of the driver's seat like we'd never met, until the cab merged into the traffic and disappeared from view.

Although I'd only been gone for ten minutes, Scene of Crime Officers had arrived when I re-entered the building. I saw a junior member of the team hauling gear up the stairs as Sutty was coming back down them.

'That's all she wrote,' he said. 'I've set the primary scene boundary in 413.'

'It should be at least the whole floor.'

'We've only got half a team. Tactical can go door-to-door as and when. It's not as though there'll be a rush on the front desk tomorrow morning, is it? I'm pushing off.' He walked past me, whistling a tune. The sound echoed through the lobby.

I carried on up, past several uniformed officers. They were visibly uncomfortable with my being there, and I thought they might even try to block my path. When I reached the third floor I saw Karen Stromer, the pathologist, descending the stairs. Stromer was an impressive woman with a reputation for withering criticism and sharp instincts. It was the first time I'd seen her since rejoining the night shift, and I got the feeling that I'd fallen in her estimation. She valued serious officers, professionals, and the look on her face said she didn't consider me one. She was wearing a pristine, plastic CSI cover-all. She stopped when she saw me and drew down her hood, revealing a narrow, bone-white face and a frown. She had short, black hair, gleaming dark marbles for eyes and an almost invisible little paper-cut for a mouth.

'Detective Constable Waits,' she said, still standing a few stairs above me. 'May I ask what you're doing here?'

'We were responding to a reported break-in . . .' I started.

She cut me off with a subliminal smile and spoke with a quiet, steady voice. 'I hadn't quite realized you were back on active duty.'

'I managed to keep a foot in the door.'

'And a foot in something else, if I recall correctly. You were arrested. You were stealing drugs from evidence . . .'

My voice sounded thick. 'They dropped the charges.'

She nodded, stared down at the space between us and smiled to herself. 'I think I'll ask you to return to the lobby, if that's OK. I don't want my crime scene contaminated.'

I started to back away. 'Is there anything you can tell us at this stage?'

'Time of death somewhere between 11.30 p.m. and 12.30 a.m. Never ideal because one doesn't know which date to record it as.

No identification on his person. And it looks as though the labels have been cut out of his clothes.'

'Cut out?'

'I'll be making a full report to your superior officer. Detective Inspector Sutcliffe, I believe?'

I nodded and started for the stairs. 'I keep trying to believe it myself.'

'There was one thing, Detective Constable.' I turned to see the smile, still playing on her thin lips. 'I wonder if you spotted the thread in the dead man's trouser leg?' She read the look on my face. 'Of course you did. The stitching's from the inside . . .'

'What does it mean?'

'It means that something's been sewn into his trousers. Something he obviously wanted to keep safe . . .' When I didn't say anything she went on. 'If I find drugs, I'm afraid I'll feel compelled to report your attempted access of the crime scene. Given your history.' She started to climb the stairs again, clearly unwilling to leave the body alone while I was in the building.

'You won't find any,' I said to her back.

She stopped but didn't turn. 'And what makes you so certain of that, Detective Constable?'

'It's something else.'

'Well,' she said. 'I suppose you'd know.'

She climbed the stairs out of sight.

Standing alone on the landing I realized I was out of breath.

The boy reached out for the woman's hand but she pulled away.

He was in the chaos of an outdoor market, between the stalls, surrounded by adults twice his size. The people were all moving in different directions and all he could see were their hands trailing by him at eye level. He reached out for the woman again but she shook him off and disappeared. The boy stopped, panting, being jostled all the while by the movements of people around him. He reached out for another familiar hand. Dark blue veins, long fingernails and silver jewellery. He held on tight this time and didn't let go, even when the woman pulled him out into a clearing. He reached his other hand up and hung on, until she was dragging him along the floor.

She stopped, gave a final tug and then crouched to look at him.

'What are you doing?' she said. The boy let go and saw that, her hands aside, she wasn't much like his mother. This woman was younger. She smelt like fresh flowers, and when she frowned it was compassionate, curious. He opened his mouth, wondering what he was about to say, when the light changed. Something blocked out the sun and a strong hand clasped his shoulder.

'Wally, Jesus, mate. Don't run off like that, yeah? Scared me to death.'

The boy watched the woman's face change. She moved dark hair out of her eyes then stood, squinting at the large man who'd joined them. The boy twisted round to look up at him. Against the sunlight he was just a silhouette. That superhero square jawline with the shoulders to match.

'He's yours?' asked the woman, tilting her head.

'For my sins,' said the man, with a rogue's grin. 'I'll never tell you what I did, though. I'm Bateman, by the by.' He held out a hand and she took it.

'Holly,' she said. 'That's a funny name he's got . . .' She was prolonging the conversation unnaturally. The boy often noticed women doing that around Bateman.

'Wanna know where it comes from?' Holly wrinkled her nose, nodded. 'Well, Wally's not his full name. It's actually short for wallet.' He reached behind the boy's ear and produced a coin, dropping it into his outstretched hand. 'Kid's a gold mine.' Holly started to laugh. When she did, the boy saw that she was more like a girl than a woman. Bateman took a step closer, offered her a cigarette. 'You live around here, Holl?' Her face changed again, and she shifted her weight from one leg to another.

It was dark by the time Bateman got back to the car.

Holly said her parents were out for the night, and Bateman had gone to look at her house. When he got back to the car he smelt like her, like fresh flowers. He sniffed his fingers and then searched his pockets for a cigarette, lighting up and chuckling to himself. He'd smoked it halfway down to the filter before he looked over at Wally. He reached behind the boy's ear as if to produce another coin, but this time took a fistful of his hair. He held him tight with one hand, edging the tip of the cigarette towards him with the other.

'Not a word to your mother, understood?' Wally nodded, eyes locked on to the flame. Bateman grunted and let him go. 'Let's see how you did at the market.' Wally opened the glove compartment and pulled out some jewellery. Some of the rings from women he'd held hands with and three wallets he'd taken from passing men. Bateman went through the wallets, stripping them of cash and cards before dumping them out the window. He put the rings in his pocket and started the engine. He looked at the boy again before he pulled out into the road.

'Fucking gold mine,' he said.

———

II
Red Eyes

1

I woke up confused by my surroundings, like I'd been moved in my sleep. The phone was ringing and I climbed out of bed to answer it.

'Hello,' I said, surprised at the gravel in my voice. There was no answer. Shafts of bright, warming sun beamed through the windows into my eyes, and everything was quiet and still. I leaned into the wall, happy to bask in the daylight I saw so little of. 'Anyone?' A moment passed. I thought I heard breathing down the line before it went dead.

I waited a second, replaced the receiver and went to the window. It was the same Northern Quarter room I'd lived in for a year but it still felt borrowed, unfamiliar. My last job had required my moving here, severing ties with old friends that I'd yet to rebind. In the months since then I'd remained on pause, sleeping through the days and working through the nights. I'd got in from my shift after 6 a.m. It was after 9 now. The morning traffic that roared daily by my window had been and gone, and the street below was quiet. I could hear the buzz of talk radio coming from a car, the tick of a girl's heels down on the pavement.

I went to the bathroom and looked into the mirror. The night shift had done its work. Drained my skin of all colour, except for the immovable black shadows beneath my eyes. Sometimes my face seemed to change, drastically, in the night, and the next day I'd barely recognize it. I knew in reality it was just me, my idea of myself, that was so moveable, but now these shifts in perception, these changes, came so fast that they were frightening. Sometimes I thought I could even see my face warping, altering in the glass. I couldn't tell if it was the drugs, finally leaving my system after all these years, or some kind of psychological trauma. It felt like finding out something terrible and undeniable about myself every day, and had become one more reason to hide out on the night shift. I could disappear into it and never be the same person twice.

Identity, I thought.

The smiling man.

I usually experienced the presence of a dead body as an absence, but in this case it felt like a black hole opening up in front of me. Stromer said there had been no ID on his person, no labels in his clothes. As though the man had intended to disappear, to strip himself of all meaning. But the room we'd found him in sent mixed signals. I'd given a lot of thought to the anonymous death. Aokigahara, the suicide forest at the base of Mount Fuji, where the trees are so dense that the world can't get in. Varanasi, India, where the blasting heat of the funeral pyre incinerates hundreds of bodies a day, or the Ganges, where you can fill your veins with cheap smack and walk up to your waist through the grotesque waters, keep on going, and vanish into the slipstream. Dying in the Palace Hotel was different. A flaw in what I saw as an otherwise perfect design. Where everything else about the man felt anonymous, there was something personal about the choice of room, the choice of view. Whether he'd made that choice himself or not was a different matter.

The phone rang again and I went back into the living room to answer it.

'Rise and shine, gorgeous.'

'Morning, Sutts.' I could almost smell his breath through the phone. 'What can I do for you?'

'Turn that Aidan Waits frown upside down and get over to St Mary's.'

'Is the guard awake?'

'He'd better not be. I want those sulky blue eyes to be the first thing he sees. Hold his hand and squeeze out a tear or two, he'll spill his guts.'

'Shouldn't we be handing this over to the day shift?' I wanted to know how involved we'd be before getting invested.

'Officially it's on DS Lattimer's desk.'

'So it's a paperweight.'

'Which is why I said you'd help him with the legwork.'

'Oh, yeah?'

'It's going in my clearance stats, Aid. Not his.'

Between Sutty and Lattimer that meant doing all the legwork. Somehow I didn't mind. 'What do you think our guard knows?' I said.

'Maybe he flat-lined for a few seconds and saw the other side? You tell me. I'm mainly interested in what happened before someone bounced a fire extinguisher off his head. Get a sense of what kinda guy he is, dirty or clean.'

'I'll head over there now.'

'And ask him about this other guard, the day guy. Name's Marcus Collier.'

'Have we got anything on him yet?'

'An address but you know what it's like. Uniform couldn't raise a hard-on in a high school. They're looking now.'

'Do you think he's involved?'

'Well, one point of interest. The key card found on the floor of room 413 belonged to him.' Marcus Collier. The day-shift security guard. I wondered if it could be that simple. He could have let someone into the hotel before Ali's shift started. He could have had his key card stolen. He could even be our dead man. 'Anyway,' said Sutty, derailing my train of thought. 'Everyone's involved until I say otherwise. That includes your boyfriend in a coma. If the nice-guy act doesn't wake him up, he might need a dose of your real personality, but please, only as a last resort.'

'Is this a murder investigation?'

'Only if it's over *my* dead body. Think of this as a pleasant

diversion from the investigation of dustbin fires. A thorough ana-
lysis of the facts designed to get the file off our desk and into my
clearance stats.'

Sutty's investigative approach was usually the path of least
resistance.

'So you're going to say it's suicide? The attack on Ali implies—'

'Implies shit,' said Sutty. 'For all we know, Smiley Face knocked him
out then topped himself. You haven't worked a case like this before,
Aidan. We're looking for a result, not a resolution. Our job's to find out
what top brass want to hear and belt it out from the rooftops.'

'And have we got anything on him?' I tried to ask naturally but
I couldn't keep the interest out of my voice. I could hear Sutty
breathing down the phone. 'Sutts?'

'We'll have the post-mortem results tomorrow. All I've heard
from that direction is Stromer wants you off it.'

'Why?'

'Why does a fly eat shit? She's a dyke, hates men.' He snorted.
'She must have you confused with one.' A call with Sutty could feel
like pouring poison into your head, and my ears were already ringing. I gripped the phone tightly.

'I don't think that's it, Sutts . . .'

'Listen, she's been muff-diving so long she's finally got the bends.
Don't worry about it.'

I changed the subject. 'Where will you be?'

'It's Sunday. Shift doesn't start for another ten hours, I'll be in
bed. Let me know how you get on.'

I started to hang up and then thought of something. 'Did you
call me earlier? About five minutes ago?' He whistled in response.
'What?'

'Two callers in one day, an Aidan Waits record. Maybe it was
Stromer,' he laughed. 'Maybe you've brought her back from the
other side?' Sutty hung up and I took a shower, mainly to wash
him off me. I drank a coffee, dressed and left for the hospital. As I
closed the door I wondered idly who else had been calling.

2

The sunlight was brilliant, beating down from a powder-blue sky. The people were all gleaming smiles and glowing skin, and their shadows danced out in all directions at once. After so long spent out of the day, it felt like a brand-new sensation to walk, unnoticed, through a beautiful one. I passed through streets of dirty redbrick buildings, through the morning bustle, feeling somehow new, somehow awake.

My shirt was damp against my body when I reached St Mary's. I approached the reception and was directed up to the first floor. I arrived on to the ward to see the uniformed officer Sutty had sent to keep watch. He was pacing back and forth, yawning into the crook of his arm. He started when he saw me, unconsciously tucking his shirt in as I closed the distance between us.

'Morning,' I said.

He looked at me strangely. 'Detective Constable.' As he spoke there was a scream from behind a closed door. 'Just some bloke with night terrors,' he said wearily.

'It's the morning.'

'Go and tell him that, he's been at it for hours.'

'How's our patient?'

'Slept through the lot. Wish they'd given me whatever they gave him.'

'A blow to the head? Don't give Sutty any ideas.'

'That was my fault . . .'

I changed the subject. 'Our man hasn't said anything?'

'Hasn't opened his eyes, but they don't think there's any permanent damage.'

'When are you being relieved?'

'Two hours from now.' He said it like a wish.

'Well, I need to be here when he wakes up, anyway. You may as well get off home. I can hang around until your replacement arrives.'

He paused. Glanced down the corridor over my shoulder, then looked at me again.

'I'm not sure I should leave him alone . . .'

'Alone?' I said. He floundered, searched for the right words. His hands were clasped so hard behind his back that I felt like I'd cuffed him. 'You mean that my reputation precedes me, Constable?' He gave me a combined look of relief and dismay as I addressed the elephant in the room. He nodded tentatively. 'That's fair enough,' I said. 'I'll find us both a coffee.'

Ali was awake an hour or so later. The doctor saw him first and, satisfied that he was OK to talk, asked a passing nurse to take me through. The nurse was a sick-looking man with grey, translucent teeth. He sucked them, audibly, as we walked. I wondered if he'd begun working here as a healthy person and then slowly absorbed the aura of madness and death surrounding him. I wondered what I was absorbing in my line of work. The patient I'd heard howling from the other side of the door fell silent when he saw us. He was rose-cheeked and sweating. He looked exhausted.

'Is he all right?' I asked the nurse.

'Ignore him, he's due for the deep six any day now.'

I stopped walking. 'I think I'll be all right on my own from here.'

'*Great*,' he said. He gave me a smile I could see through, turned on his heel and headed out of the ward. He paused by the door to exchange a few vicious words with the terrified patient and then left. I took a seat next to Ali, whose eyes were closed. He was a large man. His forearms, which rested on top of the bed sheet, were the size of my calves. It must have taken some blow to the head to put him under. He heard me sitting down and opened his eyes.

'Good morning, Mr Nasser. How are you feeling?'

He held out his hands as if to say, take a look.

'Did the doctor explain what happened?' His dark eyes moved on mine. 'You're in hospital. You were assaulted last night . . .' He put a hand to his head and nodded. 'I'm Detective Constable Aidan Waits. I was called to the Palace Hotel because something triggered the alarm.'

He spoke with a clean, considered Middle Eastern accent. 'You are the man who found me?'

I nodded. 'In the third-floor corridor. Do you know how you came to be up there?'

He frowned, concentrating on the memory. 'I heard voices.'

'What kinds of voices?'

'Men.' He hesitated. 'Shouting.' He thought for a second more and then corrected himself. 'Screaming.'

'Do you know how many voices?'

'I think two?' He shook his head. 'It sounded like an argument, a fight.'

'And what were they saying?'

He strained. 'I . . . could not tell . . .'

'Do you have any idea what time this was?'

'Before midnight, certainly. Or I would have already been on patrol.'

'So you heard the voices from the lobby?'

'Yes.'

'And that led you through to the stairwell?'

'Yes, I followed the voices.' He smiled, self-deprecatingly. 'Old fool.'

'You were only doing your job.'

'Was anything taken?' he said, trying to sit up.

'I'm afraid it's a little more serious than that. We found a body on the fourth floor.'

'I don't understand . . .'

'We're treating the death as suspicious.' I watched the news sink in, like a drop of ink in water.

'Who . . . ?'

'We haven't identified the body yet, but I have to ask, have you ever let any other people into the building?'

'Never.'

'No one at all?'

He thought about it. 'Workmen, months ago for repairs. Mr Blick occasionally for inspections . . .'

'Mr Blick's an owner?'

'Solicitor,' he said. 'Mr Blick is the man who hired me.' He was proud of the fact.

'I see, does he work with Ms Khan?'

'I believe he's her employer.'

'When was Mr Blick last around?'

'Months ago. He's been unwell, I believe.'

'OK. Did you see or hear anything unusual, anything out of the ordinary last night?'

'Not until the voices.'

'When I arrived I found a fire exit open on the fourth floor . . .'

He frowned. 'I didn't open any fire exits.'

The statement felt like a dead end so I changed direction. 'Can I ask how you came to be working at the Palace?'

He gave a cynical snort. 'How I came to be in this country?'

'If you like.'

'I am here one year, from Syria.'

'You sought asylum?'

'The devil is real there.' He looked down at the bed, his face clouded by thoughts I couldn't guess at. 'Yes, I sought asylum.'

'How did you find it?' He looked up at me. 'The process, I mean.'

'It's difficult. Like . . .' He searched for the word. '*Humiliation.* Life in the detention centre is very bad. That's why I found this security work. I can do the same job but with kindness. With a good heart.' He shrugged. 'But so far, I'm only a guard.'

'What kind of work did you do in Syria?'

He looked, almost wistfully, at our surroundings. 'I was a doctor,' he said. 'Fifteen years.'

'We've had some trouble locating your colleague, the day guard, Marcus. The description I have of him is neat, dark hair, tanned skin and blue eyes . . .' I was actually describing the dead body. There seemed no point in alerting Ali to his colleague's possible murder unless I had to, but he shook his head at the description.

'Marcus is white, pale, no hair.'

'Can you think where we might find him if he's not at home?'

He shook his head. 'Not close friends.'

'How do you get on?'

'I don't know,' he said, before amending the statement. 'I don't know him well.'

'Is he good at his job?'

'When you meet Marcus, will you ask about me?' I didn't say anything. 'Yes,' he nodded. '*Very* good at his job.'

'What do you mean by that?'

'Marcus has a business mind, entrepreneurial spirit.'

'Meaning?'

He snorted. 'You might find my meaning in the third-floor dustbins of the Palace.' I waited for more but he didn't expand on the statement. 'I'm telling you more than I know, sir,' he clarified. 'I'm telling you a guess.'

'OK. What about Marcus's key card?'

'Sir?'

'Can you think of any reason why we might find it in room 413, with the dead man?'

He struggled. 'None.'

I looked at him for a moment. 'Well, an officer will be along to take a full statement from you this morning. Until then, we'd like to leave someone on the door as well.'

'Watched?'

'It's for your own protection,' I said, standing to leave.

'Why?' he said, suddenly animated. 'Why protect me now?'

'You're a witness to what looks like a serious crime.'

'In Aleppo I saw everything. Then, when I sought asylum, no one asked. No one cared.' He laughed, joylessly. 'Here I see nothing, I am protected.'

'Sometimes we know things that we think we don't.'

He snorted again. 'And sometimes we don't know things that we think we do. Old saying,' he said. 'Shit in, shit out.'

'I think I've heard that one.'

As I left the ward the agitated patient started screaming again. I saw the grey-toothed nurse pacing down the corridor towards him, relishing the thought of an argument. I half-turned to intervene.

'Is he fighting with the patients again?' said a woman who I took to be a doctor.

I nodded. 'I think a guy in there might have given him a long night . . .'

'Well, that's the job,' she said, recognizing a fellow night owl in me. This happened more often than you'd think. We marked out the pale skin, the tired eyes in each other. 'I'll talk to him,' she said.

'Thanks.'

When I stepped outside, the heat was like a wall. I was thinking about Ali's experience, our talent for dehumanizing each other, when a large black BMW pulled up in front of me. I tried to walk around it, but the driver nudged forwards, blocking my path. The glass was tinted and I saw my own, troubled reflection before the rear window buzzed down. It revealed a familiar face, staring out at me.

'Aidan Waits,' said the man, in a low, Scottish growl. 'As I live and breathe . . .'

He looked like a grey-haired Lucifer, and I wasn't convinced he did either of those things.

'Parrs.'

'Put some respect on my name, son.'

'I'm sorry, Superintendent.'

He looked at me. His raw, exit-wound eyes. 'Where are you going?'

'Nowhere,' I said.

'Correct answer. Get in.'

3

Climbing out of the daylight and into the cool darkness of the BMW, I felt like I was stepping out of life itself. Being enveloped by something larger than me. I sat beside Parrs on the enormous back seat, leaving just enough space between us for a man to lie down and die. In my peripheral vision I could see his grey hair, grey clothes. The driver started up and I stared straight ahead, waiting.

With Superintendent Parrs you were always waiting.

He was a wiry, fatalistic spider of a man who played chess with the people around him. He was a strategist and a people user, as likely to ruin your life as to save it. He'd done both of those things with mine, before dispatching me, permanently, to the night shift. To what he must have assumed was my death or resignation. I knew that in living, in refusing to leave, I must have surprised him. And that surprising Parrs was the worst thing you could do. By not going one way or the other, I'd denied him an outcome that must have seemed inevitable. I knew that to Parrs, a man who operated several months, several moves ahead, my survival could only be interpreted as a betrayal.

The driver pulled out of the car park and smoothly into traffic.

The engine was so quiet that I could hear myself breathing, thinking. Waiting.

Parrs still didn't speak, and I was grateful not to be looking at him. Those unreadable red eyes, embedded in grey skin. All I could see were his hands. Long, thin fingers and knotted, blue-grey veins.

He clenched and unclenched them, then he leaned forward and sighed.

'Seat belt,' he said. I risked a sideways glance. He was staring out the window, his face doing the approximation of a smile. 'We wouldn't want anything to happen to you.' I pulled the seat belt around me and he went on. 'There's a lot hanging over your head, Aidan. Not many men in your position would have made it through the last few months.'

'Thank you, sir.'

'It wasn't a compliment, and try not to speak again unless I ask you a question.' I swallowed, lowered my head. 'You seem to have been learning to keep your mouth shut, though. Reports have even reached my ears that you're making a go of things with Detective Inspector Sutcliffe . . .' He paused. 'How are you getting along with the Elephant Man's ball-sack?'

'Famously.'

He exhaled through his nose. 'Don't be glib with me. I asked you a question.'

'We weren't put together to get along, sir.'

'What makes you say that?'

'I accused him of planting evidence and he offered to testify against me when I was suspended.'

'And you've decided to hold a grudge . . .'

'I've decided to remember it.'

We drove on for a minute before Parrs spoke again. 'It's water under the bridge, son.' With some dead bodies under the water, I thought. He looked at me suddenly, like he could hear what I was thinking.

I looked back.

He had a hard, gaunt guillotine for a jaw, which he clenched and flexed before he spoke. 'Don't sit there mean-mugging me. When I wipe the look off your face I'll take the fucking skin with it. Remember that every day you draw breath and a salary is borrowed time, donated directly out of the goodness of my heart.'

65

I turned, stared straight ahead again and nodded. 'Can I ask why you wanted to see me, sir?'

'Quite the opposite. I thought it might be beneficial for you to see me. You've been testing your eyesight again, Aidan. Trying to see around corners.' I didn't say anything. 'You had an interesting night. Tell me about it.'

I swallowed. 'At 1 a.m., Detective Inspector Sutcliffe and I were called out to the Palace Hotel. The intruder alarm had been tripped and the security guard was missing. When we searched the premises we found the guard unconscious. He'd been assaulted. A blow to the head from a fire extinguisher. As I was tending to him I saw an intruder fleeing the scene. I pursued the intruder to the fourth floor but they were able to escape through a fire exit. When I retraced my steps along the corridor I found that one of the rooms was open. Making a search of that room I found the dead man.'

'Go on.'

'He had no identification on his person. No labels in his clothes.'

'And the Palace is shut down . . .' he mused. 'Vagrant?'

'No, sir. Smartly dressed.'

'What do you think?' said Parrs, sounding vaguely interested.

'The guard regained consciousness this morning. He says he heard an argument, two voices. I think there were two intruders and, for whatever reason, one of them killed the other.'

'Cause of death?'

'Too early to say.'

'Could be natural. Could be suicide . . .' He said it like the lesser of two evils.

'It's possible, but even so, his presence is unexplained. And then there's the second intruder. I definitely saw someone else.'

'Hm,' said Parrs.

'We're currently trying to locate the other security guard as well, the day man, Marcus Collier.'

'He could well be your second intruder,' said Parrs. I nodded. 'So what about the owners?'

'They're trying to get rid of the place. Last night we dealt with a solicitor handling the sale.'

Parrs thought for a moment. 'Talk to them anyway. If our dead man has some connection with the Palace he might be on their radar. And let's leave Detective Inspector Sutcliffe out of that line of enquiry for the moment.'

'I'm not sure I'm comfortable with that, sir.'

'I'm not sure I care. Sutty has a certain talent for taking a room's temperature, but only by sticking a thermometer up its arse. Might not go down so well with old money. Speaking of rectal temperature, do we have the time of death?'

'Around midnight.'

'I take it you're liaising with the day shift?'

'I'm assisting DS Lattimer with his enquiries, sir.'

He snorted at that. 'Sounds like you've got yourself a case. It's fascinating stuff, but when I asked about your interesting night I was referring to your altercation with a Mr Oliver Cartwright.'

I looked at him, confused. Those unreadable red eyes.

'I'd hardly call it an altercation . . .'

'What would you call it?'

'A conversation.'

'A conversation taking place after midnight. Some flight of fancy from a teenage girl . . .'

'Cartwright had spent a night with her—'

'Consensually, go on.'

'He filmed the encounter. He suggested it might leak out on to the internet unless she went back for more.'

'And you don't think she's being dramatic?' I started to speak but he cut in. 'A re-run of your little problem from last year?'

'What are you asking me, sir?'

'I'm wondering if there's a more innocent explanation for all of this . . .'

I paused for a moment. Thought about it. When the silence became excruciating I said: 'No, there isn't. I saw the message myself.'

'Has the girl made an official complaint?'

'It's sensitive. She doesn't want to make trouble. I thought I'd give Cartwright the same courtesy. A word in his ear rather than his name in the papers.'

'Unless the girl makes an official complaint, it's none of our concern.'

'You know she won't do that.'

'Case fucking closed, then.'

'I take it that Oliver Cartwright's someone important.'

Parrs turned. 'I don't think I like what I'm hearing, son.'

'I don't like saying it, sir.'

He exhaled through his nose. 'Mr Cartwright is a media figure who deserves better than my worst man dragging him out of bed at gone midnight. Candidly, though, you'll find his name in the address book of every ambitious riser in town, including Chief Superintendent Chase. So I repeat, unless the girl makes an official complaint, it's none of our concern.'

'Sir.'

'Still,' he said, changing the subject. 'Sounds like you'll have your work cut out for you anyway. Have you got anyone for those dustbin fires yet?'

I shook my head.

'Well, I've every faith. And of course you'll be galloping sideways trying to crack open this smiling man case.'

'How did you know he was smiling, sir?'

'Well spotted,' he said. 'I knew you weren't totally useless. Unfortunately, the pathologist disagrees.'

'Karen Stromer.'

'Aye, had her talking me off on the phone this morning. What a drugs risk and liability you are.' He grinned. 'Pushing all my buttons.'

'She wants me taken off the case.'

'She wants you taken off the planet, son.'

'Can I ask what you told her, sir?'

'I said I sympathized. Really, I did, but that you and Sutty are like one of those fancy dress donkey costumes that two people need to wear. If I get rid of you I'll just have a big, fat arse running round the stage.' It was almost a compliment. 'So no fuck-ups this time. And if you could close it without swallowing the city's entire speed supply, we'd all be grateful.' He grinned again. 'Leave some for the rest of us, eh?'

4

Parrs had me dropped back at the hospital, exactly where I'd been picked up. The sun still hadn't moved in the sky and this, combined with my having nowhere pressing to be, made it seem as though I'd imagined the whole thing. It was one of the Superintendent's great talents. He was a man who casually snuffed out dreams and made nightmares come true, often without seeming interested one way or the other. Our conversation this morning had felt like life or death. Now, a few minutes later, it was as though it had never happened.

I took out my phone and got to work.

'Hello?'

'Aneesa Khan? It's Detective Constable Waits.'

'Good morning, Detective Constable.' I heard the shake in her voice. 'Are you calling about Ali? Is he OK?'

'I actually just spoke to Mr Nasser, he's doing a lot better. I was hoping you could help me, though.'

'I wanted to speak to you, too. I'm sorry I was so shaken up by it all last night. I've never been around violence like that before. I think it just gave me a shock.' She said this like a prepared answer in a job interview but, I reminded myself, that formality was in everything else she said as well. Aneesa had very briefly let her guard down around me, and I thought that was probably what had disturbed her most.

'Completely understandable,' I said. 'Don't worry about it.'

'Thank you.' She sounded lighter already. 'Now, how I can help?'

It was past time for me to inform her about the body we'd discovered on the fourth floor, but I wanted to try the owners first. Telling Aneesa meant I wouldn't get to see their reactions to the news, so I edged around it.

'You mentioned last night that your firm was handling the sale of the Palace?'

'That's correct. Although in the event of a sale it would be my boss, Anthony, leading things.'

'Is this Mr Blick?'

'Correct. How do you know that?'

'Mr Nasser mentioned the name this morning,' I said. 'I wouldn't mind speaking to Blick if you can arrange it?'

'I'm sure that by next week he'll be all over you. Anthony's in Thailand at the moment.'

'Work-related?'

'He decided to go and find himself at age fifty. Can you believe it?'

'It's never too late to start looking. What about the current owners, would it be possible to speak to them?'

She was silent for a moment.

'Well . . .' she said, finally.

The Palace Hotel was owned by the Coyle Trust, she explained, the principals of which were a Natasha Reeve and Frederick Coyle. When I suggested a meeting with them that day she told me that their schedules might not allow for it but said she'd call me back. I was almost in town when she did.

'Natasha says she can receive you now, if that's useful?'

'Sure.'

'I'm afraid I can't be there to accompany you . . .' I waited, thinking she was about to warn me that her client could be difficult. There was something unspoken but, for the moment, it stayed that way. Aneesa had already let her guard down once. That was as far as she was prepared to go.

'I'll be on my best behaviour,' I said. 'Just tell me where and when.'

5

Natasha Reeve requested that we meet on King Street, off Deansgate, and I assumed that she lived locally. The wealthy often declined to receive police officers into their own homes. Above a certain income you were always more likely to conduct interviews in cafés or restaurants. Their concern, perhaps, was how their houses and possessions might be interpreted, or even resented, by the uniformly working-class police force. Having spent time with both sides I thought they were probably right to be careful.

I knew Natasha immediately.

She was a slim, tanned woman of perhaps forty-five. She looked like she had a lifetime of good living behind her. Sun, nutrition and education. She might have been my exact opposite, and her healthy glow made me feel faintly ashamed of myself. From some other, lesser race. She wore cream-coloured jeans with a matching blouse, and her clothes brought out the warmth of her rich, brown skin. A deep tan that even the city's current heatwave couldn't have provided. At first I thought she was looking into a shop window at baby clothes. As I drew closer I saw that she was actually checking her own reflection. I thought she seemed vaguely disappointed with it, until she turned and gave me the exact same look.

She knew me immediately, too, acknowledging my presence with a minimal nod.

'Ms Reeve? My name's Detective Constable—'

'Waits,' she said, twisting away from my outstretched hand.

'Yes, shall we?' She began to walk, expecting me to fall in step beside her, and I did. 'I'm told we had a break-in at the Palace last night.'

'I'm afraid so.' I turned but she continued to stare straight ahead. 'I was wondering if you could give me some background on the hotel itself?'

'Is that necessary?'

'At this stage it's a little more complicated than a break-in.'

'Intriguing,' she said, flatly. 'Very well. The Palace has been in my family for three decades and I've been responsible for it for one-third of that time. It's always been a prosperous business but certain family commitments have necessitated its sale. Negotiations are currently inching forwards.' She spoke briskly, like a woman who'd lost interest in her own life, and it took me a moment to realize that the history lesson was over. She'd condensed three decades into as many sentences.

'I was told the hotel had two owners?'

'The Coyle Trust, which owns the hotel, has two principals,' she said.

'You're one, may I ask who the other is?'

'Frederick Coyle, my husband.'

'I hadn't realized you were married.'

'It seemed to slip Freddie's mind towards the end as well. We're currently divorcing, Detective Constable. Negotiations are inching forwards there, too.'

'Is that the reason you're selling the Palace?'

'Freddie suggested we divide it into two separate entities, per-haps a health spa and a hotel, but I can't bear to see that happen. My one condition of the Palace's sale is that it remains intact.'

'I'm glad to hear that.'

But Natasha Reeve didn't want me for an ally. 'I'm afraid your sentimental response to the problem isn't shared by the prospective pool of buyers.'

'You're having some trouble with the sale?'

'As I say . . .' She looked as though she couldn't bear to repeat herself.

'Negotiations are inching forwards. How long were you and Mr Coyle married?'

'Ten years,' she twitched. 'Why this fascination with my marriage? If you're considering it, I can suggest better uses for your time.'

'I'm just establishing the facts. Do you and Mr Coyle have any children?'

'Not including the one he walked out on me for?' I didn't say anything and she came back to reality. 'No, no children. Freddie never wanted the hassle. I regretted it, for a time, but after his conduct with the Palace I wonder . . .'

'How do you mean?'

'No doubt he'd have suggested we cut the child in half, too.' She heard herself and stopped walking, looking at me for the first time as she did. 'You must understand that I don't believe every wrong visited on me in the past is a prophecy of my future. Occasionally the cards simply fall that way. If it were up to me, we wouldn't be selling the Palace at all. I'm afraid the subject can colour my conversation.' She resumed walking. 'What does this have to do with a break-in?'

'As I said, it's slightly more complicated than a break-in.'

'So you *keep* saying,' she said, walking on.

'The security guard, Mr Nasser, was assaulted.'

'Ms Khan said as much. I take it he'll recover?'

'It looks like it.'

'I'm glad to hear that, he's a reliable man. Of course, his job will remain open should he still want it, and we can be flexible about working hours should it assist his recovery or your investigation. Anything else you need can be handled through Ms Khan or, as of next week, the returning Mr Blick.'

'I was also hoping to speak to Mr Coyle.'

'Of course you were,' she said quietly.

'Have you spoken to your husband this morning?' I had a wild idea that Frederick Coyle could be our unidentified dead man. It sounded like Natasha Reeve's life would be a lot simpler if she was the Palace Hotel's sole owner.

'Ms Khan copied us both into an email, to apprise us of last night's events. He didn't seem too interested.'

'But he did reply?'

'Of course.'

'I'm afraid that Ms Khan might not have been fully up to speed. Last night when we responded to the intruder alarm at her behest, we discovered your security guard, Mr Nasser, unconscious on the third floor. He'd suffered a blow to the back of the head.' I risked a look at Natasha but her face remained implacable. 'Upon a closer search of the premises a dead body was discovered in a room on the fourth floor. We're treating the death as suspicious.'

'I see,' she squinted. 'You don't think that Mr Nasser . . .'

'No. It looks like he disturbed them. He says he heard raised voices just before he began his midnight patrol. Two people arguing . . .'

She smiled thinly. It looked like a crack of light under a door. 'And you're wondering if it might have been Freddie and me?'

'Mr Nasser was investigating the voices when he was attacked,' I said, side-stepping the question. 'It would be helpful to know if there've been any other break-ins while the Palace has been closed.'

'None that I know of.'

'Any suspicious activity at all?'

She shook her head. 'Although I suggest you speak to Ms Khan. I've intentionally made myself absent for much of the Palace's closure and I'm sure she and Mr Blick have more insight into its day-to-day operations.'

'There's been nothing in the negotiations for sale that gives you any pause or concern?'

'Perhaps if there were more robust interest, but for the moment we're merely making eyes at one another. Could this affect a potential sale?'

'I can't think why. We'll need access to the crime scene for the next couple of days, but aside from that . . .' She nodded. Gratefully, I thought. I could see why sharing a business with your ex might make things difficult. 'Which brings me to my final question,' I said. 'You suggested the image of you and your husband being the two people that Mr Nasser heard arguing. Can you account for your whereabouts last night?'

'Happily,' she said. 'I was at home, alone.'

'Here in town?'

'I keep a flat on King Street.' We'd walked a circuit of the block and she nodded towards the street sign.

'Can I ask how you spent the evening?'

'Reading.'

'Reading what?'

'Poetry.' She said it like the only kind of book there was. 'Is that all, Detective Constable?'

'You don't seem particularly worried about not providing an alibi . . .'

'I have nothing to hide and, besides, you still have Freddie to talk to. He'll prove that the two of us weren't arguing in the Palace.' When I gave her a questioning look she went on. 'Well, I've no doubt he was curled up with something a little warmer than a good book.'

6

Natasha and I said our goodbyes and, after checking Frederick Coyle's schedule, Aneesa told me I might not be able to speak to him until the following day. I was still thinking of my interview with Ali when I arrived back at the Palace. I walked past the baleful stare of the officer stationed on the door and into the lobby. The daylight beaming through the glass ceiling and on to marble surfaces made the enormous room glow, transforming it from the sinister setting of last night's action into somewhere calm and meditative. As I crossed the room, another uniformed officer stepped in to meet me.

'Detective Constable Waits,' he said, drily. 'Can I ask what your business is here?'

'Good morning. As you know, I'm investigating the suspicious death of our man on the fourth floor.'

'And is there something I can assist you with?'

'Have the premises been searched yet?'

'Detective Inspector Sutcliffe set the primary scene boundary as room 413. It's been searched.'

'What about the rest of the building? The other rooms have all been unlocked?'

'They have. The building's been secured.'

'Searched,' I repeated. 'Has it been searched?'

'What are you expecting to find?'

'That isn't really how it works,' I said, walking past him towards the staircase.

'Hey.' He was following me. 'You can't just wander round.'

'I know, but let's pretend we're police officers.'

'Karen Stromer was very clear that you weren't to be admitted to the fourth floor without authorization.'

'That's fine, we're only going to the third.' We reached the staircase and began the long climb up. The officer kept pace, breathing loudly through his nose, trying not to give away how out of breath he was. By the time we reached the landing I thought he might pass out. Without pausing I walked straight down the first corridor and began searching rooms. Ali had mentioned the dustbins on this floor in relation to the daytime security guard, Marcus Collier. I went directly to them. Each suite had a dustbin in the main room and one in the bathroom. The first few searches yielded no results.

Room 305 was different.

Where the other beds had been completely unmade, this one had a loose sheet thrown over it. I checked the dustbin in the main room and then paced around, got down on the floor and shone my torch under the bed.

Nothing.

The officer watched me from the door. The bathroom was completely plain. I didn't want to touch the light switch, so I went by torch beam. I put my foot on the pedal of the dustbin and it flipped open. Something gleamed in the light. A torn piece of silver packaging, about one inch by one inch. I crouched down, took a clear plastic bag from my pocket and picked it up. The bright pink font on the front said: *Lifestyle*. I left the room and the officer followed me out into the corridor.

'Call SOCO,' I told him. 'We need a fingertip search of this room with particular focus on the bed.'

'Looking for what?'

I was losing my patience with him. 'Evidence of sexual activity. Hair, skin flakes, DNA. You don't know what you're looking for until you find it, but not looking at all's just sloppy work. And speaking of sloppy work, this should be tested for all of the above.'

I handed him the plastic bag I was holding and he did a double take at its contents.

'Is that a condom?'

'Only the wrapper. Don't get any ideas.'

I winked at him and left.

On my way out of the building I spoke to the officer on the door. He'd been stationed there since we discovered the body, and I asked if Marcus Collier had shown up for work that morning. He said that, aside from me and some Scene of Crime Officers, no one had approached the building. I thanked him and left. He looked relieved to see me go.

7

It was early evening when I arrived for my shift with Sutty. We met in the city centre and he landed heavily on to the passenger seat.

'Anything you wanna tell me, pal?'

I didn't know which part of my day he was angry about, but if he knew I'd been talking to an owner of the Palace without him I was in for a long night. I decided to start at the beginning.

'I spoke to Ali—'

'The Super. You were talking to the Super.'

'Against my will,' I said after a beat.

'Don't piss in my eye and tell me it's raining. If you're coming at me, come at me straight.'

'It was nothing to do with you, Sutts.'

'Why else all the cloak and dagger? Tell him I was sat at home, did ya?'

'No.' I thought about it. 'If you know he picked me up then the driver must have told you . . .'

'Dave's an old pal.' This was the police force now. A fucking infinity of Daves.

'So why don't you ask him what it was about?'

Sutty sniffed. 'He couldn't hear very well.'

'He should keep his mouth shut, then. I didn't know I was seeing Parrs this morning, either. One of the guards you had on Ali must have reported my presence upward. He was just warning me off Cartwright, anyway.'

'Warning you off who?'

'The man I questioned in the Quays last night.'

'You and those fucking girls . . .'

'It's not the girl, it's him. I guess he's a big deal.'

'Why? What is he?'

'New media, I don't know. Someone more important than us.'

'An ever-growing list,' he grumbled.

'Parrs suggested I focus on the dustbin fires . . .'

'Hur-hur,' said Sutty. 'Big case. Needs his best man on it.' He breathed heavily for a few seconds, deciding if he believed me. 'So? Tell us about Ali.'

'Says he heard voices, went to investigate and got clocked.'

'Believe him?'

'He's a first-year immigrant from Aleppo. Scared of talking to the police. Yeah, I believe him. Any word on the day-shift guard yet?'

'Two words, actually. Fuck all.'

'It sounded like there might be some tension between him and Ali.'

'Oh?'

'When I pushed Ali for his meaning, he said I should check the bins on the third floor of the Palace. I found a condom wrapper . . .'

'Marcus has been testing the bedsprings, eh?'

'Maybe. The room looked like it had been made up in a hurry. I've asked SOCO to go over it.'

'What about the wrapper itself? Too much to hope for prints?'

'Too soon to say, I only just found it. You're probably about to get a phone call about me attempting to access the crime scene . . .'

'Stromer?'

'She'd left instructions.'

'Well, I can't say I blame her. We should have a poster made with your face on it. Unwanted. Speaking of which,' he said, opening the door and climbing back out. 'Why don't you take my dinner break as an opportunity to get rid of that.' He nodded at Sophie's jacket on the back seat, which I'd taken from Cartwright's flat the night before. 'Take the car. I just don't want to see any new scratches when you get back . . .'

'How would you even tell?'

'I meant on you, hot stuff.'

8

I parked up and crossed the grounds of Owens Park. I had the same transient feeling as the day before. Like I was stepping back in time, somehow. Like the lights might hit my face on the other side and make me young again, able to live my life over. I went to Sophie's building and buzzed her flat, thinking about what Parrs had said, to forget about Cartwright.

I'd forgotten so many things for him, already.

No doubt he'd go Fukushima if he knew where I was now, but there was something else, beyond Parrs' wrath, that pulled at me. Stromer's antipathy? That had been expected. The dustbin fires? Just background noise. My mind went all the way back to that morning. That first phone call. A few seconds of silence, some breathing and then the dial tone. Calls to my landline were rare, and anyway, the breaths hadn't been incidental. They'd been the point of the call. Expelled directly into the mouthpiece for no reason other than menace. I thought about the day preceding the call. Guy Russell, Ollie Cartwright and the smiling man.

All new enemies.

I buzzed the first-floor flat again and, after a few seconds, the bolt on the door thunked open. I went up the stairs. The only part of the day that made sense to me was the disturbed man on Ali's ward, screaming in fear and confusion at the world.

When I reached the first-floor flat, I could hear young voices, music, fun. I turned off the hallway and into the communal space where I'd waited for Sophie the night before and saw Earl, on duty, making four cocktails at once. He noticed me and stopped. He was the focal point of the room, and a few heads turned in my direction. He lowered the bottle he was pouring from and his friends booed.

'Patience,' he said, holding the S sound. He walked towards me, widening his eyes to propel me back into the hallway. I stepped out and he drew the door closed behind him. 'What was your name again? Heavy?'

'Waits,' I said. 'Is Sophie around?'

'You can't just walk in here.'

'Sophie, is she in?'

'Nah,' he said, leaning into the wall and blocking my way.

'Her bike's in the hall.'

'Well, she's not here.'

'Is her room open?'

'No.'

I knew he had a problem with the police so I tried not to push it. 'I've got her jacket,' I said, holding it up.

'Oh.' He was surprised. 'Well, I can give it to her?'

'OK. She shouldn't have any more problems with this guy, but she's got my number if she needs it.' I could see that he wanted me to expand on what had happened but I handed over the jacket and turned to leave.

'Thank you,' he said, to my back.

'You're a friend worth having, Earl. Keep an eye on her.'

I went down the stairs, through the pressure cooker hallway, passing through ambient sounds of conversation, laughter and music.

'Hey, Heavy,' said Earl, following me down the stairs. 'You dropped this . . .' He handed me a folded slip of paper and I opened it.

Oliver Cartwright. Ollie. Mid-thirties.
Thinning red-brown hair, some paunch. Incognito. 7 p.m.

The note must have fallen out of Sophie's jacket, which I'd had folded over my arm before passing it to Earl.

He scowled at the sheet. 'You know that prick?'

'Cartwright? No, do you?'

'Just the name. Runs that alt-right site, Lolitics. We went to a protest outside their offices once.' Something occurred to Earl. 'Hang on. He's not the guy who Sophie got with?'

I was shaking my head. 'No, this is another case I'm working on.'

'Your lot should pull the fucking flush on him,' he said. 'There's nothing he doesn't hate.' He turned and went back up the stairs, disappearing into the communal space, meeting a cheer from his thirsty friends. I left the building and crossed the block with the note still in my hand. Sophie's handwritten description of Cartwright implied she'd known who he was before she set out for the club, perhaps even that she'd targeted him. If that was the case, she'd been lying to me about how they'd met, and why.

9

I drove back into town and decided to check in with Sutty. He was assisting the stompers, the force's tactical response unit, in bringing a violent bar fight to a close. If I knew him, he'd probably started it as well. I felt restless with new, unfamiliar energy. Like my brain had been reactivated after too many months dormant.

Parking up near the Palace, where Oxford Road intersects with Great Bridgewater, I saw lights coming from The Temple. In a past life, The Temple had been a public toilet. It had also been a notorious cottaging spot in Victorian times, taking the city's gay history back far before Canal Street. Now it was a small, subterranean bar. The owner was the frontman of a local band who'd blown up, and their biggest hit, 'Grounds for Divorce', obliquely mentioned the place.

It felt like I was being nudged back towards some old thoughts, old feelings, and I decided to go along with it. One benefit of quitting speed, cocaine and ecstasy was that it made drinking feel like a health choice. I walked down the steps and tried the door. It was locked but I could hear voices from inside. The jukebox still going at gone 11 p.m. I knocked, heard movement and stepped back so they could get a look at me.

'Who is it?' said a familiar voice.

'It's me.'

'*Waits?*' The bolt was drawn back and the door opened. I felt the warmth from inside, the simple thrill of communal drinking. Sian, the barmaid, looked out at me without expression.

I felt that too.

Sian had dark hair, pale skin and freckles. She wore black clothes and hipster glasses, and had a sleeve of delicate tattoos down one arm. 'We'd started to think you were a reformed character . . .'

'Relapsing,' I said. 'It's good to see you.' I took a step forward but she didn't move, just stood in the doorway looking up at me. I remembered seeing her for the first time, also in that doorway. It had felt like a sheer drop.

'Is it?' she said.

A moment passed and she turned, walked back through the bar. I bolted the door behind me and followed. It was one narrow room, about the length of two saloon cars. There were four or five small tables alongside each wall, with just enough space to walk down the middle. I passed a few groups but no more than ten people. The Sunday-night lock-in crowd, all wrapped up in tall tales and heated debates. Conversations that seemed like life or death in the moment, but would probably be forgotten by the next day. The jukebox was blasting out 'Brand New Cadillac' by The Clash. No one gave me a second thought.

'Guinness?' I said, sitting at the bar.

Sian looked at me. 'I might be out of glasses . . .'

'I'd drink it from a hot-water bottle tonight.'

'Don't tempt me,' she said, kicking opening the dishwasher, pouring steam into the air. She filled a glass in silence and slid it towards me. It was warm from the machine. I started to look for my wallet but she held up a hand. 'It's on the house, Aid.'

'Thanks.' I looked at her. Watched the pulse moving in her neck and knew that she felt it too, whatever it was. 'How've you been?' I asked.

'Did I die of heartbreak, you mean? What are you doing here?'

'Forgetting how to be a detective.'

'At least it won't take long, then. Seriously,' she said. 'Back after all this time . . .'

'A lot of the local places have requested my absence.'

She leaned on the bar. 'I didn't know it was that easy, is there a form I can fill in?'

'Tonight I was just working up the road.'

'You're always just working up the road. You're the only person I know who keeps worse hours than me.' She shrugged. 'You look well on it . . .'

'I've been running.' She raised an eyebrow. 'A man needs a vice . . .'

'You weren't lacking in that department, as I recall.'

'I'm clean now,' I said, wondering if I'd come here to tell her that.

She let her guard down and smiled sincerely. So sincerely that I wondered how bad I'd been the last time we met. 'That's good, Aidan. That's so good.' She poked my arm. 'What are all those speed dealers gonna do for a living now, though?'

I laughed. 'I think they're recession-proof.'

'And what, you quit girls at the same time? Or just me?'

'I . . .'

'I usually get a goodbye at least.'

'I thought I was coming back.'

'You never did, though. You're not even back now, really, are you?'

A man appeared at the bar and began ordering a large round. Sian served him brusquely, giving a small, tight smile as he began ferrying drinks back to his table. I realized I'd made a mistake in coming here. Worse, that I'd executed another flawless act of self-sabotage in disappearing from Sian's life. I drank up and turned to leave.

'I might not be here the next time you come around,' she said.

I looked at her. 'Where are you going?'

'I don't know, daylight? Above ground, at least. I'm seeing some-one now.'

'Nice guy?'

She nodded. 'And they're fucking hard to find.'

When Sian and I separated, more than a year before, we'd been in the unspoken stages of moving in together. Neither one of us quite ready to declare it, or give up their own flat, but taking it as read that we'd walk on to my place or hers when our respective night shifts ended. I'd been slowly meeting her friends, her family, and avoiding the fact that I had no one for her to meet in return. We'd been happy for a time, though. I remembered hastily prepared meals, eaten off plates that we balanced on our knees, so we could talk while we ate. Or getting on to the roof of her old building through the fire escape in the summer. Watching the stars with a bottle of wine and singing 'Drunk on the Moon'. It had been a good time in my life but I'd ended things badly, gotten into trouble at work. Derailed my life. She was right, I hadn't really come back.

'I'm sorry,' I said.

We began talking, a little more comfortably, about old times. When some regulars joined in I relaxed a little, letting the events of the last two days turn over in my mind. Arson, revenge porn and death. A varied caseload stretching all the way from bad to worse. I started on my second drink. Thought about Ollie Cartwright. Rousting him was exactly the kind of behaviour that had put me on to the night shift. On to my very last chance. It had been worth the riot act from Superintendent Parrs, though. I'd liked Sophie. She reminded me of someone I used to know.

Mostly, I thought of the smiling man.

Someone started banging at the door and Sian walked round the bar for it. Between songs I heard a gruff voice, hard and low, and turned to see a man, a shadow, trying to talk his way inside. The music kicked in again, and I didn't hear the rest of their conversation. There was a short back-and-forth before the figure in the doorway held up his hands and backed away. Sian bolted the door and called time.

I finished my drink and left to the sound of 'Tom Traubert's Blues', knowing it couldn't get any better than that, wondering if Sian had put it on the jukebox for old times' sake. I climbed the stairs feeling loose, absent-minded even, and emerged on to the street still humming the tune. Double-decker buses roared by like bright, empty boxes of light. I'd started to walk back into town when I heard a movement behind me. I turned and saw someone, the shape of a man, standing by the entrance of The Temple. He was in shadow but I must have been back-lit by the street, and I could feel his eyes on me. Neither of us moved for a moment, then I turned and walked away.

It started again with another knock on a door.

It was a Sunday night, after ten, and the boy waited a minute first. Even though they were a long way from the city, even though it was dark, there were no stars this time. The boy thought about going back down the lane to the car, where his mother and sister were waiting. He could shrug and say there was no one home. But he knew that Bateman was watching, somewhere over his shoulder, ready to detach himself from the shadows and step in. Bateman already knew there was someone inside the house.

He already knew they were alone.

So when the boy knocked he wasn't surprised to hear movement behind the door. He wasn't surprised by the young woman's voice.

'Hello?' she said. It sounded familiar, but he wasn't sure. 'Bates, is that you?' She hesitated. 'I don't think you should come here any more . . .'

The boy took a final look over his shoulder into the shadows, where he knew Bateman was waiting. 'I'm lost,' he said, sounding convincing. He heard the lock being turned from inside. The door opened and a concerned-looking young woman stared out at him. It was Holly, the same girl he'd seen in the market square, but this time she wore pyjamas, a dressing gown.

'Hi,' she said, crouching down to him. Her eyes went wide with recognition. 'Wally?' For a second she didn't know what it meant and, too late, looked over his shoulder. She got up and tried to close the door but Bateman swung his steel-toe boot into the gap. The door stopped short and he shoulder-barged it back open, sending the girl sprawling on to the floor.

'I'm sorry,' she said. 'I'm really sorry.' It took the boy a moment to register that she was talking to him. Bateman stepped past, into the hallway. He was carrying a claw-hammer in one hand and a large holdall bag in the other. He dropped the bag and took a fistful of Holly's hair, dragging her across the floor and into the next room.

'Door,' he said over his shoulder. The boy pushed the front door until he heard it click shut. He stood with his back to it, trying to breathe, sliding down until he was sitting on the floor. He could hear the rumble of footsteps from the next room. Raised voices. Furniture being thrown around. Glass breaking. Through it all he could hear Holly's small voice, saying that she was sorry over and over again.

'The bag, Wally,' Bateman shouted. 'We haven't got all night.'

The boy picked up the bag and walked into the room. He was surprised by its size, its opulence. Enormous bookcases lined the walls and there were expensive-looking pieces of furniture throughout. It was bigger than their entire flat. He followed the disarray, the overturned table, the dent in a wall, the shattered lamp, until he turned a corner and saw Holly, crying on the floor with Bateman standing over her. He was flexing his hand, gripping and re-gripping the claw-hammer.

'Now, I need a favour,' he said to the girl.

'Sure,' she nodded, wiping her eyes and trying a smile.

'I need you to get in that bag for me.' He nodded at the large holdall that the boy had dragged in.

'What?' she said quietly.

'Need you to get in that bag for me,' Bateman repeated, not looking at her.

'But . . .' She swallowed. 'Can I ask why?'

'*Can I ask why?*' he said. 'Cus we're not all born fucking rich, darling. Some of us have got work to do. I like peace and quiet, one way or the other.' He raised the claw-hammer in illustration. Holly looked suddenly out of breath. She nodded, got up and, in a blur, made a break out of the room. The boy went out into the hall and watched her at the door, shaking as she undid the lock. Bateman materialized behind him, chuckling as she stumbled out into a blinding light.

She threw both hands up in front of her face and stopped.

'Back inside,' the boy heard his mother say.

Holly's shoulders slumped, she went weak at the knees and had to lean into the door. Bateman went forward, lifted her up and carried her back into the other room. 'Told you,' he said. 'I'll have peace. One way or the other.'

The boy stood in the hallway, trying to disappear into the wall. Trying not to look at his mother as she passed. She followed Bateman into the next room and he closed his eyes, listening to their movements. All three of them grunting with effort.

'Please,' he heard Holly say. 'Please . . .'

Dizzily, the boy edged to the door. Bateman was pushing Holly down with his heel, folding her double so she'd fit inside the hold-all. She started to say something as he drew the zip up but it was muted by the bag.

The black holdall lay packed, bulging on the floor, shaking with quiet sobs.

It was impossible to see which parts of the girl were where, but some strands of her long hair protruded through the zip. Bateman took a padlock, linked it through the hoops and punched it closed with his palm.

'Shut the fuck up,' he said, touching the bag with his boot. 'We've had bigger than you in there, darling.' The boy felt the chill of his mother's eyes on him and moved, too late, back out of the room.

'Go and play with your sister,' she said flatly.

The girl inside the bag was screaming for help now but the boy kept on walking. His ears were ringing and his mouth had started to water. A haze of sunspots blistered in front of his eyes and he had the feeling that he was lifting, effortlessly, out of his body. When he got to the front door he heard Bateman lose patience with the girl.

'Shut,' he screamed. 'The. Fuck. Up.' Each word was punctuated with the sound of a steel-toe boot slamming into a person. By the time the boy was outside he couldn't hear her any more. He was lifting, floating, rising up. First walking, then running, then flying away from the house.

————

III
China Town

1

'Sorry about that,' said Freddie Coyle, re-emerging from the bedroom. When I'd arrived he hadn't been ready to receive me. He'd asked that I wait in the reception room of his spacious, city-centre loft while he changed out of his dressing gown and pyjamas. The room wasn't quite in disarray but somewhere near it. There were half-empty bowls of party food scattered around, as well as some dirty glasses still giving off a strong smell of alcohol. There was also a faint, fruity scent hanging over everything that I traced back to an e-cigarette, stuffed down the side of the sofa. While Coyle changed I paced the room and found a silver cocktail shaker, tucked behind a curtain.

It looked like it had been hastily hidden.

Watching the bedroom door, I twisted the lid off and smelt the mixture. Although the shaker was cold to the touch I was still surprised to see un-melted ice cubes in there.

It was 10 a.m.

I dipped a finger in and tasted it. Gin and juice. Either the party had only just ended, or it started to pick up again, moments before I arrived.

I heard movement behind the door and took a seat.

Coyle re-entered the room in a crisp, electric-blue suit and apologized for the delay. His thin pencil moustache looked like a crack in white ceramic, and his jet-black hair had been slicked back, welded into place with product. I thought at his age, mid-to-late forties, it must be a dye-job. When he went to the window I thought he was checking on the shaker hidden behind the curtains, but he twisted the venetian blinds closed while he was at it, filtering the sunlight so it broke through the room in strips.

'A little bright in here this morning, if you know what I mean.' He took a seat and clapped his hands together, as if to activate me. When I didn't say anything he began cautiously. 'You're here about the break-in at the Palace . . .'

'It goes a little further than that, Mr Coyle.' I wasn't sure if Natasha had apprised Aneesa or him of the details after our discussion so I let him fill the silence.

'This attack on our security chap . . .'

'Ali,' I said, helping him out.

'Ali, yes. I was sorry to hear about it. We're not liable, though, if this is related to a claim . . .'

'I don't work for an insurance firm, Mr Coyle. As I said, I'm a detective.'

'I take it you've caught the burglar if you're banging down people's doors at this hour?'

There was a sound from the bedroom. We both looked towards it and Coyle smiled, aiming for self-deprecation. Missing it by a mile.

I leaned forward. 'I'm sorry if I'm interrupting something, but we did have an appointment for this morning. A man died in your hotel, after all . . .'

I didn't think edging towards it would get the best out of him.

'Died? Ms Khan informed us he was injured . . . ?'

'In Mr Nasser's case that's correct, but I'm afraid that following the assault on him we discovered a dead body on the fourth floor.'

'What the hell?'

'We suspect foul play.'

He rubbed his index finger back and forth across his moustache for a moment. 'And who is the man?'

'As yet he remains unidentified. Any assistance you could give us there would be greatly appreciated.'

'What assistance could I give?'

'You might have an idea of who he could be.' Stromer had provided us with a facial shot of the man. I'd emailed it to Natasha Reeve to no avail. When I showed it to Coyle he grimaced.

'Not the faintest.'

'What about any unusual activity in the Palace?'

'Such as?'

'It looks as though one of your security guards might have been renting rooms.'

'Renting rooms?' he asked. 'For what?' But the answer occurred to him a moment later. 'Ah, the world's oldest profession.'

'We're keeping an open mind.'

'You must get very open-minded in your line of work.'

I nodded. 'I think it's the second or third oldest profession.'

'So you suppose this man's death is, what? Related to prostitution? Does Blick know about all this?'

'I was actually hoping to speak to him, but he's out of the country.'

A roguish look passed across Coyle's face and he dug his phone out of a pocket. 'I'll say . . .' He held it out to me. On the screen was a picture of a topless, overweight man. He was wearing designer sunglasses and was surrounded by young Thai women. 'I won't be surprised if he never comes back.' I had to admit that for a solicitor he looked pretty relaxed.

'Returning to the Palace, Mr Coyle . . .'

'Prostitution, you said?'

'That's one line of enquiry. When was the last time you visited the hotel?'

He laughed at that. 'I haven't been there in years. That's the truth.' I thought I believed him but his making the distinction this late in our conversation seemed interesting.

'And you don't have any personal enemies who might want to delay the sale of the hotel?'

The smile froze on his face. 'Delay the sale? Could it delay the sale?'

'The point is that it could be an effort to.'

He thought for a long moment, his eyes moving off and then back on to me. I thought I could see last night's booze finally breaking the surface.

He shook his head. 'I'm certain that's not the case but we have to be careful. Can you be discreet?'

'About . . . ?'

He shook his head in pity and spoke slowly so I'd understand. 'Headlines about assaults and dead bodies will only send the asking price in one direction.' He gave me an illustrative thumbs down.

'It's an interesting chain of events, though. A closed-down hotel in negotiation for sale gets broken into. Nothing's taken but the security guard gets assaulted. A dead body's discovered. You can understand why we'd want to speak to the owners . . .'

'Have you spoken to Natasha?'

'Your wife? Yesterday.'

'My ex-wife.'

'I didn't realize the divorce was finalized.'

'That only the makes distinction more important. The Palace *is* our divorce in practical terms, and she's the only one holding things up.'

'Do you suspect your wife of some involvement in this?'

'I didn't say that.' He looked at me. 'Natasha wouldn't have left any survivors . . .'

'But she's obstructing the sale?'

He ignored the question. 'I merely wish you'd spoken to me first.'

'I wanted to speak to the two of you together. You weren't available.'

'To discuss a break-in,' he said. 'If I'd known the full details, I'd have cleared my schedule.' His eyes darted about the glasses in the room. I got the impression that they were his schedule.

'Why does a dead body change things so drastically for you?' I asked.

'Because of the potential ramifications. If we're to avoid negative publicity, things need to be handled delicately. Not something Natasha has any great flair for . . .'

He invited the question so I asked it. 'What does Ms Reeve have a flair for?'

'The dramatic,' he said, reclining into the couch. 'What did she tell you about me?'

'Just the facts.'

He looked up, shrewdly. He was a man who'd been betrayed by facts before. 'So you're on her side?' he said.

'I'm usually on the dead person's side. Ms Reeve told me very little about you.' I wasn't interested in feeding his martyr complex. 'And she was pretty vague on the details of the Palace itself.'

That seemed to please him. 'Well, no surprise there. She acts as though she built it from the ground up.'

'That's not true?'

'She married into it,' he said triumphantly. 'Then remade the place in her own image. You can imagine why I'm so desperate to get rid.'

'Are you desperate, Mr Coyle?'

'For everything except money,' he said, waving the question away. 'I was using what's called a figure of speech. It's Natasha's fault that we're going through all this. I would have been content to remain a silent partner in the business. She gave me an ultimatum . . .'

'And that's what happened six months ago?' He didn't answer. 'Is that when the two of you separated?'

'We separated years ago, as far as any real relationship goes.'

'May I ask if there was someone else involved in your marriage?'

'You may,' he said, sitting upright. 'But you won't get an answer. I fail to see the question's relevance.'

'What about now, are you seeing anyone new?'

'Again, I fail to see the question's relevance.'

'Its relevance is that I'm wondering if you can account for your movements on Saturday between 10.30 p.m. and midnight.'

'We both know I never killed a man.'

'Even if we did. Other things happened that you could have done.'

'Such as?'

'Your security guard heard two voices, arguing, shortly before midnight. When he went to investigate, he was attacked. We saw someone flee the scene and found the unidentified dead man soon after.'

He smiled. 'You think Natasha and I meet there for our midnight punch-ups. Perhaps we killed a stranger on our way out to alleviate the stress?'

'You could quite easily have had an argument there and had nothing to do with the man's death. If that was the case, now would be a good time to say something.'

'It's almost worth it to take her down with me, but I haven't spoken to Natasha in months, not since I moved out. I'd love to hear what she said to this accusation . . .'

'It's not an accusation, Mr Coyle, and she simply explained where she'd been, what she'd been doing.'

'And?' When I didn't expand he went on. 'Well, I'm afraid I can't account for my movements. Saturday night? I was here. Alone.'

'Your ex-wife was on her own as well.'

'As she no doubt delighted in telling you.'

Freddie kept a jazzier, more flamboyant mask on his disappointment than Natasha, but it was there all the same. I left his apartment feeling grateful not to have seen the two of them together. They were both evasive in their own ways, argumentative too, and I wondered if that's how they'd lasted for ten years, by evading each other. I wondered why that had suddenly stopped working. As I reached the staircase I thought I heard voices, or at least his, talking to someone else. Then I heard ice, rattling inside the cocktail shaker.

2

My phone was vibrating when I reached the street.

'That rubber,' said Sutty by way of a hello.

'Good morning to you, too. The condom wrapper? Was there a print on there?'

'Yeurgh, but no hits. It's the brand that caught my eye, though.'

'Remind me.'

'Lifestyle,' he said. 'Ever come across it? So to speak . . .'

I thought for a second. 'It looked unusual, but I didn't recognize it. To be honest it's been a while.'

'Well, I'd worry if it was your protection of choice. Y'know the clinic on Hulme Street?'

Around the corner from the Palace, there was a sexual health walk-in clinic run by a charity. As soon as Sutty mentioned it I remembered.

It was branded as the Positive Lifestyle Clinic.

'I'm about a five-minute walk away.'

'All right then, but Aidan . . .'

'Yeah?'

'Get yourself checked out while you're there.'

There was a homeless couple sitting outside, sharing a bottle of fortified wine. I passed them and walked into an off-white, clinical reception area. The waiting room was an even split between young men and women. Some looked like sex workers and carried on loud, outrageous conversations as I passed them. Others looked nervously at their phones or their shoes. I went to the front desk and spoke to a woman through a battered Perspex screen.

'Hi,' I said, discreetly showing her my badge. 'I'd like to speak to whoever's in charge, please.'

She wasn't impressed. 'Name?'

'Aidan Waits.'

'Yes, he does. Someone'll be with you in a minute, Mr Waits.'

I sat down. The three escorts who'd been discussing the wilder fantasies of their regulars looked at me. Then they looked at each other. They stood up as one and walked out of the building. I couldn't tell if I looked like a cop or just especially contagious. After a few minutes a woman in a white coat came through and spoke to the receptionist, who pointed at me.

'Mr Waits,' she said, with a professional smile. 'Shall we go through to my office?'

We stepped through and I closed the door behind me. 'Sorry, I think I cleared out half your waiting room.'

'They'll be back,' she said. 'Their bodies are their livelihoods. Now, what seems to be the problem?'

'I'd like to ask you about condoms.' She raised an eyebrow. 'It's work-related. Would you happen to have any to hand?'

She looked at me for a moment then leaned off the counter and opened a drawer. She reached inside and held one out for me to take. The packaging was identical to the wrapper I'd found at the Palace.

'Are these available anywhere else?'

'There are two other Lifestyle clinics—'

'But not in the city?'

'Correct.'

'And they're not for commercial use?' She shook her head. 'So if someone's using these in the city centre, they most likely came from here?'

'Stands to reason.'

'This is a very long shot but you don't happen to keep records of—'

She was shaking her head before I could finish the sentence. 'Nothing like that, I'm afraid. First of all, we supply contraception to anyone who needs it. Usually students or sex workers. Secondly, there are confidentiality issues involved. A clinic like this is built on trust. If people felt as though they couldn't come here in confidence we'd be losing the battle.'

'I understand that,' I said. 'Thanks for seeing me at such short notice, I know you must be busy.' We both heard the disappointment in my voice.

'Not since you scared off the waiting room. Where did you say you found it?'

'A hotel.'

'A condom in a hotel?' She smiled. 'A needle in a haystack, surely?'

'It's closed down at the moment but a man died there in suspicious circumstances on Saturday night. We're trying to trace anyone who might have seen something.'

'Closed down?' She frowned. 'You don't mean the Palace?'

'I can neither confirm nor deny that,' I said, nodding.

'So if someone had been working from there, they wouldn't be in any trouble . . .'

'They'd be making my day.'

She looked at me for a moment. 'I've heard a couple of girls mention it. I think there's a room they use sometimes.'

'Even since it's been closed?'

'You'd be surprised at some of the uses these empty buildings get put to. Someone was hiring it out for a percentage. There are some real users in this city, and I do occasionally feel compelled to report things, but in this case it sounded like a good deal for the girls. A fairly safe environment. Fairly cheap. And they could just cross the road for supplies, or a check-up here if it came to that.'

'Any girls in particular?'

'I'm afraid that really is as far as I can go.' I passed back the condom and she smiled. 'It's on the house, Detective.'

I shook my head. 'I hate seeing things go to waste.'

3

I requested the address that uniform had been given for Marcus Collier, the day-shift guard, and then settled into some paperwork. Sutty and I had an unspoken agreement to spend half of each shift apart from each other, so I could ghostwrite his reports. Although this meant more work, and was in violation of several regulations, I took an odd pleasure in approximating his constipated, staccato writing style. Or at least, in spending a few hours apart from him.

When uniform still hadn't supplied Collier's address several hours later, I knew that they probably never would. Lately, my name was closing a lot of doors. I requested the CCTV from the site of the latest dustbin fire on Oxford Road, just in case Parrs decided to check up on me. There had been three of them, spread across five days. So far the perpetrator had chosen surveillance blackspots, by accident or by design, and I assumed this would be no different.

Finally, bored with waiting, I called Aneesa for Martin Collier's address. She gave it to me immediately and, with some hours to kill before my shift actually started, I decided to head out there for a look. It was still bright out but creeping towards evening. The streets were filled with rough-looking young men about my age, their arms wrapped around women so beautiful it could break your heart. I tried to look at the skyline instead. Endless regeneration cranes, vanishing off into the smog.

Marcus Collier lived at a Salford address. I saw his area code, a gun-crime hotspot, and grimaced. Almost a quarter of all reported shootings in the city took place in a one-mile radius of his street. Dynastic crime families going back generations carried out beatings, robberies and even hits with near-impunity. No one blamed the bystanders, the civilians, when they didn't make statements. A code of silence was what kept them safe. Due to this, most violence in the area went unreported, and we speculated the true gun-crime figures were much higher. When I visited it was usually to deliver Osman warnings. Threat-to-life alerts. Sutty and I had communicated dozens of such threats to men, women and even children, most of whom declined police protection.

Marcus had a room in a beat-up-looking boarding house at the dead end of a cul-de-sac. I heard the whistles as I pulled into the street, followed by a stillness that was very different from calm. The whistles were an early-warning system. Literally a boy on the corner who'd put his lips together and blow. It told his employers – the local dealers – to close the first-floor windows, where they'd usually sit dropping down zip-bags of dope for passing regulars. The whistles put everything on hold, pausing the sad melodrama of the street for a few minutes.

The original red bricks of Marcus's boarding house had blackened beneath the city smog, and several windows were covered up with wooden planks. When I knocked on the door it nearly gave way beneath my hand. The lock was bust and I stepped inside, into a damp, messy hallway. There was a disconnected washing machine blocking my path, and I pressed myself into the wall to edge round it. You saw this a lot in some neighbourhoods. People bored of being robbed would push them up against their front doors at night, to stop junkies from breaking in.

I went up the stairs and knocked on room 3, apparently Marcus Collier's.

There was no movement behind the door. From the room across the hall I could hear a game show, blaring out of a cheap TV. I listened for a moment and knocked there instead.

107

A woman's voice, thick with drink or age or both, said: 'You're early . . .'

'I'm a friend of Marcus's, any idea where he is?'

'A friend of Marcus?' There was a pause, then a low, joyless laugh. 'Now I've heard everything.' I stepped back as she came to the door and opened it. She was middle-aged, wearing a leopardskin nightie at least one size too small. I could smell skunk on her breath. '*Hello* . . .' she said, looking me up and down. 'You after some company, sweetheart?'

'Nothing like that.'

'Marcus owe you money or something?' I showed her my badge and she laughed. 'With friends like you . . .'

'What's your name?'

'Jeanie,' she said, leaning into the doorway. 'Rub me the right way and all your wishes could come true . . .'

'Have you got a key for his room, Jeanie?'

She opened her mouth but didn't say anything.

'It might distract me from what you're smoking in there . . .'

'Yeah yeah,' she said, pressing her lips together in affected disappointment and disappearing back inside the room. As an afterthought she kicked the door closed behind her and I waited a minute. She re-emerged with a key and pressed it into my hand. I felt the hot sweat from her palm and she took a step closer. 'Mates rates, if you're quick about it . . .'

'I'm a married man.'

She looked at me for a second then pulled away. 'I doubt it, shug. They're my best customers. Put the key under the door on your way out.'

I crossed the hall to Marcus's room and opened it.

It was a box, about four by eight, and smelt of damp. I could see a security uniform, crumpled on the floor, like he'd evaporated while wearing it. There wasn't much more than a bed, a chair and a desk. I looked at the bed, moved the dirty sheets about until I was satisfied that nothing was hidden there. Then I went around the room. Empty take-away boxes were taking on a life of their own in the heat, and the littered napkins and discarded payslips on the floor looked interchangeable. I checked inside the pockets of his security uniform, crushed into the floor. There was a leaking biro and some change in one pocket and a plastic package in the other. I drew it out carefully.

Lifestyle.

The condom connected him to room 305, where I suspected there had been sexual activity. Alongside what I'd learned about girls tricking in the Palace, it shed some light on what Ali had referred to as Marcus's entrepreneurial spirit.

It didn't tell me where he was, though.

As I slid the key back under the door of No. 4, I called out, 'If Marcus isn't here, where will he be?' There was no answer. 'Hey,' I said, kicking the door.

'The Inn,' said Jeanie.

'Which Inn?'

'The *Fawcett* Inn.' She laughed. 'Get it?'

4

Although the daylight was failing, the heat hung motionless in the air, and the warmth still hummed underfoot. It had been baked down into the ground and into the buildings, charging the kerbs with kinetic energy. I walked, following Jeanie's directions through failed estates and problem blocks, where hooded kids shouted at me and bass-driven music poured out of the windows into the streets.

When I reached The Inn I thought I'd been had, that it must have been abandoned. Scuffed, industrial sheet metal covered the ground-floor windows, and the sign was falling off the wall one letter at a time. The dirty off-white façade had come away from the building itself in places, exposing the no-nonsense cinder blocks beneath. It was a dilapidated roadhouse, rendered obsolete by newer motorways, and starved to death by one recession that looked like it was going back for seconds.

My fingers stuck to the door at first touch, so I pushed it open with my foot. The room smelt like a wet, drunken dog, and there were ten or so near-identical men sitting around it. White, and of a certain age, either gleaming bald or with short, close-cropped hair. Most kept their eyes on the football highlights, screaming out of a widescreen TV on the far wall. The colour was turned up so brightly that it hurt my eyes. A few of the men glanced at me as I walked in, their fists wrapped around pint glasses of piss-yellow lager. There was a crumpled, faded England flag hanging above the bar at an angle, and I saw that it had actually been nailed into the wall. Something to be proud of.

The barman pushed himself upright as I approached, baring his teeth in what might have been a smile. He had a face full of age, hate and booze, and I counted three golden teeth before he closed his mouth again. He didn't say anything, just nodded at me and waited. The roar of the TV covered our conversation.

'Evening,' I said. 'I didn't know you were open . . .'

'Some days neither do I. Got the football to thank, though.'

'I'm looking for someone.'

He stared blankly ahead. 'You think this is a place where people come to be found?'

'Marcus Collier.'

'Never heard of him, mate.' He began to turn away.

'He's a regular here.'

'A regular what?'

'That's funny,' I said. 'He's pale, no hair . . .' He laughed at that, flashing his eyes over my shoulder, at the ten or so men matching my description.

'I'll have a beer, then. You've heard of that?'

He seemed to come suddenly awake but I turned to go to the toilet. This time I caught a few hard looks from the men as I went through the room. The gents was just one filthy cubicle. It had been kicked in so many times that the top and bottom halves of the door moved independently of each other. I read some of the more legible graffiti and made my now-automatic five-point search of the space. In the light fixture I found a plastic baggy with what I took to be amphetamines inside. White power.

'Three quid,' said the barman when I returned. I put the coins down on the counter and he used his index finger to drag them towards him one at a time.

The bar mat was a dirty red, white and blue.

THERE AIN'T NO BLACK IN THE UNION JACK, it said.

Coming back through the room I'd noticed that we were one man down. I took a drink of my beer and turned to the barman.

'Out of interest, was he here on Saturday night?'

'Who?'

'Marcus Collier.'

'I've already told you—'

'His name's written all over the toilet wall. Biggest cock in the north, apparently.' He didn't move. 'Although it's a close-run thing.'

'What d'ya want him for?'

'That's between me and him.'

'Leave yer number.'

I looked at him for a second, fished inside my pocket for a pen and wrote '999' on the bar mat.

He laughed, drew himself up. 'You're no cop . . .'

'We let all sorts in these days, and we've got a pretty good sense of humour about who a skinhead shares his cell with.' He showed me his teeth again. I drained my glass and set it down on the counter. I could feel the eyes of the other men in the room, burning holes into the back of my head. Slowly, deliberately, I used both hands to sweep up the sopping wet bar mat.

THERE AIN'T NO BLACK IN THE UNION JACK

I screwed it into a knot, wrung out the stale beer on to the bartop, and forced it into my empty pint glass. When the barman didn't stop me, I knocked it on its side and rolled it towards him. It connected with his belly. He still didn't react so I crossed the room and turned.

'Thanks for the tip-off,' I said, loudly. That pushed him into action. He lifted up the bar counter and walked through, letting it crash down behind him. He had the handle of a cricket bat in one hand and the broadside resting on his shoulder. A couple of the other men stood up.

'Tip-off about what?' The football was forgotten now, and the entire room followed our argument with interest.

'I came here to ask you a straight question. Was Marcus in? You said no so I went to the toilet. While I was there you shared our conversation. I notice we're one man down now.' I took out my card and dropped it on the floor. 'Maybe you could give him a message for me?' Nobody moved. 'I'm the best chance he's got of avoiding a long jump.'

'He's not here.'

'Not if he's got any sense, but the guy I'm looking for isn't exactly a brainwave. Where else would he be?' The barman started to answer but I cut him off. 'Don't answer that. I'll be outside, and if I see him leave I'm doing you and everyone in this room for obstruction.' He went beetroot red with rage. The only sound was the football commentator, screaming about an own-goal. The men started to sink into their seats, or otherwise curl away from me.

'Marcus,' shouted the barman, finally.

'Yeah, yeah,' said a man, emerging from the stairwell. Even I would have struggled to pick him out of a police line-up of the others in the room. Sky-blue jeans, a white polo shirt and a bald head.

'Evening, Marcus. According to this guy you've never been here before.'

He shrugged. 'So?'

'So I'm trying to eliminate you from a murder enquiry. You'd better find someone who can remember where you were on Saturday night.'

5

We were sitting to one side of the bar. I had my back to the other men in the room but could still feel the waves of hate, radiating out from them. I'd decided to talk to Marcus one-on-one. So far the day, the case, had been one loose thread after another, and it was time to twist them together into something more tangible.

Collier was eating peanuts by the fistful, chewing with his mouth wide open.

His breath made my eyes water.

'We've been trying to get hold of you,' I said.

'Oh?'

'Oh. Why haven't you been turning in for work?'

'I have.'

'Not according to the officer on the door.'

He chewed thoughtfully and shrugged. 'Saw the filth, didn't I? Didn't know what it meant so I left 'em to it. I know jack shit about all this.'

'As a general rule of thumb, someone who bolts at the sight of the law usually has something to hide.' He took another fistful of peanuts and sucked them out of his hand. 'So it makes me wonder what your story is.'

'I'm a fucking eccentric millionaire,' he said. 'If I'm found out it'll disrupt my charity work . . .'

'Your shift finished at 8 p.m. on Saturday?' He nodded. 'What did you do after?'

'Came home.' I could see peanuts and beer mashed up in his mouth. 'Came here.'

'It'll hurt your case when I testify that the owner said he didn't know you, said you hadn't been in.'

He swallowed. 'What case?'

'A man's dead.'

'Ali?'

'What makes you say that?'

He shrugged. 'Only person I ever see there . . .'

'I'm wondering whether I believe that.' He didn't say anything. 'What do you think of Ali?'

'Depends if he's been murdered or not . . .'

'Not.'

'He's an officious little prick.'

'You mean he does his job?'

'And the whole world's gotta know it. They pay him more than me, y'know?'

'I heard something like that. When you can't be trusted to go round flushing toilets, you need to take a look at yourself, Marcus.'

'He's a jobsworth.'

'Someone agrees with you. They smashed his head in with a fire extinguisher the other night.'

'Hang on, you said—'

'He's alive, in hospital. We also found the body of an unidentified man, though. Did you see or hear anything unusual during your day shift?'

'Naw,' he said, avoiding my eyes.

'That's a yes, then. Have you ever let other people into the Palace, Marcus?'

'No comment.'

'Another yes. Look, I haven't arrested you yet. If I had, you'd have already perjured yourself. Think.'

'Fuck off. Why don't you?' He drew himself up, raised his voice for the benefit of the room. 'Go on, arrest me.'

I swept his peanuts off the table and looked at him for a minute, letting him sink back into his chair.

'I haven't arrested you yet because you interest me so little. Because I thought you could give me some information before I went on to the next place. But the more questions you avoid, the more interested I get.'

He didn't say anything.

I took out my phone and called Dispatch. Told them who I was and that I'd found Marcus Collier, a man wanted in connection with the events at the Palace. He frowned. I gave them the address, hung up and resumed our conversation. 'I haven't arrested you because I don't think you've got the balls or the brains to kill someone. I think you're hiding something else. Probably the sort of thing we could usually let go. You've probably been let go all your life. You've put it down to skill or charm, but I'm here to tell you that you're chronically bereft of both those things.'

He folded his arms, smirked, sniffed.

'The truth is that you've just never been near anything important before. Now you are, and now you'll talk. Whether I give you a slap on the wrist or a decade in Strangeways, I will never think of you again. So you've got until that squad car arrives to take the easy way out.'

He didn't move, but the smirk was gone.

I searched inside my pockets for the condom I'd found in his flat and dropped it on to the table. 'Do you recognize this?'

'Nope.'

'What if I were to tell you it was found on your property?' He frowned. 'The door was open.'

He sat, fuming. 'I bought it. So what?'

'They're not for sale. Try again.'

'I dunno. Some girl.'

With one finger I dragged his glass to my side of the table.

'Not done with that,' he said.

I poured his pint into the carpet. 'I'm taking this, with your

116

fingerprints, to compare against those found on a used condom wrapper in the closed-down hotel you're supposed to be guarding.' There was a hardening of the jaw. 'When I match them, and I will—'

'Wait a minute, look, I was here last night.'

'That's not what the barman just said.'

'Yeah, but he was covering—'

'Either way, it's a there-and-then-gone-again alibi from the scum of the earth.' He started to speak but I cut him off. 'Alongside this baggy of coke found in your possession, you start to look like the perfect fit for a dead man no one can explain.'

'That's not even mine, you can't—'

'I can do anything I set my mind to. Jail time isn't a threat any more, it's a promise. Do you know what happens to skinheads inside? They get used as prison pockets.' I saw the question in his face and went on. 'It's where the real bangers hide shanks, drugs, burner phones. It's your arse, Marcus,' I said, getting up. 'You'd better keep the condom.'

'Hang on . . .'

I opened the door.

'*Hang on.*'

I turned. 'You had your chance. You decided to waste my time. Now I'll waste a few years of yours. You're right, you don't know anything.'

'Slags,' he said, quietly. The whole room was watching us now.

'What?'

He stood, took a step closer. 'Slags. Girls. I was rentin' a room out for 'em in the Palace.'

'When?'

'A few times.' He shrugged, looked at the floor. 'Been at it for months . . .'

I sat back down at our table and directed him to do the same. 'How many girls?'

'I dunno . . .' he said. I looked at him. 'I *don't*. A few. Different ones. The pimps keep 'em on tour, shift 'em round towns so punters don't get bored. Started out just some locals, girls from under the bridge. Word got out . . .'

'When?'

'Durin' the daytime. In my shifts. Bit of cash in hand . . .'

'And what, you took a cut?'

'I was always in the building with 'em, though. It's nothing to do with anyone in there last night. I wasn't handin' out keys.'

'Which room were you using?'

He didn't say anything.

'That squad car must be getting close by now . . .'

'Different ones,' he said. 'Third floor.'

'Why the third floor?'

'The lift's fucked.' He shrugged. 'That's the only floor it goes to . . .' It was such a banal, lazy explanation that I knew it was true.

'The intruder I saw was on the third floor,' I said. He closed his eyes. 'Did you have a girl there on Saturday by any chance?'

'She left before I did.'

'Or she liked the spot and wedged open a fire door. Went back once you'd gone. Who was she?'

'I don't know.'

'You might have started out hiring the space, but I think you were sampling the goods as well.'

'Naw . . .'

'So your fingerprint just fell on that condom?'

'You don't know it's mine.'

'But you don't know it's not.'

He didn't move.

'Tell me what the girl looked like.'

'Just some girl. Slagged up. Red hair.'

'How old?'

'I dunno, twenties?'

'Where did you meet her?'

'She came to the door one day . . .'

'All right, Marcus. Outside.'

Collier got to his feet, leered over my shoulder at the other men in the bar and turned for the door. I followed him outside to the car park, where uniform were arriving. When he saw them he stopped so suddenly that I almost walked into him.

'Listen,' he said, turning. 'Listen . . .'

'I'm listening.'

'Cherry,' he said. 'The girl's name's Cherry.'

'Where will I find her?' He didn't say anything and I looked over his shoulder significantly.

'China Town. Y'know Legs?'

'The topless bar?'

'Yeah, there's some shithole building next door. She's in 4B.'

'If she's got a room, why does she trick out of the Palace?'

'It's not what you'd call spacious . . .'

'OK. Well, that's a big help, thank you.' He smiled. 'Marcus Collier, I'm arresting you.' I read him his rights and placed a hand on his shoulder.

'The fuck?' he said, as I turned him towards the squad car.

'These gentlemen will look after you from here.' The two officers climbed out of the car and opened a door for him. I gave the charge I wanted him held on, as well as the fact that he was a material witness in connection with a suspicious death. Then I set out back through the estate for the car I'd arrived in.

6

I called Sutty as I drove. The night had fallen like a curtain while I'd been in the bar. Our shift was technically just starting and he agreed to meet me in China Town. If what Collier said was true, Cherry had been in the hotel on the day we'd discovered the smiling man.

I parked up feeling electric.

I entered through the Paifang, a twenty-foot archway above Faulkner Street adorned with pixies, dragons and gold-leaf finishes. It felt like stepping out of sync with the world and passing through to another dimension, and as I arrived it was coming vividly to life. All-you-can-eat buffets and karaoke rooms were giving way to shot bars, strip clubs and casinos, with sombre neon lights leading the way inside.

It was an easy place to get a fix and the walking dead seemed to shuffle by on every street, dissolving in and out of reality. A recession was like boom time for the drugs trade, with people looking for new methods of escape as conventional ones evaporated. Spice was the current favourite. We were seeing eighteen-, nineteen-, twenty-year-olds have shaking fits, psychotic episodes and heart attacks.

They called it the rattle.

One man had gone on a rampage here, setting fire to cars, buildings and, finally, to himself. When the police got to him he'd said that he was desperate to get arrested, to get off the drug. It was impossible not to notice them now, coming up or down, shivering in the heat, turning blue. The highs and lows could be harmless, a man or woman, laughing or crying in the street. They could also turn people inside out. Living ghosts, well matched to the haunted, faded splendour of the buildings, the failing romance.

I found the building, as promised, beside a strip club called Legs. There were three or four dancers standing outside talking, smoking cigarettes, staring blankly into the street. They looked beautiful, invulnerable, immune to love. I suppose that they had to. I interrupted a conversation to ask where the street entrance for the flats was. I was pointed by one long finger towards a shabby doorway. The girls knew what went on in there and looked at me like I was a Spice freak or a john. I went to the entrance and searched for a room 4B on the intercom. There wasn't a button for it, so I buzzed all the others until someone let me inside.

The hallway was poorly lit and the air smelt stale, uninterrupted. I could hear Frank Sinatra, 'Only the Lonely', from behind one of the doors and it soundtracked my walk up the stairs. When I came to Cherry's room, 4B, I saw that the door was ajar. Splintered wood littered the floor from where the lock had been forced. I listened for a moment and then gently pushed it open.

It was a small, airless room. Not a flat. More like a repurposed store cupboard. There was one window, gritted by smog. Its view was crossed out by an external fire escape passing diagonally from one corner to the other. There wasn't much light, so I clicked on my torch and shone it about. It was neat, in the way that small rooms, small lives, have to be. A multicoloured poster of Marilyn Monroe on the wall. Several pairs of identical red high heels lined up in a row. A roll-mattress on the floor where it looked like Cherry slept. It was an illegal sublet, neither designed, nor fit, for human use.

Not exactly spacious, as Marcus had said.

It would be difficult for the girl to bring people back here, and I wanted to believe that she was out working, for her own good, as well as our one lead. But when I moved the torch I saw toiletries, which had been lined up on the windowsill, scattered across the floor. I saw a full-length mirror, lying on its side, fractured from an impact.

I saw a shock of bright red blood embedded in the glass.

'Shit,' I said.

I heard a movement and shone the light in its direction.

'Whoa there, hot stuff,' said Sutty. 'I take it we're one step behind?'

By way of an answer I lit up the mirror, the bloody shards.

'Seven years' bad luck,' he muttered.

I shone the light about the dismal room. 'Looks like she got it all in one go.'

We walked out into the hallway, stepping over the splintered wood. I felt a cold anger on Cherry's behalf and wondered if she was OK. I wondered what she'd seen. It felt like we hadn't missed her by much.

'Well?' said Sutty, leaning on the wall. 'Think this is who you saw at the Palace?'

'I don't know, but she was definitely there on Saturday night. Marcus was using a room on the third floor for girls and that's where I saw someone. He said he'd sent her home before his shift ended, but all it'd take for her to get back in would be an object wedged in a fire door.'

'And what? Smiley Face was a customer?'

I thought about it. Shook my head. 'He was on the fourth floor. I think he's something else. Something separate. But that this girl wandered in on it, whatever it was. There's no way she's the one who knocked out Ali, for example.'

Sutty nodded. 'If she'd seen a guard coming she'd have talked or screwed her way out of it.'

'What scares me is she couldn't talk or screw her way out of whatever happened here . . .'

We looked at each other for a moment and then parted, each knocking on a door either side of 4B. There was no one in on my side, and the man on Sutty's hadn't seen or heard anything. His

English was bad, and he was more scared about his legal status in the country than the building. We worked our way along the corridor, encountering hostility, language barriers and similar results.

I followed Sutty down the stairs.

On the ground floor a frail, nicotine-stained man was waiting for us beside his room. He had an oxygen mask loose around his neck and dragged an air cylinder behind him.

'*Good* . . .' he said, trying to address Sutty. He walked past the man, to the street entrance, waving at me to stop and talk. The man's hair was a weak, sickly shade of yellow. '*Good riddance,*' he hissed, before falling into a hacking fit. His body was wracked with coughs that didn't quite make it out of his mouth and he shook as they reverberated inside his ribcage. He doubled up and applied his oxygen mask, leaning on the wall to stay upright. When it looked like he was stable again I spoke to him.

'We're looking for the woman who lives above you.'

His milky, cataract eyes went wide. '*Woman?*'

'Girl, whatever.'

He wheezed again and I thought he was going into another coughing fit. It wasn't until his face contorted that I saw he was laughing. He held on to my arm. His fingers were thin. Cold and hard as carrots. '*Some girl,*' he whispered. There were tears in his eyes from the effort.

'Did you see what happened?'

'. . . *Saw the police drag her out of the building* . . .' I thought about the violence of the scene. The broken door, the blood.

'When was this?'

'. . . *Less than an hour* . . .'

'How did you know they were police?'

He screwed up his face. '. . . *Guy said on his way out* . . .'

'A man?' He nodded. 'What did he look like?'

'. . . *Like you* . . . *like everyone* . . .' He used his free hand to point at his thick, milky eyes. '. . . *He looked like a blur* . . .' I peeled his hand off me and followed Sutty out on to the street, crossing through traffic towards him. He was leaning on the roof of the car, watching me.

'That guy on the ground floor says the police took her . . .' I said.

'The blind bloke? He probably posts his letters into the dog-shit bin, Aid.' He exhaled out some malice. 'Police are unlikely from the busted door and the blood. Your generation haven't got that kind of get-up-and-go. What's she look like?'

'In her twenties, according to Marcus. A redhead. *Slagged up . . .*'

'Oh,' said Sutty, looking about us at all the girls matching the security guard's description. 'We'll have her in custody in five minutes, then.'

I climbed into the car and called in the crime scene, requesting SOCO meet us there. Sutty got in beside me, opened the glove compartment, found his wipes and cleaned down the radio I'd just touched. My phone started to vibrate.

Aneesa.

I thought she might be calling on behalf of Natasha Reeve and Freddie Coyle. Neither had given a straightforward account of themselves and, as a rule, money equalled trouble. As per Parrs' instructions, I still hadn't told Sutty about these interviews. Pathetically, I was still hoping to get back in the Superintendent's good books. I got out of the car and moved to a safe distance before answering.

'Waits,' I said, impatiently.

'I really wish you'd kept me updated about events at the Palace,' said Aneesa. 'Specifically the dead body. My clients have both been on the phone, asking why they were blindsided. If I'd known about the man, and that you were putting those kinds of questions to them, I'd have been present.'

'Well, now's your chance. I'd like to follow up with Natasha, if possible.' She didn't say anything. 'Ms Khan?'

She sighed. 'When?

I looked back at the car. Sutty was standing outside it, wiping down the door handle I'd just touched. 'What are you doing right now?'

7

I told Sutty that I'd been dragged away by a development on the
dustbin fires, left him waiting for SOCO, and made the ten-
minute walk back in the direction of Natasha Reeve's flat. Aneesa
met me there.

'Thank you for seeing me again at such short notice,' I said.
Natasha Reeve acknowledged both Aneesa and me with a blink
then went towards an unoccupied bench, sitting down as though
our walk round the block one day before had worn her out. We
were back on King Street but she still wasn't ready to invite me into
her home.

Aneesa sat down beside her. 'Thanks for doing this,' she said. I
sat on Natasha's other side, putting her in the middle. They both
stared at me and Aneesa went on. 'Apparently, Detective Constable
Waits has some follow-up questions. He's assured me he'll be brief.'

'I really just wanted to clarify some things about the Palace.'

Natasha waited.

'When we spoke before, you told me that you and your ex-
husband built up the hotel between you.'

'Yes?'

'Mr Coyle claims it was inherited from his side of the
family . . .'

She smiled, as though at some old adversary. 'Semantics. His
family owned the property but it had stood empty for some years
when it came to us. I won't deny that inheriting a building of that

size and stature was an enormous help, but it's the truth that Freddie and I built the business. It's also the truth that I was a larger part of the partnership than he.'

'That must have been frustrating.'

'Less so than seeing him flounder in business . . .'

'He doesn't have a head for it?'

'That was one of his tired old jokes. He said a brain was useful but it was his fingers that he really counted on.' I smiled. 'Unfortunately he was still counting on them when we inherited the Palace,' she said. 'I was only too pleased to assume the lead role.'

'He mentioned some tension with his family. Were they disappointed in his lack of business ambition?'

'I don't think they ever expected much. His parents had an unhappy marriage. On our wedding day, Gloria, Freddie's mother, took me to one side and gave me some advice: "Always expect the worst from them and you'll never be disappointed."'

'Are his parents still alive?'

'Well, we inherited all their money and property, so what does that tell you?'

'I don't have much experience in that area,' I said.

She ignored the provocation. 'They went one after another, soon after we were married.'

'Money and property,' I said. 'There was more to the inheritance than the Palace?'

'There was at first. Freddie made some bad deals. Counting on his fingers for business again.'

'So if he mentioned tensions with his family . . .'

'He was either living in the past or being glib. I'm all that's left of his family now, so I suppose he could have been referring to me.'

'Could Freddie's bad head for business, combined with his separation from you, have left him hard up?'

'Absolutely not.'

'You're sure?'

'We both draw a handsome salary from the trust . . .'

'The Palace has been closed for some time.'

'Only out of stubbornness from both sides.' Aneesa started to interject but Natasha waved her protest away. 'It's true. Freddie never cared for the business but I did. It was our baby, as far as I was concerned. But once we were dead and buried, so was the hotel. I let the staff go and stopped going to work mainly as a challenge, to see if he was capable of doing anything about it. If he had any sense at all he'd hire a new manager. He doesn't, though. Now, I see it as my little gift to myself, not earning him any more money.' She looked at me again. 'We could both retire today, though, Detective. Freddie saying he's hard up is, well, a bit rich.'

'How does the trust work?'

'Like a business. Money goes into a pot from the Palace and leaves for expenses. Those expenses might be upkeep, legal fees, salaries, etcetera. Neither Freddie or I can draw any more than the agreed amount, though.'

'You're certain of that?'

'When you're preparing for a divorce you tend to check these things. It's iron-clad, I'm absolutely certain. Of course his half of the pot will be his to spend once we've dissolved the trust. A great deal more than his monthly allowance. Why all this talk of Freddie's finances?'

'When I told him about the assault, and even about the death, his first concerns were liability and how it might affect the sale. He seemed unusually keen on that side of things for a man with no head for business . . .'

'The Palace is his last tie to me. That's what he's keen to get rid of.'

'May I ask what specifically caused your separation?'

She shook her head. 'And besides, what can that have to do with a break-in?'

I thought for a second and then tried another tack. 'Was Freddie always a big drinker?'

'I was the drinker. He never quite had the constitution for it. A glass of wine here or there.'

'When I spoke to Mr Coyle at 10 a.m. yesterday it looked like he was ending a long night . . .'

'Freddie changed so much towards the end of our relationship, I suppose he could be anything now.'

'Changed how, Ms Reeve?'

'Well, at the time I thought there was something wrong. With him, I mean. He became cold, distant. I see now he was preparing to leave our marriage. He changed more in the weeks before we parted than in the preceding ten years. I can't say how much he's changed since.'

'Do you think he could have changed enough to be involved in whatever's happening at the Palace?'

'It's a ridiculous question. Freddie's only motivation in life is to sell the Palace. He may be a fool for business but he doesn't usually throw things away.' In the silence that followed I saw her wonder why that logic hadn't applied to their marriage.

'What happened six months ago?'

'You have to keep banging away, don't you? Is this how you get your kicks? Burrowing into the lives of strangers?'

'If this was about your marriage, I'd leave you to it. We believe a vulnerable young woman's mixed up in it all, though. That she might have seen something to put her in danger. There was evidence of violence at her home, so I'll keep asking until I get an answer.'

She looked away again. 'I began to receive notes.' I caught Aneesa's eye. Her face told me that this was news to her too. 'Anonymous notes.'

'Can I ask what the substance of these notes was?'

'The same substance as all such notes, I expect. That my husband was walking out on me. That he was having an affair.'

'Do you still have them?'

'No. And they were hand-delivered. No envelopes or postmarks or anything like that.'

'Did you report them to the police?'

'The police? My husband's sex life is a little out of your jurisdiction, wouldn't you say?'

'Whoever sent them obviously did so with malicious intent. Was there any sense of blackmail involved?'

'No threats or anything like that. Just details. Times. Places.'

'Did you speak to Freddie about them?'

'I ignored them, for a time. Then the notes became pictures. Photographs. I couldn't ignore them any more. The final letter was an address, a day and date in the future. A few days from when I received it. There was a key taped to the paper. Freddie was acting so elusively, so strangely. I genuinely *was* worried for him. So I went.' She spoke as though it was the central humiliation of her life and I'd excavated it. Aneesa gave me a dirty look and turned away. 'Some absurd loft place on Sackville Street.' The same address where I'd visited Freddie earlier that day. 'I waited outside the building until someone came out, then I caught the door and went inside. I found the room and heard raised voices. So I used the key that had been sent to me . . . He was with another man.' I looked out into the street to make sure the surprise didn't show on my face. None of us spoke for a moment. 'I don't think we've ever been in a room together since.'

'Did you know this other man?'

'Ask Freddie.'

'I will. Do you have any idea who might have sent you those notes?'

She looked at me. 'Isn't it obvious? His lover, of course. No doubt he's having a good laugh with my husband about it even now.'

Unless he was murdered in the Palace Hotel on Saturday night, I thought.

'You don't really think they had something to do with all this?'

Aneesa and I were walking in the same direction, me to pick up with Sutty at the site of Cherry's apparent abduction, Aneesa to catch a cab home.

'It's pretty interesting how much they have to hide,' I said. 'I take it all that was news to you?'

'It was, actually. And it was also none of my business.'

'Do you think Blick knew about it?'

'You'd have to ask him that.'

'I will. He's back next week?'

'Next week.'

'Why this sudden urge to find himself?'

'It was one of those things that built up for a long time. Anthony's compulsive, a workaholic. It's the first break I've known him take in years.'

'The timing seems—'

'No,' said Aneesa. 'You don't get to just throw shit at people and see what sticks. Anthony went away for health reasons, if you really want to know.'

I stopped, looked at her.

'He had a heart attack,' she said. 'His break's on doctor's orders.' I thought of the pictures I'd seen of Blick, surrounded by young Thai women. I wondered if that was medical advice as well.

'Coyle's cash-flow situation,' I said, changing the subject.

She gave a small laugh. 'He'd have to be wiping his arse with it to be running out.' She could see me edging towards the question and saved me the trouble. 'Annually? Comfortably six figures,' she said. 'Very comfortably. Anyway, you've said it yourself. This death in the Palace hurts them both financially.'

So who'd want to do that, I thought.

8

I'd been gone for the best part of an hour when I got back to China Town and SOCO still hadn't arrived. Sutty and I waited, listlessly, with the doors wide open, trying to stay cool.

The acrimonious split of Natasha Reeve and Frederick Coyle ran through the case like a fault line. But Freddie's affair, and the anonymous notes revealing it, were a sudden turn into darker territory. Someone meant them harm. There was nothing so out of the ordinary about Freddie's affair being with another man, except in what it said about his state of mind. Natasha said he'd changed, even before she knew about his infidelity. Now he was a party animal, a drinker and gay. A man with no kids enjoying a mid-life crisis after a lifetime in the closet? Something to look forward to.

I knew that this side of the case was becoming too unwieldy to keep from Sutty for much longer, whatever Superintendent Parrs thought. My partner was no fool, and if he found out for himself who knew what he'd do?

I turned to him. 'Shouldn't SOCO be here by now?'

'The Pusher's struck again so they're running late.'

'You're joking?'

He shook his head. 'Someone saw a floater from the bridge on Albion Street. They're fishing him out now.'

I thought of the violent scene we'd encountered inside the China Town flat.

The missing girl.

'It's definitely a man?' I said. He shrugged and I looked at him. 'If it's a woman, it could be Cherry . . .'

'Shit,' he said, flatly. 'You'd better get over there.'

I got out of the car and slammed the door before I said anything that might get me fired. It was a ten-minute walk and another welcome break from Sutty. The Pusher was just an urban myth. The heart of the city courses with aqueducts, dockyards, quays and locks, and in less than a decade almost a hundred young men have died in them, usually drowning in canals between the hours of midnight and 6 a.m. This has given rise to press speculation of a serial killer at work, The Pusher. It sells more papers than the truth. A massive student population, vibrant nightlife and open waterways. A sad statistical inevitability.

But every crime scene has a kind of power and I felt this one before I saw it. Then I heard the sirens and saw pulsing blue lights. Uniforms in high-vis jackets had closed the bridge and were diverting traffic from both sides. I carded my way on to it and looked over the edge, down on to the waterside of the canal. The scene was confused but I could see that something had already been recovered. I waited as large lighting rigs were positioned on the pathway. When they were switched on, the light seemed to slam down on to the ground, illuminating a single black vinyl sheet.

It was about the size of a human body.

I gripped the brickwork of the bridge and felt the pulse passing through my hands. SOCO had finished videotaping the path but the scene itself was a nightmare of contamination. They wouldn't be making it to Cherry's flat any time soon. That hardly mattered if it was her body beneath that sheet, though. From the lack of activity, I guessed the pathologist hadn't examined it yet. I looked down for a moment. The water was a still, liquid-black beneath the lights.

I went to the waterside, approached the nearest officer and showed him my card. 'Did you get a look?' I said, nodding towards the body.

'First on scene,' he said, sullenly. 'Second in two years.'

'Anything you can tell me?'

'Was pretty fresh, comparatively. Last one we pulled out looked like corned beef hash.' He looked over my shoulder and took a step back.

'Aidan Waits.'

I turned to see Karen Stromer descending the bank towards us. She was already wearing the white plastic coveralls that she'd examine the body in. She set her case down and stared at me.

'Let me guess,' she said. 'You were first on the scene again . . .'

I felt the officer I'd been speaking to evaporate into the background.

'I only just arrived.'

'To check *his* pockets, too?'

I didn't say anything and she took a step closer, lowering her voice. 'You're giving me a very bad feeling, Detective Constable. Have you lost something, is that it?'

'No.'

'Are you here to plant something? You've got a reputation in that direction, after all . . .'

'I'm here because I think this might be connected to our unidentified man from the Palace Hotel.'

'Smiley Face? Isn't that what you're calling him?'

I didn't say anything.

'Turn out your pockets.'

'Excuse me?'

'It's a simple enough request,' she said. 'If you want to remain on my crime scene, you'll check the contents of your pockets. It's no less than I expect from every officer. I'm not risking contamination or planted evidence.' I looked at her for a moment and then at the body beneath the vinyl sheet. I reached into my jacket pocket, removing my wallet and warrant card, which I held up to her. 'The others,' she said. I felt inside my trouser pockets, pulling my phone out from one and feeling my keys in the other. And something else.

She must have seen my face change. 'I don't believe it,' she said. I pulled out the plastic zip-bag I'd found hidden in the Inn toilets, before questioning Marcus Collier. It was half-full of white powder.

I closed my eyes. 'It's not—'

'Leave,' she said, moving past me. 'Now.'

'Karen,' I said to her back. A few heads turned in my direction, including, eventually, hers. 'I mean it, I'm here on duty. If this is a young woman then it could be connected to the man from the Palace.' She glared at me. It felt like betting everything I had on one roll of the dice. For a moment the only sound came from the buzzing lights overhead, the water, lapping against the canalside. Finally she lifted the sheet from the body and looked at it.

'It's a man,' she said, before turning her attention to it fully and casting me out of her mind. The officers gathered round either shared smiles or looked away in sympathy. I walked back up the bank to the street, feeling my face and neck burning red with humiliation. I couldn't face going back to Cherry's flat. Sutty had eyes and ears everywhere, and he probably knew what I'd done already. He could wait for SOCO to arrive on his own. I tried to think of anything useful I could do. Collier had mentioned the bridge beside the Palace as a meeting place for his girls, but when I went there I didn't see any.

So Cherry had vanished into thin air.

When I reached my street in the Northern Quarter, I saw a car sitting outside the building. The lights were dimmed but as I got closer, the driver cranked them up to full beam, blinding me. I heard the roar of the engine and the car pulled out, missing me by inches. I went to my door and unlocked it before stopping. Remembering the zip-bag of some nameless amphetamine still in my pocket. I walked to the nearest grid and dropped it in. I paused, standing in the space where the car had been parked.

There was a pile of cigarette butts.

Fifteen to twenty of them. All smoked down to the filter and crushed before they'd been thrown out of the driver's side window. Someone had been sitting here, waiting, watching, for some time. I looked along the road, wondering who it was and what it meant.

It felt like the car might come apart when they took the corner, but it turned off the main road and kept on going. There were no streetlights any more, and the way was complicated, impossible. It was just the four of them. The man and the woman, Bateman and Elaine, and the two kids, Wally and Ash.

They could all feel it.

The desensitizing effect of details, fizzing by the window.

Wally was sitting in the back, staring out into the endless dark, until the rattle of the car, the looping, unseen turns, became hypnotic to him. It was freezing cold and he could hear his little sister, Ash, chattering her teeth in the next seat. Wally held her hand because he thought she was scared, because he knew he was. It had been a few weeks since they'd forced their way into Holly's home, and it felt like they'd been driving ever since. Sometimes they'd stayed on the floors of strangers. Sometimes they'd parked up in lay-bys and slept in the car. Finally, they'd settled in a messy terraced house. One night the grown-ups had been arguing and, when they fell abruptly silent, the boy had crept to the door and watched. On the TV he saw an emotional man and woman sitting at a table holding hands. The sound was muted but there was a large picture of Holly on the wall behind them. Bateman had been gone when they woke up and, after a few days, the boy started to hope he'd never come back. He had, though. He had something he wanted them all to see. Now the children rocked together in the back of the car, in a trance of slow movement.

'*Fuck's sake*,' said Bateman, breaking the spell.

It was the first time anyone had spoken in hours and, because he was in the driver's seat, the car stopped abruptly. There was just the sound of the engine turning over. There was just the blackness all around them. They reversed a few savage feet and then drove on in a different direction. Elaine, the children's mother, was sitting rigid on the passenger side, her body not moving an inch with the motion of the car.

The grown-ups had woken the children in the early hours of the morning and then carried them downstairs, out on to the potholed driveway, to a cut-and-shut Skoda they'd never seen before. It was a new colour, somewhere between green and rust. Once they'd fastened their seat belts, the grown-ups slammed the doors and argued behind the car. Wally and Ash stared straight ahead, listening to the hissed, 2 a.m. voices from outside. Bateman's deep, explanatory drone repeating the same sounds over and over again. He didn't stop when their mother tried to cut in and it sounded as if they were having two separate conversations.

Then one of them hit the other.

The children both jumped at the sound, like the car had gone over a speed bump. Bateman ripped open the driver's side door and climbed in. His face was flat. That trained inexpression that gave nothing away. It was his fist, flexing open and closed, that said everything.

He rolled a cigarette and tapped tunelessly on the dashboard. They heard their mother picking herself up off the driveway, felt the car rock slightly as she steadied herself on it. She got in on the passenger side without another word and shrank down into her seat. No one spoke as they drove along the motorway, the tension in the car rising, tightening like a knot. Now this sudden deviation into a country lane, the endless, looping backroads, felt like something coming undone, unravelling faster than they could keep track of. When Bateman killed the engine, let the headlights die out and coasted the car downhill, Elaine had shifted in her seat, looking from side to side.

'We're lost,' she said.

'We're here,' Bateman replied.

They were both right.

He eased the car into the side of the road and lifted the hand-brake. It was the middle of nowhere, the middle of the night, and no one said anything at first. Through the glare of the windscreen the dark looked unreal, a shining neon black. Bateman stared out of the driver's side window up at a farmhouse, while the children held hands in the back seat, hoping he'd forgotten them. Even now, ages five and eight, they knew all about Bateman's stare. They were conscious of its withering effect, of all the things they'd seen spoiling and going bad under it. There was a creak of leather from his seat. He shifted his enormous body round and looked at Wally.

'Just like we talked about,' he said to the boy. 'Pick that door and get up the stairs.' He felt around in the back seat and passed the boy an aluminium pole, about one metre long. 'Use this, go nowhere else.'

The boy looked at his mother, at the back of her head. Her knotted black hair. When the silence started to feel like a held, screaming note, she turned around. There was the start of a black eye from where Bateman had hit her.

'You heard,' she said.

Wally let go of his sister's hand and opened the door.

After the cramped confines of the back seat, he was overwhelmed by the space surrounding him. The car was parked off the court-yard of a large farmhouse, at the end of a lane. A mass of trees, just enormous, swaying shadows, stood behind him. Inside, he'd felt like they were protected, invisible, but now he saw how exposed they were. The moon hung over them like a spotlight, rendering the house, the yard, the car, in astonishing detail.

He caught his own reflection in the window and took a step back, away from everything he knew, into wide open, panoramic fear.

———

IV
Vanishing Act

1

I was watching Sutty through the corner of my eye. He was massaging the lumps about his face, neck and shoulders. Shape-shifting. After weeks of unbroken heat he was starting to look and smell like the larval stage for something else entirely. It felt like we were both changing.

We'd established that 4B, the room where Cherry had been staying, was an illegal sublet. When we'd traced the woman responsible for the building, she'd been shocked to find that someone was actually living there and, although I was relieved that Cherry's wasn't the body found in the canal, it left us with nothing. Just a vague description from Collier, a street-name.

Sutty and I were waiting in Karen Stromer's office, where she'd agreed to meet us. Although I knew we were there to discuss her findings on the smiling man, I couldn't help but feel nervous. The humiliation of the night before was still on my mind.

Sutty stopped playing with himself and started searching idly through his pockets. When he didn't find what he was looking for he sighed, half-stood and leaned across Stromer's desk. He picked up a ballpoint pen and started cleaning his ears out with it.

'Looking for your on-switch again, Peter?'

We turned to see Stromer, closing the office door behind her. If Sutty was fazed he didn't show it. Instead he collapsed back into his chair, wiped the pen on the desk's edge and inserted it into the other ear. Stromer walked round her desk and sat down. She wouldn't look at me and couldn't look at him, so she addressed herself to the space between us.

'For obvious reasons, I'd like to make this as brief as possible,' she said, opening a report and searching for a pen. Sutty offered her the one out of his ear but she ignored him, fished inside her pocket for a biro and made a note. 'With that said, we have rather a lot to discuss. The cadaver—'

'Layman's terms, Doc. Aidan hasn't got his dictionary.'

Stromer paused for a moment and then continued. 'Our unidentified man is one of the more fascinating specimens I've examined in recent memory.' She spoke with a professional detachment, as though he was an inanimate object. 'There are so many irregularities that one almost doesn't know where to begin . . .'

'Could one give us the cause of death?' said Sutty.

'Preliminary bloodwork suggests multisystem organ failure.'

He made a noise. 'And can you tell us what *caused* the cause of death?'

'Not as stupid a question as you make it sound, Peter. In a word, no. We're still awaiting the toxicology report, but I believe we'll find a foreign agent or agents in the soft tissue.'

'You think he was poisoned?'

'I'm almost certain of it, but that isn't what I called you here to discuss.' Her eyes flicked on to me for a moment and I started to sink. Stromer had said if she found drugs she'd feel compelled to report my trying to access the crime scene. That, coupled with my performance the previous night and Parrs' renewed interest in me, spelled trouble. I was relieved when she went in a different direction entirely. 'Are either of you familiar with the concept of the *missing* missing?'

'No,' said Sutty. 'We're *not* not.'

'Missing persons who are never reported missing,' I said. 'As such, they don't appear in any database. No one's looking for them and if they're found deceased, with no ID, they're generally just referred to by their clothes, or some other distinguishing feature . . .' Stromer looked at me, finally, as I tried to summon a case. '. . . the lady in the Afghan coat?'

'An enduring example,' she said, turning to Sutty. 'The lady in the Afghan coat was killed whilst hitchhiking on the A1 in the seventies. She'd spoken to a lorry driver earlier that day who said she had a foreign accent, that she introduced herself as Ann. The vehicle that struck her was never identified, never found. More crucially than that, no one ever reported a girl matching her description – young, pretty in a boyish way – as missing. She had an NHS filling in her teeth and wore a long Afghan coat with French supermarket-brand jeans. She wasn't wearing any shoes . . .' Stromer paused. 'It's funny the little details that you remember. There are hundreds of such cases every year, with few, if any, ever resolved.'

'Stop,' said Sutty. 'My bedsores are weeping . . .'

'I just want to be certain that you're familiar with the concept before I continue.'

'Course,' he said. 'Sonny and Cher.'

Stromer nodded. 'Although I never cared for those nicknames.'

Sonny and Cher were two unidentifieds from my first year on the force. A woman's body had been recovered from the River Irwell, in a pronounced state of decomposition. She'd been stabbed so many times that the pathologist stopped counting at a hundred, and there were the remains of a black bin bag wrapped around her head. Because the body had drifted through various jurisdictions, no force or department wanted to accept responsibility for her. It was decided that the caseload would be distributed evenly, and she was nicknamed 'Cher' to reflect this. No one matching her description was ever reported missing, a fact that became more confounding when the body of a little boy was recovered from the same river, some weeks later. Tests showed that they were mother and child, and so he was given the nickname 'Sonny'.

It seemed impossible that no one but their killer noticed they were gone, but the e-fit of her face, the appeal for information, and even a TV reconstruction, was met with something like the sound of one hand clapping. The missing missing were people who dropped off the face of the earth and kept on going, with no one in their lives who noticed, or no one in their lives who cared. When they were found dead, with no means of identification, it was almost as though they'd been born that way.

'We already know he's not been reported missing,' said Sutty.

'It's a little more complicated than that,' Stromer replied.

'How?'

'It's my opinion that this man has gone to great lengths to obfuscate his identity.'

I cut in before Sutty could object to her choice of word. 'You said there was no ID on his person?'

'And the labels have been carefully unstitched from his clothing. That's the least of it, though. Our man's fingerprints have been surgically removed.'

We were all silent for a moment.

'Post-mortem?' said Sutty. 'Gangland stuff?'

'The scar tissue indicates that the surgery took place some time, perhaps even some years, prior to his death. It stands to reason that our man was a willing participant in events, given that kind of timeline. *Gangland stuff* seems unlikely to me.'

'Surgery,' I said. 'That implies, what, doctors, a hospital? I assume it's not something you can just go private for?'

'I use the term surgery simply because I don't know what else to call it. In anything like a gangland body-dump we'd see, perhaps, the hands completely removed from the body. In some instances the fingertips themselves clipped off with pliers. This is much more advanced, much more thoughtful. And done some time before the man died, most likely with his consent.'

'Consent . . .' said Sutty, like it was a new word. 'I once saw some brown bloke who'd burned off his fingerprints with a lighter. Said it was to get through a checkpoint in Fuckbeckistan or something.'

'Totally different. Burns, cuts or even an amateur version of what I'm describing will go deeper than the surface tissue and leave a permanent scar, simply becoming part of a new fingerprint. In this instance, the tissue was completely removed and replaced with something else.'

'Replaced?'

'Skin grafts, Peter. They could take years off you . . .'

I leaned forward. 'Why would someone do that to their fingertips, though?'

'Why, indeed? When you stop and think of the possible reasons – a master thief, perhaps, who doesn't want to leave his prints behind – it remains senseless. This is an incredibly rare procedure and would leave its recipient with a truly one-of-a-kind fingerprint, even if it's not a fingerprint in the conventional sense.'

'So, it was less about masking his future activities and more about hiding who he was before?' I said, thinking out loud.

'That's one theory.'

'There's more than one way to skin a cat,' said Sutty.

'An excellent point. You're correct, most people sail through life without ever being printed, after all. It's certainly rare that we identify a body in that manner. Dental records are much more likely . . .' She said it like a challenge.

'Let me guess, he missed his last check-up.'

'Quite the opposite, he's had extensive work done. His birth teeth have either been removed or filed down into pegs. Those pegs have then been used for the affixation of artificial crowns. A Hollywood smile, I'm sure you'll agree. So dental records are out. Finally, on the physical augmentation side of things, perhaps you were struck by the man's eye-colour?'

'They were blue,' I said. But they'd been more than that. A piercing cobalt.

'Very good. But also incorrect. The man's true eye colour is a rather nice shade of brown. He was wearing tinted contact lenses.'

Stromer straightened her report, aligning the file's edge with the desk. She seemed satisfied that I, and especially Sutty, were dumbstruck. 'He was also a stage four.' Neither of us spoke. 'Cancer,' she clarified.

'I take it stage four isn't good?'

'There's no stage five. It was riddled through him like dry-rot. Neither his stomach contents nor bloodwork showed evidence of painkillers, though. He must have been in agony.'

Sutty stirred. 'So, whoever crossed a line through him could've just waited?'

'A matter of weeks, I'm sure. As an aside, in many ways our man was in peak physical condition. I've never seen calves quite like them. If I had to hazard a guess, I'd say he was either an accomplished free-runner or a disciplined ballet dancer.'

'Terminally ill ballet dancer with no teeth or fingerprints,' muttered Sutty. 'Got it.'

'Would you like to regroup or are you ready for the rest of it?'

We waited.

'Aidan, perhaps you could tell Detective Inspector Sutcliffe what I'd like to discuss next?' Stromer's face was blank and open, as happy for me to lose my job in the next sentence as keep it. Well, she can go there, I thought. I was tired of setting traps for myself.

'The stitching,' I said. 'There was something sewn into his trousers.'

Stromer looked into my eyes. 'Any idea what it was?'

'No,' I said.

'And how would you?' She took two photocopies from her file and handed one to each of us. I didn't know what it would be, and was relieved to see nothing but a scanned piece of text. Looking closely I could see the original fragment's edge. It had been torn from something larger. There were two words, in what looked like a foreign language.

TAMAM SHUD

146

'Professionally printed, and on high-grade paper,' said Stromer. 'I'd suggest this has been torn from a book. It translates from the Persian as "ended" or "finished".' She smiled. 'And that's probably as good a place as any for us to draw our conversation to a close.'

'Hang on,' said Sutty. 'You said sewn into his trousers? By him or by someone else?'

'Hand-stitched from the inside, so he, or whoever did it, must have done so while the trousers were off. There was one more thing in there.' She handed us each another photocopy. This one showed a scan of what looked like a cloakroom ticket. It was a number. 831.

'Any idea where it's from?' said Sutty.

'None whatsoever.'

'Well, thanks,' he said, getting to his feet. 'I hope the next time we meet I'm lying on the slab.'

'I already know what you're full of, Peter. I was wondering if I could have another moment of your time, though?' He grunted and Stromer looked at me. 'Alone,' she said. I collected my photocopies and left the room.

'Thanks for your help, Karen.'

She didn't answer. I closed the door behind me and walked to the end of the corridor. I didn't even think about their conversation. I didn't care. I looked at the first sheet and, despite it being just a photocopy, found myself running my fingers along the ornate letters.

TAMAM SHUD

Ended, it said.
Ended or finished.

2

Sutty looked thoughtful when he climbed into the car. I couldn't tell if he was reappraising me in light of something Stromer had said, or if I was projecting my own fears on to him. Either way, he didn't speak for a few minutes. I started up and began driving back into the city while he sat beside me, absent-mindedly cracking his knuckles, neck, knees and wrists. Whatever our interpersonal problems, I knew he had a sharp mind and that when he started popping his joints it generally meant he was putting it to some use. It had been a while since I saw the wheels turning.

'You returned that girl's jacket?' he said, finally.

'Two days ago.'

'Bet she welcomed you with open legs . . .'

'She wasn't even there, and that's not what it's about.'

'Stuck in the friend-zone, are we, Aidan? Stay there, son. Believe me. If the Super finds out you've been back at all he'll donate you to medical science. Luckily, you can rely on my renowned discretion.'

I drove on in silence for a few seconds. 'It's resolved.'

'Keep it that way. What d'ya make of Stromer?'

'Confused as we are. Seemed like it was something she'd never seen before.'

'If it was a cock and ball-sack it'd be something she'd never seen before.'

'For fuck sake, Sutty.'

He looked at me sharply and I knew I'd put my foot on the line. Disagreements, arguments and insults were fine but anything that touched on morality or acceptance was a no-go. I'd made the mistake of encouraging him.

'I'm just sympathizing,' he said, holding up his hands. 'Can't be easy for a woman who looks like a transsexual Bob Dylan.'

I didn't say anything.

'All right then, squeeze into your shorts and meet me on the seesaw.'

The seesaw was a favourite exercise of Sutty's, probably because it had all the hallmarks of an argument. He'd make a point about a case and I'd counter it. Sometimes it took us to interesting places. Sometimes it took us to the edge of physical violence.

'Point,' said Sutty. 'Smiley Face was looking at a bad death from the C-word. Maybe he took matters into his own hands?'

'Counter. It looks like he was poisoned. Surely if he'd done it himself we'd have found the means of death alongside the body?'

Sutty was silent for a moment. 'He could've ingested the poison elsewhere and then gone to the Palace.'

I shook my head. 'The suspicious circumstances of the scene, an unconscious security guard, suggest that something else was going on.'

'Point,' said Sutty. 'That could just be to do with Marcus and his call girls. He was running a fuck house out of the Palace, after all . . .'

'Come on. Neither of us believe that an escort knocked out Ali.'

'Marcus could've been there himself. He could've easily whacked Ali. You said there's no love lost between them.'

'But that barman changed his story once he realized I was police. He gave Marcus an alibi and I believe him. What's more, he said there was a bar-full of men who could back him up.'

We drove on in silence for a moment.

'Still,' said Sutty. 'Running girls out of your workplace takes some steel. I should talk to him. OK. Point. If someone *did* kill Smiley Face, they didn't know him very well.'

'Why not?'

'Well, if they knew he was weeks away from being worm food they'd have just let nature take its course . . .'

'Counter. The fact that he wasn't taking painkillers suggests he was pushing on as normal, maybe hiding or ignoring his illness.' I thought for a second. 'And his killer could only let nature take its course if it was personal.'

'Yeurgh?'

'Well, if he wasn't killed for personal reasons, but because he knew something, then his killer couldn't have risked waiting for him to pass away. What's more dangerous than a dying man who knows too much?'

'Point,' said Sutty. 'Fair enough, maybe, *maybe*, our man was murdered. But there's no more mystery to it than that. He could've just forgotten his ID.'

'Counter. No one's reported him missing and the labels were cut out of his clothes.'

'He might've had no friends. The clothes could be from the Salvation Army. They cut out tags with the original owners' initials on.'

'His clothes looked like new to me, and a good fit, and it still doesn't explain him sewing messages into them.'

Sutty chewed on that. 'Point. This *Tamam Shud* thing could just be his personal motto.'

'Ended or finished? Pretty ominous motto.'

Sutty laughed. 'Came true, didn't it? Anyway, that bit of paper could be our way out of all this.'

'How?'

'Suicide note . . .'

'It's not a suicide note.'

'How would you know?'

'Murder victims don't leave them.'

'Stop,' said Sutty. 'Stop saying that. We're not calling him a murder victim.'

I changed the subject. 'That other thing looked like a cloakroom ticket to me. Why sew that into your trousers unless you've got something to hide?'

'Hm . . .' said Sutty. 'We need to find that cloakroom. Any ideas?'

'Looks like your standard ticket to me. Ten a penny.'

'OK. Point. He just wanted to pretty himself up with the teeth and the lenses . . .'

'Counter. Doesn't explain the fingerprints.'

'Point. He's one of those mad men who thinks the government can read his mind . . .'

'A survivalist?'

'A failed one, yeah.'

'But what was he doing in a closed-down hotel? And why's someone gone after our one witness?'

'Point,' said Sutty, exhaling through his nose. 'In every instance, the missing missing were people who wasted air while they were alive and are wasting time now they're dead.'

I drove on for a minute. 'Counter. For us, it's the Palace break-in or the dustbin fires.'

Sutty conceded that one. 'Point,' he said. 'Stromer's a pathological dyke, hell-bent on the destruction of straight white men.'

'Counter. She's an intelligent woman who's had enough shit from the likes of you to last her a lifetime.'

'Point,' said Sutty, looking at the side of my face. 'She thinks you're an incompetent officer with a substance abuse problem and too much baggage to work cases. Furthermore that you should be removed from active duty effective immediately and face charges of corruption.'

I drove on, trying to think of a counter, but I didn't know what to say.

To accommodate her office hours, we'd met Stromer before our shift actually started. Although it was now early evening, Sutty decided to take a break. Most likely I'd collect him a couple of hours later smelling of drink, but who was I to judge? The CCTV I'd requested from the scene of the latest dustbin fire was available, and I returned to the office to make a start on watching it.

Sure enough, our burner had picked another surveillance black spot, and all I could see from the nearest camera was the other side of the road. I could tell when the fire started because a passing cyclist looked sharply in its direction as the light began to change, but I couldn't bring myself to care. I thought about ladies in Afghan coats instead, mothers and sons who could vanish without anyone noticing they'd gone. Smiling men.

The missing missing.

I was getting nothing from the CCTV and was grateful for the distraction when my phone began to vibrate. An unknown number.

'Waits,' I said, picking up.

'This the police?'

'Yeah, is that Earl?'

'I found your card in Soph's room . . .'

'And?'

He was silent for a moment. 'Dunno if I should be talking to you.'

3

Sophie had received another message from 'that man', Earl said. She hadn't told him it was Oliver Cartwright and, after his earlier reaction to the name, I didn't want to betray that either. Cartwright told Sophie he'd had the police scared off her case. He'd sent her another clip of their sex-tape to prove it, and asked her to meet him again, this time in public. She hadn't wanted to tell Earl, he'd said, but he saw her leaving the flat, looking badly shaken.

'Did she say where she was going?'

'The place they first met,' he said. 'Wherever that was.'

When I arrived, Incognito was uncharacteristically quiet. It was after eight, still early in bar terms, and there was no queue to push past. The same bouncer who'd dragged me out last time was standing on the door, and he chuckled to himself as I approached.

'Y'know, the goal is to try and get the drink in your mouth,' he said.

'I'll bear that in mind this time.'

He grinned and I saw the veins go pulsing across his skull. 'There's not gonna be a this time, pal.'

'I'm going up,' I said, walking by him. 'You decide if our names are in the paper tomorrow.'

He pushed me back and then held up his hands. 'Look, I don't want any trouble, but your fuse is too short for this place. You go in there throwing round threats and drinks, scaring people off who just want a night out, and it's me who's in the shit.'

'If it makes you feel any better I don't want to see your boss.'

'He's not in, anyway. Really this time.'

'So who's in charge?'

'I am,' said Alicia, descending the stairs. She was dressed more sedately tonight, the wild day-glo colours replaced with a smart, dark skirt and blouse. 'It's OK, Phil, I've got this.' The doorman grunted, put his hands inside his pockets and shunted out of hearing distance. I was impressed by the way that Alicia carried herself, and when she looked at me, coolly, I saw that I'd misjudged her the first time we'd met. Without the tinted contact lenses there was an undeniable intelligence in her eyes, and I thought perhaps she'd worn them to hide it. Having met her father last time, I wondered if she was the brains behind the operation.

'Miss Russell.'

'Detective . . . ?'

'Waits.'

'That was it. What can we do for you tonight?'

'A drink would be a start.'

'Off duty? I wouldn't have pictured you spending your free time here . . .'

'Where would you picture me?'

'I don't know. Somewhere dingier. Moodier. Probably sat on your own nursing something hard.' She smiled at the innuendo. 'Daydreaming about what might have been.'

'All that daydreaming led me here.'

'Of course it did,' she said, looking at me for a moment. 'Well, I suppose you'd better come inside then.' I went by her and she spoke to my back. 'This visit wouldn't have anything to do with our friends Sophie and Oliver, would it?'

'Who?' I said, turning to look at her.

She was smiling again. 'If you could just settle for throwing the book at him rather than your drink . . .'

The floor was so sticky it felt like part of the design. I didn't pass anyone on the staircase, and I could tell by the subdued, hollow sound of the music that the place would be emptier than last time. I emerged slowly, not wanting to draw attention to myself. There were only around fifteen people dotted about, most of them ensconced in booths at the far side of the room. I was grateful to see that the doorman had been telling the truth about Guy Russell's absence. His regular seat was empty.

I saw Oliver Cartwright immediately, though.

He was wearing a dark, loose suit and sitting with his back to me. Sophie was opposite him, wearing the jacket I'd returned to her, like she might get up and leave any second. She looked pale and couldn't meet his eyes. Neither of them noticed me, and I ordered a beer, watching them in the mirror behind the bar. Cartwright looked as though he was concluding some prepared speech and he sat back with a satisfied, curious look on his face. It was a look I associated with people who came from power and money. They conducted experiments on the rest of us, simply curious to see how we'd react. Alicia allowing me inside was no different, and I saw her emerging into the bar, taking a seat in the far corner for the best possible view of the action.

Cartwright swirled his drink and regarded Sophie, his girl zero. I could see his mind working. Thinking that perhaps she'd go home with him, perhaps she wouldn't, but that his findings would just go into refining the process for next time. For the Ollie Cartwrights of the world there was always a next time.

When Sophie didn't reply to whatever he'd said, his hand crawled slowly across the table like a fat, pink tarantula, enveloping hers. She blanched. I turned from the bar, crossed the room and sat down beside her. She drew her hand back when she saw me, looking to Cartwright like he'd set this up.

'Detective Waits,' he said, smiling. He was red-faced from too much drink and too little exercise, and I could see the gin blossoms, blooming in his cheeks.

I smiled back. 'Pretend I'm not here, Ollie.'

'With pleasure. Although a part of me wonders why you are . . .'

'Yeah, well, don't tell me which part.' He didn't say anything. 'Anyway, I hope you don't mind sharing the table but there's nowhere else to sit.'

He looked around the half-empty room, snorted, and spread his arms across the back of the booth. 'You're welcome to it. Sophie and I were just leaving.' She didn't move and Cartwright went on. 'It's our second date. Early days, but I think she might be the one.'

'That's not why I came here,' said Sophie. It was the first time she'd spoken since I'd sat at the table, and I was glad to hear some anger in her voice. Cartwright's smile slipped a little and he took a drink to cover it. 'I came here to say that what happened between us will never happen again. Whatever you do, I'm not going with you.'

'*Whatever* I do . . .'

I looked at him. 'And you're not going to do anything. Are you, Ollie?'

'Oh, Sophie,' he said, talking to her but looking at me. His lips were dripping wet with drink and there was naked hate in his eyes. 'I know you're feeling brave all of a sudden, sweetheart, but your friend here's only a part-time hero. I could tell you stories about him that'd curl your hair.' He looked at her. 'The hairs that aren't curled already. Did you ever hear of—'

'I don't *care* about him,' she said, raising her voice. 'I didn't ask him to come here for moral support. I didn't ask him to come here at all. Get it? I came here on my own to look you in the eye and tell you that you're a fucking animal. Nothing you do to me could be worse than another night in your company.'

'Animal, eh?' he said, swirling his glass around as his face grew redder. 'I don't know what you're talking about. I thought we had a good thing going. It's not every girl who's into what you are . . .'

'You're disgusting,' she said quietly.

'As I recall, you were the disgusting one. Oh well, good job there's no video evidence, eh?' He drank up and started to slide out of the booth. 'I'm out of the country for a few days from tomorrow night. Dubai. Hope no one steals my laptop while I'm out there.' He looked at me. 'S'pose, legally, any fallout wouldn't be my fault . . .'

'That's right,' I said. 'The law wouldn't have anything to do with what happened to you afterwards.'

'Is that a threat?'

'Threats are more your style than mine, Ollie.'

He nodded, got up and crossed the room to the exit. He paused when he saw Alicia watching our conversation, and laughed to himself. Then he descended the stairs without looking back. She raised her drink to me, took a sip and followed him outside.

Sophie sighed and lowered her head. She was shaking.

'You did well . . .'

'Do you think he'll do it?' she said quietly.

I know he will, I thought.

'No,' I said.

'I don't know how I could be so stupid . . .'

'All you did was trust someone. The rest of it's on him.'

'The rest of it's online as of tomorrow night,' she said, rubbing her face. 'Lads watching it in class, people I work with in five years finding it . . .'

'The only part of this that reflects on you is that you stood up to him.'

She thought about it. Swallowed. 'He looked surprised, didn't he?'

'He looked like you'd kicked him in the balls. You know, you could still make an official complaint . . .'

She shook her head. 'But thank you for coming. Was it Earl?'

I tried to think of a convincing white lie but came up short. 'Don't blame him . . .'

'I don't,' she said, smiling, in spite of herself, at the thought of him. I could see she was realizing something about her friend that perhaps she hadn't before. It was a nice moment and I looked away for a second to let her have it.

'Shall we get out of here?'

'Yeah,' she said. 'I'd like that.'

I walked Sophie to Piccadilly, where she began unlocking her bike. I was impressed that she'd stood up to Cartwright but I worried about what would happen next. He'd taken a blow to his ego, no doubt his most vulnerable spot, and with his impending foreign trip he might feel like he had nothing left to lose. Worse than that, he was right. If he went abroad and reported his laptop as stolen it would be almost impossible to prove that he'd leaked the tape. Perhaps I should remind him that things could be worse.

I pushed the thought out of my head.

Following those instincts had almost ruined my life, perhaps even cost other people theirs.

I looked at Sophie and thought of something else. 'Can I ask about your helmet . . .'

'Course. Do you cycle?'

'Too unbalanced, but is that a camera?'

'GoPro,' she said. 'Sort of puts drivers on their best behaviour, and if anything bad happens you've got it on file.'

As I watched her cycle out of the park, I remembered the note that had fallen from her jacket pocket. A physical description of Oliver Cartwright, along with a time and a place to meet him at. It hadn't been the right moment to ask, but I was still wondering what it meant when another thought struck me. Alicia had used Sophie's name when I was entering Incognito. She'd already known who she was.

4

I went back to the office, to the CCTV again, but this time with purpose. Sophie's helmet had given me a flash of inspiration. I clicked through to the time-stamp of the most recent dustbin burn. I could tell when the fire had started because a passing cyclist looked sharply in its direction as the light began to change. He must have seen the flamer.

The moment a case starts to break, even petty street arson, can be its own reward.

The cyclist had a camera mounted on his helmet.

I requested the footage from his likely route down Oxford Road, hoping to trace him to a destination. If he'd stopped inside a shop and paid with his card, it wouldn't be impossible to find him. Then I checked the time and bought a sandwich before heading out to meet Sutty for the remainder of our shift. I moved along Oxford Road, thinking about our case. Ali said he'd heard two people arguing. As much as I wanted those voices to belong to Natasha Reeve and Freddie Coyle, he'd been clear that they were two men. Freddie and the smiling man? Marcus Collier and the smiling man? I looked, idly, up at the Palace as I passed it.

I stopped.

There was a light on in one of the fourth-floor rooms. It looked like 413, where we'd found the body. I crossed the road and tried the door. It was locked. I started for the corner entrance, dialling Sutty as I went. The side door was closed as well.

'Yeurgh,' said Sutty, answering the phone.

'Do we still have an officer at the Palace?'

'Nah, SOCO wrapped yesterday. Why?' I was crossing the street again, looking up at the building. The light was off. From a certain angle the top-floor windows caught a reflection from the street. Had that been it?

'Ignore me,' I said.

'For Christ's sake,' said Freddie Coyle, crossing the road towards me. I'd been approaching his Sackville Street building to ask some follow-up questions about his infidelity. He had other ideas. He strode past me wearing a dark, mahogany suit, smelling richer than God. 'If this is more talk about that man in the Palace, you're wasting your time. More importantly, you're wasting mine.'

'Do you know if there's anyone in the Palace now, Mr Coyle?'

He stopped. Turned. 'How would I? Ask Ms Khan. Now if that's all . . .'

'I'm afraid it isn't.'

He held out his arms. 'Well?'

'When we spoke yesterday, I asked if you had any enemies . . .'

'Did I mislead you, Detective Constable?'

'After speaking to your wife, it seems like you might have.'

'Then you didn't listen to a word I said.' He shook his head and walked on.

I matched pace. 'What was it that I should have heard?'

'It's no wonder you missed it. All I did was as good as say the words to your face. Of course I have an "enemy". And it's no surprise that after speaking to her you suddenly have more questions for me.'

'Are things as bad as all that between you and your wife?'

'Ex-wife,' he said. 'You're here, aren't you? A divorce is one thing, breaking up the business and all that, but to set the police on me . . .'

'Do you think Ms Reeve has something to do with events at the Palace, Mr Coyle?'

'Oh, listen to yourself. Don't you get sick of pinballing between us? All this he-said, she-said shit?'

'Frankly, yes.'

'Natasha's not an instigator, not a creative or a visionary. She's a manager. She handles things. She's simply exploiting this poor fool's death to get back at me.'

'To get back at you for what?'

He stopped then. Looked at me and gave a short cynical snort of laughter. 'So that's it?' He looked me up and down and took a step closer. 'You cheap little boy. Who I share my bed with is my own business.' He started to walk again and I followed.

'I agree, but someone tipping off your wife about it sounds like an enemy to me.'

He stopped again, looked at me. Frowned. 'Tipping off my wife?'

'What did you think happened?'

'She copied my key. She followed me . . .' He almost said it like a question.

'Ms Reeve was receiving anonymous notes in the final weeks of your relationship,' I said. 'Times, dates, places.' The news seemed to hit him like a blow. 'Even pictures. You didn't know?' Coyle stared down the street. A convoy of fire engines, ambulances and police cars was blasting by us, and it bought him a few seconds to think. He looked like a man whose worst suspicion has been confirmed. I didn't think Natasha keeping the notes secret was the source of his pain. He looked angry, betrayed. People walked around us on the street like we were a quarrelling couple. 'Who was the man you were sleeping with, Mr Coyle?'

At length his eyes came back to me. 'That's none of your business.'

'With respect, it really is. I'm trying to identify a dead man found in your hotel.'

'What? You think I killed my former lover and then framed myself for his murder?'

'I didn't say that, but your wife thinks that in the weeks leading up to your separation you'd become preoccupied, distant . . .'

161

'What of it?'

'Are you in some kind of trouble?'

He looked at me and lowered his voice. 'I know you may think me cold but it's not exactly a dream to deceive your partner for years on end. To discover something so fundamental about yourself so late in life . . .'

'There's also the matter of the person writing those notes.'

'Don't you see?' he hissed, taking a step towards me. 'They're one and the same. They have to be one and the same. Happy now?'

'What do you mean?'

'I mean that no one but the man I was sleeping with knew about us. I mean that I was careful.' He was breathing hard. 'I mean that if someone tipped off my wife about our relationship then it had to be him.' Saying the words seemed to make them true for Coyle and he looked about us, as if he'd never seen the street we were standing on before. 'You must live for these moments of discount poetry,' he said at last. 'The betrayer gets betrayed . . .'

'Are you still seeing this man?'

'No.'

'I heard someone in your flat when I interviewed you on Monday morning. Can I ask who that was?'

'You can fuck off.'

I nodded. 'I can, but first I'll need the name of the man Natasha found you with.'

'Fine,' he said, walking back the way we'd come. 'I've lost my appetite, anyway.'

'I assume you refer to the precedent of Fuck All vs Never Happened?'

I'd asked Sutty about potential legal options that Sophie could explore for preventing Oliver Cartwright from leaking their sextape. He'd made a compelling argument for the impossibility of my situation, the absolute certainty of my failure.

Worse, I agreed with him.

He was eating a Subway breakfast sandwich, his favourite food, while we walked. Because it was their policy not to serve the sandwich after 11 a.m., and because Sutty was never awake by then, it meant that an argument was built in to each order, and I suspected that was what he really kept going back for.

I gave up on Cartwright for the moment, focusing instead on the comparatively simple smiling man. Coyle had given me the name of his former lover but I'd had to report for our shift before I could follow it up. It was getting more difficult to keep this line of enquiry from Sutty as a new vista of lies and betrayal opened up before me. I was wondering again if I could broach the subject with him when I saw the satisfied smile slide off his face. I followed his eyeline to the car to see what was wrong.

There was someone sitting inside it.

We stopped for a second, looked at each other and then went forwards.

'Och, fuck,' said Sutty, under his breath. The door opened to reveal Superintendent Parrs, sitting on the passenger side. He hung one leg out of the car and gave us his dark, shark's smile.

'The dynamic duo,' he said. 'Doom and Gloom.'

'Sir,' we said in unison.

'Evening, Peter,' said Parrs, talking to Sutty. 'It's been too long. How are things?'

He shrugged. 'No complaints . . .'

'That's not what the last girl you arrested said, pal. Anyway, it's late. You must be hungry. And I need a word with the boy wonder. Why don't you go and grab a bite to eat?'

'Famished,' said Sutty, looking at me gravely. He was already walking backwards, still clinging on to his sub. 'Evening, Superintendent.'

'Good evening, Detective Inspector.'

Parrs watched him go, still smiling. He didn't speak again until Sutty was out of sight, and even then he didn't look at me.

'Get into the fucking car,' he said quietly.

5

'Would you say you're still a young man, Aidan? Actually, don't answer that. Youth's a bit like beauty, isn't it? In the eye of the beholder. I'd say you are, though. I've seen a girl or two giggle in your direction. You've got a job, a jawline. Even your hair. If I were talking to someone else in your position, I might even say they had their whole life ahead of them. Hold that thought for me, eh?

'In January of this year, we had a visitor. Not really our tourist season so he turned a few heads, too. Older heads than yours, though. People with long memories who could put a name to a face. Blunt Trauma Billy, they called him.' He smiled. 'Blunt Trauma Billy's one of those names you don't really hear so much any more. Bit like Doris or Ethel. Of a time and a type. Yeah, sure enough, our tourist was well into his sixties. Retirement age for most. Unfortunately, old Billy's chosen profession doesn't provide much of a pension plan. A mechanic, these old heads called him.'

Parrs paused and smiled. 'Not the kind that fixes cars, though. They remembered him as a sort of freelancer. Headhunted for certain jobs. A specialist who moved around the country to wherever the money took him. You have to be a bit nomadic for that kind of life. Rootless, with nothing to tie you down. Nothing to lose. That's probably why he's got no family, no friends. Bit like your smiling man. Bit like you. Do you know what Blunt Trauma Billy's specialism is, Aidan?'

'He fixes people,' I guessed.

'Correct. Dozens of them over the years, although only one that ever stuck. Anyway, back in January when we kicked his door in for a chat he had his mouth full. The funny thing was that he was tucking into a piece of paper. A couple of big lads held him down and, shall we say, obstructed the nasal passage, so he spat it out. It was just an address but I think you'd recognize it. You live there, after all. And there were three words scrawled below. *Make it painful.*'

He let that sink in for a minute. I realized I could hear myself breathing.

'People keep asking me what you're still doing here, son. You're like a lucky charm that doesn't fucking work. But I tell them someone's gotta write Sutty's reports for him. That you're a gifted young detective with a bright future ahead. Obviously you and I know that's a fairy tale. The truth is that it's convenient to keep a compromised officer around the place. Someone I've got so much dirt on that I can use him for special jobs. See, I don't believe in trust, Aidan. People you trust let you down every day. But when someone understands that you can flick off their life like a light . . . *then* you've got someone you can depend on. Make no mistake about it, son, my finger is hovering over the fucking switch.'

I didn't say anything.

'A hit's slightly different, though. An imposition. In the game we're playing, us versus them, there is one sacrosanct rule. Cops die of natural causes. I'm not talking about the madmen and the users, they're a law unto themselves. I'm talking about the firms. The families. The ones who've got history and should know enough to know better . . .

'Don't get me wrong, I've wished ill on you at times, Aidan. There've even been occasions when it might've been convenient for you to go missing. Convenient for you to not turn up to work for a few weeks. Convenient to fish a headless torso out of the river, identifiable only by his thirty-inch waist and the word TWAT tattooed across his shoulders. But a hit represents a breakdown of the system. If I allow that, I'm opening the door to anarchy. Frogs raining from the sky, cats marrying dogs, etcetera, etcetera.

'Course, our mechanic, Blunt Trauma Billy, is old school. That's his USP. If he gets arrested he stands up, keeps his mouth shut and does his time. He wasn't gonna talk to us, and he'd done nothing wrong except have a bad reputation and a copy of your address. So I let him go and told him to leave town. Far as I know, he's never been back. Then I made a series of speculative arrests. I wanted to talk to the kinds of people who might've had him on speed-dial. I brought in what's left of the old families. The Burnsiders, The Franchise. Even your old friend Zain Carver. And I explained to them the golden rule of the game: *cops die of natural causes*, and I told them what happens when they break it. You're still alive, so it looks like they got the message. One hand went up at the end of class, though. Zain Carver. Teacher's pet. He said he appreciated my time, the courtesy that I'd extended, but asked, out of curiosity, if the rule would still be applicable to people who became ex-police officers. People who got fired, for example. Are they still golden? Well now, I said, that's in the jurisdiction of someone slightly less important than me. That's between you and God.

'When we first met, you were on your very last chance. Now you're past it. Your life quite literally depends upon you keeping this job. This job quite literally depends upon keeping me happy. Do I look fucking happy?'

I realized he expected an answer. 'No, sir.'

'And why do you think that is?'

'Oliver Cartwright, sir.'

'Oliver Cartwright,' he repeated. 'I didn't suggest that you stay away from him, did I? I didn't say, "Stay away from him if you feel like it", did I? I took you up the mountain with me and engraved it in stone tablets. Thou shalt not.'

He threw a rolled-up newspaper at me.

The main story was about a man who'd died in police custody. A whistle-blower had come forward, saying the stompers, the tactical response unit, had applied an illegal chokehold. There was a picture of Chief Superintendent Chase looking grave.

'Surprise surprise, the news broke on Cartwright's site. He's been sitting on it for months in agreement with our mother superior, Chief Superintendent Chase, but since my men are harassing him, he decided to put it out there. You can imagine how upset she is with me, and in turn how apoplectic I am with you. You are labouring under the illusion that your continued existence in this world is related to skill or talent. You are wrong. Do something useful and focus on those fucking dustbin fires, because the day I can no longer depend on you will be the last day of your life, Aidan. And it's getting closer.'

He turned to look at me but I kept staring straight ahead. After a minute or so he climbed out of the car, slammed the door behind him and walked away.

6

Sutty and I passed the rest of our shift sitting in deafening, heavy silence. The only sound was the wet click of his alcoholic hand-sanitizer, which he compulsively applied and reapplied as I drove. The fumes became so strong that the car felt like a hot box, and I started to see a trail on every light, a slipstream for every object. When I finally dropped him home in the early hours of the morning, he turned.

'Anything you wanna tell me?' he said. Sutty was a walking night-mare, but he'd also survived several career-ending catastrophes, constant controversy and his own rampant unprofessionalism. If I wanted to live through this, there were worse people to ask for advice.

'Parrs thinks—'

'Y'know what,' he said, climbing out of the car. 'I'm not inter-ested.' I watched him hustle up the path into his building like I was infective. I turned off his road and sat at a set of traffic lights for a minute.

A hit.

The engine was running, and the lights must have gone from red to green several times before I noticed. When another 5 a.m. driver, the first I'd seen for some time, angrily pulled around me I snapped out of it. I wound down all the windows, flicked on the sirens and tore through empty streets for an hour or so, blasting Sutty's clinical stink out of the car, the cobwebs out of my head. The sudden exhilaration was something close to a high, and I ached for the days when I could have swallowed this feeling in a pill or snorted it off the back of my hand.

When I had these thoughts I sped up, attempted impossible manoeuvres and hairpin turns. I raced towards buildings with my eyes closed and didn't stop until the last possible second. By the time I arrived back into the Northern Quarter I was shivering, and I could barely feel my arms and legs.

The night had passed and the morning commute had begun.

I parked up, got out of the car and stood in the warming morning sun for a few minutes, letting it sink into my skin and bones.

When I passed another pile of cigarette butts, each smoked down to the filter, lying on the kerb outside my flat, they carried new meaning. A health warning. I looked all around me for anyone who might have left them, then kicked them out into the street. If what Parrs had told me was true, it seemed possible, even likely, that I was being watched. The enemies I'd made had deep pockets and they could afford to wait for my next mistake. My mind went back to the man I'd seen, a few days before, watching me when I'd left The Temple.

I opened the flat and went to make myself a drink. The bottle I'd been chipping away at was empty, but I didn't remember finishing it. I looked at it for a moment before opening another and pouring a strong one, which I barely felt. I paced the room. The message from Parrs had been clear. My next mistake would be my last. Somehow, far from feeling trapped, I felt free. He'd described a sequence of events – my becoming undependable, my becoming unemployed, my becoming unprotected – that felt inevitable.

Like a clarification.

Once I'd paused, let it sink into me like the morning sun, I felt much more certain about where I stood. Who I was and what I'd do next. I thought about the arrogance of Oliver Cartwright. I didn't have the full story between him and Sophie, but I was certain he was using her body, her youth, her sex, against her. Using my own past, my own job against me. Gliding through life like my exact opposite, untouched by consequence or cause and effect, while the rest of us drowned in it.

I picked up my keys and took another drive.

7

As a younger man I'd habitually snorted methamphetamine. There's no point saying whether I did so to excess or not. In some cases I'd taken it until my nose bled. I'd taken it until I couldn't remember my own name. I'd seen and heard things as a result that I knew to be impossible, and had long, animated conversations with people I knew to be dead. Occasionally this altered perception still bleeds through into my sober life, rendering events and people as more grotesque, or more beautiful, than they could in reality be. Occasionally, my surroundings become altered almost beyond comprehension, peopled with living ghosts, phantoms and sirens.

I'd managed to kick by acknowledging privately that my abstinence likely wouldn't be permanent. I told myself that the next relapse would be different, though. Sensible. I'd take time out, draw the blinds and relax into it. Fully recover afterwards and wait another six months before I used again. And because this fantasy was what made my day-to-day sobriety possible, I nurtured it.

At irregular intervals over the course of a year, I'd withdrawn small amounts of cash, which now added up to something more substantial. It would cover the tracks of how I paid for drugs if financial forensics ever looked closely. Before leaving my flat I'd gone to the bathroom and stared into the mirror for a moment, feeling my face warp and alter, even as I unscrewed the fixture and pulled it off the wall. I'd taken the black carrier bag that had been hidden, pressed flat behind it, and carried it to the car with me. Inside was the cash I'd saved and a simple lock-pick set. Drugs, burglary and lies. My only inheritance. Now, little more than an hour later, the bag was burning a hole in my pocket.

It was still early, but the city was already bustling, and the heat felt incredible. Half weather, half malice. I was running down a Chorlton Street rumour. When I arrived, the coach station was busy and I walked inside, into a feeling of inescapable, repeating history.

I'd always come here when I was running away.

Usually with a pocket full of saved or stolen cash that had never quite been enough. As a boy I'd vanished from foster homes with this as my destination. The only fixed idea in my head. Sometimes I got as far as the next city, sometimes I was back in care before they noticed I was gone. I remembered oblivion nights, sleeping outside, waiting for the doors to open, and all of my first kisses, with girls, with drink, with drugs. I remembered running away here as a teenager, with the first love of my life, and coming to outside the next morning. The girl and the money were both gone, and she'd written a Dear John letter on my left hand in red biro.

I found myself walking through all those old faces, now. Organized, optimistic people, taking trips. Reluctant, frazzled travellers, following work or family on to the next place. Stiff-limbed rough sleepers trying to look respectable enough to use the toilets, where they'd wash up as much as possible before being moved along. The endless ebb and flow of a major city. And unmistakable in the throng, all of the lovers running away.

I took a seat facing the payphones, a rarity these days, and watched as a man raked them. He was a dilapidated, raw-faced destitute, walking painfully on one crutch. He pivoted to move, seemingly having lost the use of one side of his body, and there were so many tattoos on his neck that it looked like he wore a collar. When he reached a phone he felt inside the change slot then threw himself to the next one. Once finished, he exited the building, disappeared from view for a minute and reappeared at the door where he'd started. I watched him repeat this circuit a few times, always glancing over his shoulder in what a casual observer might have thought a twitch. When he next exited I stood, crossed the room and stuffed my rolled-up banknotes into the change slot of the first payphone.

I sat down and waited.

The man laboured back into the station thirty seconds later, wincing from step to step. When he put his hand into the coin slot, his face betrayed nothing different from the norm, and he palmed the cash with a dexterity that was impressive to see. He carried on, disappearing for another minute. When he came back around there was nothing outwardly different about him. He painfully approached the payphones, checked the slots and clicked out of the station on his crutch. I went to the first phone, picked up the receiver and dropped in a coin. I dialled my own number and let it ring. When there was no answer I hung up and heard the change fall into the slot. It didn't make the precise rattle you'd expect, but a muted thud, as though on to something soft. I put my hand into the slot, took the bag that the man had left and exited the station.

There were street dealers I knew, both personally and profession-ally, but I couldn't use them. First of all, I'd needed something harder than speed. Secondly, I'd needed total anonymity. In this case, someone's word or discretion wasn't good enough. I sat in the car, feeling the weight of the powder in my pocket. I'd always believed that there was more to me, my personality, than people saw. That one day I might surprise them with a good turn, an unexpected act of kindness. The Stromers of the world would re-evaluate me as a person. Parrs and Sutty would see me as someone who could be trusted, relied upon, perhaps even promoted. I moved the rear-view mirror so I couldn't see myself and pulled out into traffic. Sometimes you confound expectations, sometimes you grow into the thing that people think you are.

8

I drove to the Quays and parked outside Imperial Point, Oliver Cartwright's building. When I killed the engine it was with a feeling of inevitability. Like I'd reached a destination that I'd been heading to for a long time. Everything outside the car was quiet, still, bathed in light, but inside it I was tapping my fingers on the dash, looking up at the building.

Cooking my brain.

I hadn't sampled the coke in my pocket, but felt a buzz in my left leg, a contact high just from knowing it was there. I felt the right-hand pocket, the outline of the lock-pick set. I took a breath, climbed out of the car and approached the entrance. I buzzed 1003 and waited.

No one picked up.

After a few minutes I saw a young woman coming through the lobby. When she opened the door I smiled, stood to one side and allowed her to exit. Then I walked through the main entrance, past the comatose man on the front desk, and directly into a lift. I pressed for the tenth floor, stepped out into the same air-conditioned corridor as before and went directly to 1003. Cartwright's flat. I knocked, rang the bell and waited.

Nothing.

I put my index finger to the lock and applied some pressure. The loose pin-and-tumbler rattle was like music to my ears. I took the case from my pocket and unzipped it, revealing an abbreviated locksmith set inside. As a boy I'd been able to break front doors using nothing but found pieces of wire. I'd scrambled on to the roofs of buildings looking for weak spots, or spent minutes painstakingly pressing myself through narrowly open windows. Now I'd need the tools.

I selected a small torsion wrench and raker and got to work.

A pin-and-tumbler's simple. A series of brass pins which occupy a locking cylinder, preventing its movement. A correctly inserted key raises these pins so the cylinder can turn sideways and click open. Picking's an attempt to appropriate that same motion. The process took a little over a minute.

There was no sound from inside.

I entered the flat, moving quietly from room to room until I was sure it was empty. Then I approached the hardshell flightcase that I'd seen in the lounge on my first visit. I lifted it, testing the weight.

Packed and ready to go.

I laid the case sideways and unzipped it. Cartwright was leaving for Dubai that evening. His clothes, his monogrammed dressing gown and flip-flops, were strapped down and I carefully removed the clasps. Moving them aside, I found flavoured condoms and lubrication. Thoughtful.

I lifted the clothes out of the case and felt around inside the lining. Once I found a gap in the material I took the bag of cocaine from my pocket and eased it into a space where it wouldn't look incongruous, even if he decided to remove his things before travelling. Then I carefully replaced the clothes as I'd found them, re-clasped the straps and closed the case, returning it to its upright position. I backed out of the room, drew the door closed and went to the lift.

It was one of those everything-on-red moments that I always swore off until I was suddenly in the middle of them. As the lift sank down to the ground floor I felt weightless, light, after months of docile suffocation.

I walked back outside into the thousand-degree summer, staring the sun full in the face. I thought about all the things I'd done that I didn't believe in. This one was different. Something I could live with. Crossing the road, I saw that someone had parked right behind me. As I got closer, the other driver started the engine, abruptly backing off before making a hard U-turn and taking the corner. I stood in the road looking after them, breathing hard. It was the same car I'd seen waiting outside my flat two nights before. I was wondering what it meant when my phone started to vibrate and I looked at the screen.

Unknown number.

I picked up the call to the sound of someone breathing.

The boy backed off from his reflection, moved round the car and walked towards the farmhouse. There were no lights on inside and all he could hear was the wind coming through the trees. The cold air went in and out of his lungs like a narcotic, and it felt like the moonlight at his back was pushing him forwards. With each step he became less afraid, less like himself.

He started to walk faster, feeling it more certainly, this thing he'd come to think of as the rising. His transition from a small child into thin air, into the self-preservation of an out-of-body experience. First he focused on one object, like the front door of the farmhouse, then he thought about Bateman. His mouth would start to water. He'd see a haze of sunspots and gradually begin to lift above the fear, until he was watching himself from a distance. It was in this way that he could float upward when his mother gave him the belt, or drift towards the centre of the ceiling when she held his hands under boiling water. He could rise and rise when Bateman put out cigarettes on his little sister, soaring into the stratosphere until he couldn't see the look on her face.

He rose now.

It felt like being perched on his own shoulder, and from up there he could see the building more clearly. A grey-brick farmhouse, ageless and meandering, like a thing grown out of the ground. He approached the front door and craned his neck. Took two wires from his back pocket and began picking the lock, automatically going through the motions, just like all the other times. He'd gone through high windows into department stores at 3 a.m. He'd broken into chemists and emptied prescriptions into bags for Bateman. He'd crawled along the floors of old people's homes, pocketing keepsakes and cash.

But this wasn't just like all the other times and it never would be again. This time, when the boy's hand brushed against the door, he almost lost his balance. This time he had the strangest sensation, like he was watching all of this from another life, like he was remembering things that hadn't happened yet. He had the sudden fear that he'd risen too high out of his body, that he could see as far as the future. In a flash he saw the impossible, open-throated woman sitting inside this house. The slender man, bleeding from the mouth, who he knew would follow him outside. And somewhere else, even further in the future, he saw a figure sitting in a chair, staring out of a window, smiling.

With that the boy felt a fear that he couldn't rise up above. He started to plummet, crashing back down to earth, back into his own body, hearing the frantic, panic-attack breaths that were always on the other side of the rising. He collapsed into the farmhouse door and laughed at his own stupidity. Because those things hadn't happened yet. They hadn't happened yet.

They hadn't happened yet.

Inside, he felt the darkness like a living thing, enveloping him, until he was indistinguishable from it. He breathed quietly through his mouth and stood still for a few seconds, letting his eyes adjust. It was in these moments that the boy wondered if he was really alive, and he found himself thinking of the night his mother caught him praying.

'You're wasting your time,' she'd said when their eyes met. 'There's no heaven or God or anything like that. When you die the lights go off and never come back on. You're just talking to yourself.' She turned to leave but he followed her to the door, pressing her on this point, the lights. 'Before you were born,' she said wearily. 'Do you remember?'

The boy didn't move. 'Well, death's like that. One minute you are and the next minute you're not. Everything goes black.'

So in the darkness of the house, the boy ceased to exist. He breathed the shadows into his lungs and ceased to feel. He saw the outline of the stairs and in three steps he was standing at the bottom, about to climb, when he sensed something like a breath on his skin. There was a cool breeze coming down the hallway towards him. He retracted his foot from the staircase, moved around the bannister and walked towards the draught. The carpet was so thick that he didn't need to worry about his footsteps. He walked on the balls of his feet instinctively, though, because Bateman had shown him how. When he reached the room at the end of the hall, the door was partly closed. Almost in wonder at the force that moved his hand, in awe of the motion that disobeyed Bateman, the boy edged it open. He felt the air against his face and was suddenly afraid.

He was standing at the entrance of a large kitchen, whose windows looked out into a field. He knew this because of a faint light coming from outside, the kind that makes everything else seem darker. Because the shadows had gone through him so thoroughly, the boy found himself helplessly drawn to this light, and took a step forward, feeling the shards of broken glass crunching underfoot. His senses came alive and he smelt something familiar and metallic, an odour that registered in his brain as fear itself.

In the centre of the room, in shadow against the light, sat an impossibility. The motionless shape of an open-necked person. Reversing out of the room, towards the wall, the boy felt something hard press into the back of his head. A light switch. Feeling the shake in his hand, he reached behind himself and placed two slippery fingers on it.

Just a second, he thought. On and off.

It would change his life forever.

The room lit up with the exhaustive detail of a nightmare. The kitchen windows had been blown in. Sparkling shards of glass covered the work surfaces, the table, the floor. A thick, electric-red liquid cast crazy patterns on the glass, walls and ceiling, and his eyes swept across a gun on the table. There were two large, sack-like objects on the floor. Taking a step closer the boy saw that they were the fallen bodies of two men.

It felt like his heart was punching out through his chest.

The smell was overpowering now. In the centre of the room sat the impossible person. A young black woman, looking somehow pale. She was tied to a chair and her neck had been cut almost in half, spilling her blood, her life, all over the room. The boy saw in a flash that his mother was right about the afterlife. There was no heaven or God or anything like that. He recognized the metallic odour as that of his mother's bad breath. The blood-spray smelt like the lapsed fillings in her mouth. He flicked the light off again, feeling like he'd been swallowed whole by her.

Everything went black.

———

V
Came Back Haunted

1

'You're a flat tyre, Marcus,' said Sutty, winding down. 'There's no bouncing back from this. I'm just glad we found that condom wrapper. I'd hate to think I'm gonna see that face again on someone else.' We were in one of the boxes beneath the station, sweating Marcus Collier. Sutty had been talking, shouting, pacing up and down, uninterrupted, for fifteen minutes straight, when he finally left a pause long enough to get a reply.

It was like watching a small animal step into a trap.

'Are you finished?' said Collier, staring at the table.

'No,' Sutty replied. 'Now I hear it, I don't like the sound of your voice, either.'

'. . . All I did was get laid.'

'And that's all you'll be doing for the next five years,' said Sutty, slapping him on the shoulder. 'Why d'ya think they call it Strange-ways? There are blokes inside who'll take a different kind of virginity off you every night. It won't be their eyes they're undressing you with, either.'

Collier tried to ignore him. 'Is this necessary?' he said, appealing to me. 'Is it? I've told you what I know.'

Sutty leaned over him. 'For the purposes of this conversation, Aidan's your imaginary friend, pal. Ignore me again and I'll high-five your face.'

It wasn't strictly necessary but, then, Collier hadn't strictly co-operated. We'd begun, reasonably enough, by asking him to tell us about Cherry, the escort we suspected to have been in the Palace at the time of the unidentified man's death. Collier had stared at the table and folded his arms.

Then the pyrotechnics started.

It was less an interrogation of him than a form of therapy for Sutty. When the storm clouds were hanging over his head, he'd often disappear into an interview room and make it rain on someone else. Collier's flawless cooperation wouldn't have changed that.

I almost admired Sutty's self-knowledge.

The first person he spoke to on any given day would invariably take the brunt of his rage, he knew this, and had quickly tired of exhausting it on me. Increasingly, I collected him for our shifts in total silence. I knew he was holding it in, waiting to spit venom at someone he could actually break, so I kept my mouth shut and felt quietly grateful when his attention went elsewhere. It could be the girl in the coffee shop, a cold-caller or a mugger, and when he was sweating someone, the crime itself had no bearing on his mood. I'd once seen him reduce a speeder to tears and then, with the thunder out of his system, charm a wife-beater with impeccable politeness. Like a stopped clock, even Detective Inspector Peter Sutcliffe got it right occasionally, and there was a certain thrill in seeing him chew people out who deserved it. It took steel for Collier to run girls out of his own workplace. More importantly, the key card that allowed the smiling man access to room 413 had belonged to him.

'I'll appeal,' said Collier, meeting Sutty's eyes. 'This is harassment.' Occasionally we reached this point. Insults became the new normal and people got brave. This only served to fuel Sutty's anger, propelling him to new heights of cruelty.

He leaned over the table again and lowered his voice. 'Allow me to explain why you couldn't get hate mail from appeals.'

My phone started to vibrate. An unrecognized number. 'Excuse me,' I said. When I closed the door behind me, Sutty was screaming at Collier, and I walked up the corridor before answering.

'Waits,' I said.

'Aidan.'

'Sian?'

'You sound surprised . . .' She laughed. 'You deleted my number, didn't you?'

'I lost my old phone,' I said, after a moment's hesitation. 'What's up?'

'I think we need to talk.'

I looked down the corridor. 'I'm afraid it's not a great time.'

'Right,' she said.

'I just mean I'm at work.'

'Bit early for you, isn't it? On the up, are we?'

'Try the other direction. We've caught a bad one. We're interviewing someone now, listen.' I held my phone up towards the interview room I'd left. Sutty was describing Collier's demise in biblical terms.

'He hasn't changed,' said Sian.

'I don't know, sometimes I think he's getting worse.' I hesitated for a second. 'I could see you later . . .'

'I'm working tonight.'

'I don't mind, I could drop in.'

There was a moment's silence. I thought she'd been disconnected but when I heard a breath I knew I'd said the wrong thing.

'OK,' she said. 'Ricky and some friends might be around, though.'

'Ricky? The new guy?'

'My boyfriend, Aidan . . .'

'Well,' I said, somehow unable to back down. 'That's fine by me, I'd love to meet him.'

'You'd love to?' She laughed again. 'OK. Later then. Hope your old phone turns up.' She disconnected before I could say goodbye and I rubbed my eyes. I had deleted her number, to stop myself from calling at one, or two, or three, in the morning. To stop myself from wasting her time while I was getting straight. That was simply uncomfortable. Inviting myself to meet her new boyfriend was excruciating.

I was grateful for the distraction when my phone buzzed with an email. I'd spent the morning trying to identify the biker who might have seen the dustbin flamer. Unfortunately, he'd turned off Oxford Road without exhibiting any traceable characteristics. As a last resort, I'd requested the footage from further up the road, to see if I could find the start of his journey. That footage was now available.

I looked up and saw two uniformed officers lingering in the hallway, listening to Sutty's latest rant and laughing.

'Find somewhere else to be,' I said. Their faces fell and they moved along. I waited outside for another minute and, with the worst of the tirade over, opened the door and stepped back inside the box.

'I wish you'd stop saying that,' Collier was groaning.

Sutty's nostrils flared. 'You can wish in one hand and shit in the other, but I'll tell you which fills up fastest.' In the ensuing silence the walls themselves seemed to be ringing. 'OK, interview terminated,' he said, removing the tape and replacing it with a blank one. As far as I knew he collected these recordings, studied them like a touring stand-up perfecting his act. When he stood up and stretched I heard material splitting. He grunted and went for the door.

'Hang on,' said Collier. 'Don't you wanna hear what I've got to say?'

Sutty looked at him, almost in confusion. 'No, not particularly. Aidan, with me.' He left the box and I followed him outside, back down the corridor.

'Shall we give him an hour?' I said.

'You haven't got an hour to give, pal. Had a phone call from Parrs this morning . . .'

Because I'd collected Sutty in our customary silence, this was our first conversation of the day. Our first since Parrs had told me about the hit. I thought for a second that Sutty knew about Oliver Cartwright, the drugs I'd planted in his suitcase, but that was impossible.

I'd have been the one getting interrogated.

'Oh?' I said.

'Oh. He thinks you're wasted on Smiley Face. Wants you to focus on something more suited to your talents.'

We stopped walking.

'The dustbin fires,' I said flatly.

Sutty clicked his fingers and walked on. 'You should be a detective.'

'We've got a murder here—'

He was shaking his head. 'Stop saying that. I've got a suspicious death. You've got yourself on the shit list and it's up to you to get yourself off it. In addition to whatever last night was about – and, please remember, my door's always closed – Stromer's been dripping poison in his ear. Something about you turning up at that canal body-dump and making a scene.' We stopped walking to let people go by us and Sutty lowered his voice. 'Are you on airplane mode, Aid? Get the fucking message. They want you to put in your papers. My advice is: do it. This job's not for you.' He carried on walking and I watched him go. I wondered if Parrs had suggested my resignation, knowing I couldn't do it because of what he'd told me the previous day. He'd twisted the knife in my back so often that I could recognize the brand.

Sutty held up his pass to get through a door, even holding it open for the next person. Sated for the moment by his screaming fit, he was actually at his most rational, and would stay like that for the next few hours. He'd grow increasingly unreasonable throughout the shift, though, with his rage fully recharging overnight, like a lanced boil.

I went to the toilet and closed the cubicle door. There were caricatures of both Sutty and me, drawn in marker pen at eye level. I was thin, sullen and simmering with rage. That looked like a compliment next to Sutty, who was bulbous, sweating, exploding with it. In the picture we were each using a magnifying glass to stare at the other's tiny penis. The caption beneath it said:

Slutty and Toxic Waits investigate . . .

2

Geoff Short was a man who belied the height restriction imposed by his surname. He was tall and slim, with an athletic spring in his step and a healthy, clear complexion.

'Thank you for meeting me, Mr Short.'

'I hope I can help,' he said cautiously. Freddie Coyle had told me that his former lover was married with children, so I'd suggested we meet for a coffee near his Whalley Range home.

'In a way, you've helped already . . .' I explained the circumstances of the Palace Hotel break-in, and that I'd wanted to eliminate him from two lines of enquiry. In the first, I could plainly see that he wasn't the unidentified dead body we'd discovered, and in the second, he'd been able to provide a cast-iron alibi for the events of Saturday night. His wife had been going into labour, and they'd been holding hands, breathing deeply.

He looked relieved at having provided both answers. 'It's nice to help just by dint of being alive. But . . .' He looked at me curiously. 'You do know I haven't worked with Mr Blick for the best part of a year now?'

'I actually didn't know that you had at all. You're a solicitor?'

He nodded. 'It's a great firm, but I had to climb up the ladder elsewhere. Now, hang on. If you didn't know I used to have dealings with the Palace, why would you imagine . . .' The answer occurred to him before he finished the sentence. 'Ah.'

'I'm afraid that during the course of our investigation your affair with Frederick Coyle came to light . . .'

He covered his face. '*Affair*. Christ . . .' I gave him a moment and at length he looked at me again. 'OK,' he said.

'Can I ask how it started?'

He shrugged but it was with an openness I'd yet to encounter from anyone else in the case. 'The way I suspect these things usually do. Professionally, then less professionally, then what starts out as innuendo gets tested with too much drink. Finally, of course, it all ends in tears.'

'Whose tears did it end in?'

'Certainly Freddie's. When I knew him he had no one but Natasha in his life . . .'

'Now he doesn't even have her.'

'He was close to a total shut-in, then. Of course I was complicit, of course I was.' He lowered his voice. 'But he'd just realized he was gay. He pursued me and it was different. Exciting. All the old reasons.'

'Can I ask how it came to an end?' I wanted to move him on to the confrontation with Ms Reeve, but he went deeper than that.

'I'd been slowly distancing myself, slowly breaking it off. Right from the word go, if truth be told. When I found a job at a new firm, I knew that was the right time. We'd had some fun and no one had got hurt.'

'As far as you knew . . .'

'As far as I knew. Jesus Christ, that day. I'd met Freddie at his apartment. I was telling him that I was moving on, re-committing myself to my marriage. He was upset. He kissed me and said it would be easier to take if we could pass one more afternoon together. And then the door opened . . .'

'Natasha Reeve?'

'She was furious – I mean, rightly so.'

'Did she say anything?'

'That was the odd thing. She stepped inside, looked at us, did one circuit of the sofa we were sitting on and let herself out. It was like a cold fury. Like she knew already . . .'

'I'm afraid she did.' He closed his eyes. 'Ms Reeve was receiving anonymous notes about your relationship.'

Short went suddenly pale. 'Notes . . . ?'

'You didn't know anything about them?'

'No . . .'

'Both she and Freddie Coyle believe that you sent them.'

'What?' He looked speechless.

I sat back. 'You didn't send them?'

'Of course not, I didn't even know . . . First of all, I would never do that to someone. Secondly, it would wreck my life, my marriage. Why would I do that?' He realized he'd raised his voice and, although the coffee shop was empty, went on more quietly. 'I mean, I was *ending* it.'

'Freddie says he told no one about your affair, do you think that's true?'

His shoulders slumped. 'I expect it is. As I say. He was hardly a social butterfly . . .'

'So that leaves someone from your end . . .'

'But that's impossible.'

'You told no one?'

'About cheating on the mother of my children with a man? No.'

'You may have told someone without realizing it. What about your wife?'

'What about her?' he said, suddenly angry. He'd accepted my questioning his own character but drew the line at hers. It made me at least want to believe him.

'Well, she could have worked out that something was happening between you and Coyle. Sent Natasha Reeve the notes as a means of stopping it.'

'Absolutely not.' He saw the look on my face and answered it.

'Well, that's how I got into the whole mess to start with. She was working abroad. Lecturing in the US.'

I thought for a moment. 'Natasha Reeve says that in the weeks before their relationship ended, Freddie Coyle had changed. Become distant . . .'

'From her? No doubt.'

'He wasn't that way with you?'

He shook his head.

'Was he a big drinker back then?'

He paused to consider this. 'That would be something new . . .'

I asked Short for his whereabouts on Monday morning. The day I'd interviewed Coyle in his apartment and heard someone in the next room. He'd been at work and seemed quite happy to prove it.

I left him, wondering again who it had been.

At the time I'd thought of Aneesa, but everything I'd learned about Coyle since implied that he was off women for good. Directionless, I wondered if I was just pulling at this thread because I didn't have a lover of my own.

3

It was late afternoon and the heat was finally starting to ease. I went in the direction of The Temple. I wasn't happy about my phone call with Sian earlier, someone I still thought of as a friend, and I wondered if I could improve on it. Selfishly, I wondered if I might arrive before Ricky, her new boyfriend, and make it easier for us to talk. She'd seemed surprised that I was happy to meet him, and I tried to think what she wanted to see me for. I tried not to imagine it was about us, our relationship, but that aside, what else was there to say?

In the closing weeks of our living together I'd tried to get sober. To eliminate the pharmacy of uppers and downers I depended on. I had a few days of nerve-shredding withdrawals then started to feel better, physically and mentally. I looked at the beautiful, funny young woman in front of me and thought she was all I needed. My mind cleared and I started to really see Sian. The problem was that I started to see myself, too. Memories began to surface that felt like they belonged in another life, to another man. For years I'd remembered flashes of my sister, just her in isolation, but now I saw the people who'd surrounded us as children. After years of blank, medicated sleep I began to have living, vivid dreams. They grew darker, more disturbing, until one day I woke up to Sian watching me fearfully from the far side of the bed.

The Temple, where she worked, was a favourite of mine beyond her rare, friendly face behind the bar. It was unaffiliated with any gang or drugs franchise in the city, it was too small and dark to represent a club alternative to party-goers, and it had a carefully curated jukebox. Best of all, Sutty was banned, creating a sanctuary for those days when he became unbearable. After our conversation earlier, this was one of them.

When I descended the steps I saw that the bar was quiet. Sian was serving a couple, chatting happily, and I waited until she was alone.

'Hello, stranger,' she said, pleasantly surprised. 'I didn't think you'd actually come.' She was wearing her customary black with stark red lipstick. Her thick-rimmed glasses on the end of her nose.

She looked wonderful.

'You said we needed to talk.'

'I know, what was I thinking? Asking Aidan Waits to talk. When I hung up I thought you'd block my number as well as delete it.' I didn't say anything and she let me off the hook. 'You're early.'

'It's late for me. I haven't been to bed yet.' It was true. The night shift with Sutty, followed by my stake-out and break-in of Cartwright's flat had made for a long day.

'You're not up to your old tricks again?'

I thought of the night before. If Cartwright hadn't been arrested at departures, on his outbound flight, he'd be in the air by now. 'All new tricks,' I said.

She smiled but it faded from her face as she remembered what she wanted to talk to me about.

I sat at the bar. 'So what's up?'

She started to pour a beer. 'I wasn't sure whether I should tell you or not . . .' I looked into her eyes and she made up her mind. 'Well, there was some guy in here looking for you last night.'

I was surprised. 'Looking for me?'

She watched me closely, like I must know what she was talking about. 'Or, I guess, looking to find out stuff about you . . .' She slid the beer across the bar.

'Stuff like what?'

'How often you come in, if we're friends. He did it all in a round-about way but he just seemed to be . . .' she searched for the word, 'fishing.'

'Did you get his name?'

'He didn't give it. When I asked if he was a friend of yours he said you probably wouldn't remember him, but that he thought he'd seen you in here the other day. Wondered if that was *the* Aidan Waits . . .'

I took a drink, thought about it. 'Maybe that's the truth? Even I had some friends once.'

'You've still got friends,' she said, with a flash of indignation. 'Anyway, you'd remember this one . . .'

I waited.

'. . . I would've felt sorry for him if he hadn't been so weird about it. But there was something wrong with his face,' she said. 'The right-hand side. He had all these thick, overlapping scars and scabs. His mouth was all dry and chapped, and the eye socket . . . there wasn't anything there.'

I didn't know what to say.

'Look,' she said. 'He can't help what he looks like, but he can help being a creep. I had this feeling he was proud of it, y'know? Or, like, knew the effect it had on people. The whole time we were talking, he kept that side of his face pointed at me, leaning right over the bar until we were almost touching.'

'How old was he?'

'Older than us, in his fifties maybe. He looked like he was in the life.'

'A criminal?' She nodded. 'Guess I've met a few of those.'

'He was stacked as well. Like, seriously built, and a head taller than you. When he leaned on the bar I saw all these shitty, washed-out tattoos on his forearms. Like those prison ones they do with hot biros. He saw me notice them and started asking about mine. If they covered my whole body, if I had any naughty ones . . .'

'Shit, I'm sorry.'

'So was he, I poured his Guinness down the sink. Anyway, it's not your fault,' she said. 'Is it?'

'I don't know,' I said honestly. 'He doesn't sound like anyone I've put away. Or anyone I was ever friends with, either.'

'It's the second time he's been here. The first was Sunday night, when you came for the lock-in, remember? He was trying to push inside but when I saw I didn't know him I just said it was a private party.' I thought about leaving the bar that night. Someone had been standing in the shadows, watching me. 'Yesterday he came back, drank eight pints, sitting at that table, following me with his fucking dead eye. After a bit he came up and started asking about you.'

'Did he pay by card?'

'Cash . . .'

'What did you say?'

'Well after the weirdness about whether he knew you or not, and then the tattoo stuff as well, I just said *Sorry, shug, I don't really know him.*'

'Thank you.'

'Turns out that wasn't exactly a lie, though. He asked me how that sister of yours was doing . . .' I looked at the bar but Sian must have seen my jaw tighten. 'Yeah, that's what my face must've looked like as well, since you told me you had no family. You said you grew up in care.' She was silent for a moment. 'Who lies about something like that?'

When I looked at Sian again I could see a searching kind of pain in her eyes. I suddenly remembered it so well from our time together.

'I did grow up in care,' I said quietly. 'That's the truth. But I also had a sister, biologically. We were separated when we were very young.'

'So why not tell me that?'

'I don't know, it didn't seem worth saying.'

'It wasn't an omission, Aid. You lied. I really wish you hadn't.' I started to say something but she cut me off. 'I really wish you hadn't done it so well. I didn't even guess. How old were you?'

'I don't know, eight or nine?'

'So you had a sister for almost a third of your life and just forgot about her?'

'I didn't just forget—'

'What happened to her? Where is she?'

'I don't know,' I said, my descent complete. 'I never looked.' Sian frowned and I found myself justifying my inaction. 'She went to a well-off family, we had very different lives.' It was a thought that had sustained me through some bad times. For each of my care-home low points, the undiagnosed personality disorders of roommates, the casual violence and cruelty of older boys, I'd awarded the sister of my imagination with a corresponding positive experience. An attentive mother, perhaps a protective older sister. Finding her now, with her own imperfect life, her own disappointments, would mean losing all that. 'We're just separate people,' I said.

'Do you hold it against her? That she went to a nice family?'

'No,' I said, thinking about it. 'No, of course not. But she should be able to live her life.' I swallowed. 'We didn't come from a very good place. Nine out of ten times she'd have stayed there. Her being placed with a family was the only thing I ever wished for in my life, and when it happened it was like a miracle to me. I was glad. That's the truth.'

Sian put her hand on mine, but when I looked at her I saw it was for emphasis more than affection. 'She's your family, Aidan. You're hers . . .'

I shook my head. 'She has a family, and I've moved on. I'm sure she has too.' We stood like that for a moment until someone approached the bar.

'Hello-hello . . .'

I looked up and saw a man in a smart chequered suit, watching us closely. He was slim and in good shape, with skin that radiated health at first glance but looked made-up at second.

'Ricky,' said Sian, removing her hand too late from mine.

'Something I should know about?' He was smiling.

'Shut up,' she said, moving around the bar to hug him. 'Aidan was just leaving.'

'Nice to meet you,' I managed to say, watching as I held out my hand.

He shook it. His palm was cool and soft, and I noticed the clammy sweat on my own.

'The famous Aidan Waits,' he said. 'Don't think I've ever met a detective before. Can you tell what I do for a living from the dust on my shoes?'

'No, we're just like normal people.' I looked at Sian. 'But less so . . .'

'And has she been able to tempt you?' He nodded at Sian, his partner. There was some challenge in his voice and I looked at her, not knowing what to say.

'Aidan can't make it,' she said.

'Oh come on, mate. You only get engaged once.' In the silence that followed he almost certainly saw the truth of the situation but pressed on. 'Well, twice in my case, but as far as I know Sian's record's clear.'

'Well, I'll see what I can do,' I said, smiling. 'And congratulations. You're a lucky man. If you'll excuse me.' I put a hand on Sian's shoulder as a goodbye and went up the steps, out of the bar and back into the blazing heat. I walked fast, feeling the sweat run down my back.

Feeling like a criminal.

I hoped that Sian wouldn't be in trouble with Ricky. He'd caught us in what must have looked like an intimate moment and, for a second, I wondered if I should wait for him and explain. I had no right to feel hard done by. No right to feel anything but happy for them. So why did I risk my life crossing the road for a distraction?

And as for my sister, Sian had been wrong.

I saw her often, several times a day. Oxford Road was populated by young women, some with the same curled hair and serious expression I remembered from Annie's face, from twenty-odd years before. Any one of them could have been her, so I thought of them all warmly. I felt proud when I saw them well dressed, on their way to important jobs, or happy, floating down the streets with their lovers, or weird, with piercings, tattoos, blue hair. I'd seen her marching in protest against fascists, and offering expert advice on the news. I'd lost certain things in life, but I gained all of this, these twenty smiles a day at strangers, because I'd been separated from my sister. Her brother was no kind of man anyway. A corrupt detective, a criminal. A user of women and drugs.

My phone started to vibrate and I took it from my pocket. It was a withheld number.

'Waits,' I said, picking it up. 'Hello?'

There was no answer.

Straining, I thought I could hear someone breathing on the other end, but it was buried beneath the crackle of a bad signal. Then they disconnected. I slowed. My mind turned back to the man who'd been asking about me, to the Superintendent's warning of a hit. I thought about the anonymous phone call I'd received at home, and the ones since, to my mobile. I thought of the crushed piles of cigarettes I'd seen outside the flat.

And then I stopped dead in the street.

The man looking for me knew my name, my home and mobile number, and my address. He knew where I drank and who my ex was. He hadn't been fishing for information at all, he'd been telling me something. He knew I had a sister.

4

I returned, distractedly, to the CCTV. I'd watched so much of it in the last few days that I could feel the wrinkles forming round my eyes. Even if I found the cyclist, even if he'd looked right at the perpetrator and caught him on camera, I'd most likely have a blurred image of a kid with his hood up. One more for the collection. And anyway, this assignment wasn't about getting results. It was about sitting me in the naughty corner with a dunce's hat on my head, and I was bored of it.

I had a flash that I should walk out on my life. Leave a shit on Sutty's desk as my resignation letter and accept the consequences of my accrued mistakes. I'd been telling Sian the truth. I didn't know this scar-faced man. He didn't sound like anyone I'd met or anyone I'd put away, and that set me on edge. Parrs had learned about the hit and quashed it months before. So why would another mechanic surface now? It was the mention of my sister that pushed things into uncharted territory, though.

Threats against family members just didn't happen.

That kind of escalation was bad for everyone and actively discouraged from within the ranks of the criminal fraternity. Even dealers need to put their kids to bed at night. A hitman shouldn't know I had a sister at all. If he did, she should be off-limits. So what had I walked into? If it wasn't my past and it wasn't my job and it wasn't the hit, what was it? My relationship with Superintendent Parrs was at an all-time low, but I knew I had to tell him.

My mind was churning while I watched CCTV, and I traced the cyclist back to the start of his journey almost by accident. Studying the new footage, I saw him leave work and climb on to his bike a few hundred feet away from the Palace. He'd come from a florist on the other side of the theatre.

Pursuing leads in a case of dustbin vandalism was almost more humiliating than failing to do so. I picked up the phone anyway. It would be one less thing to apologize for when I next found the Superintendent in my car. I called and introduced myself. The man on the other end was disinterested until I mentioned the police. I asked if someone matching the description of my cyclist worked at the florist.

'Erm, yeah,' he said. 'Speaking . . .'

'Would you mind if I came around?'

'OK . . . Is it for a special occasion?'

Just the crime of the century, I thought.

When I arrived I found him serving a customer. I was certain he was the man from the footage and stopped to smell the flowers until we were alone. I explained that he may have been a witness to a criminal act on Oxford Road, two days previously, and that I'd noticed his cycle helmet had a camera. He was thrilled to help me, reeling off a series of offences and violations he'd caught on film.

'It's really just one thing in particular,' I said. 'I can give you the time and date?' When I did he remembered the incident immediately, as he'd stayed late that night doing the books. He was able to plug the GoPro into his work computer and we scrolled through to the corresponding time-stamp. He'd turned his head, and therefore the camera, towards the dustbin just before the blaze started.

'Guy was being really weird,' he said.

I watched the video with rising disbelief.

'Light changed,' he went on. 'Sorry I didn't get a good look at him. Is it any help? Detective?'

'Play it again,' I said.

He clicked back and we watched for a second time.

The man approached the dustbin carrying a plastic bag. He kept his head down so that no one passing would see his face. He removed a large object from the bag, which seemed to be wet cloth wrapped around something else, and dropped it into the bin. He struck a match and began to turn away. As he did so, his face looked directly at the cyclist for a split second.

I knew the man.

'If I give you an email address, would you be able to send me that file?'

'Course,' he smiled. 'You look like you've seen a ghost . . .'

I put my card on the counter, walked out of the shop and turned left, down Oxford Road, towards the burned-out dustbin. It was just a few hundred feet away from the florist's but I had to see it, and I wondered if it would still be there when I arrived. If the council would have removed it already as they had the previous two. I was frustrated at the pace of the people in front of me, beaten into listlessness by the heat, and found myself walking around them, then jogging, then running. I ran the times through my head. The man had set the fire a little after eleven. The other two had also occurred in the late evening, either shortly before or after midnight. When I arrived, I was relieved to see that the dustbin hadn't been destroyed or removed, but remained exactly where it had been. A melted cylinder of plastic which had folded in on itself.

I called SOCO and asked to speak to the Chief Scene of Crime Officer.

'Yes,' she said. It sounded like she was doing three things at once.

'The dustbin fires along Oxford Road . . .'

'If you're about to ask me what I think you're about to ask me, then no, we didn't. Neither you nor Detective Inspector Sutcliffe marked the crime scenes for collection, and nothing about them stuck out to me, either.'

'That's OK,' I said. 'But we need to trace the two dustbins that have been removed and we need SOCO on scene for the third.'

'Didn't this happen days ago? What could be of interest there now?'

'Don't know yet,' I said, hanging up. I dialled Sutty with shaking fingers and got him on the third try.

'Yeurgh.'

'I know who set the dustbin fires.'

'Wow,' he said, leaking boredom. 'Maybe we'll meet the prime minister.'

'It was the smiling man.'

That got his attention.

5

While I waited, I spoke to the fire brigade shift manager from four nights ago. The third dustbin fire had been put out comparatively quickly because the call went in immediately after it was lit. I had a flash that, for some reason, the smiling man had called the authorities himself, that we'd have a record of his phone number, maybe even his voice, but the shift manager clarified.

'Some kids over the road were meeting up for their mate's midnight vigil, that lad who got knocked down. They called it in.'

'Of course . . .'

'I hope you crucify the prick who lit it. We had a house fire on the other side of town. Had to split the team.'

I saw Sutty striding towards me. 'Don't worry, he got what was coming to him.'

I ended the call.

'Well, here we are,' he said, examining the dustbin, trying to prise it open.

'I've got SOCO on the way.'

'Pretty quick work.' He gave up on the bin and eyed me suspiciously. 'How d'ya know it's him?'

'He's on camera.'

'Not on the CCTV I've seen . . .'

'I traced a passing cyclist who had a camera on his helmet.'

'A useful cyclist? This case is getting fucking weird.' He eyed me. 'What do you think's in there?'

'Whatever he dropped looked like fabric, wrapped around some-thing else.'

'Means those last two bins were probably the same thing . . .'

'I've got SOCO tracing them now. Chances are they're in a landfill somewhere but they might still be on the back of a van. Both of them burned for longer than this one, though.'

'Hm,' he said, and we lapsed into an uneasy silence. SOCO arrived quickly. The team had still been working at the site of the canal body-dump. They didn't thank us for diverting them from a murder scene to an act of vandalism, but Sutty's look of reproach effectively got them to work. I watched as they cut apart the melted, plastic shell of the dustbin, lifting it away from the steel mesh can-ister on the inside. It smelt like stale ash.

'Take a look at this,' said the Scene of Crime Officer, with awe in her voice. Sutty and I approached the can and looked down. It was filled with burned, shrivelled and soaking rubbish.

'Good one,' said Sutty.

'This is what you called us away from Albion Street for?'

'Not to hear the sound of your voice, darling. Bag it up.'

The SOCO stared at Sutty for a second, decided it wasn't worth the fight and shrugged. She and her partner began removing items, burnt cans, blistered crisp packets and shrivelled fast food wrap-pers, placing them in evidence bags. Sutty and I walked a little further away from them.

'It was him,' I said. Sutty watched me closely. 'It was.'

'Just funny . . .'

'What is?'

'Parrs throws you off Smiley Face and on to the bins, and you manage to link them in the space of a few hours.'

'I've been following up on this for days, and if they're linked, they're linked. What can I say?'

'I just hope you've got the tape to prove it. Stromer's tight with SOCO. When she hears you've got them taking out the trash, it'll be in Parrs' ear faster than a finger in the fucking dyke.' We were standing beyond hearing distance of the other officers and after the day I'd had, being removed from the case, being told to resign, having nameless threats made against me, I thought I didn't have much to lose.

I lowered my voice and looked him in the eye. 'Do you know something, Peter?'

He stood up to full height. 'What?'

'It's a shame that bleach you bathe in only ever touches your skin. Do us all a favour and neck a bottle of the stuff next time.' I started to walk away but he grabbed my arm. I could feel his fingers digging into the bone. When I looked at him he was smiling, his eyes aglow, and I knew I'd given him what he wanted.

'*There it is*,' he hissed. 'Just keep on thinking your sack's inseparable from your body, gorgeous. Know why we're still in a job? Cus one day they'll need someone to take a fall. Which of us d'ya think it'll be?' He laughed. 'We both know who Stromer'd choose, don't we?'

'I don't care what her opinion of me is. Now get your fucking hand off my arm.' He didn't move it. 'I've got less to lose from a fistfight in public than you have, Sutty.' He must have seen that I meant it, because he smiled again, let go of my arm and backed off.

'Detectives,' said the SOCO. We both turned. She was holding an evidence bag containing two fat, singed wads of cash. We exchanged a look and walked back to the dustbin. With the trash removed, the fabric object that our man had dropped inside was visible. It had simply been a blanket, mostly burned away now, wrapped around wads of cash.

'One man's rubbish,' said Sutty.

No one laughed.

6

We watched SOCO removing currency in varying states of distress from the dustbin. Some of it was unrecognizable, some of it looked fresher than the cash in my wallet. No doubt there'd be bills somewhere which were completely untouched by fire. So far all the visible notes had been in twenties, in stacks of what looked like thousands.

I looked at Sutty. 'Still think I put it there?'

My phone started to vibrate as he gave me an evil look, and I used it as an excuse to walk down the road. It was the Chief Scene of Crime Officer returning my earlier call.

It wasn't the news I'd been hoping for.

'The two other dustbins have been landfilled already,' I told Sutty when I returned. 'They spoke to one of the refuse guys and he said they were basically ashes anyway.'

'I'd say the same thing if I found a few grand in the back of my truck, but I guess that's that.' Even Sutty sounded disappointed. It was galling to know we'd been standing so close to answers on the smiling man in each instance, and that we'd let them slip through our fingers. Even if the contents had been incinerated, a forensic examination might have told us something about him.

'How much longer?' Sutty barked at SOCO.

'We'll be here a while,' said the officer. 'But there's no chance we'll run these serial numbers today, if that's what you mean.'

Sutty exhaled through his nose for what seemed like an

impossible amount of time, but when he spoke he sounded almost calm, nearly rational. I realized he might be afraid.

'Given that both your team and mine have let crucial evidence slip through our fingers, I suggest we all get a move on.'

'Couldn't agree more. I'm doing my job. You breathing down my neck won't make it any quicker.'

I was surprised when Sutty pursed his lips, swallowed an insult and nodded.

'Collier,' he said, turning, moving like a black cloud towards the car.

I followed at a distance.

7

'There's been a development,' said Sutty, slamming the door of the box, and leaning against it. I sat at the table, opposite Collier.

He smiled. 'So I'm free to go?'

'Be still, my beating fists,' said Sutty. 'A development in the case. Not medical science. You're still halitosis on legs.'

'What's halitosis?'

'It means your breath could take that door off its hinges. Might be your quickest way out of here.' Collier looked at the table. 'Thought not. There's been a development in the suspicious death at the Palace. The short version is that there's money involved. Now, that suggests a few things to me. One of them being organized crime. So it just got a lot more important and you just got a lot more fucked. If it's nothing to do with you, tell me how your key card ended up in room 413 at the foot of a dead body.'

'What?' He looked between us. 'I left it at work, on the desk.'

Sutty watched him closely. 'What about this hooker? This Cherry . . .'

'I don't know her real name,' said Collier. 'I'm telling you the truth.'

'How'd you meet?'

'That bar over the road from the Palace, after a shift, the rock club.'

'Grand Central?' I said.

'Yeah.'

Sutty pushed himself off the door. 'She a rocker, Marcus?'

'Y'know, bit alternative, maybe a bit gothic. Anyway, she started talkin' to me. I could tell she was on the clock so I offered her a deal. Told her I worked in an empty hotel. Maybe she could use a room there to trick out of?'

'And what,' I said. 'You take a cut?'

He didn't answer.

'No,' Sutty gurgled. 'Not a cut. You wanted to make a friend. Forensics from 305 was interesting. That is the room you had her tricking out of, isn't it, Marcus? Your DNA profile was one of seventeen found in that bed.'

'So what? She's pretty,' he said. 'Colourful . . .'

'Well, I'm afraid it looks like someone's toned her down a bit.' Collier looked up. 'We're working on the assumption that this girl wedged open a fire door and went back to the Palace after your shift, when you thought you'd kicked her out. Same night some-one brained the security guard and a dead body appeared on the top floor. She saw someone, or someone saw her, or both. Now, we've been to her address and she's gone. Neighbour says the police dragged her away, but guess what? We didn't.'

Collier was sweating.

I leaned forward. 'You can do the right thing, here. This girl isn't in any trouble, she'd be doing us a favour. There's no reason not to help on this one.' I looked at Sutty. He nodded. 'It'll work for you, too. Screwing a girl's not the crime of the century, but this bloke in the Palace just might be. Help us out and we'll put in a good word for you.'

Collier looked at me. 'I'll talk to you,' he said. 'But I don't want him in the room.'

Sutty shrugged. Opened the door and stepped out. Once he did, Collier let out a sigh.

He looked miserable.

'It's the truth I don't know Cherry's real name . . .'

'But there's got to be something. A regular she was seeing, a pimp she mentioned . . .'

He looked at me. 'I don't know *his* real name.'

'His?' I said. 'Cherry's a cross-dresser? A man?'

He nodded down at the table. I was already out of my seat and going for the door.

8

Sutty hung up the phone and started sanitizing his hands. 'That canal body-dump,' he said, looking at me. 'Stromer says there's no evidence of gender realignment or anything like that, but the guy was wearing a lot of make-up. Obviously that could make him anyone from your generation, but he did have a tattoo above his groin . . .'

'Of?'

'The three winning reels of a fruit machine. Cherries. So I think it's safe to assume the queen is dead.'

'How did it happen?'

'Crushed larynx, apparently. Stromer's sending the report.'

I hit the desk. 'We must have been right behind them.'

'Hm,' said Sutty.

'Cherry saw something in the Palace. We can be sure of that now.'

'And someone must've seen her. So from the top . . .'

'The smiling man walks up and down Oxford Road for a few days, burning money in dustbins . . .'

'We don't know the others were money,' said Sutty.

'OK, burning something, personal effects. Then, for whatever reason, he breaks into the Palace and heads to the fourth floor.'

'Where either he, or someone else, brains our security guard.'

'Cherry sees whatever happens, and the smiling man ends up dead.'

'Then someone traces her, him, whatever, crushes her throat and dumps her in the canal.' He looked at me. 'Fucking us in the process.'

'If she was working out of there, and Marcus wasn't with her, it stands to reason she had another client, someone who can tell us what happened.'

We looked at each other for a second, then I got up and went down the hall looking for uniform. It took me a while to find the right person. I needed a young woman, someone the girls on the corners might talk to, and someone who knew their operation well enough not to be messed around.

Constable Naomi Black came highly recommended.

I found her in the canteen. She got points for sitting alone, even more for reading, and probably an extra few years on her life expectancy for bringing a packed lunch.

I knew her face from the backgrounds of various crime scenes in the last few months, but as far as I could remember we'd never spoken. She was brand new to the job but already had a reputation for being organized, concise in her reports and completely off-limits in her private life. She'd probably be my boss in three years.

'Constable Black,' I said, sitting down opposite her. 'How do you feel about some extra work?'

She looked at me dubiously then smiled. 'Sell it to me.'

Having explained the situation, I left my informal meeting with her somewhat cheered. We were at the absolute beginnings of a lead, and I felt like she was a good fit for following it up. When I'd told her the potential reward for her canvassing the city's street-walkers was probably me buying her a drink, she'd smiled politely.

'Can I just get the drink, or do you have to come with it?'

I smiled. She had good instincts.

By the time I got back to the office, Sutty was on his way out.

'What's happening?' I said.

'Had a call from SOCO . . .'

'They've traced the cash?'

'No, but they've worked out what it was wrapped in.' I waited. 'A towel,' he said.

'Makes sense, I suppose. He could easily bathe a towel in a spirit so it was ready to go up when he dropped it in the bin . . .'

'And that's what saved us. The spirit on the surface burned so brightly that the fire brigade were called out immediately. Part of the towel survived . . .'

'What do you mean? Was there something on there?'

'One word, embroidered, almost intact,' said Sutty. 'Midland.'

'Like the Midland Hotel? Was he staying there?'

'How should I know?' he said, grabbing his keys. 'I found out five seconds ago.' We were both going for the door. 'Question is, why would Smiley Face break into the Palace if he was staying in a hotel just up the road?'

I thought about it as we walked down the hall. 'He's got to have some connection with the Palace, something we're missing.'

'Hm,' said Sutty, pushing through a door.

'Anyway, the Midland could have a record of his name, his card details.'

'I'll be sure to ask them.'

I stopped.

'The Super was crystal-clear, Aidan. You're off the smiling man.' He walked on.

'We found that towel in the dustbin,' I shouted at his back. 'That's my case.' Even I thought it sounded weak, and he didn't stop. 'What about the cloakroom ticket?' I said. He ground to a halt. 'It could be with the concierge at the Midland. All his stuff could be there . . .'

Sutty turned, pursed his lips. 'Remind me what that ticket number was.'

'I'll tell you when we get there.'

He half-shrugged. 'Whatever.'

9

The Midland was a hotel of a similar vintage to the Palace, although certainly grander and with business still booming. Another enormous redbrick built in the early 1900s, listed, and replete with terracotta and polished granite. The hotel's name was written in large gold-leaf letters above the entrance and it dominated St Peter's Street, facing the central library and the square. They said that Hitler had wanted it as the Nazi HQ of Great Britain.

We approached the front desk at a pace. It felt like the first development in the case and had fallen out of nowhere. More importantly, we'd missed what might have been vital clues and both felt it keenly. It was early evening and well-dressed couples were entering the hotel, for rooms, drinks, spa treatments or dinners. Sutty and I stood out a mile, and the man at the front desk acknowledged us like a glitch in an otherwise flawless program.

'Good evening, welcome to the Midland Hotel. How can I help?'

'Well we don't want a room,' said Sutty. 'I'm Detective Inspector Sutcliffe and this is my colleague Detective Constable Waits. We're here in connection with a suspicious death that occurred in the Palace Hotel three days ago.'

The man frowned slightly. 'Good evening, Detectives. I'm very happy to help you in any way that I can, but as far as I'm aware the Midland has no affiliation with the Palace.'

'I understand that, sir,' said Sutty. 'But we have reason to believe that the victim may have been staying at the Midland in the days leading up to his death. There are three lines of enquiry we'd like to pursue. First of all, we'll need to see the room our man stayed in. Secondly, we'd like to speak to the concierge for any items he might have left here. A cloakroom ticket was found in his possession and it's our hope that it was issued at the Midland. Thirdly, we'll need to review any CCTV footage from the duration of our man's stay. We'd also like to speak to any staff or guests who might have interacted with him.'

'I see,' said the receptionist, looking between us. 'May I ask for this gentleman's name?'

'Well, there's our first problem,' said Sutty. 'Because fuck knows.'

The young man at the desk called his manager. When he saw Sutty and me, he acknowledged us with the same momentary wince as his colleague. As Sutty explained again why we were there he grew pale.

'Perhaps we'd be more comfortable speaking in my office?'

'How many check-outs have you had this week?' said Sutty, ignoring him.

'Without a name, you're asking the impossible. We have over three hundred rooms, over five hundred guests coming and going at all times. If this man has died, and I'm truly sorry to hear that, then he may not even have checked out at all. Even if he has, his room will have been immaculately cleaned, most likely re-booked and have entirely different people staying in it.'

'Start making a list,' said Sutty. The concierge, summoned moments before, arrived at the front desk. 'While you're at it we'll check the luggage. Our man was definitely in town as of last week, and travelling alone if that's any help. I'm sure we'll find your office.'

'Right . . .' said the manager. 'Yes, Rory, if you could help these two gentlemen, they're looking for a piece of luggage possibly left here a couple of days ago.'

We were led beyond the front desk, to a side room.

'Do you have the ticket?' asked the young man.

'We've got the number,' I said. ''831. Would you mind handling the item with these?' I passed him some latex gloves.

He nodded and disappeared into the room.

Sutty looked at me, pulling on his own gloves. 'If it's a suitcase filled with cash we split it, sixty–forty.'

'Deal, but it won't be.'

'Makes you so sure?'

'The cash was the last thing he burned because it was the least important thing to him. I think he was dismantling his life, whatever it was. He started with the important stuff.'

'Like . . . ?'

'Well, he travelled here from somewhere. With terminal cancer that must have been for some desperate reason, and he knew he'd never leave. I think he sent his documents and personal effects up in smoke in the first two fires. If he knew he didn't need them any more, and if they made him in any way traceable, they'd be the first things to go.'

'So you do think he topped himself . . .'

I shook my head. 'Someone got to him first. If he'd killed himself, we never would have found him. The cancer, the fires, the anonymity. I think he was burning his stuff because he'd run out of road.'

'Well, you'd know.'

I nodded. 'You need me on this. You couldn't find out who he was if his passport was in his pocket.'

'Someone's getting brave.'

'Maybe you're just less intimidating than you think, Sutts.'

'Why, all of a sudden? Cus there's a price on your head?'

I looked at him. 'Parrs told you.'

'The street told me. Who do you think spotted Blunt Trauma Billy back in January? Who do you think kicked his door in and pulled your fucking address out of his throat?' He was breathing hard through his nose. 'Y'know why you're with me, Aid? In the relegation zone? Come on, take a wild guess.'

But I already knew the answer.

'You're the only one who'd work with me,' I said.

'Following evidence to a logical conclusion. Maybe you're not a lost cause after all.'

The concierge emerged from the cloakroom carrying a brown leather suitcase.

'Was this the item you were looking for, sir?'

Sutty took it from him. 'Nothing else against that number?'

'Everything else is accounted for on other tickets. I did take the liberty of looking for the tickets which would have been issued immediately before or after 831, but they've all been collected.'

'Light,' said Sutty, holding up the case. He shook it and some hard objects moved about inside. 'Let's go talk to the manager.'

10

'How's that list coming?' said Sutty, as we walked into the office.

'I'm afraid it might take—'

'Out then.'

The manager did a double-take and Sutty glowered at him.

'We'll only be a moment,' I said. 'We'd like to look at the man's personal effects and don't know what they'll be yet. There could be sensitive, even disturbing or dangerous items in there.'

'Well,' he said, getting to his feet. 'By all means disturb and endanger my office.' He moved briskly past us, closing the door discreetly behind him. What a pro, I thought.

Sutty laid the luggage out on the desk.

It was a sturdy, unbranded, brown leather suitcase. The kind of vintage, worn-out steamer trunk you often see in pawn or charity shops. Completely unremarkable. It had a dark leather handle and a rigid external frame for reinforcement. There were two catches, each with a button and a keyhole beside it. It looked like it had been around the world and was scarred from decades of use, having no doubt passed through the hands of several owners.

'Prepare to be a rich man,' said Sutty, clicking open the catches. 'Unlocked? Maybe he's not your international man of mystery after all . . .'

'If it was locked, it'd mean he had a key for it. With a case this old that would have to mean he was the original owner.'

'So what?'

'It's unlocked and there was no key on his person. That means it's second hand.' I looked at the battered case, the underside edges, worn smooth by years of use. 'Or third, or fourth, or fifth hand. Completely untraceable. I bet he'd never seen this case in his life before he bought it with cash and packed it.'

'Mr Fucking Brightside,' said Sutty. The case opened with what sounded like a sigh and we both stood there, absorbing it for a second. The stale, boxed-up smell of a lonely, cornered life. There was a thin, stained paper lining, which looked like it had been inside the case for many years. There were a handful of objects. On top was a small thread card of orange yarn. I recognized it as the same colour thread that had sewn the torn paper and cloakroom ticket into the man's trousers.

'Well, that solves one mystery,' said Sutty, daintily moving the thread aside. 'He did his own sewing.' Beneath the thread were a couple of simple items of clothing. Bland, shapeless underwear and a crumpled T-shirt. Sutty only touched them to examine the labels.

As expected, they'd been unstitched and discarded.

'And he was removing his own labels, too.' He moved the clothing aside to reveal an unusual pair of scissors. They'd been Scotch-taped shut, with the sharp edges visible at the end. Beside the scissors was what looked like a normal butter knife, sheathed in more of the Scotch tape. Using index fingers and thumbs, Sutty pulled the knife free of its ad hoc case to reveal that the blade had been halved and dramatically sharpened.

We shared a glance.

Both the knife and the scissors looked like vicious, hastily improvised weapons. The only other item in the case was an old hardback book.

The Rubáiyát of Omar Khayyám.

Sutty picked it up by the spine and dangled it upside down. Nothing fell out. He disinterestedly flicked through the pages, frowning as he did so.

'Poetry,' he grumbled.

'Look at the back. The last page.' He did so. It was torn, with part of the page missing. 'That's where the message in his pocket came from. Ended or finished. It was the end of the book.'

'Hm,' said Sutty, leafing back through the book, more slowly this time. He stopped at the front, the title page, and held it out to me. It was a neat, legible handwritten inscription.

Indeed, indeed, Repentance oft before
I swore – but was I sober when I swore?
And then and then came Spring, and Rose-in-hand
My thread-bare Penitence apieces tore.
With love,
Ax

We looked at each other.

Beneath it there was a phone number written in incredibly light pencil.

'Zero one six one,' said Sutty, squinting. 'Local . . .' I started to take my phone from my pocket but he shook his head. 'We don't know who or what's at the other end. We'll get the address and go over there, rather than give them an early warning. Too much of this case has passed us by already.'

'Who do you think it is?'

'Sounds to me like we've got ourselves a smiling woman.'

The boy stood paralysed in the doorway of the kitchen, the death room. Because of the light he'd flicked on, that split second he'd held down the switch, he couldn't see in the dark any more. Instead, a neon imprint of the open-throated woman was burned into his retina, like the first seconds following a camera flash.

When he breathed again he was suddenly retching, overwhelmed by the metallic smell of blood coating the back of his throat. All thoughts of slipping quietly through the house evaporated and he stumbled, crawled, backwards from the room, gasping, as far as he could go, until he thudded into the closed front door. He pushed himself up, choking, panicking, feeling the sweat bleed out through his palms, making them so slippery that he almost slid back down the door. His chest tightened and he crushed his eyes closed, trying to breathe. He tried to re-engage the rising, to lift effortlessly out of his body and watch this like it was happening to someone else, but the floating sensation wouldn't come. For a moment he thought this was how his life would end, lost in the darkness, his chest caving in on itself. So similar to the blackness that his mother predicted.

He passed through the worst of the pain, his head shaking with the effort, and his breathing began to normalize. The blood drumming through his ears served as an unwelcome reminder that he was still alive, he was still here.

And then slowly, reluctantly, the boy acknowledged the time delay. The difference between the breaths that he could feel, moving in and out of his lungs, and the breaths that he could hear, coarse and rasping, moving in and out of someone else's. They weren't coming from the kitchen, the death room. They were much closer than that. Muted by something, a door, a wall.

The boy could hear a prisoner, crying, somewhere in the house.

The sound brought his sister to mind. He thought of her, powerless and confused, holding her bruised arm, staring at him with wide, wet eyes from the corner of a room, communicating something to him alone, and trying not to draw Bateman's attention back to herself. He thought of her now, sitting afraid in the car, waiting for him to come back.

He followed the sound to a closed door beneath the stairs. When he reached it the sobbing stopped. The boy leaned in and put an ear to the door.

'Tracy?' came a hesitant voice.

It belonged to a man, but one whose mouth was filled with pain. The boy withdrew his hands from the oak, brushing against the sturdy, iron key sticking out from it and, just for a second, felt like they were looking at each other. As though the person behind the door could see through it, into him, and acknowledge that they were both prisoners. The boy took a step backwards, on the balls of his feet. He saw the aluminium pole, discarded on the floor, and picked it up. He returned to the foot of the stairs, to the job.

'Tracy . . .' the voice called out again.

The boy put his hands over his ears and climbed the stairs to the landing.

He didn't dare turn the light on, so he edged open a door, letting the moon cast its pale glow across the room. There was a chair lying on its side and he picked it up, positioned it in the centre of the landing and stood on top of it. Then he reached the aluminium pole upward, inserted the plastic end into the hatch on the ceiling and twisted. With a pull, the hatch opened and an unfolding staircase slid down from the attic.

The hatch above the boy was a square of perfect darkness.

He dropped the pole and climbed up into it.

The attic had one small porthole window, through which the boy could see the moon, the only source of light. There were no floorboards so he walked carefully across the beams, breathing through his mouth to avoid the stale smell of cobwebs and dust. Following Bateman's instructions, he went away from the light, towards the far wall. Towards a narrow rectangle that went from the floor to the ceiling, but wasn't much wider than a football. He plunged his arm into the void, as far as it would go, and felt around. When his fingers touched nothing but air he took a breath and began forcing his body into the gap.

His fingers brushed against fabric.

Flattening his body, holding his breath, the boy pushed himself further inside the gap, plucking at this object, teasing it towards him. When he got his fist around it he knew he had the handle of a canvas bag, and pulled back with all his strength. The bag was heavy but he could hold it.

Elated for a second, he tried to move back out of the gap but he was stuck. He pulled again, still didn't move and started to panic. He thought of his sister, with Bateman and their mother in the car. He thought of the prisoner crying beneath the stairs. In a rush of anger, the boy screamed, wrenching himself free from the space and collapsing into a gap between the floorboards. He heard the buckling sound of plaster, breaking beneath his weight. As he started to move it gave way and he fell through, down on to the landing. He hit the floor hard, still holding on to the bag, trying to breathe as splinters and plasterboard hazed down on top of him.

He rolled over, spat the wood shavings out of his mouth and got up. He half-fell down the stairs, coughing, gripping the bag to his chest, keeping his back to the kitchen, the three dead bodies. He put his hand on the latch of the front door and started to open it when he heard the voice from under the stairs again.

'*Tracy?*'

The person was crying. The boy thought, once again, of his

sister. He thought that when he walked out, they'd leave. Bateman would start the car and they'd be lost in the endless, looping back-roads, impossible to follow and never coming back. He felt the electricity in the tips of his fingers, still gripping the latch. The blood thumping through his ears.

He understood that this was a decision.

He made up his mind and moved before he could change it. He went back to the door under the stairs and felt for the key. He turned it all the way, as far as it would go, until he heard the unmis-takable click of a lock opening. Then he went back to the front door, opened it and ran.

———

VI
Wolf Like Me

1

It was five in the morning and we were watching a house on a quiet terraced street in Rusholme. The phone number found in the smiling man's possession had brought us here. There was no answer at the door and, until we knew whose home it was, the only thing to do was wait. Sutty and I had each slept briefly, in shifts, with some unfortunate overlap in the middle where we'd made conversation. He'd expanded on his theory that the world was ending. The heat was an early warning sign, he said. The steam escaping from grates was the city short-circuiting, behind the scenes. Now, in the cramped confines of the car, I watched his morning regime. Dowsing himself in hand sanitizer, his skin cracking, red raw from the alcohol. He dabbed some on to the tip of his index finger and ran it back and forth across his gums.

I wound down the window as his phone started to ring.

'Yeurgh,' he said, picking up. He listened intently for a minute. 'Fuck.' He recited our location to the person at the other end and hung up.

'What's happening?'

'Uniform have been showing Stromer's still of Smiley Face to staff at the Midland. Blank looks until the cleaners arrived this morning . . .'

'And?'

'And one of them recognized him. She walked into his room to clean it on Friday night and he rushed to push her back out. We know it was Friday because afterwards he called the front desk to lodge a complaint. Wanted assurances that no one would be walking in on him while the Do Not Disturb sign was up . . .'

'Probably soaking his towels in paraffin,' I said. 'Do they know who he spoke to from the front desk?'

'They're looking into it. But best of all, he still has two days left before checkout . . .'

'The Do Not Disturb sign's still up?'

'Still up,' said Sutty, looking at me. 'He's staying in room 413, by the way.'

The same room we'd found his body in at the Palace.

'What's his name?' I tried to keep the excitement out of my voice but I was desperate to know.

'The room's booked under the name Robert Sole,' said Sutty.

I thought for a second. 'R. Sole. Funny.'

A squad car pulled up while we were still talking and Sutty climbed out. 'Hilarious,' he said. 'I'm gonna be there when they break the lock. If anyone turns up here, talk to them. Find out what the fuck's going on.' He slammed the door behind him. I couldn't help but wonder what they'd find at the Midland, what the relevance of the room number was.

I passed another slow hour watching the street.

The humidity, which had eased during the night, was coming back with a vengeance, and I was sitting with one leg out of the door when I heard the voice of a child. I looked into the rear-view mirror and saw a little boy coming along the pavement with a woman, his mother I assumed. They were holding hands, speaking quietly to each other, and when they stopped beside the house I'd been watching, I was almost too excited to react.

The woman was a little older than me, with tanned skin and dirty-blond hair. At first glance there was something new-age about her appearance and as she moved I heard the click and rattle of the thick, coloured bracelets on her wrists. The bo-ho image was somewhat undone by her sucking the absolute last drag out of a cigarette, closing her eyes as the tip glowed red. She took it from her mouth, slowly exhaled and looked down at her little boy. She smiled tiredly.

'Excuse me,' I said, as gently as I could. The woman took a step back and her expression hardened in a way that surprised me. Like I'd walked in on her naked. The boy disappeared behind her, as though he'd been taught to do so.

I held my hands open.

Tried to look like I hadn't spent a night sleeping in a car.

'I'm sorry to surprise you, I'm Detective Constable Aidan Waits.' I showed her my badge. The boy peered around his mother to look at it, and I was struck by the dark rings circling his eyes. His mother must have noticed this, because she dropped her cigarette and tucked him back behind her. 'Can I ask if you live at this house?' The woman frowned, nodded. I was starting to think she looked familiar, somehow, but I couldn't place her. 'I'm wondering if you can help with my enquiries . . .'

'I doubt it,' she said impatiently. 'We've been out all night . . .' Her voice sounded strange, like she wasn't quite used to it. I wondered if English was her second language.

'It's nothing to do with your home, Ms . . .'

'Mrs,' she said. 'Amy Burroughs.'

A.

The initial that the book in the smiling man's case had been signed with.

I tried not to react but I needed more time with them. 'I have a slightly complicated story to tell you, Mrs Burroughs.' I smiled at the little boy, who was peering back around her. 'We might all be more comfortable inside.'

I followed her into a small, brightly coloured hallway, made narrow by the bookcases jammed in either side. Nothing matched, and the furnishings looked like the kind you might find left on a street. The shelves were painted different colours, the ceiling was sky-blue and the walls, what I could see of them, were bright yellow. They were covered with framed pictures, all at different, haphazard heights. These pictures were either of the boy, or child-ish cartoons which I assumed he'd drawn.

I felt like I was intruding on their private universe.

We turned into a small kitchen-cum-living room which smelt dimly of incense and was decorated in much the same way. The pictures on the wall were larger than those in the hallway, with each one prominently featuring the little boy. It looked like a shrine to him, and it reminded me, uncomfortably, of the homes of bereaved parents. In the dead centre, above the mantelpiece, was a large picture of Amy Burroughs, her boy and a man who dwarfed them both. Where they smiled brightly, he winced into the camera.

Mrs Burroughs and her boy sat on the sofa and I took a seat opposite them. The boy was staring at me, wide-eyed, so I took out my badge and held it out to him. He looked at his mother to see if he was allowed to take it, accepting it with awe when she nodded.

'As I said, my name's Aidan.'

'Amy,' she said, snapping the word off before it was quite out of her mouth.

'I'm sorry to intrude on you like this so early, Amy. Can I ask what you do for a living?'

She frowned. 'Isn't that why you're here?' She went on, answering the question in my face. 'I'm a nurse practitioner. I think we met a few days ago . . .'

The woman I'd supposed to be a doctor when I was visiting Ali in hospital. She'd noticed one of the nurses barking at a patient and gone to have a word with him.

She looked like a different person in her own clothes.

'St Mary's,' I said, belatedly. 'I'm sorry, it's been a very long week.'

'Can I get you a coffee or anything?'

I shook my head. I was wide awake.

'May I ask if you were working on Saturday night?'

'Saturday . . .' she said, absent-mindedly playing with her boy's hair. 'I think I was on the late . . .' She searched inside her bag for a diary, found the date and handed it to me. 'Yeah, late.'

'What hours does the late shift cover?' I said, glancing at the diary before handing it back to her.

She gave a cynical smile. 'It covers about as many hours as you can stand. I would have started at eight p.m., got home probably about the same time as today, gone six in the morning, when I collected him.' She rubbed her boy's head again. He was drawing his fingers back and forth across my badge.

'And people can confirm your movements?'

'Patients, nurses, doctors.' She shrugged. 'Of course, if they have to. You're starting to make me feel like a criminal . . .'

'I'm sorry,' I said. 'Professional hazard.' I felt wired. Excited. 'You're not in any trouble, I just need to establish some facts. May I ask if you've ever been to the Palace Hotel?'

'The Palace . . .'

'On Oxford Road.'

'The one with the old clock tower?' I nodded and she strained to remember. 'Maybe. But years ago, there's a bar there . . .'

'There was. The hotel's actually closed at the moment but at around midnight on Saturday night a body was discovered.'

'I don't understand. Someone I know?'

'We're struggling to identify the man,' I admitted. 'He had no ID on his person but we have recovered his suitcase. There was a book inside it that I'm hoping you can tell me about . . .'

'A book?'

'There was an inscription in what looks to me like your handwriting.' I nodded at the diary I'd just examined. '*The Rubáiyát of Omar Khayyám.*'

I watched the colour drain out of Amy's face. She took my badge out of her boy's hands and gave it back to me. I thought she might ask me to leave but she recovered. 'So?' she said.

'Am I to understand that you gave a copy of this book to a man?'

Her eyes drifted towards the pictures of her family on the wall, then she closed them and nodded.

'Can you give me the name of that man, Amy?'

She glanced at her boy. 'I'm not really comfortable talking about this.'

'Can I ask why?'

A shadow went across her face and she looked at her watch, mainly to buy herself a few seconds, I thought. To look at something besides me, her boy, the man on the wall. 'Mark's due home any minute,' she said.

'Your husband?' She nodded. 'Mrs Burroughs, if you've got nothing to hide then I'm sure we can be discreet, but this is very important. A man's dead.'

'Ross,' she said. 'His name's Ross Browne.'

A name. The smiling man had a name. It sounded more realistic to me than Robert Sole. 'Can I enquire as to the nature of your relationship with Mr Browne?' I said. I was trying to keep the excitement out of my voice.

'I don't really know.' She was twisting her hands around each other. 'We went out a bit, just dating.' She frowned at the look on my face. '*Before* I met my husband. I haven't seen him in years. We were a flash in the pan but he was a nice guy.' Her eyes softened on the past tense. 'I'm sorry to hear he's dead.'

'How did you meet?'

She looked at me for a moment, then took her boy's hand and led him to a play box in the corner of the room. She kicked it over, scattering toys across the floor and he immediately fell to them, bored of our conversation. She returned to the sofa and lowered her voice.

I still couldn't quite get a grip on her accent.

'It was all very *English Patient*. Ross was in the army, the King's Division. He was being treated for post-traumatic stress disorder.' She gave another small shrug. 'We went out a few times.'

'Was this here in the city?' I asked. She nodded. 'And do you know if he stayed in the area?'

'He couldn't take the noise. He went down south, to the coast. He thought it might be good for him.' She said the words with some feeling, as though it hadn't been so good for her. 'He said the sea could surprise you. It was always changing . . .'

'And when was the last time you spoke?'

'It's years,' she said. 'I think the last time I saw him we went for a drink in town. That was when he broke it off. He said I shouldn't waste myself on a long-distance relationship.' As she spoke both her hands closed into fists, and they looked tiny against her over-sized hippy bracelets. 'It must be five years ago now, because it was before he came along.' She nodded at her boy. 'Ross isn't the father, by the way.' She said this casually, and I believed her. She went quiet for a moment, thinking about her former lover, until questions began to occur to her. 'So . . . what would Ross be doing in the Palace? It's closed, you said? How did he die?'

'We suspect foul play.' I let it sink in for a second. 'I know this must come as a shock but I have to ask. During the time you knew Mr Browne, was he involved in any illegal activity?'

'Of course not. He was a young man, shaken up from the war. He was . . .' She searched for the right words. 'Damaged. Sensitive.'

'I'm afraid as well as a formal statement, we may need you to identify Mr Browne's body.' I was talking too quickly now, eager to progress the case, and this caught her off guard. She started to speak then looked at the pictures on the mantle, her boy, like I'd suggested taking it all away from her.

'I've got to get him to school, I've got to . . .'

'This wouldn't be until tomorrow anyway, at the earliest.'

She looked about. Swallowed. 'Fine. I'm off work tomorrow. Look, my husband said he'd be right behind me . . .'

'You work together at St Mary's?'

She nodded, getting up, looking out the window.

'OK,' I said, standing. We exchanged details and I made to leave. 'One quick thing,' I said in the doorway. 'Can I ask what the relevance of the book was?'

She rubbed newly tired eyes and leaned on the bright yellow wall. 'I first read it at a very special time. It's about escape. Celebrating life. I thought Ross deserved some of that after what he'd been through.' I nodded and left. As I crossed the road to the car I saw that Sutty was back, sitting on the passenger side. I was tired but buoyed by the news that had upset Amy Burroughs so much. We'd finally put a name, a past, to our unidentified man.

2

As we drove I filled Sutty in on what Amy Burroughs had told me. He nodded along, not really listening. He popped his joints for the entire journey, thinking of something else, and I wondered what they'd found at the Midland Hotel that made the smiling man's full name a footnote.

The manager crossed the lobby to meet us when we arrived.

'Detectives, I was wondering if I could have a moment of your time?'

'What's up?' said Sutty.

'Please, follow me.'

The manager took us to a side room and closed the door. It was a security office, and sitting at the desk were a uniformed guard and a small middle-aged woman. I assumed she was the maid who'd walked in on the smiling man's room and had a complaint made against her.

'You said there were no cameras on the floors . . .' said Sutty, looking at the TV screen.

'Correct, but we do have two cameras on the ground floor, one of which is positioned above the front desk. When Mrs Nowak recognized the man from your picture, I thought I should ask her to look through the front-desk footage from the day he checked in . . .' The security guard cued up the footage and played it.

It felt incredible to see Ross Browne, the smiling man, move.

He had an awkward, limping gait which reduced his height

considerably, and he kept his head angled down, away from the camera, like he already knew it was there. He was wearing the smart brown suit we'd found him in, and he was carrying the case which had been left with the concierge. From the way he held it, the case looked much heavier than when Sutty and I handled it the previous day. I wondered what was in there. He spoke briefly to the young woman at the desk, checked in, signed and then walked out of view.

'Well, thanks,' said Sutty, thoughtfully. 'If we could get a copy of that tape—'

'That wasn't what I wanted to show you,' said the manager. 'Saul . . .' The security guard cued up another video file. 'The second camera covers the rest of the floor. You can only see the back of people when they go for the lifts so it wasn't worth looking at until we knew exactly what time the man entered.'

Our man, Ross Browne, walked towards the elevators with the same awkward gait, staying close to the wall. When a door began opening in front of him his posture changed. He stepped back and melted smoothly out of view into an alcove, and the edge of something became visible in his left fist.

The improvised knife we'd found inside his case.

It had been in his palm the entire time. The people who'd walked through the door passed him. He re-palmed the blade and resumed his shuffle towards the elevator. Sutty and I looked at each other. It was like watching two different people inhabit one body.

There was already activity around room 413 when we reached it. A uniformed officer was stationed at the door and Sutty and I climbed into plastic anti-contamination suits before entering.

There was something he wanted me to see.

I didn't know what to expect but was surprised by the room's mundanity. It was neat, seemingly untouched, and the bed was made. Two Scene of Crime Officers acknowledged us with nods. Both they and Sutty watched me as I craned my neck to take in the room. I stayed standing on the spot, not wanting to move until I'd been given permission, but from there, nothing seemed unusual or out of place.

'He was definitely in here?' I asked.

'Oh yeah,' said Sutty. 'Even put a credit card down at the front desk.' I'd been too preoccupied watching his movements on the check-in video to notice. It was surprising. A card was so traceable that I assumed he would have talked his way around it. We had a former lover, video evidence and now a bank account. Perhaps he was human, after all. Sutty must have seen the disappointment in my face.

'Show him,' he said. The SOCO officers both stood at the foot of the bed and lifted that end away from the floor. Beneath it was an enormous bloodstain, soaked deep into the carpet.

'No corpse,' said Sutty. 'But pints and pints of the stuff . . .'

I took a step closer. 'Human?'

'We'll know soon enough, but unless he was into animal sacrifice, someone died badly in this room.'

'Who?' I said, almost to myself. 'How would he even get a body out of here?'

'Can't help ya with the first one, but if you'd like to follow me into the bathroom . . .'

At first glance the bathroom seemed untouched, aside from a strong smell of paraffin or petrol coming from the bath itself. We'd expected that because of the dustbin fires. When I looked inside the tub it told a different story. Sutty watched me closely. The bath was gleaming clean but scarred along the bottom. Coarse, overlapping nicks and scrapes alongside several deep, straight incisions.

Something big had been cut up inside it, using very sharp objects.

Sutty walked to the toilet and lifted up the lid. I followed him and looked down.

The water was red.

3

We returned to the station to file reports, liaise with forensics for the Midland and arrange identification of the body for the following day. More importantly, to begin the search for the real Ross Browne. Who he was and the life he'd left behind. We'd found records of a man by his name living in Brighton. The years he'd been in town, and his proximity to the coast, matched what Amy Burroughs had told us.

Local authorities had visited Browne's flat to no response.

The fact of his military past threw up interesting possibilities about the death, while muddying the water of our investigation. We'd requested his military records from the Ministry of Defence and the paperwork was currently inching its way through layers of bureaucracy. I imagined a brown file being passed, endlessly, from desk to desk.

I checked in with Constable Black, who'd been approaching streetwalkers, known sex workers and pimps. If Cherry had been inside the Palace, she had to have been with a client. Black had been spreading the word about the murder but, so far, no one had even admitted to knowing our victim.

I could hear her flicking through her notebook as she spoke to me. 'Closest thing I've had is the nickname of a regular for Cherry's kind of service.'

'Run the nickname by me?'

'Mr Hands . . .'

I thought for a moment, wondering if it might apply to anyone I'd met in the case so far. 'Doesn't mean anything to me,' I said. 'But that's a good start. Keep trying.'

When my phone rang a few minutes later, I hoped it was Black, calling back with a breakthrough.

'Waits,' I said, answering. I could hear someone at the other end but they didn't say anything. I waited for a second and snapped. 'Listen, I'm fucking sick of this—'

'Aidan, it's me, Ricky. We met the other day? Sorry if I'm getting you at a bad time, man . . .'

'Ricky.' Sian's boyfriend. Her fiancé. I closed my eyes. 'I thought you were someone else.'

'Yeah. Well, I got your number from Sian's phone . . .'

'Does she know you're calling me?'

'No, and I'd appreciate it if we could keep this between the two of us. We need a word.'

'Today's not great.'

'It's important, man. It's really important.'

'OK,' I said, slightly taken aback. 'I was hoping to talk to you, too. It'd have to be later, though.'

'I can't do now anyway. Let's grab a drink tonight.' He sounded more like he wanted to clear the air than start a fight. I thought it was an unusual move, to get an ex's number from your partner's phone, but Sian obviously meant a lot to him and if pushed I was willing to explain the scene he'd walked in on. We agreed to meet at the Rising Sun later that day, when Sian would be working in The Temple.

'I'll see you then.'

'*Sick,*' he said. I hung up and looked at Sutty.

'So, Amy Burroughs,' he said. 'What did you think?'

'She was jumpy, right from the word go. Nervous about her husband coming home and at pains to point out that Browne wasn't her little boy's father. But I guess a cop approaching you on the street at five in the morning could do that . . .'

239

'Hm,' said Sutty. 'Did she say anything else about the balls and chain?'

'Only that he worked at St Mary's with her, that he was due home any minute.' I shrugged. 'No one wants their sexual history broadcast to a partner.'

'Says the expert.' There was a trace of malice in his voice but it was habitual, half-hearted. We were wiped out from a night spent cramped together in the car. From catching two additional deaths, Cherry and whoever the blood patch belonged to, in as many days. I kept thinking of the splintered door in Cherry's room. I couldn't help but wonder how far behind her killer we'd been, and what she'd seen that had put an end to her life so violently.

Now, the blood in the Midland was a piece of the puzzle that didn't seem to match anything else. It had been confirmed as human, and forensics estimated the quantity soaked into the carpet as four to six pints. Comfortably enough to kill someone. It looked as though the body had been dissected, and disposed of through the drains. Not all of it could have gone that way, though, and it added new frustration to our not fully investigating the first two dustbin fires.

We had to know who died in that room.

We had staggered towards one answer, though. Ross Browne was the smiling man. I wondered what had happened after his relationship with Amy Burroughs disintegrated to make him go so far off the grid, to hide his identity, and what it was that had finally caught up with him now. There was a knock at the door and I got up. Opened it to a young, uniformed officer with neck acne and a large coffee stain on his shirt.

'Detective Constable Waits?' he said.

'Yeah.'

'You're wanted on the top floor. Superintendent Parrs . . .'

Sutty groaned and got to his feet. 'Yeurgh, yeurgh,' he said.

'Not you, sir,' said the officer, returning his gaze gravely to me. 'Just him.' I pulled on my jacket, it felt about as crumpled as I did, and I wondered, tiredly, if this would be another warning. The death threats against me were starting to feel more like a petition.

Either way, I was going to have to talk to him.

There was a strange man in the midst of all this tracing my movements, watching my house and calling my phone. His comment to Sian was the tipping point, though. An oblique threat against my sister was too much of an escalation to ignore. The officer didn't speak again until he knocked on the Superintendent's door and took me inside.

'Detective Constable Waits, sir,' he said, without looking at either one of us.

His voice was shaking.

'Very good,' said Parrs. The officer backed out of the room and drew the door shut. The office itself was uncharacteristically chaotic. Papers had been pushed off the desk on to the floor, and the two chairs which usually sat opposite the Superintendent were tipped on to their sides, looking as though they'd been thrown against the wall. Parrs was sitting, rigid, behind the desk, grey suit, grey hair, grey face. His tie was askew at his neck, and his raw, red eyes flicked about the room, as if inviting me to observe its disarray, before settling on mine. 'Take a seat,' he said with his shark's smile. His Scottish accent was just a low growl. I picked up one of the chairs, set it back on its legs and sat down.

'At around six o'clock this morning, GMT, the MAN–DXB non-stop to the United Arab Emirates touched down in Dubai International Airport. It's a seven-hour flight but had the wind at its back, so it landed a little ahead of schedule. Ever been to Dubai, Aidan?'

'No, sir.'

'Dry country,' he said. 'Not really your style, eh? I'm told it's the busiest airport in the world operating on just two runways. Needless to say, being ahead of schedule can present a headache in such cramped confines. Ground crews started to process the luggage.' He smiled again. 'That can be a bit of a headache there, too. Dubai

International has what's generally acknowledged to be the most state-of-the-art surveillance system for incoming drugs of any airport on the planet. Makes Heathrow look like a fucking honesty box. Obviously, the travellers themselves get finger-fucked through security, but it's behind the scenes where the real magic happens. Those unloaded bags are screened, re-screened, sniffer-dogged, you name it. A girl with half a gram of ketamine only just avoided the firing squad last year on appeal. Big risk to take carry-on. So I was surprised to receive a call this morning from the British embassy, saying that a thirty-six-year-old man from my city had been optimistic enough to think he could take a bag of the good stuff on holiday. I was less surprised when they told me his name. A Mr . . .' Parrs pretended to read from the sheet of paper. '. . . Oliver Cartwright. No, it all started to make sense once they told me his name. It started to look almost elegant.' Somehow, in my plot against Cartwright, I hadn't quite thought ahead to this confrontation. Parrs lowered his head and looked at me. 'Does it make sense to you, Aidan? Does it start to look elegant?'

'No, sir.'

'*No, sir,*' he laughed. I wasn't sure I'd ever seen him laugh before. '*No, sir. You told me to stay away from him on pain of death and I followed orders, because I'm Aidan Waits and that's what I do. I wouldn't take a personal vendetta and turn it into an international incident, would I?*' He paused, breathing through his nose for a few seconds. 'It will, no doubt, give you great pleasure to hear that Mr Oliver Cartwright will, for the next few years, be engaged in a miasma of legal proceedings, in a second language, which will more than likely see him imprisoned abroad for the rest of his life. The sex-tapes in his future will be of an altogether different variety. Do you think that punishment fits the crime, Detective Constable?'

I didn't say anything.

'You're a cold fish, son, has anyone ever told you that? At this moment in time, a latex-gloved Arab is *wearing* Ollie Cartwright like a fucking wristwatch. Have you got anything to say to that?'

'Good,' I answered.

He stared at me. 'There was a time when I thought you might be useful to me. I'd turn that chilly disposition loose on to the people who deserved it. You needed to keep your head down a bit after your last disaster, but some time spent with Inspector Sutcliffe could take care of that. Maybe it'd even give you a few lessons in what not to do. I think I made a mistake, though. I think there's too much missing from you.' He let that sink in for a minute. 'Cartwright's going nowhere. Fuck him. But you and I trusted each other once. Tell me what happened here. And make it good, eh? Make it fucking brilliant.'

'I don't know anything about it, sir.'

'Playing dumb? Well, they say the best lies always have some truth in them. Who'd believe the most amoral man on the force would grow a conscience over some teenage tart spreading them for a guy off TV?' He looked at me, his red eyes stabbing into mine. 'I'd believe it, though, wouldn't I, Aidan? I'd believe you've got a soft spot in that direction. I'd believe you can lie through your teeth for months on end and rip off everyone around you. I'd believe anything but you sitting there telling me that you don't know how a bag of *weapons-grade* cocaine ended up in Cartwright's suitcase.'

'You said it yourself, Superintendent. He's a guy off TV. Thought the rules didn't apply to him. He was bound to go under the wheels one day.'

Parrs smiled darkly. 'In spite of what you may think, I have no time for Oliver Cartwright. He speaks for, and to, human waste. I'm happy he's out of my hair for good. I hope they lock him up with nothing but his sturdiest leather belt for company. But I assume you know who he's connected to? The white knight of the alt-right, they call him. For your sake I hope he doesn't reach the same conclusion I have. Because if he does, he might take that sturdy leather belt from round his neck and put it to a different use. Sell it to some lifer for the mobile phone up his arse, make a few calls while holding his nose. No, I'm prepared to turn a blind eye on this one, let you kids work it out between yourselves. What I really called you here to ask is why your thorough and wide-ranging investigation into the Oxford Road dustbin fires necessitates the MOD's involvement?'

'It's related to the unidentified man from the Palace, sir.'

'And how's Smiley Face related to some dustbin fires?'

'I just filed my report. It seems he was the one setting them.' Parrs didn't move and I went on. 'I have video evidence, sir.'

His jaw tightened. 'No doubt.'

'The man was burning objects in the dustbins, including, in at least one instance, a large sum of money. The surrounding objects led us back to the Midland Hotel, where we found the man's personal effects. They led Detective Inspector Sutcliffe and me to a woman who used to be in a relationship with a Mr Ross Browne. We believe Browne's the dead man found in the Palace. He's ex-military. Rotated out with post-traumatic stress disorder.'

Parrs sat back. 'Good work,' he said. 'I mean it, good work. You'll be pleased to hear I had Stromer on the phone earlier as well. Retracted some of her more vitriolic remarks on your character. You were right about that body-dump in the canal being linked to the smiling man, too. It's almost as though you've got a sixth sense on this one . . .'

His red eyes burrowed into mine.

'. . . She still thinks you're a car crash, don't get me wrong. But in this instance you've rolled the vehicle and landed back on your wheels. Maybe they're the same wheels Ollie Cartwright went under. So for the moment you're three for three. I shouldn't be wasting your time, should I? In fact, let's sever ties completely, eh?'

'Sir, I need to bring Detective Inspector Sutcliffe in on the owners of the Palace. Events are unfolding that—'

'I think not, Detective Constable. I'd rather not waste two bodies. Sutty's talents are better deployed elsewhere . . .' He saw the look pass across my face. 'Something to say about that, Detective Constable?'

'No, sir.'

'If you've got concerns about a serving officer, now's your chance to air them.'

'The sound of my own voice doesn't interest me so much.'

'Could have fucking fooled me.'

'Handling the owners alone is too big a job, sir.'

'Maybe so, but you just do your own thing. Really get stuck in there. Tell you what, I'll even make you a bargain. You've got no time for Sutty, so show me some real detective work. Tell me who this smiling man is, a name, and I'll find Sutty a new partner . . .'

Parrs was always making these double-or-nothing bargains.

'. . . And if the gangs haven't got the message about the price on your head, and if Cartwright's friends *have* got the message about you planting drugs in his suitcase, and if these smiling man developments take you to unexpected places . . .' He smiled darkly. 'Well, you'll be on your own, won't you? That's how you like it best, after all.'

4

I left my meeting with Parrs trying to think of new angles of enquiry for the Palace. My unanswered questions were mainly about Natasha Reeve and Freddie Coyle. Reeve had been receiving notes about her husband having an affair with Geoff Short. Someone had wanted to hurt them, and they had two people in common that I knew of.

Aneesa Khan and Anthony Blick.

I called Aneesa.

'Detective Constable Waits, I can't say I'm thrilled to hear from you.'

'If your clients had been honest with me at the start of all this I wouldn't have had to shake the truth out of them.'

'But we keep returning to the same question. What does an affair have to do with a dead man in the Palace? Have you had any progress on that front at all?'

'One fact in isolation tells us nothing. That's why we need them all. Speaking of which, I still need to talk to your boss.'

'He's due back from Thailand next week—'

'That's too late. This case is changing every day and now it's putting other people at risk.'

'Fine,' she said after a moment's silence. 'But it's the middle of the night there now, and I want to be there when you speak to him.' I agreed to meet her at the firm's office the following day where we'd set up a conference call with Blick. I wanted to ask her about the affair that had been going on under her nose as well. Earlier that day, at a loose end as to who the blood in the Midland could belong to, I'd found Blick's Facebook profile. I was almost disappointed to see he was still living it up. Topless, surrounded by another group of young Thai women.

5

I walked to the Waterstones on Deansgate looking for a copy of *The Rubáiyát of Omar Khayyám*. After being directed to the poetry section, I found several editions, some with different publishers and translators, even different languages. I bought the one that looked most approachable and left, by now late to meet Ricky, Sian's fiancé. When I got to the Rising Sun he was hunched over a pint, sitting at a small table facing the door.

His glass was half-empty.

'Sorry I'm late,' I said, approaching the table.

'Don't worry about it. Get us another of these?'

'Sure.' I went to the bar and looked back at him. He'd avoided my eyes and I thought he looked drunk. I realized how I might look to him. A stubbled, perma-scowled detective with a bad history, who was suddenly hanging around the woman he loved. I realized I might look like a bully. His calling me and coming here had obviously taken some courage and I felt faintly ashamed for provoking it. I paid, put our drinks down on the table and took a seat opposite him. He swallowed the remainder of his beer and reached for the fresh one.

'Listen, Ricky. I'm glad you called.'

'Yeah?'

'Yeah. Look, I don't know what you think you walked in on the other day, Sian holding my hand, but it wasn't anything romantic.' He made eye contact for the first time. 'The truth is that some guy had been in the bar earlier that day, talking about me. He told Sian something that contradicted what I'd told her.'

He frowned. 'I don't follow . . .'

I went all-in. 'I lied to Sian when we were together. If you want to ask her about it, that's your business. I don't know how much you know about me . . .' His eyes flicked up again. A quick google would have revealed articles about my suspension. Drugs-related corruption charges that had mysteriously vanished. 'Anyway, Sian was upset with me. When you walked in she'd grabbed my hand, angrily, to make a point. That's all there is to it.' He still didn't say anything and I found myself filling the silence. 'I hadn't seen her in over a year until the other night, and the first thing she told me was that she was seeing someone. That she was happy. I'd hate to think I'd affected that in any way.'

Ricky was nodding, still not meeting my eyes. 'OK,' he said. 'Yeah, thanks.'

'It looks like you've got something else to say.'

'Look, I appreciate all that. I believe you. You didn't have to say it and you did.' He shrugged. 'She told me about it anyway. You lied to her about having a sister or something. Weird.' He took another big drink and reached inside his pocket. He pulled out an envelope and placed it on the table between us. 'I wanted to talk about this, though.'

My name was scrawled across the envelope.

'What's going on?' I said.

'This shit about your sister. It did annoy me a bit, but I trust Sian. I believed what she said. That's nothing to do with this.' I opened the envelope and looked inside.

Photographs.

I poured them out on to the table. They were all of me. Taken from various distances, as some kind of surveillance, while I moved through the city. At first I thought it was a nameless, shapeless threat. Related to the hit that had been hanging over my head, apparently for months.

But I saw that they told a story.

The first picture showed me leaving my flat with a black plastic bag under my arm. The next few showed my car driving across town to the Chorlton Street station. Then there were several of the crippled man who'd been raking the phone machines, pretending to look for change, while I watched. Next, a series of pictures showing me leaving cash in one of the slots and collecting something afterwards. I knew what the rest would show and I went through them reluctantly.

Their inevitable chain of events.

Driving out to the Quays. Waiting outside Cartwright's building. Going inside with the bag. Leaving with nothing. The final picture showed me staring, directly at the camera. The car I'd seen pull away as I got outside. Somehow this one, with my face perfectly visible, looked most damning of all, like an admission of guilt. The times and dates were stamped in the corner of each picture.

I looked at Ricky. 'What's going on here?'

'Shouldn't I be asking you that?' I waited for an answer and he went on. 'I went to The Temple earlier, to see Sian. Found that envelope on a table. I was about to hand it in when I looked inside. Lucky for you I did . . .'

I thought he was telling the truth.

'When was this?'

'Today, when I called.'

'Who left them there?'

'I don't know.'

'Did you see anyone it might have been? Anyone acting weird?'

He shook his head. 'You're buying drugs, though, aren't you?'

I tried to think of a response but finally ignored the question. Swept the pictures back into the envelope. 'Have you shown these to anyone else?'

'Nah,' he said.

'Sian?' He shook his head and I looked inside the envelope again. 'Was there anything else in there?'

'There were some negatives,' he said, looking away.

'I want them,' I said, jamming the envelope into my jacket pocket.

'They're not here. Look . . .' He risked a glance up from the table. 'Sian hasn't seen them. I hope she doesn't . . .'

I tried to stay calm. 'Don't fuck around with this. Whoever left them there could be dangerous.'

'Dangerous to who? Not dangerous to me.'

I stared at him but his eyes remained fixed on the table. 'What do you want, Ricky?'

'I don't want anything, you've got that wrong.' I watched him, waited. 'It just looks like something really bad. And whoever took them, whoever left them obviously has it in for you. They obviously want to hurt you. I love Sian. We've got something really special going.' I could see him edging towards it. The real reason he was here. 'I don't want anything bad around her . . .'

'Right,' I said. 'You don't think she should have some say in who her friends are?'

'I suppose we could show her the pictures and ask?'

I looked at my untouched drink. 'I want those fucking negatives, I mean it.'

'Or what?' he said. 'You'll beat me up as well?'

I heard a sound, like something snapping in my ears. 'What did you just say?'

'I told you, Sian tells me everything.'

I couldn't speak. I shook my head, got up and walked out on to the street. Mainly to avoid introducing his skull to the wall. To avoid what he'd just said. I found myself looking over my shoulder as I went, turning my head at sudden movements. The sun blazed, indifferently, overhead, catching the angles of every object I passed. I felt like there were cameras, flashing, all about me.

6

I got back to the flat hot, distracted and stiff from another long day. My conversation with Ricky had been unnerving, and I could feel the weight of the envelope in my pocket, thick with pictures that could send me to jail. Or worse. I almost didn't want to think about who'd left them there.

The list was getting too long.

The top half was made up of people who'd now faded into the background of my life, criminals and acquaintances I'd wronged. The same people who'd put a price on my head. The rest of the list was made up of more recent additions. Oliver Cartwright, or at least his alt-right friends, felt likely until I stopped to think about it. Surely if they knew that I'd set him up, and if they could prove it, they'd use that information to begin legal proceedings against me. To free him. Then there was the smiling man. An aura of dread and uncertainty hung over the case, and discovering his name, hotel room, the blood patch, had only increased it. What had Parrs said? That I was on my own if the investigation took us to unexpected places. Perhaps he already knew it would. Then, of course, there was Ricky. I thought I believed his account, however much I might dislike him, but it was clear he wanted me out of Sian's life at all costs, and I'd been wrong about people before. As I got the key into the lock I heard a scuffed footstep behind me.

There was someone at the end of the street, watching.

He was unmistakably the same man who'd been into The

Temple the day before, asking about my drinking habits, my friends. He was built solid, with the purposeful, unshowy muscle and simple prison tattoos that Sian had described. He wore blue jeans and a black T-shirt, pulled tight across a large, well-developed chest. I could see half-crescents of sweat under his arms and moisture glistening off the sides of his neck. His hair on one side was neat, buzzed short. On the other side it looked like it had been burned away, with odd, untended tufts protruding at crazy angles. His skin on this side ranged from light purple to dark, except for the area surrounding his dead eye. There, the skin was caved in, cratered and scabbed over with near-black scar tissue. It was this side of his face that he had turned to me and, as with Sian, I got the impression he was inflicting it, aware of its power. His head moved slightly, and I felt his left eye, the good one, searching my features.

And just like that, I knew him.

He spat a cigarette on to the kerb, crushed it beneath his boot and then walked, easily, towards me. I tried to get my key in the door but my hands were sweating, my fingers wouldn't work. The man stopped a few feet away, and I smelt the second-hand smoke. It had been more than twenty years but I remembered it so well. It was blended with a new aroma. Urine, I thought, sweat.

'Can I help you with something?'

We both heard the shake in my voice and he smiled.

His mouth looked like a wound, ripped right across his face.

'Aidan Waits,' he said. His speech was impeded by the damage to his skin, coating his words in a wet clicking sound. 'Lives here . . .'

I looked at him.

Felt the heat beating off his skin.

'I don't know him,' I said.

He turned his face, as though using his dead eye to look down the street. He was allowing me to take in the unscarred side of his head. The living eye that I'd always tried to avoid. I turned back to the door, opened it and went through, slamming it behind me, feeling sick. I went up the stairs, feeling sunspots wash in front of my eyes, the blood doing laps of my veins. When I got inside and went to make myself a drink I saw that the bottle I'd recently opened, that I'd had one drink from, was empty. I went to the window and looked out. The man was gone.

The boy was running away from the house and down the path. He didn't need to rise out of his body now. In spite of the bag's shifting weight at his shoulder he felt lighter than air. His senses came alive, overwhelming him with information in one generous rush of blood to the head. The night, the moon and the stars. The cold air, stabbing in and out of his lungs.

He stopped when he saw a man, a shape, sitting on the car bonnet. The shape threw its cigarette and rose up, detaching itself from the shadows. It drew closer to the boy, meeting him in the middle ground between the car and the house.

'Is that it?' said Bateman, stepping into a patch of moonlight. The soft blue hue of his stubble looked like the flame from a blowtorch. The boy nodded. Bateman let out a breath and reached a hand behind the boy's ear. He retracted it, holding a coin out for him to take. 'Fucking gold mine,' he muttered, reaching for the bag. He froze then, staring over the boy's shoulder at the house, the smile on his face twisting into a grimace.

There was a skeleton standing in the doorway. The figure was uncomfortably tall, like a thing on stilts, and its emaciated, stick-insect legs didn't look like they could support even the frail body on top of them. It ducked under the doorway, transforming from something unreal into a pitifully tall, slender man. The man moved towards them, walking with the frightening, illogical gait of an arachnid. When he lifted an arm there was a flash of steel and the gun was suddenly visible. Bateman placed a hand on the boy's shoulder, his grip tightening as the figure took a final step into the light.

He was barefoot and his clothes were the rags that might once have been a suit. There was no shirt beneath his haggard, balding jacket, and his torso, a series of tight, grey double knots, was exposed to the elements.

There was something wrong with his hands.

It looked like he was wearing dark, sloppily applied nail polish, but the boy realized he was bleeding. The man's fingernails had been removed. The skin on his face was pulled tight, and his eyes were buried so deep inside his skull that they were just two black holes.

'*Bagh* . . .' he said.

The boy recognized the voice from behind the door that he'd unlocked. He saw that the figure's lips were loose, hollow and caved in. That what he'd taken at first for stubble was a beard of dried blood. Someone had pulled out the man's teeth. When neither Bateman nor the boy moved, the man threw his head to the other side and shouted.

'*Bagh!*'

'All right,' said Bateman, drawing the boy towards him. 'We're going back . . .'

'*Bagh!*' screamed the slender man, spraying red spit. '*Bagh! Bagh! Bagh!*' Bateman and the boy stopped, hypnotized by the gun, which was drifting from side to side. With a frown of concentration the man raised his free arm, so both hands were wrapped around the grip. Breathing deeply, focusing his attention, he swung the gun barrel downward, pointing it at the boy.

'*Bag,*' he said with effort.

Automatically, the boy started to slip the strap off his shoulder, but Bateman's hand moved on top of it, gripping it into his skin. They stood like that for a moment until a woman's voice, tired but gloating, came from the forgotten car behind them.

'Give him the bag, Bates,' said the boy's mother. 'Face facts.'

Bateman's grip on the boy's shoulder tightened.

'No chance,' he whispered.

The boy's mother raised her voice. 'Give him the ba—'

'*No chance*,' screamed Bateman. He pushed the boy forward and projected himself at the thin man. 'Gonna smoke a kid, are ya?' The boy stared into the gun barrel. Felt the ground sinking beneath him. After what felt like forever, the gun started to shake, finally drooping down at the ground in answer. 'Didn't think so,' said Bateman, touching the boy's shoulder.

As he did so, a new light emerged. Waves of pulsing blue, washing through the trees.

The sound of sirens.

The figure's head turned in their direction and his body started to convulse. '*Hur*,' he said. '*Hur-hur-hur*.' His laugh revealed blackened, bloody gums. Bateman's mouth fell open, watching the lights draw closer. A mechanical roar surprised him and he turned to see the Skoda starting up, its headlights flashing momentarily. The boy's mother made a three-point turn and drove in the opposite direction to the sirens. He saw his sister, wide-eyed, pressing herself into the rear window as they got further away. After a moment Bateman laughed, squatting down like he'd forgotten the thin man, the gun, the police.

'Wally, mate,' he said to the boy. 'Them trees. Go as far as you can, hide that bag, remember where you've gone and mark the spot. Tell no fucker. We're coming back for it.' He stood and looked at the figure. The boy didn't move. 'Go,' said Bateman, without looking at him. When the boy still didn't move the man stepped between him and the gun.

'*Run, Aidan, you little shit!*'

At the sound of his real name the boy started across the road, breaking towards the woods where the car had been parked. He felt the gun like a pair of hateful eyes, burning into the back of his head, and burst through the foliage, feet beating wet ground.

The sirens were on top of him, louder now.

He smashed into clawing thorns, thumping through bushes and tree trunks. He saw blue lights from the road, illuminating a possible path, and threw himself down a bank, clearing the way with one hand, holding the bag with the other.

The sirens were going off in his head.

He crashed down into a dirty stream, and felt the cold water up to his waist, tasted the blood and soil in his mouth. He started to crawl backwards, out of the mire, breathing hard, holding the bag up over his head. The sirens were screaming.

Then a gunshot cracked, unmistakably, through the trees, and everything stopped. Everything but the boy. He pulled himself on to dry ground and staggered deeper into the woods. Away from the house, the thin man and the gun. Towards anything as long as it was away from Bateman. He could still hear him like a broken record in his head.

'*Run, Aidan.*'

———

VII
Ultraviolence

1

You forget things after a while, and I pieced together my understanding of that night from three main sources, none of which were entirely reliable. The first was from my own memory, which I'd consciously felt morphing throughout my lifetime, starting as a series of facts featuring people I'd known, and ending as a story filled with characters, infected by my imagination. My memories had become unreliable on the subject through years of drug and alcohol abuse. Over time, they absorbed the violent, menacing tone of my nightmares, until they were entirely transformed from a linear sequence of events into a swollen dream sequence that grew with me. Warping and altering like my face in a mirror. They were important for understanding the feeling, though, which had never changed or gone away.

The wide open, panoramic fear.

The second source was through my interpretation of the police and social services interviews which I'd given at the time. As a child I hadn't understood them, but the questions were designed to build a consistent narrative, and, through repetition, had made me certain on some points. My sister and I had been woken in the middle of the night. Taken to a car we'd never seen before by our mother and the man she shared a bed with. We'd driven for a long time, out to a grey-brick farmhouse. There, I'd been sent inside by the man I knew as Bateman to retrieve a bag from an attic. I was told not to enter any other room but had disobeyed him when I felt a breeze coming from the kitchen. The windows had been blown in by gunfire and the room itself was the scene of explosive physical violence. I saw a woman who looked as though she'd been tortured. Whose throat had been cut, saturating the walls with blood. Leaving the kitchen, I'd heard the sound of someone crying behind a locked door. Once I'd retrieved the bag, I'd been frozen by this sound. Whether through simple humanity or as a conscious act of disobedience against Bateman, I'd turned the key in the door and left the house.

The final and most illuminating source for what I knew of that night came in the form of newspaper articles I'd searched out as a teen. For years I'd carried around the fear and the facts, as I understood them, devoid of the context. In the late nineties, Nicholas Fisk had been a powerful player in the Northern drug scene, a precursor to the more business-minded success stories that followed him. He eschewed violence where possible, building respect, and a rumoured fortune, through negotiation and deal-making.

Then one day, no one arrived to collect Fisk's two boys from school. Three men had kidnapped their parents, taking them to a remote, dilapidated farmhouse which, it later transpired, Fisk owned. He'd kept it secret from everyone but his wife as some kind of safe house. The kidnappers had watched him for weeks, believing he stored a part of his vast, illegal fortune there. Locked inside, they'd started a campaign of intimidation against the Fisks to coerce information from them.

I still remember the moment.

Fifteen or sixteen years old, hunched over a newspaper reel in the local library, feeling the world stop when I saw Bateman's face staring out at me from a black-and-white front page.

He'd been one of the three kidnappers.

Press speculation was that he'd discovered the whereabouts of Fisk's wealth himself, and betrayed the others. Anonymously tipped off Fisk's organization and, at the very last second, warned his friends inside the house that there were men approaching. He'd left to a safe distance, watching, while they wiped each other out. Speculation was all the press had, because Bateman had never spoken at his trial or in prison.

It was difficult for him to speak.

The reports all ended the same way. When Bateman had returned to pick over the spoils, Fisk had got loose, found a gun inside the house and shot his kidnapper in the head. There'd been a child on the scene, whose name, sex and age couldn't legally be reported. But he'd been an eight-year-old boy. He'd run into the trees and hadn't been found until the following day. Bateman had needed him to get into the attic, to edge inside the narrow space that only the slender Nicholas Fisk, or a small child, could manage. Bateman had been using the boy in con jobs since moving in with his mother. The size, the perceived innocence of a child, was what he thought of as his innovation to the field. He thought of the kids in his care as untapped gold mines, and he called the boy Wally, which was short for wallet.

Everyone else called him Aidan.

2

We were in a hospital waiting room, preparing for the formal identification of Ross Browne. The smiling man. There was Sutty,
myself and Amy Burroughs, the nurse who'd been in a relationship
with Browne before he left the city.

The only person we'd found who could identify him.

The Coroner's Officer was explaining her role to Amy, but I
wasn't listening. I'd slept badly and been awoken by another phone
call with nothing but breathing on the other end. When I'd looked
out of my window on to the street there was no one there, but I
knew it was Bateman.

I was wondering why he was back.

What he wanted and why me. If it was for money, he was about
to be sorely disappointed by a policeman's salary. Revenge? On an
eight-year-old boy who'd opened the wrong door? That didn't
make sense, either. And he'd been watching me. Waiting. His
arrival coinciding with that of the pictures set off a series of internal
alarms through my nervous system. All of them saying the same
word over and over again: *Fuck*.

'Aidan,' said Sutty, clicking his fingers in my face. I looked up at
the Coroner's Officer who'd been talking to me.

'Mrs Burroughs would like you to accompany her inside.'

'Yes,' I said, looking at Amy. 'Of course.'

The Officer turned to her. 'And do you have any questions for
me now?'

'I don't think so,' she said.

'OK. Do you think you're ready to go through?' Amy suddenly looked very pale and the Coroner's Officer smiled. 'We're a little early, anyway.' We all took a seat for a minute, adjusting to our surroundings. The strangest thing about identifying a body is how normal it all seems. You're sitting in a standard waiting room that could serve any purpose, have any kind of news, good or bad, on the other side of it. It's just someone's job and it happens every day. This time it's your turn. Tomorrow it's someone else's.

'I think I'm ready,' Amy said quietly.

The Coroner's Officer smiled again and led the two of us to the door. As ever, the first thing I noticed on the other side was the impossible taste and smell of formaldehyde. The second thing I noticed was Karen Stromer, watching us from the corner of the room like a gargoyle. When she looked at me it wasn't with prejudice or dislike. It was with disappointment, I thought. The Officer led us to a gleaming stainless-steel table on wheels. There was a dull-green sheet drawn over a body and an ageless, pale man standing beside it. When the Officer turned to look at us I realized Amy had remained by the door, hadn't walked any further.

'Amy?' said the Officer.

'It's not him . . .'

It sounded like denial. The assistant hadn't even drawn back the sheet.

'Amy,' said the Officer. 'I know this is distressing—'

But she was shaking her head, smiling. 'It's not him.' She looked at me, then at the body on the table. 'His feet,' she said. They were the only part of the smiling man's body that were visible. 'Ross lost his right leg in Iraq. That's how we met, he had post-traumatic stress.'

The Officer and I looked at each other. She recovered well. 'OK, well, that's good news. Can I ask you to formalize the identification?' My mind was coming slowly back to the scene in front of me. The dead body didn't belong to Ross Browne. We'd lost our positive identification on the smiling man.

'Of course,' said Amy, stepping forward with a shake in her voice, but also some lightness, some relief. She stood beside me as the assistant drew back the sheet from the man's head.

I recognized him, of course.

The Palace Hotel.

He'd been sitting there in that room, absorbing the kaleidoscopic lights of the city, emitting a strange energy of his own, as if he was at the centre of something awful. Here, naked on a slab, he was stripped of all that. He seemed mundane, pale and powerless. I looked at Amy. Her mouth had fallen open in shock and I wondered if she'd been wrong somehow.

'Is this man Ross Browne?' said the Coroner's Officer.

Amy Burroughs didn't speak, and she slowly began to double up, like she'd been punched in the stomach. She tried to reach out for the table but didn't quite make it. She passed out and I caught her before she fell.

We were back in the waiting room. Amy was drinking a glass of water, being attended to by the Coroner's Officer. Sutty and I were looking on from the corner of the room.

'Take it we've got our man,' he grunted.

I shook my head. Kept my voice low. 'She said not.'

'What? A nurse fainting at the sight of a dead bloke she's never met? My arse.'

I turned. 'She said Ross Browne couldn't be the man in there. She said Ross Browne lost a leg in Iraq.'

Sutty closed his eyes.

'I know. But when they pulled the sheet back she had an intense reaction to the body, whoever it was.'

'Well,' said Sutty. 'Even if we can't pull Browne's full military record, we should be able to find out how many limbs he shipped home with. Was she telling the truth?'

'I thought so, but . . .'

'But what?'

266

'Her reaction says not. It was too much. She saw something in there.'

'Find out what.' I looked at him but he kept his eyes locked on Amy. His voice was a whisper. 'You can be a shoulder to cry on, but a cold fucking shoulder. Take her home and make her talk.'

3

I was driving Amy Burroughs home after the negative identification of Ross Browne. Sutty was chasing down his military records, or at least confirmation that Browne had lost his leg abroad. I was rattled. Tired and confused. I couldn't quite shake Amy's reaction to the body, and it filled me with uncomfortable questions. Either she was lying about the identification or, worse, something even more complicated was going on with the dead man.

'I need to know what happened in there.'

'Nothing happened,' she said after some time.

'That was quite a reaction for nothing.'

'It's not him,' she said, definitively.

But my patience was gone. 'You're keeping something back. What did you see?' I pulled up around the corner from her street, remembering that things were sensitive at home. When I killed the engine and looked at her she was watching me out of the corner of her eye. She turned to face me fully.

'You're imagining things, Detective.'

'I didn't imagine catching you in there.'

'My hero . . .' She looked away.

'Well, answer me this at least. Are you OK?'

'I'm fine, I'm just overworked. Just tired.'

'I'm not asking about your constitution. I'm asking if you're safe, if your boy is.'

'From what?' she said, toying with the mass of thick, plastic bracelets at her wrist.

'From whatever just scared you out of consciousness.'

The set of her jaw hardened and she smiled bitterly. 'I get it,' she said. 'You're *here* for me . . .'

'I—'

'My husband's not home so you want to come inside? Very subtle . . .'

'What?'

'You're not as slick as you think you are,' she said. It sounded like she was talking to someone else but it still landed. 'I want to get out, I want to go home.'

I started up again and turned on to her street. When I pulled up she left the car without another word, not looking back until she'd got her front door open and stepped through it. Standing there in the hallway alone, I thought she looked like a woman with a secret. She paused inside the house and then turned, took a step, as though there was something she wanted to say to me. Then she disappeared inside, leaving the door ajar.

I was thinking about following her to continue the conversation when there was a knock at the window. I turned to see an elderly woman in a dressing gown, a neighbour of Amy's. I buzzed down the glass.

'Can I help you?' I said, a little too sharply. I was tired and the question marks were ganging up over my head. I wasn't in the mood for rubberneckers.

'Oh, sorry to bother you,' she said, pursing her lips. 'But you are a police officer?'

'No, I'm sorry,' I said, really meaning it. 'I am a police officer, yes.'

'Yes,' she said, restored somewhat by my gesture towards civility. 'I saw you and your partner sitting out here the other night with nothing better to do . . .'

'How did you know we were police?'

'Shifty eyes,' she said. 'Put it this way, you'd both go hungry as salesmen. Do you not need to speak to me?'

'Speak to you about what?'

'About the prowler.'

I got out of the car and walked her back to her front door. 'What prowler are we talking about here?'

'Well, like I told her,' she said, nodding towards Amy's house. 'He was sniffing round like a dog with two dicks. Shuffling up and down the street, staring at her house. Except, when he thought no one was watching, his shuffle went away. He'd look through the windows and the letterbox, then when he saw someone coming, he'd shuffle off again.'

'When was this?'

'Last Friday.'

The day before the smiling man died.

'Can you describe him for me?'

'Well . . .' She paused for maximum effect. I tried to stay calm. 'Now let me see. He was a good bit older than you. Wore a brown suit, asylum-seeker tan. There was something about his eyes, though . . .' She frowned in concentration. 'Blue. Very blue. They didn't go with the rest of him. Stood out from across the street.'

I kept my voice level. 'Did this man speak to, or otherwise interact with, Ms Burroughs?'

'Not that I saw, sweetheart, but I told her to report him to the police. Men these days—'

'You've been a great help,' I said, crossing the road to Amy's house, where the door remained ajar.

The smiling man had been here, and on the day before he died.

His secondary connection to Amy Burroughs was already established. Her phone number found in his possession. The book that she claimed she'd given to someone else. There were possible mundane explanations for that. Theft. Obsession. But a visit here was too much to overlook, especially given that Amy's neighbour had told her about a suspicious man watching the property. Especially given that she'd failed to mention it. I pushed the open door and stepped into the hallway.

I felt glass cracking under my shoes.

The picture frames lining the walls had all been smashed in.

'Amy,' I called out.

There was no answer.

I couldn't decide if I was looking at a psychotic breakdown or an intruder. I was about to call for back-up when I saw that the person in each of the smashed picture frames was Amy's little boy. I felt certain she hadn't done it herself.

As I took another step I heard whimpering from further inside. When I reached the end of the hall I saw her. She was pale, sweating, with tears streaming down her face. Her hand had been nailed into the wall. As I stepped around the corner I saw a man in a black balaclava holding a nail gun to her temple. He turned and I took a step back. He hissed a few more words into her ear and bolted through the kitchen.

'Try not to move,' I said, approaching her. She was clearly in pain but nodded. I followed the man through to the kitchen and out the back door. I was just in time to see him vault over the fence. When I got to it and looked after him he was gone. I went back into the house, called Dispatch for back-up and an ambulance for Amy. As I tried to talk to her she continued to stare over my shoulder in shock. Following her eyeline I saw that all the photographs of her little boy above the mantle had been nail-gunned into the wall, through his eyes.

4

Amy had been taken to hospital and officers had been sent to secure the safety of her boy. He was fine, still with the friend who babysat for her while she and her husband were at work. Both of them would need protection until the threat, whatever it was, had passed. The man with the nail gun had got away and Amy was too traumatized to tell us anything. When I'd asked what the man had been saying, hissing, into her ear she'd started to tell me something and then stopped. Her eyes had settled on the pictures of her boy.

The nails sticking out of his eyes.

'He didn't say anything,' she said.

I returned to the station to fill Sutty in, finding him on the phone, mid-conversation. 'Yeurgh,' he said. 'Yeurgh. Actually, someone just arrived who I'd like you to talk to. Thanks for your help.' He threw the receiver at me and I caught it, then he dropped into his chair like a depth charge and watched.

'Hello,' I said. 'Can I ask who I'm speaking with?'

'This is Ross Browne.'

I rubbed my face and glanced at Sutty, who was smiling. Browne confirmed everything that Amy Burroughs had told us. They'd dated, briefly, five years before, when he'd rotated out of Iraq with an injury. When the city's insomnia started amplifying his own, he'd moved to the coast and they'd split up. He'd never been back since, so he claimed, and had an airtight alibi for the events of Saturday night, and for all the incidents since.

For fuck's sake, I thought.

He didn't even know she'd had a kid, so I left questions of paternity unasked.

Sutty waved for my attention. 'Ask about the book . . .'

When I did, I expected a story about how it had been lost or stolen. Something that would at least give us the smiling man's first interaction with the text. I was surprised when Browne said he had his copy there in his lap.

'We're talking about *The Rubáiyát of Omar Khayyám*, given to you by Amy Burroughs?'

'Only copy I ever had,' he said.

'You're certain it hasn't been replaced?'

'Course.'

'Could you check the last page for me, Mr Browne? Read me the final line?'

I heard him turning pages. '*Tamam Shud*,' he said.

I looked at Sutty, who was blowing out his cheeks. 'And nothing's been torn from it or amended?'

'I know it's the one Amy gave me cus her writing's there at the front. She's OK, isn't she?'

'As well as can be. Could you read me that dedication?'

Haltingly, he did so. It was word-for-word the same as that found in the unidentified man's copy. As he talked I lowered myself into a chair, resting my head in my hands. Either it had been counterfeited or she'd dedicated two copies. The local police had taken a statement from Browne and it all checked out. He hadn't been near the city in the last few days. I thanked him for his help and hung up.

I looked, flatly, at Sutty.

He looked, flatly, back at me.

I couldn't even get the first swear word out before the phone started ringing again.

It was Aneesa Khan.

'Good morning,' I said, not really feeling it. 'We're still on for later?'

'That's what I'm calling about. I'm afraid it looks as though our conference call with Anthony might not be possible.'

'Really,' I said.

Aneesa told me she'd been trying to get hold of Anthony Blick all morning to no avail. She said she'd last spoken to him, briefly, over a week before, but this morning his phone just rang out. Or at least it had at first.

Now it didn't ring at all.

Sutty eyed me suspiciously while I tried to talk around the facts of a side-investigation I was keeping from him.

'Are you still in the office?' I asked Aneesa.

5

Blick's was the respectable city-centre workplace you'd expect. A light, open reception area with biometric security measures and ergonomic chairs. A young woman on the front desk took me through to Ms Khan's office, asked if she could get me anything and then left, closing the door behind her when I declined. Aneesa looked like she was sleeping badly, too, but she greeted me with a tired smile and I took a seat.

'You said you last spoke to Mr Blick over a week ago. Can I ask what your conversation was about?'

'Nothing special. As you know, Anthony's made a point of taking some time out. So we have a monthly phone call where I brief him on any developments at the firm. Long-term clients, personnel, office politics . . .'

'And he sounded OK?'

'He sounded like he was having the time of his life.'

'He didn't say anything that struck you as odd or out of the ordinary?'

'Nothing . . .'

'Are you in charge of the office in Mr Blick's absence?'

She nodded. 'We've always worked very closely together.' My face didn't change but when she looked up she said, 'Strictly professional.'

'Does Mr Blick have a partner?' She shook her head. 'Any close friends or family?'

'He works extremely hard . . .'

'You're telling me there's no one in his life who'd notice his absence?'

'Anthony lives for this place, but that's partly what this trip's about. His health scare last year. He wanted to go and see some of the world before he felt too old . . .' She sounded like she was trying to convince herself of something. She was worrying a thread at her sleeve.

'Do you have his home address?'

'What's going on?' she said, her eyes moving on to mine.

'As far as we know, his phone's run out of battery, but that's no reason for us not to check up on things.'

We drove out to Anthony Blick's Carrwood home, while Aneesa described it to me in glowing terms. The venue for the office's annual Christmas party, where her boss curated an evening of fine wine and dining. Last year's had been particularly grand, with Blick treating his employees to several expensive bottles and a catered, eight-course meal.

'What does he make of the events at the Palace?' I asked. Aneesa was silent for a moment. 'You have told him?'

She stared straight ahead. 'I emailed him about the break-in . . .'

'But not about the body?'

'He never replied,' she said quietly. We both began turning scenarios over in our heads.

'There's something else I need to ask you,' I said. 'Do you remember a Geoff Short? Worked for Blick's up until last year . . .'

'Geoff, of course.'

'How well do you know him?'

'What are you asking? He was a colleague, a friend.'

'So you didn't know he was having an extra-marital affair with one of your clients?' I chanced a look at her.

'What? No . . .' She connected my statement with what Natasha Reeve had told us, about discovering Freddie's affair. 'Oh my God. But Geoff's married . . .'

'His wife's in the dark, and I said as long as it wasn't relevant to the case she could stay that way. Do you know her?'

'Only socially. I haven't seen her in a long time, though. She was teaching out in America for most of last year.'

'Apparently so.'

'. . . You don't think she sent those notes to Natasha?'

I shook my head. 'I checked her out. She was definitely in Washington, teaching at the time, and the notes were hand-delivered. Obviously she could have had a surrogate, but it all starts to feel unwieldy.' When I chanced another look at Aneesa she was frowning, turning over who else might be responsible, I thought.

The list of people connected to both Frederick Coyle and Geoff Short wasn't a long one, and her name was on it. Freddie Coyle preferred men, but for all I knew she might have had a pre-existing affair with Short. She might even have sent the notes out of loyalty to Natasha, but that felt like a leap. From what I'd seen, Natasha Reeve treated Aneesa no more warmly than she treated me.

'You don't mind, do you?' said Aneesa, breaking into my thoughts.

She was holding up a cigarette.

'No, go ahead. The vaping didn't work out, then?'

'I don't know where I left it – my mind's all over the place.'

She lit up and took a drag. It was the first time she'd looked relaxed since I'd met her.

The house was a large, detached property with bay windows and a herringbone wood door. A long driveway wound through the garden, which was brilliant green under the sunlight, looking sharp and well loved, considering its owner was out of the country. There was a cream-coloured Lexus beside the house, and a messy handyman van next to that.

'Is the car Anthony's?'

Aneesa frowned. 'I don't think so.'

There were voices coming from the hallway, the sound of a portable radio and the smell of paint. I knocked lightly and pushed it open. A man on his knees with a paint roller looked up at me with a questioning face.

'Hi, we're looking for the owner . . .'

'Mrs Hardy,' he shouted over his shoulder.

A woman stuck her head round the corner and, seeing us, walked down the hallway.

'Can I help?' she said, leaning comfortably into the frame.

'I'm Detective Constable Aidan Waits, we're looking for Anthony Blick . . .'

'Anthony Blick?'

'I believe he owns the house . . .'

She was already shaking her head.

'Excuse me,' said Aneesa, incredulously. 'I had Christmas dinner with him here . . .'

The woman looked between us with a smile. 'And he sold it to me in January.'

6

According to the rest of his office, no one had been in contact with Anthony Blick since Aneesa, over a week ago, and no one had seen him since he left for his trip, six months before. I didn't raise the fact that the timing coincided with the breakdown of Natasha and Freddie's marriage, the vicious, anonymous notes, but it played on my mind.

By the time we got back to the firm it was last thing on a Friday afternoon, and the small team were already filing out for pre-weekend drinks. We went to the office. Trawled through Anthony Blick's address book for a half-brother Aneesa vaguely remembered. When we got him on the phone he claimed they'd fallen out years before and not spoken since. Aneesa got up from the desk abruptly and started for her own office.

'Facebook,' she said. 'He's been all over it.' She logged on to her own computer and sent several messages in quick succession, none of which were acknowledged or answered. We were both staring at the screen, at a loss, when it refreshed.

A new picture was posted to his account.

It was similar in style to the one Freddie Coyle had shown me when I'd first interviewed him. Similar in style to the one I'd seen when casually searching for Blick's page the previous night. It was Anthony Blick, a large, red-faced man, with his shirt wide open, and his arm around a young Thai woman. Aneesa and I looked at each other in confusion, and I checked the time.

279

It was 6 p.m. exactly.

'Scroll back,' I said. 'I want to see what time the others were posted.'

The previous picture, showing Blick with a street vendor, had been posted at 6 p.m. the day before. The one before that, showing Blick stood by a body of water, was posted at 6 p.m. the day before that. Blick at a restaurant: 6 p.m. Hotel lobby: 6 p.m. Roof terrace: 6 p.m.

'Oh, fuck,' Aneesa said. 'They're auto-posting.'

Aneesa had officially reported Anthony Blick missing, and I'd called Natasha Reeve and Freddie Coyle to tell them the news. I also wanted to know when each of them had spoken to him last. Both had supported his decision to take some time out in the wake of his health scare the previous year, and apparently neither had anything but email contact with him since.

My next job was to begin tracing his movements. Phone, bank and flight records. Mobile information was simplest. The rest would take time. As a precautionary measure, and with Aneesa's consent, I asked SOCO to attempt the collection of DNA from Blick's office. He'd seemingly walked out on his life with some level of premeditation, and I wondered if he was tied into the smiling man's murder. The real revelation came when I viewed his mobile data.

Anthony Blick's phone had never left the city.

Anthony Blick's phone had been switched off since the day he'd been due to leave for Thailand.

I was trying to come to some kind of conclusion on this when my own phone started to vibrate.

It was Sian.

It had been a long day, and the last time we spoke she'd been angry with me. That wasn't the real reason I hesitated, though. The photographs that Ricky found had kept me awake for hours after my last shift, then when I'd finally closed the curtains on the morning sun, finally closed my eyes, someone buzzed for my flat. There was no one at the door when I went, cautiously, down the stairs, but someone continued to buzz it, at irregular intervals, until I gave up on sleep, showered, and left. Knowing that Bateman was the man behind my harassment only made things worse. He could have gone back to the bar. He could have shown Sian the pictures of me, and she could have come to the same conclusions Ricky had.

That I was using drugs again.

'*Beat me up as well?*' Ricky had said. '*I told you, Sian tells me everything.*'

I thought of the final night we'd spent together. We hadn't talked about my newly emerging sleep troubles. The night terrors that left me exhausted by morning, and left her cautious around me, afraid, I thought. I'd started spending more time away, more nights, making poor excuses for why I couldn't meet her at the end of a shift and why I couldn't spend a day off in her company. After some weeks of this, she'd arrived on my doorstep one night with a bag of shopping and a smile. She'd kissed me on the cheek and walked inside like there was nothing wrong between us, and I got some idea of what I must mean to her. I remember standing in the doorway, watching her go inside, and getting some idea of what she meant to me. We fell back into our old routine that night, laughing about her regulars, worrying and wondering about mine. Finishing the bottle and then going to bed.

That night I dreamt of a family of four, driving out to a house in the middle of nowhere. I dreamt of a terrifying slender man and a woman with a wide-open throat.

I woke up to the sound of a gunshot.

When I did, I was at the foot of the bed. My head was in Sian's lap and she was talking quietly, telling me it was OK. The room was a mess and my first thought was that an earthquake had hit the building. Then I saw the marks on my hands. Broken nails, cuts and bruises. I got up, unsteadily, and looked about. The curtains had been ripped off the wall, a lampshade had been smashed. There was a crack in the window.

I'd gone into the bathroom.

Watched my face warp and alter in the glass, and thought I was going to be sick. I opened the toilet, saw bloody tissues inside it and tried to think. Sian was straightening up when I went back into the bedroom. She smiled at me and I noticed that her hair was down.

She never wore her hair down.

What a time to start thinking like a detective. I asked about it and she tried to walk around me. When I took a step closer, she took a step back. I pinned her up against the wall and moved her hair while she fought me off. There was a large plaster on the side of her face, covering a cut or a bruise.

I took a step back. My ears were ringing. 'Was that me?'

'It's OK . . .'

But I felt sick. I was walking out, getting dressed, going for the door.

'Aid,' she said. 'Aidan—'

'I want you gone when I get back.'

I'd said it without turning around.

I came, slowly, back to the present. The phone had almost vibrated off the table when I picked it up.

'Aid,' she said. 'Aidan . . .'

'Sian.'

'He's here again. That guy who was asking about you.'

7

My sister had a chubby face, intelligent, heart-wrenching blue eyes and a perpetual thinker's frown. Some of my earliest memories are of warming my hands on her head, which always seemed to be hot with thought or feeling. Too hot with thought and feeling for a five-year-old girl, but I only realized later that she was a preoccupied, sickly child. Malnourished and so scared of our mother that it could make her physically sick. To me she was simply my sister and to me this was simply our life.

I learned more about her from the reactions of others. The children in new schools, laughing because she wore her brother's hand-me-downs. Concerned adults, bending or crouching down to her height, quietly asking me how much sleep she got. The bags under her eyes looked like bruises. If questions persisted we'd stop going to school. We'd move house in the middle of the night, carrying our things in bin bags. Occasionally we stayed with friends, with friends of friends. Occasionally we stayed with strange, new men.

I was my mother's son. A hiding place within myself and a born liar, immune to new people and desensitized to our surroundings. But Annie was a human being. A musical child capable of thought and feeling. Around the houses, the various flats and homes, she was always humming or tapping out anxieties. Singing lovely, sad little songs of her own invention. I see now that it was her acknowledgement of our environment, its undeniable cause and effect, that so incensed our mother. I was older and she'd grown used to me, my numbness. My ability to dissolve in and out of rooms or situations.

Annie, on the other hand, couldn't hide her thoughts and feelings. She burned them out in fevers, turned them over all night in her head, until they were as plain to see as the frown on her face, the bags under her eyes. So our mother started to leave the room whenever Annie sang nervously to herself. She started to leave the house, locking us inside. Sometimes she'd be gone for an hour, sometimes she'd come back the next day, dancing through the front door all glass-eyed, still wearing her going-out clothes from the night before. This became normal, with the periods lengthening each time, until finally she didn't come back. We were locked inside, and we ran out of food on the second day. On the third, when Annie was too tired even to sing or tap, I dialled 999, dizzy with hunger, knowing on some level that it would make things worse. I don't remember who came for us or how they got inside. I remember being sent to a home with hard, damaged children for one week, before being released back into our mother's care.

She collected us wordlessly and never spoke of it again.

When we returned home I saw where the door had been kicked in to get us out. Deprived of her coping mechanism for the outward expression of her daughter's despair, our mother simply found a new one. And so my sister became accident-prone. At first, these accidents were minor. A fall, resulting in a bruise, a cut or scrape. Soon she started to really hurt herself. Broken fingers and toes. I didn't realize for some time that our mother was responsible. When I did I became inseparable from my sister, temporarily solving one problem and unknowingly sowing the seeds for something worse. One day we came home from school to the smell of cigarettes.

One day Bateman arrived.

We never knew him by any other name, and at first his presence, his antipathy towards children, brought more stability into our lives. He didn't want us around the house so we attended school more regularly. On weekends, if he was there, we'd be sent outside until it started to go dark. It was impossible to avoid him at all times, though. He was an enormous man with dirty, invasive eyes that could always see the worst things you were thinking, and he projected his anger at whatever happened to be in front of him. Sometimes that was our mother. Sometimes that was me. To his credit, he came to my sister last.

As Bateman segued from verbal to physical abuse, so I began to segue from reality into the rising. A haze of sunspots would wash in front of my eyes. My mouth would start to water and I'd lift out of my body. I'd drift up to the ceiling and ignore the six-foot-two man slapping, pushing down and hitting an eight-year-old boy. I'd watch my little sister instead, crouched down facing the wall with her hands over her ears. At first this was agreeable to Bateman, an uncomplaining human punchbag, but where my detachment from events had suited our mother, it didn't truly suit him.

Bateman had no internal life.

Outside of cruelty he ceased to exist, and he became agitated when he couldn't see the effect he was having on things. The rising, my passivity, became my only form of defence against him. So when he made lewd comments to my mother, I wasn't there. When he verbally threatened me, I wasn't there. When he physically assaulted me, I wasn't there.

But one day he noticed my head turn, sharply, when he took a step towards my sister, and from there began his experiment in making me react. She was smaller than me, small for her age, and I never saw him hit or sexually abuse her. He was more interested in fear, and in terrorizing Annie he got two for the price of one. My sudden, futile, pleading anger and my sister's wide-eyed, thoughtful, comprehending terror. Sometimes he'd tell her how stupid or ugly she was. Sometimes he'd put cigarettes out on her arms and call her names. The constant smell of tobacco burning about his person just fed the perception that something smouldered inside him. A kind of fire, generated out of spite, kept alive by constant chain-smoking, and witnessed occasionally through his eyes.

With our fear secured we settled into a dysfunctional family unit, with Bateman at our head. He stayed with my mother because we represented new opportunities to a conman. He'd have me approach remote homes with sob stories. Telling them I was lost, training me to steal whatever I could see while I was inside. He had me crawl into people's homes at night. Just to see if it was possible at first, graduating to theft and even home invasions, where I'd unlock the front door, let him in and sit down while I heard the elderly people he targeted plead with him not to hurt their partners. We sat outside chemists and department stores at 3 a.m. and then he'd feed my body through high windows or skylights. When it became useful for me to pick locks, he taught me that too.

The night he and my mother woke us, took us downstairs to a car we'd never seen before and drove us out to the middle of nowhere was the last time I saw him. Annie and I were taken into care and separated shortly afterwards. She was successfully placed with a new family, and after that I never saw her again, either.

Bateman had re-entered my life before, but until now only in the vivid nightmares that made me a lifelong insomniac. He was the archetype, the logical conclusion, of every bully and every abuser I'd ever met since. When I think of him now, I feel a limitless, cold hate. He'd been crippled by a gunshot and sent to prison for the rest of his life where, if my childhood wishes came true, he'd die shrivelled up like a cold scrotum. But, as Sutty always says, you can wish in one hand and shit in the other. Only one of them ever fills up.

8

'He's in the toilet,' said Sian, nodding towards the back of the room.

'Are you OK?' I said it distractedly, because I knew I should.

I was nervous, looking over my shoulder.

'Sure,' she said. 'He kept asking for shots of Jack Daniel's. Dropped some notes on the bar and said to just keep lining them up so he could watch me pour. In the end I took the notes, pulled the bottle off the wall and sat it next to him.'

'Sounds better than the alternative.'

'I don't know . . .' She nodded at the bottle on the bar. It was half-empty. 'Who is this guy? What's his problem with you?' Before I could answer I saw her eyes move, smoothly, over my shoulder. Widening slightly. I felt Bateman's entrance into the room as a change in air pressure. A psychic gasp going through the bar. I turned to see him crushing a cigarette out on the wall, dropping what was left and walking through the tables towards us.

The people either side of him glanced at the ruined face, the empty eye socket surrounded by darkened, concave scar tissue, then they looked quickly away. He held his chin out like a challenge, daring someone to say or do something. When he reached the bar he shoulder-barged past me and I felt the power of his body. The heat that seemed to pour out of him, the hate.

'Jim Beam,' he slurred, through the wet click of his speech impediment. Close up, his face was painful to look at. A gunshot will do that. Sian glanced at me for a split second but I didn't react.

'You've got half a bottle of Jack,' she said.

'Changed mind . . .'

When he spoke he sounded like a deaf person but I wasn't sure how much of that was real and how much of it was for show. My impression was that he enjoyed unnerving people. Sian took a nervous step back from the bar, pushed a glass up to the optic and measured out a shot. Bateman made a show of watching her move. She looked back at him and he nodded to make it a double. *'Slower,'* he said. She turned to give him the glass. 'Make it a threesome . . .' he said.

'Nope, that's your lot.' She slid the drink towards him so there was no chance they'd touch. I could see the pulse moving in her neck. He gave her his painful, flesh-wound smile, dropped more notes on the bar and ran his hands back and forth across it.

'Could watch all day,' he said, his fingers leaving slug trails of grime on the wood. He picked up the drink, threw it back and slammed it down. 'More glasses. You and friend can help with bottle.' He nodded in my direction when he spoke, but he still hadn't looked directly at me. Sian hesitated then put two more glasses on the bar, watching as he poured large measures into each. 'Cheers,' he said, raising his in toast to her.

'Cheers,' she said, lifting hers and pouring it down the sink.

Bateman scowled. 'Paying a compliment . . .'

'You pay me money for drinks,' she said. 'That's it.'

He screwed up his face, literally, folding it in on itself. My skin itched standing so close to him, and I wondered how we must look to Sian.

Inseparable, I thought. Like the fucking cause of each other.

He broke eye contact with her suddenly. 'Bet this guy drinks.' He was so tall that he had to look down at me and I saw saliva bubbling out of his damaged mouth. He sucked it noisily back in. 'Have we met . . . ?'

'Come on,' I said, taking my glass and sitting at a free table. My back was against the wall and he followed me, sitting opposite.

I leaned into him. 'What the fuck are you doing here?'

'Like the barmaid . . .'

'Well enjoy your drink, because it's your last.'

'Says who?'

I looked at him. Waited.

'Told you, Wally,' he said, hunching up over the table.

'Aidan,' I replied.

'Told you to hide the bag. Tell no fucker where. Told you we were going back for it.'

'You're not serious . . .'

'*Said*—'

'It was twenty years ago.'

'Yeah?' He drooled the word out of his mouth. 'I wasn't counting . . .' His inability or unwillingness to articulate certain sounds ignited a natural sympathy in me. But whenever I looked at his one living eye I knew the person behind it hadn't changed.

'They say that by fifty a man gets the face he deserves. How old are you now?'

'*This*,' he spat, pointing at the dead eye. 'This was for you. I stepped between that gun and you.'

'Bullshit. You stepped between that gun and the money.' It was so plainly true that he paused and took a drink while considering his next line of attack. He dribbled bourbon into the side of his mouth. 'How's your sister?' These words were difficult for him to get his mouth around, and it looked like he was chewing them.

'I don't have a sister,' I said.

'Funny—'

'No, Bateman,' I said, lowering my voice. 'Get this into that fucking squash you've got for a head. I don't have a sister. We haven't seen each other since then, either. She's nothing to do with me, and I'm nothing to do with her.'

He did his best impersonation of a smile. 'Maybe I'll pay a visit. You lived together afterwards.' He caught my look. Smirked and went on. 'You might not have kept track of me . . . but I kept track of you . . . Maybe you told your sister where that bag went in The Oaks.' The Oaks was the home we'd been sent to, and not something he should know about. I tried not to react. 'Your mother told me, by the way.' He smiled again. 'Sends her love.'

I didn't know if he was telling the truth.

I didn't even know if she was alive, but the revulsion working its way through my body felt so strong I thought it must be visible. A light haze of sunspots washed in front of my eyes and I held on to the table to stay in control. Bateman was still talking but I couldn't hear him. I looked about the room. It seemed to be in motion. Sian was serving someone, distractedly, watching us through the corner of her eye.

I looked at Bateman, interrupting him as my senses snapped back.

'Do you remember what you used to call her?'

'Your mother? A few things . . .'

'My sister,' I said, my voice thickening. 'Do you remember what you used to call my sister?' He looked away. Shrugged. 'A nickname,' I said. 'You had a nickname for her.' All traces of smirk fell slowly from his face and a look of overwhelming exhaustion replaced it.

'Twenty years ago,' he said. 'How would I remember that?'

'I remember it.'

'This sister you're nothing to do with?' The saliva was boiling at the corners of his mouth. 'I'm counting on that memory. You in those trees . . .'

'Count on this. You've been inside for two decades. The bag's gone. The trees probably aren't even there any more.'

'They're there.' He nodded. 'I've been back. Looked round.' He smiled again, globs of spit dropping on to the table. 'No mention of that bag in papers. No mention ever since . . .'

'I threw it in the water.'

He shook his head. 'I don't think so.'

'Why?' I said. 'Why don't you think so?'

'You were too scared of me to throw in water. Still scared now.'

'Most people are probably scared of you, weren't there any mirrors inside?'

'I was a celebrity inside,' he said, drawing himself up. 'Not many men eat a bullet and live.'

'Well, if you ever feel like going back for seconds . . .' I felt a jolt of self-loathing. I was actually sitting here having this conversation.

Meeting him on his own level.

'Anyway,' I said, getting up. 'Let's do this again in twenty years.' I went back to the bar, leaning on it with both hands. I'd take the pictures to Parrs myself rather than interact with him again. When I moved my hands from the bar-top they left perfect prints in sweat. Sian touched my arm and I looked up.

'Are you OK?' I nodded. 'Hang around for a minute, yeah?' she said, with a smile.

I nodded again. My eyes were wet.

She frowned over my shoulder.

'Aidan, save me bother,' said Bateman to my back. He was intentionally hamming up his speech impediment now, into a caricature of a man with learning difficulties. 'Where's sister?' I turned. He was looming over me. Neck, chest and arms swollen with muscle. People at the surrounding tables were starting to stare. 'She'll talk to me . . .'

'We've got nothing to talk *about*,' I clarified. 'And you've got even less in common with her.'

'Wrong,' he said, slapping a sloppy wet kiss on my forehead. 'Wrong. Wrong. Wrong.' I put a hand out to stop him getting any closer. His chest felt like a rock face. He looked at me momentarily and took another step as though my arm wasn't there. He gripped the back of my head tightly and tore his hand away.

He pressed a sweaty coin into my palm.

Then he reached around me, poured a final shot of Jack Daniel's and drank it off.

291

'Places to go . . .' he said, winking his good eye at me. 'People to see. Annie's my daughter. So we must have a few things in common . . .'

He put a cigarette in his mouth and started to leave.

'Bateman,' I said. He half-turned. 'If you go anywhere near my sister, your eyesight will deteriorate in a serious fucking way.' He looked at me. 'I swear on my life, you'll never come back from it.'

He laughed and looked at the cigarette in his hand. 'I've remembered her nickname.' As he said this I saw that he'd been telling the truth. That he was capable of forgetting something like that. He looked at the cigarette again and did his pitiful impersonation of a smile. 'Ash,' he said. 'Short for ashtray.' He spoke deliberately, making the effort to enunciate every word. 'Nothing put a smoke out like those fat little arms.'

He turned to leave.

I looked at Sian. Leaned on the bar to stay upright.

She was talking to me. 'It's OK,' she was saying, her voice shaking. '. . . it's OK.' But something snapped in my ears and all I could hear was ringing. My mouth watered and white-hot, electric sunspots roared down in front of my eyes. Sian moved her hand on to mine but I was already rising, lifting up out of my body.

I picked up the bottle of Jack Daniel's by the neck, followed Bateman and swung it with both hands like an axe, in the highest possible arc. I felt the whisky, glugging out on to my wrists, before bringing it down on the back of his head with every ounce of strength in my body. The bottle exploded in a red mist of blood and broken glass, and an incredible shock wave travelled up my arms. He didn't go down. He put both hands out to steady himself on the wall then turned, touched his head and gave me his flesh-wound smile.

I was still holding the broken bottle by the neck.

I heard a guttural scream and I was charging it at him.

His arm belted out like a piston and struck me the hardest blow I'd ever felt. I crashed back through a table and into the couple who'd been sitting there. Bateman threw himself at me. I rolled to the side and he flattened the man I'd landed on. I was still on my knees when he turned, and I swung an uppercut for his groin. He moved in time and it caught him in the thigh, knocking him off balance rather than off his feet. He leaned back on the upturned table and swung a kick at my head. I felt my body travel up and back down again in a perfect arc, then he dropped on top of me with all his weight.

He gripped me by the jaw and started banging my skull into the concrete. I struck two blows to the back of his head but he didn't even notice. His grip tightened. His body felt like one enormous taut muscle, crushing me to death. I spread both hands wildly along the floor, searching for purchase, for anything that would help me roll away.

Anything I could hit him with.

My right hand found broken glass from the destroyed table. As he brought my head down on the concrete again I wrapped a fist around the shards, feeling the blood bursting out from my hand. Then I forced my palm into the good side of his face. Pressing the glass into him, into me, as hard as I could. He threw back his head in an animal scream, let go of me and lifted himself to a crouch. This time when I kicked him in the groin I didn't miss, and I saw the pain climb all the way up his body. I got to my feet on another overturned table.

He was bleeding out of his good eye, and his face turned the colour of old money.

I buried a fist into his stomach and he doubled up, retching over my shoulder. I linked both hands behind his head and kneed him so hard in the face that my entire leg went numb. I stepped back, holding my own head, watching him falter. He drooled out a long stream of blood on to the floor and collapsed into it, face first. I fell down on top of him, tears blurring my vision, and hit him, repeatedly, in the face, the neck, the chest, until I couldn't breathe.

I felt a hand on my shoulder and slapped it away, then another and another, until I couldn't move my arms any more and I was being lifted up from the floor. When they pulled me off him I had both hands inside his mouth, trying to rip it apart, and I was screaming incomprehensibly. As the hands pulled me upright and dragged me backwards through the room I saw that the bar was destroyed. Terrified men and women pressed themselves into walls, covered their mouths. Some consoled each other. Some were sitting on the floor, holding injuries. And at the end of the room, growing smaller as I got further away, was my friend, Sian. She had both hands over her mouth and she was crying.

9

By the time they turned the key on me I'd painfully re-set my jaw, but it was too late to start a conversation with the desk sergeant, or to request a phone call. I couldn't think of anyone who'd pick up anyway.

I couldn't think of what I'd tell them.

I'd been thrown into the back of a squad van by four stompers. During the drive I'd felt the bumps in the road like pneumatic drills at my temples, with the pain reaching an almost transcendental pitch. At the other end I imagined for a moment I might wake up out of a nightmare. Instead I was arrested, booked and detained.

A fresh arrival in hell.

The stompers were subnormal men kept on continual call. They scored non-existently on tests of IQ, emotional intelligence or intuition, so of course there was a place for them in the modern police force. They spent their shifts drinking protein shakes, lifting weights and shit-talking each other. When they got the call, they burst on to scenes of ongoing violence and brought them rapidly to a close.

Almost always by taking it up a notch.

I was probably lucky to be alive, but that depended on how you saw things. The mingling smells of blood, sweat and bourbon turned my stomach. I was dragging one leg from where I'd driven my knee into Bateman's face and my head felt like it had been cracked open, then glued back together again in the dark. It was unfamiliar to the touch, with a whole new terrain of ridges, scars and bumps. I could almost see the concussion stretching out in front of me like an enormous, never-ending skyline, and my hands, when I looked at them, were unrecognizable with deep cuts and grazes, those of a psychopath, I thought, a madman. My right palm still glistened with the shards of glass I'd forced into Bateman's face, and I was still picking them out when I heard the bolt go.

'Stand away from the door, please,' said the desk sergeant. He was smooth and chinless. Literally the most humourless man I'd ever met, and I could never remember his name. He looked like a stage of evolution we'd had to go through to reach humanity.

'Give me a minute,' I said, with some difficulty. I almost didn't want to know who was outside. Superintendent Parrs would probably send me into the main population with a sign on my back that said 'police officer'.

'Stand away from the door, please,' the desk sergeant repeated.

'Give me a fucking minute.'

It sounded like I had cotton wool in my mouth.

I was lifting myself up off the bunk when the door opened anyway and Sutty stepped inside. Next to me he looked pretty together, and I was actually glad to see him.

'Don't get up on my account,' he said. 'Give us a minute, yeah?' The door slammed shut behind him and I slumped back down.

'Get me out of here, Sutts . . .'

'No can do, pal,' he said, working alcoholic sanitizer into his hands.

'I haven't had a phone call.'

'Unless you've got God Almighty on speed-dial, it's not much use to you. You've been locked up with your belt and shoelaces, though. What's that tell you?'

'That they don't expect me to be here long.'

'In a way . . .'

I looked at him. 'What? They think I'm going to hang myself over a bar fight?'

'More than a bar fight from what I heard. What was it, Aid? Is the hit back on?' I didn't say anything. 'Or is it drugs again? Always multiple choice when it comes to you . . .'

'It's neither.'

'Anyway, do they think you'll hang yourself? They're counting on it, pal.' He laughed. 'No, really. They're running a book from the front desk, taking bets. They all think tonight's the big one.'

I didn't say anything.

'I was outraged. Said that's my partner you're talking about, there. Put a tonne down on you seeing daylight.' He smiled. 'Hanged? Not your style. Not your style at all. When a guy hangs he kicks out the stool, shits his pants and presents himself to the world. *Here I am.*' He shook his head. 'That doesn't sound like Aidan Waits to me. If they'd locked you up with something messier, a chainsaw or a shotgun, that'd be different . . .' When he saw I wasn't in the mood he changed the subject. 'Do you want the good news or the bad news?'

'I've got a feeling I won't tell the difference . . .'

'The bad news is that your data requests on a Mr Anthony Blick started to drop into the office after you left. Luckily, while you were in the pub I was able to pick them up. That led me to speak to Aneesa Khan, which was very illuminating. Turns out there's an entire line of enquiry you've been keeping from me. You've been interviewing the owners. Playing them against each other. Even making allegations. And now I know all about it. So, that's the bad news.'

I didn't say anything.

'The good news is that due to my tireless work on this case, I've managed to close the book on our smiling man.'

I looked up at him. 'You what?'

'Yeah, well it's obvious, isn't it? Him and this Blick guy had some crooked deal at work. Drugs most likely, although since Smiley

Face burned the evidence in those dustbins you failed to investigate, we'll never know. But Blick's financial records show he's up to his arse in debt – apparently, that's why him and his brother fell out – so it's easy to see how he might go over to the dark side. I think they betrayed each other. Blick poisons the smiling man. Smiling man cuts up Blick in the bath. Afterwards he realizes he's been spiked. Staggers to the Palace, knowing it'll lead us back to Blick.'

'That doesn't even start to make sense,' I said.

'Well, this helps. The cash found inside the dustbin was fake.'

'Fake?'

'Quality stuff but fake nonetheless. And the card that old Smiley Face put down at the front desk of the Midland was a clone. Also under the name R. Sole. He was some con artist, Aid.'

I was shaking my head. It hurt. 'So his dying act is to implicate someone he'd just cut up and flushed down a toilet?'

'Human nature's always been beneath you.'

'And if they took each other out before we even started investigating, who killed Cherry?'

'Random sex case. Who cares? One less chick with a dick on the streets, I'd throw him a fucking party.'

'And who had a nail gun to Amy Burroughs' head?'

Sutty was tutting now. 'It's a shame you can't cash all these reality checks, Aid. You'd be a fucking a millionaire. Amy Burroughs doesn't want to take things any further.'

'What?'

'Declined protection and all. She wants to move on. Parrs is impressed. Thinks I've tied it up like a kid in the basement. Bound and gagged the fucker.'

'You didn't take it to Parrs . . .'

'I felt, given the circumstances, I had no choice. I was updating him on your current lodgings and it just slipped out. Forensics were able to match DNA found in Anthony Blick's office to the blood found in the Midland Hotel, by the way. So there's no doubt he died there. That was smart thinking, Aid. You should've been there to receive the results, though.' He banged on the door and the bolt opened again. He stepped out into the hallway and looked back at me. 'That bloke you battered? He got up and walked away. I hope he doesn't know where you live. They'll turn you loose tomorrow morning if you make it through the night, but expect to face charges from the bar owner.' He smiled again, his eyes aglow. 'And if you decide to take the coward's way out when you get home, then do medical science a favour, yeah? Stab yourself through the heart so they can study your fucking head. Sleep tight.'

The door crashed like a gong behind him.

10

I passed a bad night trying to stay awake through my self-diagnosed concussion. I didn't know what time it was but I could see the moon in a grubby window, slicing through the sky like a scythe. I listened to conversations, screams and echoes passing through the walls and tried to imagine the lives they were attached to. I'd have swapped places with any one of them. I must have slept, because when I removed my forearms from my face, the sky outside had tinted like an old photograph, catching the scuffed, dull colours of my cell.

It was morning.

Everything hurt.

They banged on the door an hour later and I called a taxi to take me home. I paid extra for a slow drive. Climbing painfully out of the car, I stopped on the street. Sian was standing by my front door, looking pale and tired. She opened the fingers of one hand in a small wave. When I got to the door she reached out and lightly touched my face, her eyes taking it all in. Then she looked directly at me, stood on her tiptoes and gently hugged me.

*　*　*

We lay on the bed, listening to music, drifting in and out of sleep. Sian had gone, wordlessly, to the record player. Removed *Blackberry Belle* by the Twilight Singers and replaced it with Max

Richter's *The Blue Notebooks*. She hesitated for a moment before lying down next to me, shifting herself closer. She ran a hand through my hair, exploring the new bumps and seams in my skull. I put a cautious arm around her shoulder, watching the pulse move in her neck, trying to memorize the freckles on her radiant white skin.

It felt like the end of something.

'Those were the dreams you were having,' she said.

'He was always like that,' I said. 'Not his face but the rest of him. He hasn't changed.'

Sian thought for a moment. 'It's like he's a part of the heatwave.'

'What was she like, anyway, your sister?'

'A thinker,' I said. 'Stubborn, lovely.'

'I walked out when Ricky told me about the pictures.'

'I think he was just trying to look out for you.'

Sian's fist closed around my hair.

'You used to talk in your sleep,' I said.

'Not like you did . . .'

'What kinds of things did I say?'

She laughed. 'We haven't got that long.'

'You were buying drugs, weren't you, in those pictures?'

I was silent for a moment. 'Yeah,' I said, finally.

'What's it about?' She was leafing through the copy of *The Rubáiyát of Omar Khayyám* that had been beside my bed.

'Living life, apparently.'

She put it down and shifted against me. 'Only you'd need a guidebook.'

'Was there anything else that you lied to me about?'
   'I don't know,' I said. 'I don't remember.'

She was thoughtful for a moment. 'You could be so many things, you know . . .'
   I looked at my scarred hands and closed my eyes.

'We'll see each other less and less,' she said.
   'I know.'
   'We'll drift apart again.'
   'I know.'

Sian was sitting on the edge of the bed, her back to me.
   She turned slightly. 'And what are you gonna do?'

VIII
A Pair of Brown Eyes

1

Sian and Ricky's engagement party was held at the home of his parents. Their back garden was crammed with people. Resplendent with hanging lanterns, bunting and colourful bouquets of flowers. There was a large tent set up in the centre of the lawn, from which a band was playing 'Brown-Eyed Girl', and small children were doing laps of it, scuffing up their Sunday best with grass stains. Guests held perspiring glasses of Pimm's or Prosecco, or paper plates of barbecued food, and there was laughter, skin, sunlight, everywhere you looked.

Sian wore a shimmering silver dress with her hair pulled up and her porcelain shoulders on show. The sun had started to catch her skin, and a light constellation of freckles was visible about her cheeks. Greeting old friends, pausing for photographs and talking to large circles of people, she was impossible not to look at, impossible not to love. She moved through the party like an aura, and even the places she'd been and gone from held something of her radiance, her afterglow. Occasionally her eyes went to mine from across the field and I nodded at her, I smiled. I'd never seen her looking so happy. A lot of heads had turned at my arrival. I was talking to a friend of Sian's, explaining away the bruises on my face, the scars on my hands, as a hit-and-run.

She put a hand on my arm. 'You must feel so powerless . . .'

'I don't know. When I look back at all the times I've deserved a kicking and not got one, I can't be too angry.' She laughed. 'I think I'm still basically ahead.'

'So you did have it coming?'

'It's the heat, I think. Fate turns into karma at forty degrees.'

'Excuse me,' said Ricky, interrupting us. 'Can I borrow you? Need a strong pair of hands for the keg . . .' He started off towards the house before I could answer.

'Do you think he was talking to you or me?' I said to the girl. She smiled and I followed him. We stepped into the cool shade of the porch, standing between stacks of cakes, bottles and buffet foods, in a corner. When Ricky turned he looked as stiff as his starched shirt.

'What happened?'

'An old friend . . .' I said.

'Very funny. Sian said it was at The Temple. You wrecked the place.' I nodded. 'She had to go to the owner and beg him not to press charges against you.' I didn't say anything. 'She could have got hurt.'

'I know that.'

'She thought you'd gone mad.'

I hesitated. 'I know that.'

'And I thought we had an agreement.' When he said this he sounded so much like a little boy doing an impersonation of his successful, business-class parents that I felt sorry for him.

'And she told me that you showed her the pictures anyway,' I said. He reddened. 'That's a good thing. It means you're not start-ing this off on a lie. I'm here because she asked me to be, and because I owe her that much. But I agree with you. She could have got hurt. So when I fade out of the picture, it'll be because I decided to. And in ten years' time when you're happy together, you won't have to wonder if it's because you blackmailed her ex. Look after her,' I said, backing out of the room. 'We probably won't be seeing each other around . . .'

'Hang on, have a drink.' He pulled a fresh bottle of champagne from an ice bucket. I shook my head and walked away. 'Did she spend Friday night with you?'

I stopped. 'I spent Friday night in the cells, partner.'

'Saturday day, then. You know what I mean.'

I turned around. 'Only because you always mean the same fucking thing. What did she tell you?'

'She said she went to see if you were OK . . .'

'So why don't you believe her? Has she ever given you a reason not to?' He didn't say anything. 'Look, I've got to go,' I said, taking the dripping-wet bottle of champagne from him. 'I'll be needing this, though.' I walked out into a wall of heat and crossed the luminous-green lawn, over to the driveway. I popped the bottle when I was halfway down it and started to drink.

'You're not leaving, are you?'

I turned. It was Sian's friend, who I'd been speaking to earlier.

'Duty calls,' I said, unsuccessfully trying to hide the bottle. I gave up and turned to face her. 'Go back and have some, yeah?'

She smiled and shook her head at me. 'You're a lost cause, Aidan Waits.'

IX
Turn on the Light

1

I buzzed the first-floor flat and waited. It was almost lunchtime and Owens Park was quiet, with most of the students either still in bed, sleeping off Sunday night, or attending their first lectures of the week. I'd walked through one or two groups on picnic blankets. Golden-skinned girls, gleaming with suntan cream, their male counterparts going stoically red.

I heard the bolt on the door release and pushed it open.

There was a girl at the top of the stairs who I recognized from my last visit here, when she'd been waiting for a cocktail. It looked like she'd just returned from a morning run. She was sweating, out of breath.

'Hey,' she said. 'Earl's friend?'

'Is he around?'

'Work, I think . . .'

'That's OK, I was actually hoping to speak to Sophie . . .'

'Who did you say you were?'

'If you tell her Detective Constable Waits is here she'll know what it's about.'

'Oh . . .' She backed off down the hall and I climbed the stairs. When I reached the top I could hear low voices from Sophie's room. I pushed the door open enough to talk through.

'Morning,' I said. 'Can we have a word?'

The friend edged out past me and Sophie appeared. She looked trapped, I thought. 'Sure,' she said, moving back inside the room. I followed. She sat on the bed, folding her legs beneath her and placed both hands on her lap, each holding the other. I sat on the absurd pink chair at the desk. When she looked at me properly for the first time, she sat up with concern. 'Your face . . .'

'I walked into a door.'

'A door?'

'A revolving door. I wanted to give you an update on Ollie Cartwright.'

'What's left to say?'

'Well, he left us on the threat of releasing the sex-tape once he got abroad. That looks unlikely now.'

'Really? Why?'

'Mr Cartwright was arrested when he reached Dubai.'

'I said I didn't want to make anything official . . .'

'It was on an unrelated matter. The local authorities found a large quantity of cocaine in his possession. They take that pretty seriously out there, so it's unlikely he'll be back any time soon. For the next few years we'll be the least of his problems.' When Sophie's face altered and she allowed genuine relief to flood into it, I realized her guard had been up since I entered the room. Maybe since I'd first met her. This would probably be our last interaction, and I needed to make something happen.

'Thank you,' she said.

'Don't thank me. Thank his dealer.'

'If I could, I would,' she smiled. 'I don't know what to say. It feels wrong to be happy . . .'

'I don't know. Sometimes it's a relief when a guy hits his natural level. There was one other thing I've been meaning to talk to you about, though.'

'Oh?' she said, re-clasping her hands.

'When I went round to see Mr Cartwright last week, after our first conversation, I found your jacket hung up in his flat . . .'

'Yeah, I left it there. I told you. My student ID was inside, that's how he found me.' She sounded like a drama student reciting her lines.

'When I returned it, this fell out of your pocket . . .'

I unfolded the note and handed it to her.

Oliver Cartwright. Ollie. Mid-thirties. Thinning red-brown hair, some paunch. Incognito. 7 p.m.

I saw her breath quicken. 'Where did you get this?' She said it with a flash of genuine anger, genuine confusion, that I was surprised to see.

'Like I said—'

'I . . . just . . .' She swallowed. Tried to recover. 'I just didn't think it was in my jacket pocket . . .'

I didn't want her to lie to me so I gave her a nudge towards the truth. 'That is your handwriting, isn't it?'

She hesitated. 'Yeah, I remember now. It was weird. When we were talking in Incognito, he took out a pen and paper. Asked me to write that down . . .'

'He asked you to write down his name, his nickname, an unflattering description and where and when to meet him?' I saw the pupils contracting in her eyes. She didn't say anything. 'You know, Sophie, if you actually arranged to meet Ollie Cartwright before he filmed the two of you together, if it was a date or something, that wouldn't make it any more your fault . . .'

'I didn't,' she said, fully committing. The pupils were like pinpricks in her eyes. 'Like I said, he asked me to write it at the table. He wanted it as a memento or something, but I must have left it in my jacket pocket.' As if to prove the note's meaninglessness, she lifted it for me to take. She was holding it so tightly that her thumbnail turned white.

'Keep it,' I said, as reassuringly as I could. 'He should be out of your hair for good now, but any problems and you know where I am.' She didn't say anything but closed her fist around the note. 'Don't you, Sophie?' She swallowed, nodded. I gave her a half-smile and went to the door.

'Thank you,' she said. 'For everything.'

She sounded sincere but I thought she looked afraid of me. I descended the stairs with more questions than I'd had on my way in. I decided I needed a cocktail.

2

The Alchemist was doing brisk business for a bar on a Monday lunchtime. The outdoor terrace, blinding white beneath the sun, was fully occupied, with groups sitting down to gourmet burgers off pieces of driftwood, ice-buckets filled with Corona, or complicated, hair-of-the-dog cocktails. Inside, it was darker, cooler, lit by hanging clusters of lightbulbs. They bestowed a kind of alchemy on the hammered-copper bar-top itself, and it seemed to glow golden beneath them.

The barman was putting the finishing touches to a theatrical cocktail involving dry ice, and a thick, smoke-like vapour was pouring out of the beaker. It looked like a science experiment. The menu was designed to resemble a dreamy, Victorian gentleman's periodic table, illustrated with sketched intersecting geometric shapes, fossils and kraken tentacles. I was trying to interpret it when the barman eased into position opposite me.

'What's good?' he said, in a cool monotone.

'Afternoon, Earl.'

He took a step back. 'What happened to you?'

'Nothing a drink wouldn't fix. Anything you can recommend?'

'I'd usually say something tall and strong, but it looks like you've had enough of that for one day . . .' I didn't say anything. 'You look serious.'

'It just hurts when I smile.'

He shrugged. 'What kind of thing do you like?'

'When it's a cocktail I want it to taste like static, y'know? Like white noise. I want to feel the brain cells dying.'

'Sure.' He hesitated, then turned and got to work, drawing on several bottles from the alcoves around him. Finally he handed me the drink. 'Barrel-aged corpse reviver,' he said. It was served in a long-stemmed glass and when I took a sip I tasted Sapphire gin and Cointreau.

'What do I owe you?'

'On the house.'

'Really? In that case, you must owe me something. I thought you hated the police . . .'

'You were good with Soph,' he shrugged. 'What brings you here, anyway?'

I smiled. It did actually hurt. 'Some days it seems like I'm magnetically attracted to liars.' He turned to go but I grabbed his arm. 'You're not walking away from this. She's your friend, remember?'

He nodded and I removed my hand.

'Is she OK?' he said.

'For now. But I want to talk about you. There are a lot of reasons people lie, Earl. Even some good ones.'

'What've I lied about?'

'Come on,' I said, taking a drink. 'Don't double-down on what we both know. We're talking about why you did it. Like I said, I've heard good reasons before.'

'What do you think mine is?'

'Well, that's just it. My job's to build cases. Theories. Gather evidence. But motive? You never know that unless someone comes out and says it.' His expression still hadn't altered so I said the hardest thing I could think of. 'Worst-case scenario? You're a manipulator, wasting police time, fucking around with a girl you pretend to care about and getting off on watching her twist . . .' I thought I'd hit a nerve. 'Either that or you're the man I thought you were. Someone who doesn't like to see a friend getting used.'

He made eye contact for a second.

'If I believed that, I couldn't care less about you lying to me. In your shoes, I might have done the same thing.' Earl swallowed. 'That note never fell out of Sophie's jacket, did it?'

He shook his head.

'You found it in her room?'

He nodded.

I softened my voice. 'And you know what it means?'

He lowered his eyes to the bar and nodded again.

'I need to hear you say it, Earl . . .'

'That she went to meet him,' he said with sudden intensity.

'Who?'

'The fucking prick. Cartwright. She went and fucked him.'

He looked desolate.

'So she didn't meet him on a night out?' I asked. Earl didn't move. 'Had you really been to a protest outside his building? Or did you just want to be sure I knew who he was when you gave me that note?' He nodded, covering it all. 'This wasn't really about a sex-tape when you called the police, was it? What kind of trouble's she in?' He didn't answer. 'Cartwright's in jail, Earl.' He looked at me. 'They found a bag of coke in his possession when he got off a flight to Dubai. They're not big on second chances out there . . .'

'He's not the problem, though.'

'So tell me who is.'

'That club,' he said. 'That place. Incognito.'

'You told me you didn't know where Sophie met Cartwright . . .'

He shook his head. 'I went there. Went down there myself when I found the note. When I saw that club, his name, and realized how revolted she was about this guy she'd been with, this tape they'd made, it all clicked.'

'What happened when you went down there?'

'I didn't even get inside,' he said. 'I asked the doorman to speak to the owner. Said I knew what was going on. He laughed at me. Pushed me down and said no Irish, no dogs, no blacks.'

'What's Sophie's problem?'

'Money, same as everyone else's,' he said. 'You grow up in a shit town and if you wanna break out, you need a degree. To get a degree, you need money. They've got it locked up.'

'I thought she came from a good family?' He frowned. 'She told me that's why she didn't want to make her complaint official. Her parents would kill her.'

'That's what I told her to say. All she's got's a deadbeat dad she doesn't see.'

'So why'd you tell her to say that?'

'Because she freaked out. When I told her I'd called the police she fucking freaked out. You were waiting in the next room and she was having a full-blown panic attack. She said I'd landed her in the shit, she'd get a criminal record, go to jail, her life was over. But I couldn't let that guy post pictures of her on the internet. So I said she should tell you she didn't want to make it official because her family would kill her. I fucked it, didn't I?'

'I don't know. You got Ollie Cartwright off her back at least, and stopped him from blackmailing her.'

'But he's not the problem. Is she gonna go back there? Does she even have a choice?' He hesitated. 'She won't talk to me any more . . .'

'She won't talk to me, either.' I got up. 'Thanks for the drink, Earl.'

3

I crossed the road towards Incognito. The doorman I'd dealt with twice before saw me coming, and stepped in front of the entrance.

'You look like—'

I headbutted him then stepped over his body, inside the club. When I got to the top of the stairs another doorman approached, one hand on his earpiece. I kicked his knee out from under him and crossed the dance floor towards Guy Russell's usual seat. I wanted to force my fingers inside his eye sockets. I put my hand on the shoulder of the man sitting there, but when he turned it wasn't him.

I walked through the dance floor.

People were giving me a lot of space.

'Where's Guy Russell?' I said to the barmaid.

'He hasn't been in,' she said, her eyes drifting up to the doorman's blood on my forehead. I wiped it with the back of my hand.

'It's the truth, Detective.' I turned to see Alicia, Russell's daughter, watching me. She was smiling and the bottoms of her perfect white teeth looked like pearls against her tanned skin. 'Perhaps I can buy you a drink . . .'

'I'm afraid of what you might put in it.'

She stopped smiling. 'Then perhaps I can convince you that those days are behind us?'

We went to an office in the back room. Its furnishings were dark and mirrored, or made from cheap, creaking leather, and the ceiling was so low it felt like it was pressing down on us. It was like sitting in the back of an old limo. Alicia had entirely abandoned the wild neon of our first meeting. Now she seemed more comfortable in a smart black dress and minimal make-up. Her dark clothes made the whites of her eyes look brilliant. It wasn't just her clothes, though. She was different. She sat and watched me taking the tiny room in from the doorway.

'This is my dad's idea of cool . . .'

'He has some strange ideas,' I said, joining her on the sofa.

'And some good ones.' I looked at her. 'Oh, come on. You have to admit that as business plans go, matching well-off, middle-aged men with broke teenage girls isn't bad . . .'

'His opinion of it might change after I've spoken to him. When are you expecting Daddy home?'

'I don't know,' she shrugged. 'On about the same timescale as Ollie Cartwright. What would you say? Twenty years or so, with good behaviour?'

'What are you talking about?'

She regarded me for a moment and slipped off her heels, so she could stand up without banging her head. She went to a small desk in the corner of the room and opened a drawer. When she came back to join me on the sofa, she handed me an envelope with my name scrawled across it. She shifted closer until our knees were touching, as though eager to see what was inside. I opened it and poured the pictures out into my palm. They were the same ones that Ricky had found in The Temple. They showed me leaving home with a bag of cash. Buying drugs, anonymously, at the station, entering Cartwright's building. When I left I didn't have the bag any more. The final picture showed me staring, directly at the camera.

The car that had been parked behind mine.

'You took these?'

'No . . .' She laughed. She touched my leg and looked at me with real pity. 'I don't find you that interesting.'

'Explain,' I said, moving her hand away.

She smiled. 'After you came to the club screaming sexual harassment, Daddy put a private detective on you.'

'Why?'

'You were a threat, but maybe one he could neutralize. Plus blackmail really turns him on. All that power. Anyway, the private dick – that's what you call them, don't you? – the dick knew what was up when you bought the drugs, but he didn't know Imperial Point was where a friend of my father's lived. He thought you were just some bent cop acting as a middle-man, selling them on. When I saw the pictures I was one up on him. I knew Ollie lived there. I knew you were trying to help Sophie. I knew different . . .'

There was a rumble of footsteps from the hallway and I turned to see the two doormen bursting into the room.

'That's enough,' said Alicia. They stopped.

'Miss Russell—'

'I said fuck off, thanks.'

They trudged out of the room.

She took the pictures from my lap and began sorting through. Reinserting them back into the envelope. 'My mother left when I was fifteen,' she said. 'At sixteen, Daddy decided I should become the face of the business.' She handed me the envelope. 'The rest of my anatomy followed soon after.'

I accepted the pictures. 'You're not serious?'

'Oh, he wasn't my pimp,' she said, impatiently. 'He just encouraged me to spend time with customers. Get my face out there and make them feel good. As the club got more popular, he got more ambitious. He realized he'd tapped into something here. It wasn't just the age difference, he said. In a lot of ways that was the least of it. It was the power balance that our customers enjoyed. Things had changed in his lifetime. He said women were more like men now, loud and crass. Premium call girls were a step in the right direction, but watching the men out on the floor, he realized they wanted something deeper. An experience. They didn't want to hand over old notes in a travel lodge for a dry handjob. They wanted to pay premium membership fees for a club where they could sit down at a table and some pretty thing would join them. Touch their arm and laugh at their shitty old jokes. The question was, where to find the right kind of girl? Young, pretty, naïve and broke . . .'

'Students,' I said.

She smiled. 'Economic doom and gloom, exploding tuition fees and a town with three universities in close proximity. Daddy says geography's destiny. He got girls through the door with free drinks then started to give them credit. Once they were comfortable with that he'd lend them money. Payday loans at 60 per cent interest. When they couldn't pay, he offered them some work. Sex was never mentioned. Never once. He just let them off their repayments to come here and act natural. He'd give them the names and descriptions of certain men, his gold *members*, and tell the girls to hang off their every word.'

'And the men paid?'

She laughed. 'Happily. What's a couple of hundred a week when they can come here and have someone half their age fawning over them? They don't even need to talk to anyone. To set anything up or feel seedy. They just buy a drink and sit in one of our reserved booths. It almost feels real . . .'

'But some girls did go home with the men.'

'Nothing to do with us,' she said, holding up both hands. 'But of course, Daddy knew that a night of drink and small talk would give us a good enough hit-rate to keep things going. He knew some girls would want to make bigger dents in their loans than others. The kind of clients he had were always going to expect more . . .'

'What kinds of people are we talking about?'

'Businessmen, politicians, press. Even some friends of yours . . .'

I frowned and she eyeballed me.

'What's it worth?' she said.

'I might not arrest you on the spot.'

'Big words for a man holding pictures of himself planting evidence.'

Now I smiled. 'You don't know anything about me, Alicia.' I stood, crouching away from the low ceiling. 'I'll take these to the police myself before I'll be Guy Russell's man.'

Her lips parted and I heard the strain in her voice. 'I hoped you'd say that . . .' She thought for a moment and stood, went to the desk. '*This* friend of yours . . .' She handed me another picture of myself, on the street, talking to Freddie Coyle. 'He's a regular here.'

'I didn't realize your father was so broad-minded.' She frowned and I explained. 'Freddie Coyle's gay.'

She laughed. 'If Freddie's gay then, well, I'm a man.'

'He's a regular here?'

'Like clockwork,' she said, drawing closer. 'And I'd rather you didn't take those pictures of yourself to the police.'

'Why not?'

'I thought it was cool, what you did for her.' She smiled to cover some genuine emotion. 'I was glad to see it, anyway. Gerry, the private dick, came here the day Daddy was travelling to Dubai.' She must have seen my face change. 'You didn't know? Daddy and Ollie are best buds. They do everything together. I wonder how they're getting on now? The dick came here while Daddy was at home getting ready. I said I'd pass on the message, the pictures. Must have slipped my mind. I liked your style . . .' She looked up into my eyes. 'I found it inspiring.' She put her head on my shoulder and whispered into my ear. 'So I bought a bag of coke, too. I went home to kiss him goodbye and slipped a little something into his suitcase.'

I stepped back.

'The opportunity of a lifetime. And like he always said, geography's destiny. So while he's in a Dubai jail, fighting drugs charges, he'll have to transfer the business over to me. I see Incognito going in a slightly different direction from now on . . .'

'So you've got nothing to gain from these coming out,' I said, holding up the pictures.

'I've got everything to lose. I just wanted to rattle your chain a bit by leaving them at your local . . .' She touched the bruises on my face. 'I hope you didn't get yourself into trouble, blaming other people?'

'No trouble,' I said.

'Good . . .' She was right up against me, looking into my eyes. Then she turned dismissively away like it had never happened. She'd got what she wanted.

'The night we first met, when you followed me outside to the street . . .' I said to her back.

'What about it?'

'You weren't angry that I'd poured a drink on your dad's head.'

She shrugged. 'It looked good on him.'

'You wanted to tell me where Cartwright lived, how to get to him. What happened between the two of you?'

Her eyes were hard when she turned. 'A girl always remembers her first time,' she said. I realized why she didn't wear the lenses any more. She didn't need them.

I looked at the floor. 'The loans your dad gave out . . .'

'Cancelled,' she said. 'But some of those girls'll be back anyway. Even when you give people the choice, they get it wrong half the time. Enough to keep the roof over my head, anyway.'

'Are you going to be OK, Alicia?'

She closed her eyes and nodded. Somehow I thought she would be. 'If this is our last conversation, then look after yourself, Detective Constable Waits.'

'You too,' I said, making to leave.

'What happened to you, by the way?'

I paused in the doorway, touched my face. 'I was in a fight.'

She smiled, but genuinely this time. 'I meant before that.'

4

'Yeurgh,' said Sutty, mopping his brow. 'It's a drought, all right.' He was talking to Dispatch as we drove because he couldn't get a word out of me. 'I'm just hoping the black cloud over Aidan's head starts raining soon . . .'

I'd collected the pool car for our shift early.

Sutty despised the sound of music and had something close to a panic attack if the dial ever turned to it. He preferred talk radio and phone-in shows. Cabbies complaining about asylum seekers. He murmured to himself and nodded along, like it was the latest hit. I'd performed my daily routine of changing all the pre-sets to hip-hop and R'n'B stations, something I'd been doing for so long that he thought there was a ghost in the machine. Then I'd gone to collect him and waited until he turned on the radio.

I thought he might throw himself from the car.

Sutty's appearance in my cell two days before had been perfectly in character but somehow I'd expected more of him. Some kind of gesture towards our partnership. For his part he acted as though nothing had happened, and continued to drawl into the handset about me like I wasn't there.

I was driving, on autopilot, when I looked up at the Palace. Sutty's elegant solution had solved one murder with another. He said the smiling man had killed Blick and vice-versa, for all the sense it made. One body with no name, and one name with no body. Between the two of them we almost had a real person. It was another victory for Sutty's clearance stats.

'Yeurgh,' he said, still talking to Dispatch. 'If he keeps giving me side-eye I'll go in looking for his cataracts . . .'

I looked up at the Palace. Squinted. Then I stopped the car in the middle of the road, ripped off my seat belt and climbed out.

I could hear Sutty shouting after me, cars braking and blowing their horns. I crossed through traffic, straight to the main entrance and tried the door. It was locked. I started to bang on it, kicking and shaking it as hard as I could. Finally I heard some movement, the lock opening.

'Yes?' said Ali, looking out at me. I was surprised to see him back at work.

'I need access to this building now.'

'Sir?'

'Detective Constable Aidan Waits. We spoke in the hospital after you were assaulted.'

'I hadn't forgotten,' he said, taking a step back.

'Is there anyone besides you in the building, Mr Nasser?'

I thought I saw a shadow cross his face. 'No, sir . . .'

'Then can you explain why the light's on in room 413?'

'Impossible,' he said, but I'd already pushed past him and started across the lobby towards the stairs. I could hear him locking the door behind us and following. Shouting after me. There were two enormous flights between each floor, and I was pulling myself up by the bannister. When I looked down the centre of the staircase, I saw Ali, in pursuit one floor behind me. I reached the fourth floor breathing hard, wiping sweat out of my eyes, and went cautiously towards the room.

The door was open.

The light was off.

I looked about me, trying to see something, anything, that was out of place. I heard footsteps coming down the corridor, Ali, breathing hard. Because the light was on in the hallway he was just a silhouette.

'Sir . . .' he said, trying to get his breath back. 'I told you, no light. No one else is here. I must ask you to leave . . .'

We stood like that for a moment, looking, but unable to see each other. Then I dragged a chair to the centre of the room, watching his enormous shadow filling the doorway as I did. I stood on the chair and reached up to the lightbulb.

It was hot.

* * *

The boy was running through the trees, his legs were wet from the stream and the strap of the bag was biting into his shoulder. His ears were ringing and there were sunspots roaring past his eyes. He started to lift up. At first his feet were still skimming the ground, then he rose above it, up and up, until he was soaring over the woods.

I woke up panting for breath.

The phone was ringing in the next room.

'Hello,' I said, picking it up. It was early. Seven or eight in the morning, I thought.

'You're out?'

I gripped the receiver. 'Bateman, this has got to stop.'

He breathed in and out for a few seconds. 'Can't stop, Wally. Can't stop.'

'My name's Aidan, and there's nothing I can do for you.'

'Drive,' he said.

'No.'

'Drive with me.'

'There's nothing out there.'

'Hurt sister,' he said. '*Love* sister, kiss sister, fuck sister—'

I closed my eyes and hung up the phone. When it started to ring again I ripped the cord out of the wall.

X
Demon in Profile

1

I was waiting outside Stromer's office. She looked up from a clipboard when she saw me and opened the door.

'You know, it's unlocked . . .' she said.

I followed her in. 'It's you I needed to talk to.'

'I'm very busy, Detective Constable. Perhaps you could adhere to procedure and arrange a meeting through your senior officer.'

I shook my head and sat down. 'Sutty couldn't arrange his own funeral.'

'Pity,' she said, perching on the desk and looking at me. 'Yours looks more likely from where I'm sitting. You've been in the wars again . . .'

'Tell me about the poison that killed the man from the Palace Hotel.'

She was staring at me like I'd risen from the dead. 'Smiley Face, you mean?'

'Sutty's nickname, not mine.'

'A carbon atom triple-bonded to a nitrogen atom,' she said. 'Cyanide, a classic. I was under the impression that this case was closed?'

'Do you know how it was administered?'

'It was mixed into his drink.'

'Which was?'

'A blended whisky. Jameson's, if I had to hazard a guess . . .'

'You can tell that from the stomach contents?'

'Nothing so advanced,' she said, tapping her nose. 'There was also an empty bottle found in the room . . .'

'So someone could have easily spiked it without his knowledge?'

'Of course. He'd have started to feel symptoms soon after.'

'So he'd have known?'

'That something was wrong, certainly. The ensuing muscle-paralysis probably accounts for the grimace on his face.'

'Either that or he died happy. How long would he have had from ingestion to death?'

'Perhaps twenty to thirty minutes. Why?'

'What about Cherry,' I said. 'The sex worker from the canal . . .'

'Real name Christopher Jordan. His larynx was crushed.'

'Cherry chose to live as a woman, Doctor. Was it a professional killing?'

She bristled. 'Quite the opposite. Someone trying to silence or strangle the poor thing, and doing a good deal more damage than was necessary.'

'Could a woman have done it?'

'With the proper motivation.'

'Sutty wants to clear it as a random sex-crime.'

'He has an enviable clearance rate.'

'Were you able to tell if she'd had sex on the day she died?'

'Was there something between you and this Cherry?'

'Were you able to tell if she'd had sex on the day she died?' I repeated.

'No,' she said. 'There was no evidence of sexual activity from the day she died. Was there something between you and this girl?'

'What about the blood from the Midland Hotel?' I said.

She sighed. 'Anthony Blick, yes.'

'It's definitely his?'

'Ninety-eight per cent probability.'

'How much blood was there?'

'Over six pints soaked into the carpet.'

'Was there any human matter recovered from the toilet?' She

didn't answer. 'That is the working hypothesis? That he was cut up in the bathtub and flushed down the toilet?'

'It's one hypothesis,' she said. 'We may never know what became of Mr Blick's remains because neither you nor Detective Inspector Sutcliffe thought to have those first two dustbin fires forensically analysed. He could just as easily have been dissected and disposed of in them.' I waited. 'No. Currently no human matter, but SOCO are still filtering the drains at the Midland. It pains me to ask this, Detective Constable, but are you quite all right?'

'Never better,' I said, getting up to leave.

'I feel like you haven't heard a word I've said.'

'I feel like neither have you. Thanks for your help, Karen.'

2

I knew something was off about Amy Burroughs' house before I even got to the door. I knocked, waited a minute and rang the bell. There was no answer. I went to the window, made a visor of my hands and looked into the living room. The pictures of her son that I'd seen on the wall had been taken down, but the nail gun's damage was done. I could see a series of holes in the plasterwork, like five or six full-stops in a row. The bookcase was empty.

I crossed the road to the home of the neighbour I'd spoken with the previous day. I needed a curtain twitcher. She answered the door in the same tired dressing gown.

'Good morning,' I said. 'I'm looking for Amy Burroughs.'

She yawned without covering her mouth. 'Left like shit through a goose in the middle of the night . . .'

'Did she say anything before she went?'

'If she'd come to my door I'd have slammed it in her face. From what I saw, she just rammed some stuff in the back of her car and tore out.'

'What time was this?'

'Three or four in the morning. We used to have real families here—'

'Was she alone?' I said, already walking backwards to the car.

'Had her boy with her.' She drew her gown tight around her. 'It's about that prowler I saw looking through her windows, isn't it? Will he be coming back?'

'Definitely not,' I said, grateful that she'd asked the one question I could answer with any certainty. Amy Burroughs had been polite to me, even courteous the first time we'd met, on Ali's hospital ward. But as soon as I'd arrived at her home with questions she'd become stand-offish, a closed book. Her reaction to the smiling man had been emotional, though.

He was the last person she thought she'd ever see again.

I went to St Mary's, straight to the front desk. The woman there glanced up and winced at me.

'That looks nasty . . .'

'I'm actually here to speak to someone, Amy Burroughs. She's a nurse practitioner.'

'May I ask what it's regarding?'

'I'm a police officer,' I said, digging out my badge. 'I've got reason to believe that Ms Burroughs might be in danger.' I was hoping to inject some life into her but the news barely registered. She told me where I could find Amy then craned her neck to look at the next person in line. I had a second thought and stopped. 'Actually, can you tell me which department I can find her husband in?'

3

I found Amy's office on the Accident and Emergency ward. The waiting room was packed out with people, all sitting round fanning themselves, stupefied by the heat. I stood outside her office and waited for someone to leave. My phone started ringing and I looked at the screen. An unknown number.

'Waits,' I said, picking it up.

Bateman, breathing. He sounded drunk. Exhausted and at the end of his rope. I thought about his time in jail. Two decades, disfigured and ageing, with no friends or family outside. With just the imagined contents of a stolen bag to sustain him. The breathing this time was different. More incidental than menacing. It sounded like he'd worn himself out.

Somehow that felt more dangerous.

'Can't stop, Aidan. Can't stop . . .'

I held the phone away from my ear and quietly ended the call. I realized I was scowling when an elderly man on a Zimmer frame laboriously changed course to avoid me.

A few minutes later the office door opened and a man with an eye-patch emerged. I stepped past him, inside, and closed the door. Amy Burroughs was standing by the far wall, craning her neck to smoke out of a small window. When she saw me she took a final drag and dropped the cigarette outside. She looked pale and blotchy. I realized she was wearing no make-up, exposing deep lines beneath her eyes. Her hair was unwashed. Greasy and flat. I wondered if she'd slept in her car. I wondered where her boy was.

'Oh, you,' she said.

'You're moving house, I see.'

Her eyes didn't move from mine. 'Well, it's not safe there, is it? I've got a boy to think about . . .'

'You declined protection, though.'

'That's my way of protecting him. That and staying away from the police. No one was breaking into my house and nailing my hands into walls before all this.'

'Bolting in the night won't solve anything.'

'Oh? What will, then?' she said, dropping into a chair. She sounded absolutely exhausted. I'd noticed her bandaged hand, but it was the other one that caught my eye. Her arm was flat on the table and her sleeve had ridden up. Without the thick, overlapping bracelets she wore off-duty I could see healed, intersecting scars on her wrist.

'Just tell me what's going on,' I said. She was silent. 'Has running from it really worked?'

'Until you turned up . . .'

But her resolve was broken.

I pulled out a chair and sat opposite her. 'Who was the man with the nail gun, Amy?'

'I don't know . . .'

'I find that hard to believe.'

'It's the truth.'

'The problem is you've lied about so many other things that it's hard to tell.'

'I didn't know him,' she said, looking right at me. 'I didn't know his shape, or his voice, or his smell, or his anything.'

'What did he say?' She looked away again. 'Did he tell you not to talk to me? Are you going to let someone like that intimidate you?'

'Right. I should only let someone like you intimidate me. By the way, you've gone softly-softly for a minute now so it's probably time to start up the threats again.'

'Well, it's true that you're not safe.'

'I know that.'

'Your son's not safe, either.'

'I know that,' she said, this time with more heat.

We were silent for a moment.

'What does your husband think?' When her eyes moved on to mine again they were so altered from the ones I recognized that I almost sat back. They were sharp and cruel. The calculating side-look of a mugger. I thought she might throw herself at me. 'Can I meet him, Amy?'

'No, you can't meet him.'

'And why's that?'

She folded her arms. Gave me a smile about as comforting as thin ice. 'Because I'm not married, Detective.'

'Who's the man from the picture? The one on your mantle, you, your boy and another guy . . .'

'Fuck knows.' She shrugged. 'It's fake. I don't know, I never even met him.'

'Is the boy yours?'

'What do you think all this is about?'

'People keep asking me questions like that rather than telling me. You didn't know the man who attacked you?'

'No,' she said quietly.

'You're not really married?'

'No.'

'You were nervous when I came around asking about Ross Browne. Your husband was due home any minute, you said . . .'

'I needed time to think, whether I should just run or not.' She closed her eyes, toyed unconsciously with her wrist. 'I thought about killing myself . . .'

'Think about your boy.'

'That's all I do, I just wish . . .' She swallowed. 'I just wish I'd been born dead. I wish we both had.'

I started to say something but saw the self-reproach already working its way through her. I changed the subject. 'Who was the dead man at the identification? I've spoken to Ross Browne and he backed up what you were saying. The two of you dated, then broke up when he left town. So you had to have dedicated a different copy of *The Rubáiyát* to someone else. The way you reacted, it had to be someone you thought you'd never see again.'

'Why are you doing this?' She was scratching at her scarred wrist now. 'What have I ever done to you?'

'We're way past that. At least two more people have died because of what they did or didn't know about this case.'

She put her hands over her eyes like a child hiding.

'And I'm not adding you or your boy's name to that list. If the only place I think you're safe is in a cell, then that's where you're going. The dead man from the Palace Hotel,' I said. 'He's the boy's father, isn't he?' She heard me but she was still processing the fact of additional deaths. She stared at the hospital lime wall. She'd aged a decade since I walked through the door. After a minute or so, she started to speak, telling me what she'd run from and where it took her, finally arriving at her meeting with the unidentified man from the Palace Hotel. Her accent, which had always felt rigid, held in place by sheer will, started to slip, until it was recognizable as something from the southern hemisphere. Australia or New Zealand, I thought.

4

'By the time I got to Marseille I'd run out of money, and I was pretty low on everything else. If I think of it now I start itching all over, like all the lice and dirt and shit from that time in my life got inside me and kept on burrowing. I'd been sleeping in the same clothes for so long they were practically alive themselves, probably more than the rest of me by then. I'd had my birthday on board the trawler, in a sleeping bag with Seb, grinding my teeth and coming back down from whatever it was, just sweating it out and feeling awful, feeling like it'd never end.'

She looked at me.

'It never did, really. Life's one big fucking come-down. I didn't dare look in a mirror until we'd docked in the old port, gone into this tavern that was right on the water. I remember I burst out crying because my jaw was so swollen up, like, to twice its usual size. Seb and the rest were supposed to be getting us a lift into town but when I came out of the toilet they were all gone. I think they left me the sleeping bag.

'I couldn't speak a word of French so I started walking, further inland, towards the buildings. The men had told me all I needed to know was the name of the place where we were staying. They'd made me memorize it and say it back to them so many times. So I started saying that to people on the street. *Sans Abri, Sans Abri.* They're probably still laughing about it now. I think I was laughing too by the time I got directed to the homeless shelter. You sort of start to see life for what it is from that angle.

'They gave me a shower there, and some clothes, and something to eat. They gave me somewhere to be. I was there a few weeks, but it wasn't hard. It was a relief to stop running, to be clean. I was the sanest person I met, which was really saying something. It was mainly all these wild-eyed boys with track-marks on their arms, plus a few dilapidated old Romeos who'd hunch up on their crutches to hold the doors open for girls. There were older women there as well, but I steered clear. They carried round photos and bits of old wedding dresses like artefacts, to prove their sob stories true. And that was it. The boys had to be tough, the men had to be gents and the women had to be tragic. I was a girl, but I was the only one, so I was sort of my own thing, somewhere in between all the rest of them. I suppose all that made me stick out.

'There was only one guy who didn't fit in with the rest. He wasn't there all the time, and he never stayed either. He sort of held himself apart from the rest of us. He had this kind of natural gravity, this kind of power over the others. I never saw him laugh or relax. He watched people and then attached himself to them. He'd sit next to someone and start talking. This soft murmur, not even looking at them. Then they'd leave together or both disappear for a while. The man wouldn't come back but when whoever he'd been speaking to did, it was like they'd borrowed his status, like they'd been chosen or something. Whenever I tried to talk to him he looked uncomfortable or embarrassed, he sort of winced himself out of the room, and I assumed he didn't speak English, or didn't like girls. I had all kinds of ideas about him, like, he was a secret millionaire or a drug dealer or a writer. He seemed above it all. Like he'd been out to the edge of life and now nothing could really surprise him.

'I was maybe even a little bit sad when he did talk to me, a few weeks after I'd arrived. Those mysteries mean a lot to you when you're lonely like that. He explained that he was a businessman but his trade wasn't for everyone. If it wasn't for me I should get up and go. His English was so good, better than the people I'd grown up with, better than mine. He was interested in buying personal documents. He said it was illegal, there were risks involved, but they mainly sat with him. I sold him my passport for 500 euros. When I looked at my real name for the last time I felt like it was me who was ripping him off.

'I had the money in my pocket for five minutes flat. We'd left the shelter to make our agreement and, of course, he wouldn't be going back there that day. So I turned on to the square feeling good, feeling rich for the first time since I ran away. There was a man sitting on the doorstep with his head in his hands. As I got closer I realized he was holding his nose. It was broken and bleeding, and he was crying. It was Seb, the guy I'd come over with. And I knew they'd caught up with me again. I turned around and walked right into Tedge, my big brother. He . . .'

She took a breath and swallowed.

'. . . He asked me how I was, said our old dad had been worried sick. Then he punched me in the stomach. He went through my pockets, found the money and took it. Said he could guess how I'd earned all that. Then right in front of me he slotted it down a drain like it was nothing. He asked where my passport was, he'd need it to get me home, and I told him it was back inside the shelter. In my locker.'

She smiled. The shake had moved from her hands, to her face, to her voice.

'I'd been keeping a case in there for when they found me. A plastic bag and a reel of duct tape that I could wrap around my head. Good, thick razor blades for my wrists and ankles.

'So he said to go inside and get it. We had time. He sat at a bench and smiled at me. He always liked it when I ran. So I went back inside. Sebastian was still crying, saying he was sorry. I went past him and up two floors to the lockers. I opened mine and took out my case, my escape kit, and I realized someone else was in the room with me. It was the man who'd bought my passport.' She looked at me. 'The man you asked me to identify. He asked if I was going with that boy outside. I told him I'd cut my own throat first. And just like that he nodded, turned to leave. I followed him through the back door. He never hurried or rushed, he hailed a cab like we were day-trippers. In ten minutes we were at an apartment. Not his, I don't think. There was nothing there. Not even the plainest furniture. I asked him who he was. He said that wasn't important. What he could do was the important part. So I asked him what he could do. He told me he was a vanisher. He provided people with new names, new identities, new lives, for money. I told him that I'd lost the money he'd given me. He didn't smile but his tone of voice changed slightly, I heard the smile there. He said this one was on the house . . .'

The woman I knew as Amy Burroughs stayed in the apartment for another week, during which time the man brought her fresh clothes and books. He asked if she'd have any doubts about never returning to her former name, her former life, and she told him she had none. He told her that once she left Marseille she'd never see or speak to him again. That anonymity was his life's work and something he'd fought hard to maintain.

On her final night there they became lovers.

She hadn't felt compelled or obligated, but felt a genuine attraction and surge of emotion for this stranger who'd decided to save her life, apparently on a whim. The only thing she had of her own was a battered second-hand copy of *The Rubáiyát of Omar Khayyám*. She hadn't even read it herself then. Just picked it up in a charity shop one day. But she chose a passage and dedicated it. She mainly wanted to give him a gift. She mainly wanted to sign something with her new initial. *A*. She knew he'd probably destroy it the second she walked out the door. Re-dedicate himself to anonymity, but apparently he hadn't. Apparently he'd thought of her since.

'What about Ross Browne's copy?' I said.

'Once I was here, settled, I did read it. It did come to mean those things to me. Reinvention, freedom, escape. I thought if I'd had that, Ross deserved it, too.'

I nodded.

'Who killed him?' she said. 'The man who saved me . . .' I thought her emotions were closer to the surface than she'd let them get in years, and I could see how scared she was. 'Was it my brothers? My dad?'

I was still trying to bring it all together. 'I think it's something else. When your neighbour told you that someone had been at your house, looking through windows, you thought it was them, didn't you? Your family?'

She nodded.

'It was actually him, your vanisher.'

She frowned.

'I think he kept tabs on you. He certainly kept the book that you gave him. He'd looked up your phone number, written it beneath your dedication. According to the autopsy he was terminally ill. It was only a matter of weeks. I wonder now if he just wanted to see his son, maybe to see you, before he died.'

'So . . . what? He died of natural causes?'

'He was poisoned. A man living his kind of life could make a lot of enemies. The intruder who had the nail gun to your head, you said you didn't know him . . .'

'Definitely not. I'd have known if it was Tedge or one of the others.'

'What did he say?'

'To forget all about the man from the Palace. He said if I talked to you he'd hang my little boy on the wall by his eyes.'

'Your family wouldn't care less about the dead man, they'd be out to get you. It's not them, Amy.'

'I can't go on the record,' she said. 'I can't go in, I can't give statements—'

'No,' I said. 'I won't ask you to. Thanks for talking to me. I'd like to arrange for someone to watch you and your boy now.'

'I can't go back to living like that. Having them hang over me.'

I felt the same way. It was past time for things to come to a head.

The smiling man was a vanisher. A man who helped people disappear. It made sense that he'd eradicated all traces of his own life, even as he was living it. It felt cruel that his one concession to himself, to see Amy and his boy before he died, had been taken away. Discovering his real identity felt unlikely now. But someone had murdered this man. He'd staggered to a closed-down hotel to die, then Anthony Blick's blood had been found in his room. Cherry had been murdered for what she'd seen.

Everything led to the Palace Hotel.

'Another day,' I said. 'Twenty-four hours at the most.'

5

I left Amy's office, walking through the baleful, hot and bothered stares of the packed-out waiting room, and out on to the street. My body and mind were buzzing. The smiling man being a vanisher made a lot of sense, but it meant that identifying him, especially without naming Amy as a witness, would be impossible. I'd tried not to get my hopes up when Parrs made his bargain. Floated the possibility of my moving on from the night shift. Of re-partnering and leaving Sutty behind if I cracked the smiling man. Now that even the possibility was gone I felt bereft.

There was still the matter of the smiling man's killer, though.

Still the final lead that he'd been helping people change identity.

I needed to check Ali's legal status in the country. Desperate and disenfranchised by the asylum process, who knew what a person might turn to? There were other questions of identity hanging over the case, too. Cherry had been born under one name, one gender, and lived under another. Freddie Coyle had two different sexualities between his wife and his lover, a third with his membership to Incognito, where he was apparently straight again, a ladykiller. There was his lover, Geoff Short. As much as I'd liked the man, he'd deceived his own family. He'd broken up someone else's marriage and moved jobs as a result. Then there was Anthony Blick, a solid businessman with the respect of his peers who'd been up to his eyeballs in debt, who'd somehow met his end in the smiling man's hotel room. His remains, the enormous blood patch, pointed to a violent death, but did that make any kind of sense? Was the anonymous stranger, the business-like shadow that Amy Burroughs had described, really a butcher? The man who'd seen a young woman suffering and saved her life? The man who'd made a last, desperate journey to see his son before he died?

There were other, unrelated questions of identity too. Bateman in my own life, who I'd known as a handsome rogue, a whip-crack around the ladies, whose face had been turned inside out by his own greed. There was my little sister, who also got her new name, her new life, her getaway. And then there was me. A man whose face warped and altered in the mirror, who couldn't identify his own hands or the violent temper that had transformed them. A man who'd become unrecognizable to his own friends.

My phone started to vibrate.

A feeling I was beginning to associate with Bateman.

'Waits,' I said.

'Good afternoon, this is Constable Black.' There was an edge of excitement to her voice that didn't usually go with interviewing escorts and pimps all day.

'Hi, Naomi, please bring me good news.'

'Possible lead for you . . .'

'I think I've forgotten what a lead looks like.'

'I'd say it's about five foot five. Loose shirt and khaki slacks.'

'Cherry's regular? Mr Hands?'

'He's here at the station. Should I notify Detective Inspector Sutcliffe?'

6

I was standing outside an interview room, talking to Constable Black. 'Unfortunately, Sutty can't make it,' I lied. 'Where'd you find this guy?'

'Well, I've been talking to street-girls in the area, which is how we got his nickname in the first place. Usually we can't even get a smile out of them, but a death tends to bring the community together. Sounds as though this Cherry was well liked. When the news finally got back to our regular, Mr Hands, he brought himself in.'

'Thank you,' I said. I paused at the door. 'I have to know, how did he get the nickname?'

'Likes to speak German to them.'

'I don't get it . . .'

'Mr Hans,' she said with a smile.

I nodded, opened the door and walked inside.

The man we'd been looking for, Cherry's regular, was sitting at a table, noisily draining a glass of water. He was small. Probably the 5' 5" that Constable Black had guessed, and somewhere in his mid to late fifties. He had an open, honest look on his face. It had been so long since someone told me the truth on their first try that I wondered if I'd even recognize it. I took a seat opposite him.

'Good afternoon, Mr . . .'

'Neild,' he said, thrusting his hand across the table. 'Larry Neild.' I shook it with some curiosity.

'Thanks for coming in, Mr Neild. A lot of men in your position probably wouldn't have . . .'

'Quite,' he said. 'Well, I felt horrible about that poor girl. They say she was killed?' There was some awe in his voice, for life and death and how a person could force the latter on to the former. I liked him for it.

'I'm afraid that's true. Can I start by confirming a few details?'

'Of course.'

'What do you do for a living?'

'I'm an IT consultant.'

'And your age?'

'Fifty-four.'

'You were a regular of Cherry's, is that right?' He nodded. 'How long had you known each other?'

'I don't know if I'd honestly say that we did. We'd met several times, but of course not strictly for conversation.' He re-clasped his hands. 'I first picked her up on the Oxford Road, probably a couple of months back. I think we've seen each other three or four times since . . .'

'Last Saturday being the final time?' He nodded and I stopped in my tracks. It was Tuesday now. It had been just ten days since the events at the Palace Hotel. 'First of all, I'd like to eliminate you from our enquiries into Cherry's death. Can you confirm your whereabouts on Monday?'

'May I take my phone from my pocket?'

I think he thought I might shoot him.

'Be my guest.'

He took it out, moved his glasses to the end of his nose and scrolled. 'Monday night I was working until gone one in the morning.'

'Can anyone confirm that, Mr Neild?'

'No point working late unless people notice you,' he smiled. 'Remember that.'

'I'll try,' I said, more tersely than I'd intended, and he stopped smiling.

'Various people passed in and out through the evening.'

'I'll need their names.' He nodded like the day he'd been dreading had finally caught up with him. 'There's no need for me to tell them why I'm eliminating you from an enquiry, Mr Neild, as long as you're telling me the truth.'

'Of course, of course.'

'Can you tell me about your last meeting with Cherry? Saturday night? I believe you went to the Palace together . . .'

'I'm afraid we did.' He closed his eyes. 'She wouldn't have even been there if I hadn't picked her up.'

'Had the two of you been to the Palace before?'

'Once, but in rather different circumstances.'

'Which were . . . ?'

'Well, of course you know the nature of our relationship. She simply said she had a friend working there who let her use a room. The first time we went in the front door it was unlocked for us. The second time we were sneaking around and I knew it. We got in through a fire exit that she said her friend had left open for us.'

'What time was this?'

'Around midnight . . .'

That accounted for the alarm which had taken Sutty and me there in the first place. 'OK,' I said. 'Go on.'

'It led up to the fourth floor but the rooms on that level were closed. Cherry said she had a room on the third floor, which we went to. I believe it was the same room we'd been to on our previous visit but I'm not certain. Once we'd finished up, we had to go back up to the fourth floor to exit the building through the fire escape. Well, the stairs there are impossible. I'd have been scared to death walking around with someone I didn't trust. When we got to the fourth-floor landing we heard voices. Two voices coming up behind us. I thought my heart might stop. Cherry took my hand and led us down the right-hand corridor. By this stage I was feeling—'

'Did you see them?' I said. 'The people that the voices belonged to?'

'Just the back of them, just for a second. One wore a dark suit, I think, and the other . . . I got the impression that the other was a security guard, from his clothes and so forth.'

'Could you see the guard's skin colour?'

'I'm afraid not . . .'

'What did they do?'

'They walked down the corridor, went to a room, opened it and went inside.'

'Using a key card?'

'I'm afraid I couldn't see.'

'OK,' I said. 'They go inside the room . . .'

'They go inside the room and by this point I've had quite enough excitement. I crept straight to the fire exit and left.'

'Alone?'

He twisted his hands on the table. 'Cherry was interested. She wondered if another girl was working out of the building.'

'Did you see or speak to her again after that night?'

'I waited outside. I couldn't run away without knowing she was OK.'

'And had she seen anything? Did she say anything at all?'

'When she got to the door it burst open and one of the men saw her.'

'Did she say which one? Did she use any words to describe him?'

He thought for a moment and shook his head. 'Not that I remember. She said the man was furious. He chased her, and she ran back to the landing and down the stairs. When they got to the third floor they both heard more voices, coming up the stairs. She ran down a corridor and the man froze on the landing. Then he walked after her, trying all the doors for a room he could get into, to hide. Then she said he'd taken a fire extinguisher off the wall and struck himself over the head with it.'

He stopped talking. I was staring down at the table. When he cleared his throat I realized I hadn't spoken in over a minute.

'Excuse me, Mr Neild. She said the man pursued her down to

the third floor and, when he heard more voices, struck himself over the head with a fire extinguisher? You're certain of that?'

'I'm certain it's what Cherry told me. Then someone came along the corridor with a torch and she bolted. Got back up to the fourth floor and out the fire escape.'

7

'Hello, Ms Khan, this is Detective Constable Waits.'

She exhaled into the phone. 'I've been dealing with your superior, Detective Constable. He told me that you'd been acting beyond your remit in investigating Natasha and Freddie. I'm afraid I won't be allowing you any further access to them without legal representation, and only then in receipt of a written request, signed by your superior.'

'That's fine,' I said. 'But I'm going to need access to the Palace Hotel tomorrow morning.'

'Why?'

'We've received credible intelligence that the dead man from room 413 left an item in the room. Once we recover said item, I can assure you that we'll be out of your hair for good.'

'Item? What item?'

'The man was murdered. It's our belief that he left evidence relating to the identity of his killer. It's all very clear. As I say, I'll need access tomorrow morning with a SOCO team for recovery.'

'I'd like to know what intelligence has led you to this item.'

'A witness has come forward, Ms Khan.'

'What witness? The Palace was empty . . .'

'Not even close. There were two witnesses inside the building, as well as Ali, at the time of the man's death. I'd appreciate it if you could alert the owners so there's no confusion. Of course, I could do it myself . . .'

'No,' she said. 'I'll notify them. If that's all?'

'It is.' I hung up abruptly. Felt the pulse moving through my body. I'd call in sick to my shift with Sutty. He could write his own reports for one night. I'd station myself outside the Palace and see if anyone felt like paying it a visit before my make-believe forensics team arrived in the morning.

'Oh, by the way.' I turned to see Constable Black leaning against the wall watching me, smiling. She'd changed into her own clothes and was going off-shift, happy about it. 'Had someone asking about you today, Detective Constable . . .'

'Who?'

'Pretty little thing. Ann something? I'd have to check my notes.'

I frowned and saw her face change in reaction. 'Ann, you say? Why did you see her?'

Constable Black moved backwards, along the corridor, and I realized I'd taken a step towards her.

'There was a break-in,' she said. 'At her place on York Road—'

Ann. Annie. My sister.

'Is she OK?'

'Yeah, she was out when it happened. Someone kicked the door in and trashed the place. Kids probably—'

'What did she say?'

'You know, was it common in the area . . .'

'About me? What did she say about me?'

I could see Black regretting that she'd opened her mouth.

'She just asked if I knew you . . .'

'What did you tell her?'

'I said I knew of you, I'd seen you around. Look, I didn't mean to get between you or anything.'

'No,' I said, trying to breathe. 'I'm sorry. Thank you for letting me know.' I could feel her looking after me as I thundered down the corridor. It felt like the walls were closing in. I walked out into the suffocating heat. Pulled out my phone and scrolled back through various missed and received calls.

Looking for Bateman.

He'd always withheld his number but now we needed to talk. He'd sent me a warning. I stared at the screen, willing him to call me there and then.

'See ya,' said Black, passing me.

'Constable,' I called after her.

She turned. 'I'm off duty . . .'

'Naomi. What are you doing now?'

'Why?'

'I need a favour.'

I told Black that I was down for surveillance on the Palace Hotel, but something urgent had come up. I must have looked desperate, because she agreed to cover it for a couple of hours.

'If anyone goes in or out, call me. Don't go near them.'

I wanted to be there, to watch it unfold, but it had sunk to the bottom of my list. Bateman had broken into my sister's house and trashed it. As far as I knew, Ann's only connection with me since childhood had come a year before, when she'd seen my face in the papers. My name next to words like corruption, drugs and disgrace. She'd tried to reach me then but I hadn't responded. I'd been ashamed. I thought of her speaking to Constable Black earlier, probably nervous, daring herself to ask about someone who'd gone out of his way to ignore her.

Bateman had put us back in touch.

I tried to think of anything I had on him. Anything at all. The only connection that came to mind was so objectionable I almost rejected it out of hand. Then I thought of my sister, asking about me after a psychopath had kicked her door in. I hoped she didn't know what kind of danger she was in. I hoped she never would. I took a breath, got in the car and drove.

8

The first time I'd come to this house it was the beating heart of an empire, and I'd been drawn, briefly, into the orbit of the untouchable monotone man who owned it. He was young, handsome and charming. He had no past that anyone could point to, and a calculating, salesman's eye for human weakness.

He wore his brilliant white smile like a mask and had a series of questions hanging over his head. Why were the police always so interested in him? What was the source of his incredible, independent wealth? And what happened to the string of young women who chose to spend their time in his company? At first they were worshipped and celebrated, displayed on his arm at restaurants and nightspots, until they said or did or thought the wrong thing and then disappeared from view. Sometimes they'd re-emerge in the sad, industrial satellite towns they'd originated from, perhaps with a black eye or a broken sternum. Sometimes they were never seen or heard from again. The house had been famous for its parties, the bass-driven music pounding through windows and walls like a pulse, but it was quiet now. I was surprised when a young, heavily pregnant woman opened the door. She was beautiful. Black, with the clearest complexion I'd ever seen. She must have noticed my surprise because she was forced to prompt the conversation.

'Yes . . . ?' she said.

'I'm looking for an old friend.'

The house had been transformed from the moody bachelor's pad

I'd known and into something lighter, more respectable. Original artwork hung in the hallway and when the woman took me through to the living room I saw there was no television. Neoclassical music played from an unknown source and the walls were lined with bookcases.

'I'll go and find him,' she said with a smile. I sat and waited, trying to believe what I was doing. When the man entered the room he paused in the doorway for a fraction of a second. He was trying to believe it too. Then he came towards me, pressing a hand into my shoulder, smiling.

'Aidan Waits,' he said. 'How long's it been?'

'Feels like a lifetime. I'm sorry to intrude . . .'

'No, not at all. Nia,' he said, turning to his partner as she came in behind him. She smiled in answer. 'Aidan's an old friend. Would you grab us a couple of drinks?'

'Of course. It's nice to meet you, Aidan. What's your poison?'

I smiled. 'I only ever drink what he's having . . .'

The man's look contained every moment of our history.

'If I recall correctly, Aidan's a cognac man,' he said.

'Two cognacs coming up,' said Nia, leaving the room. 'You'll have to have one for me, Aidan.' She drew the door closed behind her and the man sat opposite me.

'Congratulations,' I said. 'She seems nice.'

'The fuck's it mean,' he said, flatly. 'You coming here?'

'I didn't know you'd settled down.'

He smiled. 'You didn't know about her because I didn't want you to. That doesn't change because you show up here unannounced. Tell me what you want.'

'I need your help,' I said.

There was no other way to put it.

He was thoughtful for a moment. Unlike most criminals I'd met, Zain Carver didn't operate out of emotional stupidity, but from a comprehensive understanding of it. A terrible empathy. He understood immediately. 'Things must be bad for you to have come here,' he said. 'Obviously, that's appealing to me. But as you can see, I'm not running with that kind of crowd any more.'

'What are you doing now?'

'This and that.'

'It's about an old head. I just need to know how to find him.'

He considered this. 'What was it in our last meeting that made you think I'd be talkative?' He leaned forward. 'Was it when I told you about Cath? Was it when I left you crying on the street?' Catherine had been one of his best girls, once, until she saw the man behind the mask. His lies were such a success because he genuinely believed them, so when his disguise failed, when he saw a reflection of the real Zain Carver in someone else's eyes, he was as shocked as the rest of the world. His solution wasn't to fix himself, to feel regret or remorse, it was to fix those people who'd caught a glimpse of his true nature.

'This isn't work-related,' I said. 'If that's what you're asking.'

'You're in trouble again, aren't you?' The door opened and Nia came back into the room, carrying two cognacs on ice. Carver's face changed like a screen switching channels. We accepted our drinks and she leaned into the doorframe. 'So come on, how do you two know each other?'

'Aidan's got to tell it . . .' he said, like he had as much control over my words as his own.

'He's too modest,' I said. 'At the time I was working for a local charity, a homeless shelter in the city. Month after month our highest donation came from one man.' I pointed at him. 'This guy. I wanted to meet him, to thank him personally. When I did, we hit it off.'

Nia turned to her partner. 'You've never told me that. Wow . . .'

'You should check his bank statements,' I said. 'All kinds of things coming and going.'

He looked at me, amused, raised a glass and smiled. 'To the less fortunate.' We drank and he went on. 'That's how Aidan got his nickname,' he said. 'Charity Case.'

'I won't tell you what we used to call him,' I said to Nia. 'And I'm sorry for intruding like this.'

'It's no intrusion at all. I've still met so few of Zain's friends.'

'Well, a lot of them have dropped off the radar,' I said. 'In fact, I'm trying to look up one in particular. Luckily it sounds like the big guy's got a lead on him . . .'

'Remind me of his name,' said Zain flatly.

'Nicholas Fisk.'

'The thin man?' he said. 'Now that really has been a lifetime. I didn't think you'd met each other . . .'

'Just the once, but I think he'll remember me. I want to look in on him, make sure he's doing all right.'

'Same old Charity Case. Sure. I can give you the last address I've got for him, anyway.' He took another drink, got up. 'Excuse me,' he said, leaving the room with an affectionate squeeze of Nia's shoulder.

'How did the two of you meet?' I asked her.

'I was working in the Light Fantastic, in town. After he met me, he bought a stake in the club. Kept coming back until I said I'd go on a date with him.' She touched her bump. 'Things progressed from there, as you can see . . .'

'Do you know if it's a boy or a girl?'

'We want it to be a surprise but I think we're both hoping for a girl. He's got girls' names for days . . .'

'Good luck with it all,' I said, with more emphasis than I'd intended. I saw a question starting to form on her face, but before she could say anything else Zain re-entered the room with a slip of paper.

'Best I can do,' he said, holding it out. 'He used to own this place.'

'Thanks,' I said, accepting it. 'Listen, I should really get going. Nia, it was great to meet you, and congratulations.'

'Thanks. You too. Next time we'll have to make a night of it.'

'I'll see you out,' said Zain.

When we reached the door I turned to him, lowered my voice. 'Is this genuine?'

He nodded. 'I don't play games, if you recall correctly. You might as well shit into a desk-fan as go out there, though . . .'

I started to leave.

'I know you won't believe me,' he said. 'But I never wanted to see you hurt, Aidan. It was you who wanted that, it really was. The worst part is that nothing's changed.'

'Is that why you put a price on my head, Zain? To give me what I wanted?'

He smirked. 'I wouldn't know anything about that.'

'Go through with it,' I said. 'I'm sure they'll let you see the kid once or twice a year.'

He stopped smirking. 'Doesn't like you, y'know, your boss. Said he'd crucify the lot of us if it happened while you still had a badge. But if you got fired there'd probably be no arrests . . .' He tailed off. 'How are things at work, Aidan? They must be really bad if you're coming here.'

'As I said, this is personal.'

'It always is with you. Tell you what. Because I don't want Nia opening the paper seeing you've gone missing. I could talk to some people. I could make all those hit conversations go away. Probably give you your first decent night's sleep of the year . . .'

'And how would that benefit you?'

'Just tell me where Cath is. I've been wanting to catch up with her . . .' Part of my deal with Cath was that I'd never know where she went to when she finally got away from Zain. For the first time, I was happy about it.

I smiled. 'What was it about our last conversation that made you think I'd be talkative?'

He shrugged. 'It's your funeral. Good to see you, though, Aid. I was starting to think you'd forgotten . . .'

'That's the rest of the world, Zain. Not me.'

'Good luck,' he said, closing the door.

9

The address that Carver had given me was on the outskirts of
Rochdale, half an hour from Fairview if I really went for it. I knew
I couldn't trust him but had no choice. I was testing the speed limit
when my phone started to vibrate. I picked up, hoping for Bateman. The thought of him inside my sister's house had rattled me. I
was ready to agree to whatever he wanted.

'Detective Constable Waits?'

'Hello . . .'

'This is Constable Black, reporting from the Palace. I wanted to
let you know that an IC4 male just entered the building.'

'Dressed as a security guard?'

'Correct. Can I ask when you'll be arriving?'

'As soon as I can, Constable, I'm following a lead. If you need
relief, call someone you can trust, but don't leave the building
unattended.'

'. . . Received,' she said.

'If you see anything unusual, don't approach the building without calling me first.'

'What exactly am I doing here?'

'Surveillance,' I said. 'Keep an eye on the top floor. If a light goes
on in any of those rooms, let me know.'

My plan for the Palace had been a gamble, committed to in the
heat of the moment. Now I was starting to have my doubts. Learning of the smiling man's profession, and speculating how it might

have brought him into contact with certain people, I'd looked anew at Sutty's theory. That his place of death had been a conscious act.

A pointed finger.

The problem was that so many people were involved with the Palace that the finger could point at anyone. The owners, Natasha and Freddie. Their solicitor, Aneesa. Freddie's lover, Geoff Short. Short's wife, who could still be behind the notes sent to Natasha, whether she was out of the country or not. And the two security guards, Ali and Marcus. Of the three hundred or so rooms in the hotel, 413 was the only one I'd seen with the light switched on since the murder. Twice now. In both instances, by the time I was able to investigate who was inside the room, that light had been switched off.

Someone was drawn to 413.

Someone was nervous about it.

By asking Aneesa to inform the owners that a forensic team would be re-examining it the following day, I'd been hoping to flush that person out. But now the tangle of who could be responsible, or why, seemed impossible to navigate. Worse, Bateman's move against my sister meant that I couldn't be there. I hadn't been able to intercept Ali, and he was already inside. There was nothing outwardly suspicious about him arriving early for work, but because of Cherry's testimony, of Ali hitting himself over the head with the fire extinguisher, he was the prime suspect for the smiling man's murder. I tried not to think about the case sliding down the drain. I pressed my foot flat on the pedal, it didn't matter any more anyway.

10

I pulled up outside Nicky's, the address that Carver had given me. It was a boxing club built into the alcove beneath a viaduct. I killed the engine and watched a freight train passing over the tracks. When it had finally gone by, everything fell silent. It was the tail-end of another humid day, of hanging, muggy air, and when I climbed out of the car my shirt was already pasted to my body. I went to the front door not knowing what to expect and I was surprised by the silence from inside.

Something was wrong.

The boxing clubs I'd known had been about community and continuous movement. They were impossible to imagine without the sight and sound of young people perfecting stances, head weaves and mitt drills. Without rap blasting out from the speakers. I walked past an unmanned front desk and into the gym itself. There was no one in the ring, and no one working any of the bags that I could see hanging from the ceiling. It wasn't completely abandoned, though. The air was thick with the smell of fresh sweat and testosterone. My shoes echoed off the gleaming parquet floor, which I could almost see my face in. I was about to call out when I heard the staccato blast beat of someone working a speedbag.

Walking slowly around the ring I saw a young black man, naked to the waist, and streaming with sweat. He was striking the bag in small circles, rolling his shoulders and bouncing, minimally, on the balls of his feet. His stance was loose and easy, leading with the left, chasing with the right, laying a foundation and then steadily increasing his rhythm. He didn't stop as I came into view, but began embellishing the drill with elbows and double-strikes, his eyes glazing over in total commitment to the bag. His speed and technical timing increased until he was a blur. He held this pitch for a minute before slowing and steadily decreasing his hit rate, finally coming to a stop. Steam rose off his body through shafts of light from outside and, breathing deeply, he looked like a man coming back down from a high. He'd tuned out his surroundings and only looked in my direction when I cleared my throat.

'You're fast,' I said.

'Could be faster,' he muttered, grabbing a towel, getting his breath back. 'Help you?'

'I wasn't sure you were open . . .'

'We had a fire alarm earlier, cleared the place out.'

'I'm looking for the owner.'

'You've found him.' He frowned at the scrapes and bruises on my face. 'Not sure this is your game, though . . .'

'Nicholas Fisk?'

'Nicky Fisk,' he said. 'Junior.' I knew from the old newspaper articles that Fisk, the thin man, had two sons. They'd been the ones who reported him and his wife missing. It felt incredible to interact with a character from this time in my life, like it proved my sanity. He pulled off his gloves and held out a hand. I'd wanted to keep him at arm's length but I went forward and shook it.

'In that case, I think I'm looking for your father . . .'

'I know you fucking are,' he said, crushing my hand and stabbing a left into my stomach. He hit me so hard I felt the blow in my spine. I folded on to the floor and he dragged me by the leg through to the next room where I was lifted up and thrown, roughly, into a chair. I heard duct tape being torn off a roll, and then felt it, binding my wrists behind my back.

I tried to speak.

Felt the bile climbing up my throat and clenched my jaw.

When I looked around I was in a shambolic, out-of-time office, sitting opposite an empty chair.

A spit bucket was emptied over my head and when I opened my eyes, gagging, Nicky Fisk Jr threw a right at me. I winced and he stopped one inch from impact, laughing strangely. The taste of stale, bloody spit in my mouth was making me retch, and he pushed me back against the chair so I stayed upright. He grabbed a sports bottle from the desk and sprayed my face with water. When I opened my eyes again the chair opposite me was occupied.

Nicholas Fisk, senior.

The thinnest man I'd ever seen in my life.

The tragic, emaciated figure I remembered so vividly from twenty-odd years before had become somehow sharper, somehow more angular. It looked like he hadn't eaten a meal since. He had his legs crossed and I could see the bones in his knees outlined through his trousers. Despite being so slender, so tall, every visible part of his ashen skin sagged.

'What do you think, Nicky?' he said. 'We got a contender?' He sounded like Johnny Rotten giving elocution lessons.

'Guy's faded,' said Nicky, his son, leaning against the far wall with his arms folded. 'Some journeyman who's reached his final destination.'

'I don't know,' said Fisk, jerking his head to the right. 'Maybe he's not much of a technician but he looks like a brawler. You didn't do that to him, did you?'

'The bruises?' said Nicky. 'Naw. Guy's just got one of those faces . . .'

'I have to apologize for the boy,' said Fisk. 'He got the hip-hop patois from his mother's side. Now every word out of his mouth sounds like an insult. And I suppose I should apologize for him gutting you before you could get to me. But there's an old boxing saying I try to live by. Be first.'

I looked up. 'Carver told you I was coming . . .'

'I'm glad he did,' he said, using his cynical, false-toothed smile as a full stop.

'Listen—'

'No, you listen.'

I heard the hammer being drawn back on a gun next to my head. I heard myself breathing in and out for a moment, then I turned to stare down the barrel. The gun was being held by another young black man. Nicky's exact double. They were twins.

'Fool really turned up, then?' said the twin.

'What's left of him,' said Fisk. 'Which isn't much. He thinks we should listen to him . . .'

The gun pressed into my temple. 'Why's that?'

'Carver's playing you . . .'

Fisk sucked his false teeth for a moment and jerked his head to the left. 'Carver says you're not to be trusted. Says you're an informant. Says you've come here to kill me . . .'

'I'm a police officer,' I said. I felt the pressure of the gun at my temple increase. 'I'm serious, check my ID.' Fisk nodded at the twin, who felt inside my jacket pocket, found my wallet and threw it at his brother. He caught the wallet and picked through the various cards and receipts inside it, dropping them on the floor as he went.

'Well, fuck me . . .' he said, handing my badge to his father.

Fisk examined it then jerked his head to the right. 'Is that supposed to get you out of my bad books, Detective?'

'No, but it proves I'm on the level and Zain's pouring shit in your ear.'

He squinted. 'Why does he want you dead, I wonder?'

'It's about a girl,' I said. 'You know what he's like.'

'This girl didn't get herself killed, by any chance . . .'

'The opposite.'

'The one that got away?' He gave me his false-toothed smile again. 'Well, I shouldn't wonder he's upset with you, he usually likes to brick his little problems up into the walls of old houses. Sometimes while they're still breathing. Which begs the question: if Mr Carver's telling me porky-pies about you coming here to kill me, and if he wants you dead so badly, why didn't he do it himself?'

The gun was pressing back into my temple.

'He tried to. My superior told him if anything happened to me, he'd go down for it.' Fisk didn't say anything but his head kept feinting from side to side, like a fighter trying to provoke a reaction. 'As we speak, Carver's making a scene in a very public place, creating a cast-iron alibi, praying one of your boys decides to be his triggerman. You're doing his dirty work for him.'

'So, why are you here?'

I didn't even know where to start so I got straight to the point. 'Bateman,' I said. The gun was removed from my temple and Nicky's twin spat into my ear.

'Don't even say that fucking name in here.'

Fisk gave me his false smile. 'Bad form,' he said. 'It was a man called Bateman killed the boy's mother, my wife.' He watched me cautiously. 'What about him?'

'He's out,' I said. 'He's walking the streets.'

Fisk didn't move for a minute, until his boys had both turned to look at him. Then he shuffled forward in his chair. I saw that he was holding a walking stick and, with difficulty, climbed to his feet. He was so tall that he had to hold his head to one side so it wouldn't hit the ceiling. He swayed there for a moment then walked slowly to the door, leaning heavily on the stick.

'Thanks for letting me know,' he said gravely, his back to the room. 'But it looks like I owe you another apology . . .'

'Wait a minute—'

'What do you think, Nicky?' he said.

'Fuck him,' said Nicky, pushing himself off the far wall with his strange non-smile.

'Donny?'

The gun was pressing into my temple so hard I thought it might pierce the bone. 'Guy's got no etiquette.'

'Sorry, friend,' said Fisk. 'But you're a cop. You've been beaten up by my boys. Heard their names, seen their faces . . .'

'Wait—'

'Another boxing term, I'm afraid. Unanimous decision.'

'*Wait*,' I said. 'They were holding you in the cellar. You got out, you called the police, you found a gun on the kitchen table.'

'You've read the papers, well done—'

'Tracy,' I said. He stopped in the doorway. 'You were crying and you heard someone behind the door, someone in the hallway, and you called out for your wife.'

Fisk turned to look at me.

My vision was blurring, my voice was shaking. 'Bateman sent a little boy into that house to get the bag and he heard you behind that door.' The gun pressed harder into my head. 'He couldn't take it,' I was shouting now. 'He couldn't take it so he unlocked the door and let you out.' I saw them exchanging glances. 'He saved your fucking life.'

Fisk was breathing heavily, staring straight into me, leaning on his stick. He tilted his head again, but this time to get a better look. His eyes focused on mine. Neither of us moved for a moment. Acknowledging, perhaps, that we were both prisoners.

'Untie him,' he said, with some feeling. 'Now.'

11

I was driving away from Nicky's Gym as fast as I could. I had all the windows down, blasting the smell of sweat, spit and fear off myself. What I really needed was a shower. Ten hours' sleep and a locked door I could rely on. Instead, once my hands were shaking too much to drive, and once I'd put enough distance between myself and the Fisks, I pulled over to a lay-by. I stepped over the guard-rail and walked out into the botched roadside land-scape, and was sick, repeatedly, until there were tears in my eyes. Returning to the car I saw I had a missed call from Constable Black.

The smiling man was the furthest thing from my mind.

I leaned into the roof, breathing deeply, trying to force the shake out of my voice, then pressed call. 'Constable Black . . .' I said.

'Waits. I was calling to tell you that an IC1 female, mid to late forties, just entered the Palace.' That sounded like Natasha Reeve. I looked out at the road for a moment.

'OK,' I said. 'I'll be right with you. Keep an eye on that top floor for me.'

'Copy that.' She hesitated. 'Are you OK?'

My phone beeped twice, indicating another incoming call.

'I've got someone on the other line,' I said. 'Stay in position, I'm twenty minutes away.' I hung up and answered the incoming call. 'Waits.'

'. . . Can't stop . . .' said Bateman.

'You went to my fucking sister's place.'

'Can't stop now, Wally,' he said. '. . . Aidan . . .'

I swallowed. 'We'll drive out to the house tomorrow. Look for the bag, whatever. You win.'

12

Constable Black was sitting on the first floor of the Metropolitan University media hub, over the road from the Palace. I parked illegally, carded my way through the front desk and approached the table she was sitting at, by the window.

'Constable,' I said. She took in my dishevelled appearance without comment. What were a few more bruises?

'I was about to text you. A couple, a man and a woman, just entered the building—'

'OK,' I said, trying to think. 'OK, call for back-up. When they arrive, cover all the exits. You'd better get hold of Detective Inspector Sutcliffe as well.'

'What should I tell him?'

'That there's been a development in the Palace Hotel death. To get down here immediately.'

Black nodded. As she did, her eyes went to the building across the road. I looked. Saw that the light in room 413 had been switched on.

'That's where they found him, isn't it? Smiley Face?'

'Back-up,' I said, going for the stairs. I pushed my way out of the building and crossed the road through screaming traffic, holding my hands up to stop cars and cyclists.

Everything was moving too fast.

I reached the entrance and pushed the door.

To my surprise, it was open.

I stepped inside the lobby and called out to no answer. As with my first visit here, the only light came from the front desk. It was hopeless against the enormity of the space, gleaming off the glazed stone floor, and shrouding the rest of the room in darkness. I looked about me. At the gathering shadows, the pillars lining the walls. Then I started toward the light, stopping in the centre of the room, beside a pool of dark liquid. I crouched and put a finger to it. Against my skin it was brilliant, bright red. Unmistakably blood. It was still warm, and I could see spots beyond it, leading away from me.

'Hello . . .' I called out.

There was no answer.

I went forward, towards the corridor that led away from the lobby and to the grand staircase. Turning the corner I saw a man standing over a prone woman.

There was more blood on the floor.

'Step away from her, Ali,' I said. He had his back to me and for a moment he didn't move.

'She's hurt . . .' he said.

'I can see that.'

Ali drew himself up, turned around and glared at me. I went towards them. Saw that the woman was Natasha Reeve. As I got closer he stepped back, leaning into the wall with his hands in his pockets. I crouched beside her, feeling for a pulse. She was alive. I took out my phone and called an ambulance, keeping a protective arm on her shoulder and both eyes locked on to Ali. When I was done, I took off my jacket, rolled it up and supported her head.

Ali stared at me, unblinking.

'What happened here?' I said.

'You tell me . . .' His formerly smooth accent was hardened with cynicism. I watched him. Waited. 'I found her,' he said finally.

'Like you heard two men arguing on the night someone died here?'

'Just like that . . .'

'If there was any truth in that at all, one of those voices belonged to you.'

'Whatever I say, you'll hear the same thing.'

'I think I'd have heard it if you'd told me that you knew the dead man.'

'I did not.'

'You were seen with him,' I said, standing up. Ali looked, smoothly, both ways down the corridor, as though weighing up his options. 'The exits are covered. No one's leaving unless I say so. It's time for the truth.'

His gaze fell to the floor. 'The prostitute . . .' he said. 'She shouldn't have been here.'

'Marcus brought her here earlier that day. She wedged open a fire door and came back after his shift ended. She'd still be alive if she hadn't seen you, wouldn't she?' He took a heated step towards me, stopping when he saw that I wanted him to. 'Not tonight, Ali. It'd take more than a fucking fire extinguisher to put me down. Do you know what happened to Cherry?' He shook his head. 'Someone crushed her throat and dumped her in a canal like she was fuck-all.'

'Shit in, shit out,' he said, but I thought he was trying to convince himself.

Natasha stirred on the floor.

'Turn around,' I said. He didn't move. 'Turn around,' I repeated. He did and I handcuffed him. I crouched to Natasha as she opened her eyes. 'It's OK. There's an ambulance on the way.'

'He hit me . . .' she said weakly.

'Who was it? Ali?'

Her eyes went to the security guard. 'A stranger,' she said. 'At least, I thought . . .'

'You knew him?'

'He knew me,' she said, frowning, trying to interpret the memory. 'He looked at me with such hate . . .'

I looked at Ali. 'Tell me the truth. Did you find her like this?'

'I already told you the truth.'

'What about the dead man?'

He looked at the ceiling, at me. 'I never saw him before last week.'

'And?'

'And he came to the door. Slurring. Drunk, I thought. He said he was sick, dying. He looked like it. He said he spent his honeymoon in a room in this hotel, many years before. He offered me a large sum of money to let him see the room for a final time. I'm ashamed to say that I accepted it.'

'Except, when you took him up there he dropped dead . . .'

He shook his head. 'When I took him up there he was insane. Laughing. He told me that the money wasn't real. Nothing was real. Life was an illusion.'

'He'd been poisoned. Did he say anything about that?'

Ali closed his eyes. 'He said many things. He was laughing. Screaming. Talking to himself like he was many people at once. I was afraid, and when I left the room I saw the prostitute. She'd been watching us, listening, and so I chased her, to make her go. But then more voices.' He looked at me. 'You. Coming up the stairs.'

'You hit yourself over the head . . .'

'It had to look like I was nothing to do with the man.'

'Sounds drastic to me. What did he say to you in that room?' Ali didn't answer. 'Did you kill Cherry?' He shook his head. 'Then you told someone about her.'

'I had nothing to do with the rest of it.'

There was a sound from the lobby and I turned to see Constable Black approaching, truncheon extended.

'Watch him,' I said. 'There's an ambulance on the way for Ms Reeve.'

She nodded and I went towards the grand staircase.

Natasha had been assaulted by a man she hadn't recognized, which counted her husband, Freddie Coyle, out. When I reached the second floor I saw Aneesa Khan, one staircase up, coming back down. I stopped but she didn't see me for a moment.

She looked like she was in shock.

'Oh,' she said simply.

'Oh,' I replied.

She was on the opposite flight of stairs, with the gap between us, and I didn't want to get any closer.

'I wish you weren't here,' she said.

'The building's surrounded. There's nowhere to go.'

She thought about this for a moment and nodded. She climbed over the bannister and, holding on to it, looked down at the drop.

It was at least fifty feet to the floor.

'Don't be ridiculous,' I said.

'Why? Why shouldn't I be ridiculous?' There were tears in her eyes.

'Because you're a young woman, your whole life ahead of you, this is—'

'What?' she laughed. 'What is it?'

'Something you can still come back from.'

'Now who's being ridiculous? What do they give people for murder?'

'It depends if they did it, it depends if they were coerced or threatened.'

'Let's say that they weren't. Let's say they were in love and got swept up in the whole thing . . .'

'Years,' I said. 'A decade at the most. With good behaviour, you'd be out in less. Still you, still young.'

She barked out another laugh. 'To do what? Stack shelves until I'm eighty-five? I'd rather fucking die.' As she said this I looked at the hand she held the bannister with. The wrist it was connected to. It seemed at the time like I'd never seen such a slender body, such thin fingers and bones.

'No you wouldn't,' I said as she looked at the drop again. 'No, you wouldn't,' I said more urgently. 'The first time we met, do you remember how you felt when you saw the violence against Ali?' She looked at me. 'Death's worse. It's a thousand times worse in every way.'

She looked at me pitiably. 'I *was* concerned and upset. I *was* horrified. I knew it was all fucked. Even then. I knew it had caught up . . .' She looked at me. 'I was worried about myself, Detective. And death? I've seen that close up, too.'

A heavy thought occurred to me. 'Cherry,' I said.

'Cherry? He was a man in a fucking wig. He was disgusting.'

'What happened?'

'He'd heard everything,' she shrugged. 'He'd heard the man in 413 telling Ali about us. He was laughing. He was going to leave a mystery behind, he said. With any luck it'd make us sweat. Lead the police to us.' She looked at me meaningfully. 'After, when you lot arrived and saw the body, we knew we could rely on Ali not to talk. But *Cherry* . . .' she said, satirising the name. 'He wasn't hard to find from Ali's description. A man in a pink wig and a miniskirt, selling his arse on Oxford Road. I did offer him money, I did try.' She momentarily lost her balance and then gripped the bannister tightly. I could see her knuckles turning white. 'He actually thought I wanted to *fuck* him.'

'Where was this?' I said, taking a step closer.

Her slip had made me feel light-headed.

'Some disgusting room in China Town. He said he didn't want money. I laughed at him and he got offended. He had the nerve to be offended. I knew he only wanted more, and I knew he'd never keep his mouth shut. So I shut it for him.'

'We have a witness who says Cherry was taken from her flat by a man,' I said. She looked up at me. 'I think it was the same man who just assaulted Natasha Reeve.'

'Freddie Coyle?' she said with a smile.

'I wonder why his wife didn't recognize him?'

The smile slid off her face. 'Well, that was the problem, wasn't it? Another problem. His solution was to meet her here and kill her.'

She swallowed. 'That was why I had to come. Cherry was one thing. Killing Natasha was just stupid. Insane. I tried to stop him . . .'

'You did,' I said, but her eyes had glazed over and she wasn't listening. 'She's going to be OK. If you were the one who intervened then you probably saved her life down there.'

'That's good, isn't it?' she said, looking down, breathing heavily. She smiled. Nodded. 'That's good to know.'

She looked directly at me.

'Please—' I said.

She let go of the bannister and vanished. I closed my eyes. There was a terrible silence before her body crashed down on to the marble floor, fifty feet below. I didn't move for a moment. At length I opened my eyes, remembered to breathe. I steadied myself and put both hands on the bannister, hoping my senses were wrong. Hoping for a miracle. When I looked down I saw that there hadn't been one.

13

The door to 413 was open. I climbed the short staircase leading to it. I heard the traffic and street sounds from Oxford Road, felt the breeze on my skin. I walked through the doorway and stepped back against the wall. The light came from a desk lamp, giving the room a moody, intimate tone. The glare of the city outside cast moving, kaleidoscopic shadows across the walls.

At the far side of the room, sitting in a chair, facing the open window, was the solid, immovable silhouette of a man. He looked like a negative image of himself.

'It's over,' I said.

He didn't move.

The room had been completely torn apart, as though in a frenzy, a rage. Clearly the man had been looking for something. The smoking gun that I'd implied was hidden here somewhere. He turned and looked at me. I felt like I was seeing him for the first time.

The man I'd known as Freddie Coyle.

'Is she alive?' he asked, disinterestedly.

'It depends who you mean.'

'Natasha,' he said. 'My wife . . .'

'I'm afraid so. She's even lucid. She didn't recognize you, though, Freddie . . .'

'Funny that,' he said with a weak smile.

'Which means you must have changed quite a bit in the last six months.'

'Be the change you want to see in the world . . .' he said, staring at nothing.

'He was helping you to change identity, wasn't he? The man you murdered?'

He looked at me. 'That's quite a leap, Detective . . .'

'Speaking of which, Aneesa just threw herself down the centre of the stairs. She's dead,' I said bluntly. 'So maybe you'll get it if my patience is a bit thin.' It was the first time anything I'd said had registered on his face. I thought the news hit him hard and decided to exploit it. 'Tell me what all this was about.'

He shook his head like he barely knew it himself. I was angry. I went forward, took him roughly by the arm and marched him out of the room. 'This is unnecessary,' he said. 'I don't feel like talking.' When we reached the landing I pushed him towards the bannister.

'Look at her,' I said.

He gave me a desperate smile. 'I don't want to.'

I grabbed him by the scruff of the neck and dragged him to the bannister. 'Look at her,' I repeated. He did. From where we stood, Aneesa was a shadow, a smudge on the ground floor. He screwed his eyes shut and began to shake.

'Let's get closer,' I said, pushing him towards the stairs.

'Listen . . .'

'Too late for that. Let's go and have a look at your handiwork.'

'Don't speak to me like that.'

'Get used to it. In prison they'll have a different nickname for you every day. Maybe that'll suit someone going through an identity crisis.'

'I don't know what you're talking about.' I took him by the arm and dragged him down the stairs with me. 'I said I didn't want to look.' He was starting to sound hysterical. Perhaps we both were.

'There are two ways down,' I said. 'You're more than welcome to follow her.'

'I don't feel well . . .'

'I don't care.'

'What do you want? You said you wanted to talk . . .'

'You could always try, but I want to get up close to her. See what that kind of impact can do.'

'What do you want to know?' He was panicking now, trying to pull away from me.

'How did you meet the man who died up there?'

'Through an old client, a man living in tax exile.'

'But you needed something a little more complicated, you needed a complete reinvention . . .'

'Freddie was ripe for it. He had no friends, he never socialized. When he started having the affair with Geoff, I found out.'

'So you decided to put a wedge between him and the only people in his life?'

'Just some notes sent to his wife. I couldn't have predicted the rest.'

'You must have, because the real Freddie Coyle ended up dead, didn't he? The divorce already in progress, a lot of cash at stake, no one in his life to miss him once he split from Natasha.'

'Ding, ding, ding. Now can we stop this? I've told you I don't want to see her.'

He was almost crying now.

'You were the one who showed me the first picture of yourself. A red-faced, overweight man surrounded by young women. You had to lose a lot of weight, maybe even get some work done, but that only put more distance between you and your old life.'

'What the fuck's going on here?'

Sutty was standing one flight down, staring up at us.

'You were right,' I said. 'The smiling man did die here as a way of pointing the finger at Anthony Blick.'

'Have you lost the fucking plot, Aid? That's Freddie Coyle. Blick bled to death in the Midland Hotel.'

'Right,' I said, looking at the man beside me. 'Then he was cut up in the bathtub and flushed down the toilet. Funny we never found any human remains, though . . .'

'Probably went up in the dustbin fires,' said Sutty.

'But they didn't. The smiling man was a vanisher. He helped people assume new identities. He was helping Anthony Blick become Freddie Coyle.'

Sutty looked between us, frowned. 'The blood . . .'

'I don't know what their original idea was, but half the battle was making it look as though Anthony Blick had died *without* providing a body. I think he and the smiling man took blood at regular intervals. More than a man could live without if was all spilt in one go, so anyone who found it would naturally assume the person it came from, Anthony Blick, was dead.' I looked at the man standing beside me. 'Something must have gone wrong, though . . .'

Blick sat down on the stairs. 'It was really quite mundane. He found out the money I gave him was fake. He said unless I paid up he'd expose me. I had almost everything in place by then anyway, so I spiked a bottle of whisky and gave it to him. After a few drinks he must have realized. He sabotaged everything, poured my blood out in his hotel room and came here to die. Left himself in 413 so you'd find your way back to the Midland. To me.'

'Aneesa,' I said. 'I take it you were together?'

He nodded, looking at the floor. 'That wasn't really her down there . . .'

'I'm afraid it was.'

'I don't want to see her.'

'You're under arrest for the murders of Freddie Coyle, the unidentified man from room 413 and Christopher Jordan, who went by the name Cherry.' My voice shook as I spoke. 'Also for the attempted murder of Natasha Reeve.'

Sutty stared at me for a moment then nodded.

He turned and walked back down the stairs.

XI
Something to Remember Me By

1

'So Blick lures Natasha Reeve to the Palace posing as Freddie Coyle,' said Parrs. I was sitting in his office, explaining the case as I understood it. He was at his desk, his red eyes lit with attention. Stromer was standing in the corner of the room watching me shrewdly.

She didn't believe a word I said.

'That's correct, sir. According to the emails we've seen, he hinted at a reconciliation.'

'So she goes expecting her husband back,' said Parrs. 'She finds a man impersonating him who tries to kill her.'

'I don't know what his plan was for afterwards. If he even had one. He attacked her but Aneesa Khan interrupted it. Then Blick went up to search room 413 for the evidence I'd implied would bring the smiling man's killer to justice. It was a mess. He'd torn the place apart. Aneesa went as far as the room with him, probably trying to calm him down. But by the time I saw her I think she'd already made her mind up to leave.'

Parrs glared at me. 'She probably hadn't decided on the express route to the ground floor, though. What did you say to her?'

'I asked her about Cherry.'

'This trans hooker who saw everything?'

'Cherry heard the smiling man in room 413. He was ranting to Ali, about his relationship with Blick, about making his new life impossible.'

'How?'

'Blick was supposed to be on the other side of the world. The smiling man left his blood all over a hotel room he should never have been inside. Then he left himself, an unidentifiable dead body, in a hotel that Blick was financially involved with. At the very least Blick would be sweating for the rest of his life.'

It was only part of the truth.

'You're telling me Smiley Face lives his entire life in secret. Anonymity to the extent that even Interpol can't pin a name on him. But he suddenly draws attention to himself over an argument with a client . . .'

It seemed that the real answer for so many of the smiling man's actions lay with Amy Burroughs. In coming to the city perhaps he'd been hoping to make contact with her, with the son he'd never met, and been robbed of the chance. When he was poisoned he'd thought fast. Going to the Palace led us to Blick. The note sewn into his trousers led us to Amy. He knew she could deny knowing him, that she could protect herself if necessary. But that his presence in the city, and his final reference to *The Rubáiyát of Omar Khayyám* would tell her that he'd tried.

Parrs leaned forward. '. . . And why did Blick feel the need to kill him?'

'He says it was an argument over money, but that doesn't stack up to me . . .'

'Why not?'

'The smiling man was terminally ill, weeks away from death . . .'

'You think they had a philosophical disagreement . . .' said Stromer, speaking for the first time since I'd entered the room.

'This began as identity fraud but turned into something more sinister. I think Blick was realizing that Natasha Reeve was a danger, that she could identify him. I think he wanted to solve that problem ahead of time.'

Parrs smiled. 'You think our dead man objected to her murder?' He turned to Stromer. 'Aidan can get very sentimental around death.' His eyes flicked back to me. 'This is a career criminal we're talking about. Don't go looking for redeeming features. That said . . .'

'Sir?'

His red eyes were locked on to mine. 'The slip of paper, sewn into his trousers. Almost feels like a message to someone . . .'

'Maybe so, but we don't know who to. We probably never will.'

'Hm,' said Parrs. 'And Blick maintains that the real Freddie Coyle died of natural causes?'

I nodded. 'But he's not saying what he did with the body. Without that, who knows if that's true? Either way, he took Coyle's death as an opportunity to gain control of his assets. While the hotel was a going concern he could only take his monthly allowance from the trust. But if the trust was dissolved he'd get half of the proceeds from the hotel's sale. Coyle was a shut-in and Blick was his solicitor. Knew his affairs inside out.'

'Literally,' said Parrs.

'He faked a health scare, dropped off the radar, lost almost a hundred pounds and began to become Freddie Coyle. The real Coyle's estrangement from his wife made it easy.'

'With the help of our smiling man.'

I nodded. 'Apparently an expert in identity fraud.'

'So Blick tells us,' said Parrs. 'What I don't get is how you made the leap, though, Aidan? For this trap of yours at the Palace, you had to know that old Smiley Face was, what? A vanisher? You had to know his killer would be nervous about him sending us a message . . .' I saw where he was going but I'd agreed with Amy Burroughs to keep her name out of it. I knew that she wouldn't go on record with her story about the smiling man saving her life, and I knew that if she were forced or coerced into doing so, that it could put her in danger. Back on the radar of the people she'd spent years running from.

It wasn't worth it.

'Through an unrelated investigation I discovered that Blick, posing as Freddie Coyle, had become a member of an exclusive gentlemen's club in town. That was odd, given that Coyle had just painfully and publicly realized he was gay, and the club only catered to straight men. That, alongside Blick's caginess, set off alarm bells. There was the light, repeatedly being switched on in 413 after the murder, too. It made me realize someone was searching the room, nervous about what might be found in there. That had to be someone with access to the building. Coyle was just one of several possibilities.'

There had been hints.

A detail which had pulled at me was that Coyle hadn't been a big drinker. When I went to visit him for the first time, the man I met was having cocktails at 10 a.m. I'd found a vape kit down the side of the sofa and heard someone in the next room. I now believed that person was Aneesa Khan, and might have connected them sooner but had discounted the idea upon finding out Coyle was gay. When Alicia had told me he was in fact a fully paid-up member of Incognito's Gold Member system, that changed everything. Aneesa smoking a cigarette on our drive out to Blick's, having lost her vape kit, sent the same chill down my spine.

Stromer detached herself from the wall. 'What about the attack on Amy Burroughs?'

I'd been trying to lead our conversation away from her. I was almost certain that the man with the nail gun had been Anthony Blick. Either the smiling man had discussed his connection with Amy, or Blick had followed us to her home, or both. He had every incentive to silence the one person who could provide the missing link to the case: that the smiling man was a vanisher who'd assisted him in changing identities.

'It seems as though that was unrelated,' I said. 'A family matter. We're looking into it.'

Stromer looked at me dubiously. 'What about her reaction at the formal identification? Either she knew that man, or she held something else back from us.'

'She was holding something back,' I said. 'It turns out she was in love with this Ross Browne, the man we originally thought to be the victim. When she realized he wasn't dead, she was so relieved she passed out.'

'I know what relief looks like, Detective Constable,' Stromer said flatly.

Parrs sat back in his chair. 'I'm afraid the truth according to Aidan Waits is a little like an iceberg, Doctor. What shows above the surface is only about a tenth of it. So this nurse can't help us with the identity of the smiling man?'

'I'm afraid not, sir.'

'Shame that. My challenge to you was to bring me his name. It seems like with all this Blick-Coyle-Khan-Reeve intrigue, that's the one thing that we're missing. What was our wager, again?'

'You said you'd reassign me to a different shift. Find me a new partner.'

'That was it.' He gave me his shark's smile. 'So close.'

'Well, I've still got a lot to learn from Detective Inspector Sutcliffe.'

'And believe me, you'll have plenty of time to do it.'

'If that's all, sir, I've requested a day's leave.'

'So I see, Detective Constable.' He nodded. 'You are dismissed.'

I stood and left the room. I was halfway down the corridor when I heard footsteps behind me. I turned to see Karen Stromer and stopped.

'You've done good work, Detective Constable,' she said with some difficulty. 'But if this nurse knows something . . .'

'She doesn't.'

'I'm afraid I don't believe you.' She looked at me. 'I'm only pursuing this out of concern for her position. When she identified that body she didn't look heartbroken or in shock. Stacked up next to someone breaking into her home and threatening her, threatening her son, that troubles me.' When I still didn't say anything she went on. 'Why wouldn't you volunteer information that could save her life? Perhaps even your career?'

I stood to one side of the corridor and lowered my voice.

'Because that might be the one thing that could put her in danger. I won't insult your intelligence, Karen, but if asked I will deny this conversation ever took place. I'm telling you this because I hope you'll understand. As long as Amy Burroughs isn't compelled to go on the record or draw attention to herself, she's safe. After what she's been through she deserves that much. You were right, she wasn't heartbroken or in shock. She was scared for her life.'

Stromer's expression softened and she nodded. Gave me her thin paper-cut of a smile. 'Perhaps I was mistaken about her reaction in the formal identification,' she said. 'Perhaps people aren't always what they appear.'

'Perhaps not.' I wanted to acknowledge the moment, and the trust she was putting in me, but my phone had started to vibrate in my pocket. I knew with a heavy certainty who it would be. 'Thanks for all your help, Karen.'

2

We turned off the main road and kept on going. The way felt complicated, impossible. Meandering roads became unmarked streets, then lanes and then nothing at all.

I drove.

Bateman sat in the back seat but we could both feel it now. The desensitizing effect of details, fizzing by the window. We'd left the city in the late afternoon, with at least a two-hour drive ahead of us. The weather forecast had predicted that the heatwave, the shared fever dream that had passed more like a nightmare, was ready to break.

It hadn't happened yet.

Every object, building or person we'd passed was alive under the sunlight, looking like the best version of itself. When the landscape began to change, blasts of green foliage after miles of failed, grey towns, Bateman dug a pint of whisky out from his jacket and started sipping at it in silence. He was a brooding, ominous presence. Like a tumour on life itself, and I knew that this trip couldn't really be about the bag, or whatever he thought was in it. It was about me and him. It was about power and fear. Neither of us had spoken as we drove along the motorway, the tension in the car rising, tightening like a knot. Now this sudden deviation, these endless, looping backroads felt like something coming undone, unravelling faster than I could keep track of.

So far nothing but the feeling had been familiar to me.

As I made the final turn towards White Gate House, all of that changed in an overwhelming rush of memory. I stopped the car in the narrow driveway, the engine still running. Bateman stirred. Shifted to stare over my shoulder, through the windscreen. It was early evening now, but still bright out and it was clear that the farmhouse had been abandoned. Perhaps as long as we'd been away from it. I drove us closer, parking beside the enormous bank of trees I remembered so vividly. I'd turned the rear-view mirror so I couldn't see Bateman, but when I switched off the engine I could hear his loud, rasping breaths.

It felt like he was inside my head.

I opened the door, got out, and started towards the house.

'Where you going?' he said bluntly.

'I want to look around.'

He snorted and followed me.

I tried the door once and then pushed my shoulder into it. When it didn't move I stepped back and Bateman kicked it in with one powerful boot. I tried not to look rattled by it. The interior was as I remembered, but warped by time and damp.

'After you,' said Bateman, drooling down himself, still breathing like an old bulldog. The windows in the kitchen were just holes in the wall and the sun, descending in the sky, blinded us both. I walked towards it, into the death room. It didn't hold the same power I'd expected it to. Buildings forget. When I turned, I saw that Bateman was watching me from the doorway, as though he didn't want to cross the threshold.

'What happened in here?' I said.

His good eye moved on to me. 'They killed her.'

'Fisk's wife? Why?'

He shrugged. 'Fisk wouldn't talk,' he said slowly. 'Wouldn't tell where the bag was . . .'

'How did you know where it was, then?'

'What?'

'I said how did you know where the bag was if Fisk wouldn't talk? You drove us out here and told me exactly where to go . . .'

Bateman's proportions seemed to change, like those of a shape-shifter, and he drew himself up, filling the doorway.

'Where's the bag, Aidan?'

'If you're honest with yourself, I think you already know.'

He smiled. 'All gone . . .'

I nodded. 'I fell down a bank and hit the stream. When I heard the gunshot I threw the fucking thing in.' He was nodding like he understood. 'If you knew that, then why all this? Following me, phoning me, fighting me . . .'

'Even walking round your flat while you were out,' he said with a smirk. 'Reading your mail, drinking your drink. If you're honest with yourself, I think you already know . . .'

'I was only here because you dragged me out of bed. I was a kid.'

'A man now,' he said. 'Knew bag gone. Years gone. Life gone.' He drew a hand tenderly across the ruined face that had once made women weak at the knees. 'Gone,' he said. I remembered then that Bateman had no internal life. Outside of cruelty, he ceased to exist. 'You shouldn't have come here, Aid . . .'

'You broke into my sister's house, you didn't give me a choice.'

He smiled, nodded.

'I wanted to talk to you, y'know?' I was backing away. 'I thought I'd try and talk to you about violence, where it comes from. It's usually a cycle. One bad choice after another. If a few people started breaking the chain we could probably be without it.' I'd backed all the way to the window. 'I trace the violence in me back to you, I'd be interested to know where yours came from?' Bateman snorted so I went on. 'Anyway, like I said, it's a choice we don't have to make. I thought I'd tell you I won't do it any more. I'd say that if we came here to fight then you win. You can kill me, I'm better than it.'

'Moving . . .' said Bateman, taking a step inside the kitchen.

'You turned on the other kidnappers because they didn't want to hurt Fisk's wife. They didn't want to kill him.'

He took another step.

'Stay the fuck away from me,' I said.

He roared with laughter. 'Mr Non-Violent. Mr Break the Cycle . . .'

'You're not listening, Bateman.' He took another step. 'I said that's what I thought I'd do.'

'But I killed a woman,' he said, miming tears with his hand.

'You killed us both,' I said. 'You did this to yourself.' He scrunched up his face in question. 'You broke into my sister's house, you didn't give me a choice,' I repeated.

We both heard it then and he stopped.

The sound of a large vehicle coming up the path.

Bateman turned, stomped down the hall to the front door and saw the top of the white van coming towards us. He started to laugh. Not the cynical snorts and twitches from before, but the real stuff, right from the gut.

'Back-up?' he said, putting his wrists together miming his arrest. 'For what? Being mean to you on the phone . . .' Most of his speech impediment had fallen away now, and I saw that it had always just been for effect.

'No,' I said. 'Not for that.'

'For breaking and entering? I'll be out before you're back in the city . . .'

'I know,' I said, walking down the hallway towards him. He reached behind my ear and, instead of a coin, produced a crumpled-up piece of paper, dangling it in front of me.

I saw my sister's name.

An address.

He dropped it at my feet.

'Keep that, I've got it memorized,' he said, spitting in my face.

I looked past him. At the doorway he still had his back to. 'What would you say your eyesight's like, Bateman?'

He turned to look.

Nicky Fisk Junior had climbed out of the van's driver side. He walked round the cab and opened the passenger-side door, helping out the thinnest man I'd ever seen.

His father, Nicholas Fisk Senior.

Bateman's broken mouth fell open. He took a step backwards, tripped and fell heavily on the floor. He scrambled to his feet, grunted and ran the other way, down the hall towards the kitchen and the wide open spaces where the windows should be. I heard a wet thud and saw him stagger back into the hall holding his bloody nose. Donny Fisk emerged from behind him, holding a claw-hammer, as his father reached the front door.

'Hello, Bates,' said Fisk. 'You're looking well . . .'

Bateman stood, breathing blood into his cupped hands for a moment, then burst towards the door. Nicky dropped him with a devastating right. Then he picked him up by the legs and his brother took the shoulders. Where Fisk Senior jerked and bucked, his sons flowed like shadows. They went to the cellar door under the stairs. Where I'd turned the key on their father so many years before.

'This the one?' asked Nicky. Fisk nodded and they disappeared into the pitch-black rectangle of the door.

I looked at Fisk.

He hadn't stepped inside the house and, for a moment, kept his eyes locked on to the cellar where he'd been held prisoner. He looked down the hall to where his wife had been murdered. 'If it's all the same to you, I think I'd rather wait outside,' he said.

I didn't know where the two of us stood, but I was glad to join him.

I took his arm to offer support as we walked down the path into the perfect, still day, away from a muted sound that might have been a man screaming. I hadn't been certain that they'd come. And hadn't known that Donny was already in position when we arrived. I still didn't know what they planned for me, but it felt likely I'd follow Bateman down into that cellar.

It was a chance I'd had to take.

His aggression towards me had been one thing. His move against my sister was another. Fisk and I had only walked a few feet when a gunshot cracked, unmistakably, through the air. Then another. He gripped my arm more tightly and we went on without comment.

'That bag you took from the attic . . .'

'I threw it in the stream,' I said, too quickly.

He eyed me shrewdly. 'You didn't look inside?'

I shook my head. I wondered if my life depended on it.

Before he could say anything else his boys emerged from the house, walking towards us. They went to the van, took two canisters of petrol each and walked, wordlessly, back, disappearing inside. When they re-emerged, Nicky approached their father and handed him a slip of paper.

'Found this on the floor,' he said.

Still leaning on me for support, Fisk used his long, thin fingers to massage the scrunched-up ball of paper open.

'What is it?' he said.

'It's my sister's name and address. He was threatening to hurt her.' Fisk looked at me for a moment then extended the piece of paper. I took it and balled it back up. I walked to the house and dropped it in the doorway.

When I turned, Donny was staring at me, gripping the bloodied claw-hammer.

'Guy said he's your dad, by the way. That true?'

I think I shook my head.

Unable to look at them any more, I went to the car and sat inside it. I was blocked in by their van. Fisk leaned on one of his boys, said something to the other and watched him disappear inside. At length, plumes of smoke emerged. Fisk and Nicky walked past me without a look and climbed back inside the van. They started up and began to drive down the lane, back on to the main road. When I heard another engine I realized that Donny had been parked in his own car around the back. I started up and followed the van.

Donny followed me.

In the middle of the lane the van's brake lights flashed red and our strange convoy came to a sudden, claustrophobic stop. I looked in my rear-view. Saw Donny's car right behind. I looked left and then right. Acres of wide open fields either way, tinted by the day's dying light. There was nowhere to go. One of the van doors opened and I saw Fisk climb out, leaning on his stick as he walked towards me. I was gripping the steering wheel, trying not to panic. When he reached the car he draped himself on the roof and used his stick to tap on the window. I buzzed it down.

He gave me a hard look and then held out a fist.

Inside it was the scrunched-up piece of paper.

He dropped it into my lap. 'The boys think this is careless,' he said. 'Use it or don't, but I wouldn't leave anything of value in that place.' He nodded back towards the house and when I looked into the rear-view mirror I could see flames drifting out of the windows and doors, reaching for the sky. 'It was just a pair of gloves, by the way,' he said.

'Sorry?'

'In that bag you stole. They were my dad's. Hidden away cus Trace hated boxing. There was never any cash here. I just told your old man about it cus it was all I could think of . . .'

'He wasn't my old man,' I said.

Fisk squinted. 'There's a certain resemblance, but my eyesight's not what it was . . .'

He walked, laboriously, back to the van and climbed inside. They started up again, signalled for a turn and went right. I followed for a few miles, with Donny driving close behind. Then I pulled over and let him pass. He didn't look at me.

I killed the engine and sat a while, watching the light change.

I jumped at the first tap on the glass, and saw with relief that it was just a fat spot of rain. There was another, then another, until the weather seemed to break all around me, pelting the windscreen and enveloping the car. It sounded like a hundred thousand voices, screaming in the distance.

XII
Kill For Love

1

It was late by the time I got back into the city. I'd spent something like ten hours behind the wheel of a car. My eyes burned and my skin smelt salty, and I drove around for a while deciding what to do. Helplessly, I opened the ball of paper and looked at my sister's address.

I was nervous when I parked up, two streets over from her house. I imagined knocking on the door and introducing myself to her, for the first time in over two decades. I ran through what I might say, how she might see me. How she might react. I forced myself out of the car, dropped my keys trying to lock it and had to laugh at myself.

The house was a terrace that it looked like she shared. There were a couple of lights on inside, the muted sound of a television. I checked the time and saw that it was just after 10 p.m. Just about respectable. Walking up the path I saw a haze of sunspots wash in front of my eyes. For a moment I thought I might start to lift, effortlessly, from my body and watch this as though it were happening to someone else.

I didn't, though.

When I got to the door and raised my hand to knock I saw my own reflection. The dark, lived-in suit. The bags under my eyes that I could never quite sleep off. The deep cuts and bruises from my fight with Bateman, like he'd reached out from inside my head and made the mental scars physical. I waited for my face to warp and alter in the glass but it didn't change. It had finally settled on a look and, after months of doubt and confusion, I suddenly recognized myself so well.

I was my father's son. The violent man I thought I was pretending to be.

I waited a moment, feeling the electricity leave me, and took an unconscious step back. Then a conscious one. Then I was walking down the path, away from myself.

Two young women passed me when I was out on the street. They'd been talking, laughing. I kept my head low but felt my breath catch as I went by. One of them had looked familiar. Untameable, curled hair and big, thinker's eyes which I felt pass over my face. I thought I'd seen her expression change.

I kept on walking.

Oliver Cartwright and Guy Russell were each handed life sentences for attempting to smuggle drugs into the United Arab Emirates. As far as I knew, they were still waiting to hear if they could appeal. Russell's daughter, Alicia, took ownership of Incognito. She relaunched the club as *Russell's*, shaking its existing clientele as she did so and forging her own path. When I returned to St Mary's to speak to Amy Burroughs, I was told that she'd handed in her notice and left. Late one night I called her former lover, Ross Browne, to find out if he'd heard from her. When a familiar voice answered the phone I smiled to myself and hung up. I only saw Sophie and Earl again once more. They were walking through the city centre, talking, holding hands, smiling. They looked young again. Anthony Blick maintained that Freddie Coyle had died of natural causes right up until the day when remains were discovered, buried in the back garden of Blick's former home. Coyle's skull had been caved in. Natasha Reeve decided to take the Palace off the market, reopening it under a new name as the sole owner.

And Nia gave birth to Zain Carver's daughter.

They named her Catherine. Nia couldn't have known what that

name meant, and even I wondered at Carver's motive. Was it remorse or revenge? Or another long-game piece of manipulation? I wondered if he planned on replacing every girl who'd vanished from his life.

I returned to the night shift with my superior officer, Detective Inspector Peter Sutcliffe. It was a few weeks later when I saw a request from Cumbrian police cross our desk. A dead man had been found in the cellar of a burned-out farmhouse. He'd been kneecapped by a high-calibre handgun and then left to burn alive. They were looking for any information that could help identify him but there wasn't much to go on. I was reading the request when Sutty tore it out of my hand, balled it up and dropped it in the bin. He said he only wanted to investigate people with full names from now on. So Bateman became the stuff of legend. Joined those other enduring mysteries. The lady in the Afghan coat. The smiling man.

The missing missing.

When I got to the corner I stopped and looked back. The two young women I'd passed were standing beneath a streetlight, twenty feet away, and I could see them both perfectly. They'd also stopped, turned to look at me. My sister was frozen, pale, her mouth open, her eyes wide with recognition.

She was unbelievable.

Her friend was looking between us, trying to work out what was happening. We stayed like that for a moment until I nodded, minimally, and she nodded back. Started to smile. I raised a hand. Saw the criss-crossing scars embedded into my knuckles and took an unconscious step back. Then a conscious one. In a perfect universe perhaps we're still on that street corner, staring into each other. Perhaps there we get no closer, perhaps we get no further apart.

About the Author

Joseph Knox was born and raised in and around Stoke and Manchester, where he worked in bars and bookshops before moving to London. He runs, writes and reads compulsively. His debut novel *Sirens* was a bestseller.

The Smiling Man is the second in the Detective Aidan Waits series.